THE STORY OF RUSTEM
AND OTHER PERSIAN HERO TALES

"But thy doom is fixed, thou Cruel One, and even now the avenger's hand
is at the door.   Behold, and tremble!"

THE
STORY OF RUSTEM

AND

OTHER PERSIAN HERO TALES
FROM FIRDUSI

BY

ELIZABETH D. RENNINGER

ILLUSTRATED BY J. L. S. WILLIAMS

Fredonia Books
Amsterdam, The Netherlands

The Story of Rustem:
And other Persian Hero Tales from Firdusi

by
Elizabeth D. Renninger

ISBN: 1-58963-537-X

Reprinted from the 1909 edition

Fredonia Books
Amsterdam, The Netherlands
http://www.fredoniabooks.com

DEDICATION

ONCE upon a time, not so many years ago, a librarian in one of our large cities conceived the idea of forming a hero club for the boys of her neighborhood. So it came to pass that for two years, every Wednesday evening, between thirty and fifty young heroes assembled in the club-room of the library to listen to the story of some great hero, told either by the librarian or by some visiting story-teller.

Now, as the object of the club was not only amusement, helpful entertainment, and inspiration, but also to influence the boys' reading, they were introduced first to the Greek heroes: Theseus, Perseus, Hercules, Jason, and the heroes of Troy. And after these came the heroes of chivalry: Charlemagne, Roland, Oliver, Ogier the Dane, and the four Aymon brothers. Then followed Siegfried, King Arthur, and the Red Cross Knight. Yea, and even that gay little fellow in green—brave Robin Hood. And sprinkled in with these more or less mythological heroes were those of a more practical type: Father Damien, Livingstone, Lincoln, Peter Cooper, and a number of every-day heroes who so well exemplify the growth in heroic ideals in our century as contrasted with those of primitive times. Boy Heroes were also presented, and finally, in her search for good story-hour material, the librarian decided to introduce the boys to some of the great Persian heroes—they being not so well known.

And, since the boys' delight in this series of stories really inspired the thought of making it possible for other story-tellers and older boys and girls to enjoy them too, therefore this book is appropriately and affectionately dedicated to the Hero Boys of the Bushwick Branch of the Brooklyn Public Library—a more appreciative and promising set of youths than whom never resolved to do, and dare, and be—good, practical, every-day heroes.

FOREWORD

THE aim of this series of stories which, through the medium of Firdusi, mirrors so fascinatingly the legendary history of Persia, has been, not only to provide for the story-teller a treasure-house wherein may be found pure gold, refined for ready use, every coin of which may be stamped with the narrator's own individuality for the inspiration and entertainment of any group of children, but also, indirectly, to present to older boys and girls, in attractive form, the story of the Shah-Nameh in miniature.

When the material for the stories was originally collected, the author's idea was simply to work out for her own use in story-telling to children a picture presentation of a delightful series of tales little known to the young. Accordingly, like the fabled busy bee, she scrupled not to enter the most exclusive Persian gardens, dipping into the cup of each bright posy containing the least mite of the sweets for which she was delving—her desire being to give to this particular jar of honey not the Atkinson, or the Mohl, or the Arnold flavor alone, but a composite which should be all of these, and yet distinctly individual and unique, the point of view being not the usual one of the translator, the paraphraser, or the raconteur working upon the lines of the epitomist, but rather that of the moving picture artist and the story-teller combined.

The debt of the author, consequently, is large, and acknowledgment difficult. For while original translators of

the great epic, as Mohl, in French, and Atkinson and
Helen Zimmern, in English—and Arnold in his noble
poem "Sohrab and Rustem"—have contributed most liberally to this series of word-pictures, yet many additional
treasures also have been discovered and secured, even from
general works such as, for example, Benjamin's "History
of Persia," and altogether from sources too varied and
fugitive, and too thoroughly woven into the fibre of her
own text, to be individually acknowledged. The debt,
however, is none the less great.

It only remains to be said that if, when started upon
their mission, these stories give to children at large as
much pleasure as they gave to the particular group of
"heroes" for whom they were worked out, they will not
only justify their right of being, but also their method of
preparation, which, though without scholarly pretensions,
may yet serve to make better known and loved one of
the masterpieces of literature, alas, too little familiar to-
day even to grown-ups well versed in European classics.

E. D. R.

NORTHUMBERLAND, PA., *September*, 1909.

CONTENTS

ILLUSTRATIONS

xi

INTRODUCTION

THE world has few great epics. In fact, it has been said that there are perhaps but six in all. Yet the materials for an epic are to be found among all nations in those traditions, half-fact, half-fiction, which cluster about the great national heroes whose deeds of prowess make the era in which they lived stand forth before our eyes, clear-cut and brilliant, the canvas filled from end to end with deeds of daring, scenes of love, violence, and romance which, through all ages, thrill and make their own appeal to the heart of man.

Epics are written, as a rule, in the infancy of a race, and they all have this in common, that they are not the invention of a single individual, but being founded upon national traditions, are handed down orally from one generation to another, until, in the fulness of time, one of the world's great poets stretches forth his hand, gathers together all the beautiful flowers that have blossomed in the fancy of his people—as has been so happily said of Firdusi—and having breathed upon the precious blossoms, plants them in new beauty in the Gardens of Paradise, there to bloom on among the immortals, a joy and delight forever.

Among the truly great national epics, two fall to India—the Mahabharata and the Ramayana; two to Greece—the Iliad and the Odyssey; one to the North—the Nibelungenlied; and one to Persia—the Shah-Nameh.

The Shah-Nameh—without question the greatest of the Eastern epics—is seven times the length of the Iliad, being in fact much longer than the Iliad and the Odyssey together, comprising in all 60,000 couplets, and having occupied Firdusi thirty years in writing. The poem presents us, in most musical rhythm, with a complete view of a certain definite era of civilization—the Persia of the Heroic Age; an age of chivalry rivaling in mighty deeds of prowess and romantic interest the mediæval chivalry of Charlemagne and the glorious Peers of France. And, moreover, we have here a portrait gallery of distinct and unique individuals, the bright, particular star being Rustem, the great hero whose superhuman strength, courage, and loyalty prevented Persia, for hundreds of years, from falling into the hands of her foes.

In writing the Shah-Nameh it is said that, in addition to his poetic and historic incentives, Firdusi had a distinctly patriotic motive. For, being an ardent lover of things Persian, he hoped thus to keep alive in the hearts of his countrymen the glories of their ancestors, in order that they might not degenerate into mere puppets under Arab domination. Now that Firdusi had this end in view is shown not alone by the theme and spirit of the epic, but also by the diction employed, for the poet adheres rigorously throughout to the native Persian, using few Arabic words, the consequence being that no work in the literature of Persia is so free from foreign admixture as the Shah-Nameh.

Unfortunately, no complete copy of the great "Iliad of the East" is known to exist, though there are innumerable MS. copies, some of them wondrously beautiful, the scribes having used Egyptian reeds, and the blackest of ink which never fades; the writing being done on the finest of silk paper, powdered with gold and silver dust; the margins richly illuminated; the whole perfumed with sandal-wood, or some costly essence; and the title-page of elaborate design.

The best known translations of the Shah-Nameh are: an abridgment in prose and verse, by Edward Atkinson; Jules Mohl's French translation, which is perhaps the most scholarly work; Helen Zimmern's excellent paraphrase; the versions given in Reed's Persian literature, Benjamin's "History of Persia," and various other partial adaptations.

As for Firdusi (Abul Kasim Mansur) the "Poet of Paradise," who gave to the world the Shah-Nameh, many are the poetic legends that cluster about his name, making it extremely difficult to give any authentic account of his life. Authorities differ as to the exact date, but he is said to have been born at Shahdab, a suburb of Tus in Khorassan, somewhere about A. D. 930. His father's name is quite unknown, but he seems to have been one of the Dihkan, or landed gentry of Persia. It is also said that he was a gardener, and that Firdusi received his name from the spot which he cultivated (Firdus, *i. e.*, Paradise). However that may be, the legend goes on to relate that, it having been communicated to the father in a dream that his son would have a great future, he had given to Firdusi the best education the time and place could afford. The boy was carefully educated, therefore, in the Arabic language and literature, the Old Persian, and the history and traditions of his country.

Firdusi seems to have been a dreamy youth, for it is recorded of him that he spent many hours beside the canal which ran through his father's grounds, perusing eagerly the old legends of the early wars of his country as exemplified in the splendid deeds of her heroes; or in dreaming of the great things which he, himself, meant to accomplish

one day for the glory of Persia. Yea, and the lad was
practical, too, for aside from his own personal dream of
greatness, his great hope was that, having himself achieved,
he might be able to build for Tus, his native city, a great
dike of stone which should prevent the fearful inundations
which, from time to time, wrought such devastation and
ruin to the poor people of Tus.

Little seems to be known of Firdusi's younger manhood,
but it appears that his poetic gifts were early perceived
and fostered, and that he spent not his time in idle dreaming. For suddenly it came to light that, while at the Court
of Mahmud, the Sultan's poets were laboring under the
direction of that great patron of literature to produce from
the records already accumulated a history of Persia in
rhyme, all unaided, in an obscure village, one unknown to
fame was attempting the same great undertaking. Now
thus it came to pass that Mahmud who had the records,
and Firdusi, who possessed the gifts, were brought together.

And this having come to pass, Firdusi basked from this
time forth in the royal favor. A beautiful house was given
him by the Sultan, the walls of which were decorated with
martial scenes painted by the great artists of Persia, in
order to fire the imagination of the poet; the Bustan-
Nameh, a collection of the chronicles and traditions of
Persia, together with other valuable records were placed at
his disposal; and thus, happily equipped and surrounded,
the poet worked unhampered upon his great masterpiece.
Yea, for thirty long years Firdusi wrought, and when at
last the 60,000 couplets of the great Shah-Nameh were
completed, he rejoiced, for was he not to receive a reward of a thousand pieces of gold for each thousand

couplets? And with this princely sum could he not now carry out his long-cherished dream of a dike for his fellow-townsmen?

But, alas! Firdusi, while at the Court, had incurred the enmity of the Sultan's prime-minister, who resented the fact that he, the great prime-minister, was not also mentioned in the eulogy to Mahmud which prefaced the great epic poem. Poisoning the mind of the Sultan against Firdusi, therefore, the spoiled favorite of the Court managed that the money promised the poet should be paid in silver instead of gold. Now Firdusi was at the bath when the money was brought to him, and in his anger at the insult thus offered him, he immediately divided the money into three parts, giving them respectively to the keeper of the baths, the seller of refreshments, and the slave who brought the money. "The Sultan shall learn," he said proudly, "that Firdusi did not spend the labor of thirty years to be rewarded with silver."

Of course this independence of spirit upon the part of Firdusi angered the haughty Sultan, who, when he learned that his gift had been despised, condemned the poet to be trampled to death by an elephant upon the following morning. But this vile deed came not to pass, for the outraged poet fled, first giving into the hands of the prime-minister a sealed paper containing a bitter satire upon Mahmud, which he desired to be inserted in the epic in place of his former eulogy.

The chronicles relate that, as a result of this most unfortunate incident, Firdusi, like Dante, became for long years an exile and wanderer, being driven by the persecutions of the Sultan from court to court, from country to country. Finally, however, after many weary years of banishment and harassing care, friends of Firdusi, with great difficulty, extorted from the Sultan a pardon, and the ill-starred poet, old and broken, returned unobtrusively to his native town. Here the days of the immortal bard soon drew to a close. It is related that, hearing a little child singing in the streets of Tus some of his own verses, his bitter wrongs and sufferings were so vividly recalled to him that he was seized with faintness, and, being carried to his home, soon after expired. His death occurred A. D. 1020, in the eighty-ninth year of his age. Being refused burial in sacred ground, the Sheik also declining to read the customary prayers over his grave, the old poet was buried in the beautiful garden where so hopefully he had dreamed the long, long thoughts of poetic youth. Now, alas! thus ended the earthly career of grand old Firdusi, the "Oriental Homer," as he has been called; also greatest poet of Persia, and one of the greatest of all literature.

But, though Firdusi was now peacefully laid to rest, his story runs on. For, according to one of the legends, it is related that the Sultan, having at last learned of his minister's treachery, banished him from his court forever. And not only this, for being stricken with remorse at having driven unjustly from his side the poet who had made his court "resplendent as Paradise," as he himself had said, Mahmud determined to make reparation. Learning, therefore, that Firdusi was living obscurely at Tus, he sent him the long-delayed payment, together with camels loaded with princely gifts—but too late! The royal retinue met the funeral of the great poet at the city gates. Firdusi being no more, the Sultan's gifts were offered to the poet's daughter, by whom they were disdainfully refused. Other relatives, however, accepted the peace offering, building with it a bridge, the dreamed-of dike, and a house of refuge for travellers—all of which memorials are now gone.

But Firdusi's fame lives on, growing brighter with the years. When the storm-tossed, unappreciated old poet, therefore, in self-justification said that he had written what no tide should ever wash away, what men unborn should read o'er oceans wide, he made no idle boast. For to-d y, not only Persian boys and girls, but the young people of the world—as well as all lovers of good literature—are reading with delight the fascinating legends of Persia, as mirrored forth in the Shah-Nameh, or Book of Kings, of the grand old poet, Firdusi the Persian.

KAVAH THE BLACKSMITH

ONCE upon a time, so the old chronicles relate, during the reign of Jemshid the Shah, there dwelt in the deserts of Arabia a King named Mirtas. Now Mirtas was rich in flocks and herds of goats, sheep and camels which yielded up a bounteous store of balmy milk; and this milk the generous King always distributed in charity among the poor. So God was pleased with Mirtas, and increased his favor upon him accordingly.

Now this King, smiled upon by the Almighty, had one priceless possession, his only son, Zohak, who, in his youth, seemed destined to rival his father in nobility of character. But, alas! upon this noble young cypress, so luxuriant in buds of promise, there suddenly fell a blight, disastrous alike to the house of Mirtas and to the land of Persia. And this is how it came about.

One day Iblis, the Evil One, roaming the earth in search of mischief, chanced to stray into the palace of Mirtas, and, in so doing, he happened upon the charming young Zohak. Now Iblis was disguised as a noble, and so eloquent and full of guile was his discourse, that the young prince, fascinated, eagerly besought his new friend to let the music of his voice continue to delight him.

Then Iblis, who saw here a fertile field for his guile, was pleased to see the charm work so well. So, his tongue dropping honey, he thus spake unto the youthful Zohak:

"O Pearl of the East, alas! for though I am master of still sweeter converse, I may not address it unto one so

1

young unless thou wilt first enter into a solemn compact with me never under any pretence to divulge what I shall tell unto thee."

Alas! Zohak was guileless and simple of heart, and so, suspecting no evil, he sware unto Iblis that he would obey him in all things, for he believed him to be noble and good. Judge, then, of his surprise and horror when, the oath taken, Iblis said unto him:

"O Light of the Universe, thou who art fair and wise and valiant, give ear unto the voice of thy friend, and soon thy stately young head shall be raised above the stars. Listen! Thy father hath become old, and longeth to enter into his reward. While he liveth, necessarily thou wilt remain unknown. Let him, therefore, no longer stand in thy way. The robes of sovereignty are ready, and better adapted to thee. But raise thy hand, therefore, and the name of Mirtas shall be naught but a beautiful memory in the world. The leaves in the Book of Fate turn slowly, but who can change what is written on its pages?"

Thus spake wily Iblis and as the meaning of this fiendish suggestion dawned fully upon him it would be hard indeed to picture to you Zohak's horror and dismay. Enough to say that at first he refused utterly to be a party to his father's death, but, though the struggle was long and obstinate, Iblis finally terrified and subdued the youth by telling him that if he refused, his own life would be the forfeit. Then, in order to make it easier for him to agree to the proposal, Iblis assured Zohak that he need not perform the deed with his own hands, but merely consent to it.

So Iblis dug a pit on the pathway that led to Mirtas's house of prayer, and covered it over with grass. And presently, when night was preparing to throw her dark mantle over the earth, as the King, according to his custom, was going unto the house of prayer, it came to pass that he fell into the pit, and his legs and arms being broken by the fall, he shortly after expired.

Thus, according to the legend, perished Mirtas, that father whose tenderness would not suffer even the winds to blow upon his son too roughly. And thus also Zohak, in his tender youth, sold himself unto the Evil One.

Now Iblis, having succeeded in getting Zohak into his power, continued to bestow upon him the most devoted attention and flattery, with the view of moulding him entirely unto his will. Among other things, therefore, he taught him the art of magic; and, having done so, he assured him that through it he should become the greatest monarch of his time. But though the ear of Zohak was ever open unto Iblis, he ruled his people in both good and evil, for he was not yet wholly given over unto guile.

Seeing this, therefore, Iblis imagined a new device in his black heart, for he was not yet satisfied with the degree of authority which he had obtained over the young King, desiring above all things to see him completely given over unto evil. Consequently, with this end in view, by the aid of magic, he took upon himself the form of an engaging youth, and, appearing thus before Zohak, he craved permission to serve him as director of the royal kitchen. Pleased with the guileless manners of the youth, and with the delicious and savory food which he caused to be spread before him, the King finally commanded that the keys of the great store-rooms be given him, and that he be allowed to reign supreme over the royal board.

You must know that up to this time, men had been nourished with bread, and fruit, and herbs alone; Iblis, however, prepared flesh for Zohak, and invented the art of cooking. And cunning indeed was this device, for the King was delighted with the new dishes made from every variety of bird, and four-footed animal, and lived but for each new repast. Every day, therefore, something dainty and rare was prepared for the royal table, and every day Iblis increased in favor, for the flesh gave unto the King courage and strength like unto a lion, and the fame of his table was great in the land.

But of all the new dishes prepared for the King, an egg was unto him the most delicious of all. "What can be superior to this?" he cried in ecstasy, rolling his eyes toward heaven, and heaving a sigh of profound content.

"Speak not so," replied Iblis, smiling, "for to-morrow thou shalt partake of something still more savory."

The next day, therefore, the magician of the King's kitchen brought unto his majesty's table delicious fare, served exquisitely to please the eye as well as taste, partridge and pheasant, a banquet for a prince. Then Zohak, delighted beyond measure, exclaimed impulsively:

"O Prince among Cooks, verily for this new wonder wrought in our behalf, whatsoever thou desirest, and I can give, is thine. Thou hast but to speak the word."

Then Iblis, glad and little anxious, replied unto His Majesty that he had but one request—one unimportant wish. It was to kiss the mighty monarch's naked shoulder—a mere whim!

So Zohak, unsuspicious, stripped his shoulders, glad to gratify a wish so flattering and so simple. Then cunning Iblis quickly stooped, and twice he kissed the King with fiendish glee, and, having done so, vanished from the sight of men.

But alas, alas for Zohak! for forth from his shoulders, at each salute, sprang hissing serpents, venomous and black, whose fiery tongues darted unceasingly about, as though in search of prey. And at this, imagine, if you can, Zohak's horror and dismay! his angry cries of fear and rage! the frenzied haste with which he gave command to have the ugly creatures severed at the roots! But vain their utmost haste; vain all their zeal, for no sooner were the writhing things cut off, than quickly forth once more they sprang, like veritable jacks-in-a-box. And though the King's servants wearied not, but struck again and again, and yet again, it was all to no purpose, for every time that the vile creatures were severed, they sprang forth bigger, blacker, and uglier than before, each new pair writhing and hissing yet more angrily, as though, like Iblis, they longed for naught so much as to lodge their poisonous venom deep in the hearts of men.

And now, indeed, was there tumult in the King's court! And well was it for Iblis that, though the most diligent search was instituted, he was nowhere to be found throughout the whole dominion. Useless, therefore, was their search; and all to no purpose did the King's ministers offer mountains of gold as a reward for him who should rid His Majesty of the awful evil laid upon him. In response to the proclamation the most celebrated magicians and wise men of the East flocked unto the court of Zohak, but, among them all, not one was found able to charm away the dreadful vipers.

Every sunrise a new magician, every sunset failure reported; this was the record of the wretched days of Zohak the King from this time forth, until hope was almost dead in his heart. Then one day, as the unhappy monarch sat upon his gorgeous throne, sunk in the most abject misery, Iblis, in the guise of a skilled physician, once more presented himself before the King, and, after examination and mature deliberation, thus spake the cunning one unto his prey:

"O Shelter of the Universe, I have searched the heavens diligently concerning the horrible evil which hath fallen upon thee, and in thy horoscope I read a bitter tale. For behold, in the Book of Fate it is written that from this time forth thou shalt be known among men as the 'Serpent King,' since the stars have decreed that the hissing, writhing vipers shall remain connected with thee throughout thy life, involving thee in perpetual misery. Hope not, therefore, by the arts of magic to avert thy fate, for charms are of no avail when pitted against the stars."

Alas! As Zohak heard this dire interpretation of his horoscope, he uttered an exceedingly bitter cry, and gave himself up utterly to despair; seeing which, Iblis smiled, for he knew that the hour of his triumph was near. Concealing his satisfaction, however, he thus spake unto Zohak:

"O Heaven Accursed, despair not yet so utterly, for one faint ray of hope saw I glimmering for thee from afar, which, if thou wilt, thou mayest cause even yet to burst forth into a sunbeam of promise. For lo, it is written, that if yonder writhing creatures be fed daily upon human brains, which would be the same unto them as poison, in the course of time they may die; at any rate, in this way only can thy life be prolonged and made easy. It is for thee to decide."

So, having thus cunningly lodged this evil suggestion in the mind of the King, Iblis once more vanished, evidently through the ceiling, for there floated down thence unto the ears of the unhappy monarch the mocking refrain:

"If life hath any charm for thee,
The brain of man their food must be!"

Now the truth was, Iblis hated the human race, and he was, therefore, greatly delighted to think that as a result of his cunning, in time a great portion of mankind would be destroyed by the dreadful serpents. For well he knew that Zohak had now become so desperate that he would do anything to obtain release from his misery. What he did not know was that all his craft and cunning were powerless to affect God's plans for the children of Adam.

But alas for Zohak! And alas also for his subjects! For the chronicles relate that from this time forth was he given over wholly unto evil, and that each sunrise saw two young men of the flower of the land slain to gratify the furious hunger of the serpents. And lo! the fear of the King was great in the land.

Nor did the fame and fear of the Serpent King confine itself to his own borders. Alas, no! for Persia was also to suffer at his hands. And now you must hear something of the Shahs of Old, but particularly of the great Shah, Jemshid, whose fate was so closely bound up with that of Zohak.

In the old chronicles of Persia we read that Kaimurs was the first Shah of Iran, and that he was chosen by the people to rule over them. Prior to his time, each man lived for himself, in the most primitive way, owning allegiance to no one but Ormuzd, the great God of the Persians.

Now the legends tell us that Kaimurs was so wise and good that even the animals assembled to do him homage, and to help fight his battles. Yea, it is even said that, when he was crowned, great lions and tigers came forth from their lairs in the distant forest, and that with them there crouched low before the monarch wolves and leopards, together with the fierce wild boar, and the fleet-footed ass of the desert. A strange coronation pageant, surely!

But Kaimurs was loved by men, as well as beasts, and so he prospered and grew strong. Unfortunately, however, he had one very powerful enemy, the great King of the Deevs, who ruled over Mazinderan, a province to the north of Kaimurs's kingdom. And since not only Kaimurs, but, later on, many other of the Shahs and heroes of Iran were called upon, again and again, to battle with this wily race, you will be interested to hear what they were like.

Well, these wicked Deevs, according to the descriptions given of them, appear to have been a strange mixture of man, and animal, and evil spirit. They walked upright, like men, but were possessed of horns, long ears, and tails; and many of them are described as cat-headed. Great numbers of them too are said to have been small and black, but there were also many giants among them, and as one and all of them were past masters in the arts of sorcery and enchantment, it required very great courage indeed to fight against them, since in battle they could, at will, call up whirlwinds and great fires, while they, themselves, could vanish whenever it pleased them to do so. You can easily understand, therefore, that it took the courage of a real hero to go forth to battle against the Deevs.

This, however, Kaimurs's subjects were called upon to do, since a day came when the King of the Deevs sent out

against Iran a great army of cat-headed men, giants, and
other monsters of horrible aspect, with the command
utterly to subdue the land. Now in this emergency, the
son of Kaimurs, who was very brave, was sent at the
head of a large army to repulse the invading host. But
alas! the young prince was slain at the very beginning of
the battle, and his army scattered unto the four winds.
Then was Kaimurs forced to flee, and Persia was given
over unto the Deevs.

Now long and bitterly did the Shah of Iran grieve for
the loss of his son, and the overthrow of his kingdom. But
presently, in the far-off cavern where he lay hid from his
enemies, he heard the voice of the Angel Serosch, which
said unto him:

"O Beloved of Ormuzd, come forth into the sunshine of
the world, for lo! victory lieth in the hands of thy grandson. Send him forth, therefore, to grasp it."

So Kaimurs took heart, and calling before him his
dearly loved grandson, the youthful Husheng, he commanded him to go forth to meet the mighty Deevs in the
name of Ormuzd the Blessed, who promised a sure victory
unto his children.

Before going, however, Husheng, who was wise, as well
as valiant of heart, in addition to his loyal subjects, summoned to his assistance all the wild beasts of the forests,
and even the birds of the air, whose duty it was to confuse
the foe by flying in their faces, and by making fearful
swoops at their eyes.

A strange sight, therefore, must have been Husheng's
army, when drawn up in battle array; but a yet more terrible thing to see was the mighty host of advancing Deevs,
enveloped as it was in lurid flames and clouds of smoke.

But the sight caused brave Husheng not a tremor, so filled with courage and the certainty of victory was he.

And, in the fiercely contested battle which ensued, so great was the heroism of the Persians, inspired as they were on all sides by their brave young leader, that not even the Deevs could stand before them. Husheng himself, also, performed marvels in valor, slaying in single combat, not only the King of the Deevs, but also the most important members of his family. Whereupon, in dismay, the remnant of the Deevs betook themselves to ignominious flight. Howbeit, few escaped; for, by the orders of Husheng, they were pursued by the tigers, wolves, and panthers, which tore them to pieces as they fled.

It was indeed a glorious victory, and as a result of it, the kingdom of Persia was at last secure; and from this time forth, under Husheng's mighty sway, civilization grew apace, reaching at last a climax in the long reign of Jemshid, who was grandson of the valiant Husheng.

Now it is related of Jemshid that for seven hundred years he sat upon the throne of light, during which time Persia enjoyed her Golden Age of prosperity. And not only was Jemshid girt about with power and glory, but the whole world was happier for his sake; since, smiled upon by Ormuzd, during all this period, no one died or was ill, and the King, along with his subjects, remained ever in the prime of youth and strength, old age, death, pain, and sorrow being unknown.

During this period, also, the Deevs were subservient unto the great Shah, building for him magnificent palaces, inside of which were lofty halls with springing fountains, silken carpets covering soft divans on which to lie, and walls hung with pictures, embroidered silks, and jewelled hangings, all of which were fashioned by the Genii. They also erected for Jemshid a most glorious throne, upon which they transported him from one city to another in the twinkling of an eye. Now so gorgeously beautiful was this throne that it became the wonder of the world.

Jemshid, however, was not a valiant warrior like Husheng, but a builder of civilization. He first separated men into classes, divided the year into periods, encouraged building, and likewise is credited with the discovery of perfumes, the art of healing, the invention of ships, and many other useful means of benefiting mankind. It was he also who instituted the Neurouz, or New Year, at the time of the spring solstice, a festival still celebrated in Persia with many ceremonies during ten days.

You will not be surprised to hear, therefore, that Jemshid's power increased continually; for, learning of his wisdom and goodness, men flocked unto his standard from all corners of the earth. And small wonder, since he was indeed a most beneficent and glorious King. But alas! the time came, so the legends tell us, when Jemshid's head was turned by the height of power that he had reached. Then it came about that pride took possession of the heart of the King, and he forgot unto whom he owed his power and the source of his blessings. It is even said that the time came when, so great was his arrogance, he beheld only himself in the world, and he named himself God, and sent forth his image to be worshipped.

Alas for Jemshid! When the Mubids, who are astrologers and wise men, heard this decree of the King, they bowed their gray heads in sorrow, for they feared that the downfall of the Shah was near, since, forgetting his

Creator, he assumed himself to be the sole architect of his greatness. But their words of wisdom only resulted in driving the King, who seemed possessed of an evil Deev, into still greater folly.

So there finally came a day when Jemshid commanded by proclamation that all his subjects should assemble in the great square in front of the royal palace, and there, at the appointed hour, a wonderful scene took place.

Howbeit, in order to appreciate what happened, you must know that the Deevs had made of the royal abode a palace like unto a fairy dream. Indeed yes; for all the outside walls, we are told, were covered with beautifully painted tiles, while the many windows and balconies were made of fretted stone work, encrusted with cut and polished glass, so that the whole glorious building, whose towers seemed almost to pierce the heavens, glittered and sparkled as though besprinkled with diamonds.

But in front of the beautiful palace, there glittered something still more gorgeous: it was the throne of the mighty Jemshid, studded, not with glass, but with every precious stone you have ever heard tell of, and a great many that you have not. In fact, so resplendent was it when lit up by the brilliant Eastern sunshine, that it became almost too dazzling for mortal eyes.

On the morning in question, however, the gorgeous throne was empty, though about it were stationed, as guards, a great company of cat-headed Deevs, gigantic Afreets, and fearsome-looking Jinns; while the magnificent, jewel-studded awning was held in place by graceful Peris, a kind of fairy. All of which indicated that the Shelter of the Universe would soon appear.

But though yet quite early, already every inch of standing room in the great square, as far as the eye could see, was crowded with dark faces and eager, upturned eyes. So impatient were the people to behold the Glory of the World and to learn his purpose in so calling them together!

And presently, the trumpets having been sounded, and the tom-toms beaten, the glorious Jemshid deigned to gladden the eyes of his loyal subjects. Slowly he mounted the gorgeous throne, and, as he did so, all the people fell on their faces before him, performing obeisance. As they rose to their feet, however, so majestic and magnificent was Jemshid's presence that, with one accord, the people burst forth into a loud and prolonged "Bah! Bah!" of admiration, which form of expressing astonishment and pleasure is said to be customary among the Persians still to-day.

But you must hear how Jemshid looked to cause such a "Bah! Bah!" of approval. Well, to begin with, the great Shah wore many silken coats, one over the other, and a beautiful fur mantle outside all the rest. As for his gorgeously embroidered, baggy trousers, behold, they were tight at the ankles, while his slippers were of pure gold. Yes, and upon his head he wore an immense, many-colored turban, in the front of which blazed a huge diamond, set about with rubies and pearls. As for the rest, he was tall, and dark, and majestic, looking every inch a king.

As he raised his sceptre, therefore, commanding silence, the tumult at once ceased, while all awaited breathlessly his words. But the great Jemshid merely asked his people a simple question. He said:

"Long, long, O my people, have you basked in the sunshine of a Golden Age. Now tell me, unto whom do you owe this marvellous prosperity?"

In response to this query, at once the air rang with shouts of, "Hail unto Ormuzd the Blessed! Hail unto the great God of the Persians!"

Alas! This was not the reply that the arrogant Jemshid had desired or expected, so with a frown as black as the cloud of smoke which one could see curling lazily up into the blue from the great volcano Demavend, not far distant, the great Shah thundered forth at his people:

"O Foolish Ones, blind as moles or worms, know you not, then, that there is but one God of the Persians, even Jemshid the Glorious? Bow the knee unto him, therefore, and not unto Ormuzd."

Now the wonder of such arrogance held the great crowd breathless for one intense moment; then, suddenly, a shiver ran through the vast multitude, and the cry went up: "Demavend! Look at Demavend! The volcano! Oh, the volcano!" Then all eyes turned unto the mountain. And lo! the snow-covered crest was all aglow with dusky red, while a huge black cloud issued from the crater, and moved with lightning speed down toward the plain, finally hovering like a great black bird of ill omen over the awe-struck people, who turned in their terror for aid unto Jemshid.

But in vain, for even as his subjects gazed upon him, the grandeur and glory of the proud king vanished as if by magic. There was no thunder and no lightning, but suddenly, without a sign of warning, the gorgeous palace fell silently into a heap of unsightly ruins; the gem-studded throne, the wonder and glory of the world, crumbled into a heap of worthless dust; and Jemshid's royal robes became fluttering rags, such as the very beggars of the streets would disdain.

However, this was not the most terrible thing that happened upon that eventful day, for along the ground glided venomous snakes and loathsome lizards, which quickly sprang up out of the ruins, while down from the black clouds there rained a veritable army of huge scorpions, tarantulas, and swiftly running centipedes.

Now it is unnecessary to say that very soon these loathsome creatures had the great square to themselves, for verily in their mad terror and anxiety to escape, the people fairly flew from the spot. And thus ended their allegiance to Jemshid, for recognizing in the day's happenings a sure sign of the displeasure of Ormuzd the Blessed, they cried out in their anger that they would no longer obey Jemshid as their Shah, since through his pride and presumption he had forfeited the favor of the Almighty.

So it happened that the people of Iran and Turan, having heard that in the land of Arabia there reigned a monarch mighty and terrible unto his foes, now turned unto Zohak, and Jemshid, fleeing upon his milk-white charger before the Arab host, became a wanderer upon the face of the earth, without a friend, and with many foes. And Zohak, the Serpent King, ruled in his stead.

But though the royal wanderer carried a high price upon his head, the chronicles relate that for the space of twice fifty years no man knew whither he was gone, for he hid from the wrath of the Serpent King. Howbeit, such was the zeal of his enemy, that in the course of time Jemshid could no longer escape the spies of Zohak, who finally captured him, as he wandered upon the shores of far Cathay, and brought him in triumph before the Serpent King.

Yea, like the narcissus bent with heavy dew, oppressed with shame, his hands behind his back, and ponderous chains passing from neck to feet, thus stood before the cruel King the once so glorious Jemshid. But alas! the sorry sight awakened in the breast of Zohak not the lightest thrill of pity as, gazing with a scornful smile upon the fallen monarch, tauntingly he said:

"O Lord of the World, and Heaven, behold thy worshippers at thy feet! But—where is thy diadem? thy throne? Where is thy kingdom now? Where thy sovereign power? Alas, I see them not!"

At this cruel speech, the drooping figure straightened, and kingly Jemshid, gazing unflinchingly into the serpent eyes of his tormentor, thus calmly spoke:

"O Serpent-haunted One, unjustly am I brought in chains before thee, betrayed, insulted—thou the cause of all. Feign not, therefore, to feel my wrongs, but work thy cruel will, and thou shalt see that still I am a King."

Imagine Zohak's rage at this defiance mixed with royal scorn! His inward fury! Though smiling, still he said:

"Most Kingly King, bereft of throne and power, one thing at least remaineth yet unto thee: to choose the manner of thy passing. Shall I behead thee, stab thee, impale thee, or with an arrow's point transfix thy heart? What is thy kingly choice?"

Now seeing the evil intent of the King, and scorning to cringe before a thing so base, Jemshid, raising high his royal head and smiling proudly, said:

"O Slave of Iblis, since I am in thy power, do with me what thou wilt. Why should I dread thy utmost vengeance? Why express a wish to save my body from a moment's pain? True, I have lived too long, but Jemshid's memory in the world will live, undimmed by thee."

Then Zohak, realizing from these words that it was not

in his power to break the spirit of proud Jemshid, resolved upon a most horrible deed of vengeance. Ordering, forthwith, that two planks be brought, the royal prisoner was fastened between them, and his body divided the whole length with a saw, making two figures of Jemshid out of one.

So perished the great Jemshid, because he was presumptuous, and in his pride would have lifted himself above his Maker. But the good deeds which he wrought in the first half of his reign have caused his name to live, and even to-day the Persians look back with pride unto the splendor of their country in the days when the great Shah Jemshid sat upon the throne of light, comparing it with the glory of King Solomon.

But Persia groaned under the tyranny of Zohak, who day by day continued to pile evil upon evil until the measure thereof was full unto overflowing, and darkness had settled over all the land because of his wickedness. Shedding blood had now become the evil King's pastime, and he hesitated not at committing every species of crime, until despair filled all hearts.

> "The serpents still on human brains were fed,
> And every day two youthful victims bled;
> The sword, still ready, thirsting still to strike,
> Warrior and slave were sacrificed alike."

Howbeit, things could not go on thus forever, and so, in the course of time, thanks unto Ormuzd, there sprang forth from among the Persians a hero who should avenge the wrongs of his countrymen, and add new lustre unto the glory of Persia. And of this you shall hear.

For behold, it happened that, all unheeded by Zohak, there lived in his dominion at this time a man named

Kavah, a blacksmith, remarkably strong and brave, and possessing a large family of fair sons, who were the joy of his life. One by one, however, they were taken from him to be killed to feed the King's serpents, until but one remained unto him, and finally the lot fell also unto this last of his sons to meet a like death. Then Kavah arose in his wrath and sought the court of the Shah.

But you will not be surprised to learn that about this same time, Zohak was having evil dreams; and so, oppressed by terrors of conscience, he called together an assembly of his nobles, and insisted that they sign a document asserting that he, Zohak, had ever been unto Persia a just, wise, and beneficent King. And behold, it was even as this remarkable paper was being signed that the cry of one who demanded justice was heard at the gates.

Wishing to show unto his nobles, therefore, that he stood ever eager to do justice, Zohak commanded that the petitioner be brought immediately into the audience-room. And lo! Kavah, the avenger, stood before the King, and the assembly of the nobles. Now so terrible was the aspect of this deeply wronged man that, for a moment, all gazed at him in wonder. Then Zohak, the Serpent King, opened his mouth and thus addressed the sturdy Kavah:

"O Brawny One, I charge thee give a name unto him who hath done thee wrong!"

Then Kavah, knowing by the two writhing serpents that it was the Shah who questioned him, smote his head with his hands and uttered a savage cry. But, by a mighty effort, regaining his self-control, he once more faced the King calmly, as he said:

"O Serpent King, thou beholdest before thee Kavah the blacksmith, a blameless man, who hath come into thy presence to sue for justice. And lo! it is against thee, O King, that I raise my cry, and with reason. Seventeen brave sons have I called mine, yet to-day but one remaineth alive, and even now the mouths of thy brain-devouring serpents yawn to feed upon him also, to still their demon hunger. Thou art the King, 'tis true, but why on innocent heads cast fire and ashes? If Iblis, for thy evil deeds, hath given unto thee the form of hissing dragon, why to me be cruel? Why give the brains of my fair sons as serpent food, and then dare prate of doing justice? But thy doom is fixed, thou Cruel One, and even now the avenger's hand is at the door. Behold, and tremble!"

Now so fierce and sudden was this assault that Zohak, appalled by the rage and sorrow of a father whose language sounded indeed like a cry of doom, at once ordered that the son of Kavah be brought forth and restored unto him. Then, regaining somewhat his arrogance, he bade the brawny smith inscribe his name upon the lying register, already signed by some of the mightiest nobles of the land.

But Kavah, when he learned the purport of the register, hesitated not, but turned wrathfully upon the assembled nobles, crying indignantly:

"O Feeble-hearted Ones, are you then men, or what, leagued with this human monster? Only a common man am I, and yet never will I lend my hand unto such a lie, and no more shall you, nobles though you be!"

Seizing the hated register, therefore, to the astonishment of all, Kavah tore it fiercely into bits, and trampled it under his feet with rage and scorn. Then, pausing not, he strode forth from the palace, taking his rescued son with him. And so majestic and fearless was his bearing as he passed, that none, not even the King, dared raise a finger to detain him.

So, feeling that at last the time had come for action, from the palace, Kavah went straight unto the market-place. Here he rehearsed unto the people what wrongs the nation suffered, urging them to shake off the yoke of the cruel Serpent King, who was not even of their land. And so confident of success was Kavah, so eloquent and so brave, that multitudes, whose children had been sacrificed unto the brain-devouring vipers, flocked eagerly about the blacksmith, shouting madly: "Justice! Give us justice!"

Then Kavah, feeling the need of a standard about which the people might rally, took off the leathern apron wherewith blacksmiths cover their knees when they strike with the hammer, and, raising it aloft upon the point of a lance, cried out joyously:

"Behold, O my countrymen, the banner which shall lead us on to victory, delivering us from out the hands of the cruel Serpent King."

Then a glorious shout, the music of which reached even unto the palace, went up from the people, who thronged eagerly about their brave and brawny leader, mad for revenge. So Kavah led them forth from the city bearing aloft his standard—that standard which, later on, adorned with gold and jewels, and called the "Flag of Kavah," became a sacred symbol, honored by every Persian king in succeeding generations as the true sign of royalty.

But Kavah knew that not unto him was it given to be the real liberator of Persia from the tyranny of Zohak. He had kindled the flame of revolt, but a greater than he must make of the spark a devouring fire. Howbeit, the hero was ready, as you shall hear, thanks unto Serosch, the blessed Angel of Pity.

For you must know that this angel, who each night flieth seven times around the earth in order to watch over the children of Ormuzd, saw and was moved with compassion for the sufferings of the people; and so, presently, a grandson was born unto Jemshid, whose horoscope decreed that he should not only be the deliverer of his country, but should reign long and gloriously upon the throne of light. And this Kavah knew, for the Blessed Angel had made it known unto him in a dream, after he had proved himself brave and fearless of heart.

And since the Orientals say that a secret known unto two is one no longer, you, too, shall know that the name of the coming hero was Feridoun. But of how, by his splendid deeds, he earned for himself the title of "The Glorious," you must hear in another story.

FERIDOUN THE GLORIOUS

UPON a starry night, during the festival of roses, long, long ago in the land of Persia, the Angel Serosch, flying through the night, brought unto the home of Abtin, son of Jemshid, a charming babe, destined for mighty deeds. Now the name of the child was Feridoun, and it is related that upon the night of his birth Zohak, the Serpent King, had a terrible dream, which you shall hear.

Behold, it came to pass that as the King lay upon the royal couch, suddenly, in his sleep, he felt himself attacked by three warriors, two of them of powerful stature, but the third a mere youth, slender like unto a·young cypress. In his hands the stripling bare a huge, cow-headed mace, and with it he felled Zohak pitilessly to the ground. And useless was all resistance, for though the frenzied monarch struggled madly, the doughty youth bound his hands, and casting a rope about his neck, dragged him rudely along in the presence of crowds of hooting, gibing people. Now at this crisis, so great was the King's anguish that, screaming horribly, he awoke. And lo! it was all a dream.

But in those times dreams were considered portentous; so now Zohak, springing up terror-stricken from his bed, hastily called together his Mubids, although it was still the dead of night, and, having related unto them the particulars of his frightful experience, he demanded a faithful interpretation of his dream.

22

Now the Mubids saw in this vision the approaching overthrow of the tyrant, but they were afraid to tell the truth unto Zohak, fearing for their lives. So three days were allowed to pass under the pretence of studying more scrupulously the signs, and still no one had the courage to speak out. Then the King grew angry, and in this dilemma, Zirek, one of the wise men, finally stood boldly forth and said:

"O Lord of the World, much we deplore it, but the stars foretell for thee a bitter fate, since thy dream announces the coming of a great and glorious prince, who shall hurl thee from thy throne, and bind thee in chains upon the mountains. Feridoun is his name, and he shall add lustre unto the house of Jemshid, and unto the land of Persia, though naught but woe shall he bring unto the Serpent King, whose day is already darkening into endless night."

Alas for the King! Hearing this interpretation of his dream, he fell senseless upon the ground, and the Mubids fled from before his wrath. Now long he lay as one dead, and when consciousness did finally return unto him, he could neither eat nor sleep, but continued overwhelmed with fear and misery. And from this time forth, the legends say, Zohak knew neither rest nor joy, the light of his day being already darkened.

But instead of checking the King in his evil course, this experience seems only to have stimulated him to further cruelty. For, warned by the prophecy of the Mubids, Zohak now issued a decree that every person belonging unto the race of Jemshid, wherever found, should be seized and fettered and brought to him; for he hoped thus to secure the fateful prince of his dream. Sending out his spies everywhere, therefore, he caused the world to be scoured for Feridoun, but in vain.

Nevertheless, the young prince was passing his first baby days peacefully in the King's dominions, watched over tenderly by his father and mother, and daily growing in strength that should fit him to carry out the noble task assigned unto him by Providence.

For Abtin, the father of Feridoun, knowing of the King's decree in regard to the race of Jemshid, had avoided discovery by continuing to reside in the most retired and solitary places; but one day his usual caution forsook him, and he ventured beyond the limits of safety. Now this was most unfortunate at this time, for Zohak had learned of the glorious son born unto Abtin, and his spies were everywhere searching for him. Abtin's imprudence, therefore, was dreadfully punished, for, being recognized, he was carried before the King, in whose presence he was foully slain.

But not so was Zohak to secure the desire of his heart, for when Faranuk, the mother of Feridoun, heard of the dreadful catastrophe which had befallen her husband, at once she took up her infant and fled, pausing for naught. Then, footsore and weary, her heart torn with fear and sorrow, day after day this brave young mother kept up her flight, traversing burning sands and dark, demon-haunted forests, seeking a place of safety for baby Feridoun, who, realizing not his peril, cooed and laughed and slept, always clasped close in his mother's arms.

Finally, one evening just as the sun was kissing the world good night, away in the depths of the forest Faranuk came upon a beautiful spot of pasture ground. And presently, the soft tinkle, tinkle of a bell falling upon her ear, she hastened forward, and behold! an old, old man, gentle of face and mien, milked a wondrous cow, whose hairs were like unto the plumes of a peacock for beauty. Now the name of this cow of remarkable lineage was Purmajeh, and the keeper of the pasture gave away in charity the abundance of milk which she supplied.

Gently accosting the old man, therefore, Faranuk was assured a welcome; and so here she rested for the night, thinking to continue her flight in the morning. But, as a consequence of the grief and distress of mind which she had suffered, the poor mother was unable to supply her child with food, and so, urged by the gentle old man, she decided to remain in this quiet retreat for a time, at least.

But, continually afraid of being discovered and recognized, Faranuk knew not a moment's peace. Finally, it was borne in upon her, she knew not how, that it would be safer for little Feridoun if she were not with him, and so, resigning him to the protection of God, she left the pasture, and continued her flight alone unto Mount Alborz.

Now the keeper of the pasture, into whose care the mother had confided her little one, cherished the child with the fondness and affection of a most devoted parent; and so, for three happy years, Feridoun rolled and tumbled in the pasture, and Purmajeh was his nurse. A wondrous playfellow, also, was Purmajeh, and well indeed was it for Persia that the baby shouts of glee reached not unto the ears of the Serpent King.

But better still was it that Feridoun was in the guardianship of Ormuzd, and that Serosch, his messenger, neither slumbered nor slept. For it happened that one night, the Angel of Pity, resting for a moment upon the battlements of Zohak's palace, after having flown seven

times around the world, heard issue thence a fiendish laugh
of triumph, which sent the Gentle-hearted One speeding
upon swift wings toward Mount Alborz. And there,
Faranuk, thinking that she dreamed, listened unto the
voice of the Angel, which warned her that Feridoun was no
longer safe in the pasture.

As the morning dawned, therefore, Faranuk, with swift
feet, hastened back unto the forest hiding-place, confiding
unto the gentle old man of the pasture her intention of
conveying Feridoun unto a safer place of refuge upon
Mount Alborz. But the keeper, who loved Feridoun above
all else in the world, remonstrated with the young mother,
saying sorrowfully unto her:

"Why, O Faranuk, dost thou take the child unto the
mountain? Alas! he will surely perish there, while here
he is so happy!"

But Faranuk dared not disregard the warning of the
Angel Serosch, and so, comforting the old man, with her
boy in her arms she once more took up her flight. And
wise was she in doing so, for intelligence had reached
Zohak that the young prince was being nourished and
protected by the keeper of the pasture, and, like a hungry
tiger, he was preparing to spring upon his prey.

That same day, therefore, at the head of a force of
picked men, he proceeded secretly unto the pasture, hoping to surprise the keeper, and thus secure the Prince.
But once more his prey had escaped him, and when he
discovered this, verily, he was like unto a mad elephant in
his fury. For, not only did he cruelly slay the keeper of
the pasture, and the wondrous cow Purmajeh, but so great
was his frenzy that he stopped not until he had slain every
living thing around about, and made of the beautiful

spot a desert. And this done, diligently he continued his
search, but neither sight nor tidings could he get of Feridoun, and his heart was filled with rage and despair.

Now upon Mount Alborz at this time there dwelt a
pious hermit, and unto him Faranuk committed her boy,
informing the old man that her son was destined for
mighty deeds. So, being gladly welcomed, from this time
forth the mother and child abode with the pious old
recluse, who generously divided with them all the food
and comforts which God gave him, at the same time, as
Feridoun grew older, developing and storing his mind
with various kinds of knowledge. Yea, and he also consulted the Books of Fate concerning him, after which he
said unto Faranuk:

"O woman, I perceive that the Prince foretold by wise
men and astrologers as the destroyer of Zohak and his
tyranny, is thy son. Rejoice, therefore, and be glad of
heart, for

"This child to whom thou gavest birth,
Will be the monarch of the earth."

But Faranuk's heart was filled, not only with joy, but
also with foreboding, upon hearing her own convictions
thus confirmed, for well she knew and dreaded the fearful
power of Zohak. Nevertheless, her days were happy, for
had she not her boy still with her? And was he not under
the sheltering care of the Almighty?

But the years tarried not, and so when twice eight summers had passed over the head of Feridoun, he was no
longer a child, but a bright, handsome youth of sixteen,
strong and valiant of heart. Then one day he sought out
his mother, and questioned her as to his lineage. So
Faranuk, seeing that the time was ripe, told unto her son

stories of Iran and the Shahs of Old; of the valiant Husheng; of the glorious reign of Jemshid, his illustrious grandsire; of the cruel Serpent King; and, last of all, of his father's tragic fate.

Now Feridoun listened intently unto his mother's tales; then, standing up straight and tall, with blazing eyes and flushed cheeks, he said unto Faranuk:

"O my mother, verily I will uproot this monster from the earth! Yea, I, Feridoun, will cause his name to be blotted from the Book of Kings, so that soon he shall be no more than an evil memory in the world. For long enough hath Iran groaned under his tyranny, and too long hath my father's blood cried for vengeance."

But Faranuk, troubled because of the blaze she had kindled, replied warningly unto Feridoun, saying gently:

"O Pearl of my Heart, let not thy youthful anger betray thee; for how canst thou, friendless and alone, stand against the master of the world? Be not, therefore, precipitate. If it be thy destiny to overcome this tyrant, in due time the Almighty will bless thee with means sufficient for the purpose. Wait, therefore, for the sign."

But his mother's words of caution found no echo in the heart of this youth who, hearing for the first time of the cruel monster who had robbed him of a father, and made of his mother's life that of the hunted, would hear of naught but the immediate overthrow of the tyrant. Therefore he replied unto Faranuk:

"'Tis Heaven inspires me, mother, therefore be not so fearful. As for the Serpent King, not even he, with all his demon host, can stand against a valiant heart and a sturdy arm, guided by the great God of the Persians. Wherefore, then, delay?"

Howbeit, though glorying in the spirit of her son, Faranuk still tried to dissuade him from immediate action, but
in vain; for, even while she spake, a mighty throng was seen
approaching Alborz, led by one who bore aloft, as a standard, an apron uplifted upon a lance. Then both mother
and son knew that the time for action was at hand, and
glad was Kavah's welcome. And presently, Feridoun, the
helmet of Kings upon his head, sought once more his
mother's presence, saying proudly unto her:

"Behold, O my mother, thy warrior-son, who goeth
forth unto the battle against the mighty Zohak! Unto him
it is given to fight, but it remaineth unto thee to pray God
for our safety, and for victory."

So Faranuk, understanding, as she gazed, that it was
useless to try longer to hold this bold young eaglet in the
mountain eyrie, since he sensed power in his wings, blessed
her son, bidding him go forth in the name of God to free
his country, and to avenge his father's death.

But, before going, Feridoun caused to be made for him
a mighty club, the pattern of which he traced for Kavah
upon the ground; and the top thereof was the head of a
cow, in memory of Purmajeh, his nurse. He also did
honor unto the standard of Kavah, causing it to be en-
cased in rich brocades of Roum and hung about with
jewels. Then, when all was ready, the little company set
forth toward the west to seek Zohak, the two elder brothers of Feridoun accompanying them.

Now Faranuk, when she beheld her warrior-sons in full
battle array, looking so brave and splendid, wept with
pride and joy; but fear was in her heart too, and her every
breath was a prayer unto Ormuzd, imploring his blessing
upon the great undertaking.

But fear was far from the heart of gallant young Feridoun as, at the head of his brave followers, he rode forth upon his patriotic mission. The way was rough, the men poorly equipped, but their hearts were full of courage and hope, and new recruits were added daily.

Nor was the sign of God's blessing withheld. For, one evening, in the course of their progress, as the valiant host neared the place where it was to camp for the night, suddenly, upon the heights above them, they beheld a shrine, or place of pilgrims, erected for the worshippers of Ormuzd. Placed upon a grassy slope, high above the turmoil of the road, the spot seemed to breathe peace and serenity; so much so, indeed, that, coming upon it unexpectedly, a hush fell upon the horsemen as they gazed; for, bathed in the glory of the sunset, a touch of solemnity thrown about it by the stately old cypresses whose heads soared majestically up into the blue, it seemed indeed a place in which God might delight to meet his people.

Profoundly impressed by the beauty and sacredness of the spot, Feridoun decided at once to visit the shrine, since he felt the need of inspiration and guidance. And in response to his prayers, it is recorded that there appeared unto him a radiant Angel who foretold unto him the varied fortunes he was to encounter, and bestowed upon him a magic power that should enable him to overcome the wiles of his foes. And so radiant was the vision that, when the hero returned from the shrine, all noticed his changed appearance.

"Bright beamed his eye, with firmer step he strode,
His smiling cheek with warmer crimson glowed."

But alas! When the two brothers of Feridoun saw his altered mien, the pomp and splendor of his appearance, the demon of envy took possession of their hearts, and they privately meditated his destruction, saying one unto the other:

"Are not we, also, princes of the house of Jemshid? and older by birth! Why, then, should Feridoun lord it over us?"

So it came to pass that one day when the two envious ones spied Feridoun asleep at the foot of a mountain, immediately they hastened unto the summit and rolled down upon him a heavy fragment of rock, with the intention of crushing him to death. But the clattering noise of the stone awoke Feridoun, and instantly employing the knowledge of magic which had been communicated unto him, the stone was suddenly arrested by him in its course of destruction.

Now the two brothers, who were eagerly watching to see the result of their effort, beheld with astonishment and fear this event out of the course of nature. Hastening down from the mountain, therefore, they said stutteringly unto their brother:

"We were on the mountain, but we know not how the stone became loosened from its place. God forbid that it should have done injury unto Feridoun!"

Well aware, however, that this was the evil work of his brothers, the young Prince was yet wise enough to take no notice of the conspiracy; and, instead of having them punished, he raised them unto higher dignity and consequence, for he thought of his mother, and wished to fill her cup with naught but joy.

So all went well with Feridoun, and presently the little army, directed by Kavah, arrived at Bagdad, which is upon the banks of the Tigris. Here they halted, and Feri-

doun called for boats to convey them across; but the
ferrymen refused their aid, saying that it was the King's
decree that none should pass save only those who bore the
royal seal.

Alas! This angered Feridoun, and so, regarding not the
foaming stream, nor the dangers hidden within its treacherous breast, boldly the young leader plunged with his
steed into the rushing river; and lo! all the army followed
after him. And now, indeed, was the struggle sore, for
again and again it seemed as though the waves would
bear them down; but the gallant war-steeds struggled on,
and finally all stepped out in safety upon the farther shore,
where they rested for the night, giving thanks unto Ormuzd
for bringing them safely through so great a peril.

On the following day, however, they turned their faces
toward the city which is now called Jerusalem, the proud
capital of Zohak, whose glorious palace raised its towers
unto highest heaven in beauty. Here, Feridoun giving the
signal by striking the brazen gates with his cow-headed
mace, the army stormed the walls, burst in the gates, and
put the garrison to flight. Then, entering the palace, the
youthful leader cast down the evil talisman of miraculous
virtues that was graven upon the walls, and slew the wicked
Deevs who guarded it. He also destroyed or vanquished
with his cow-headed mace all the enchanted monsters and
hideous shapes that appeared before him, and released,
with his own hands, all the black-eyed damsels that Zohak
had imprisoned there—among them, the two beautiful
sisters of Jemshid.

And behold! having accomplished this marvellous feat,
Feridoun was hailed by all the people of the city as their
deliverer, for they were sick unto death of the cruelty

and tyranny of the Serpent King. So, with shouts of rejoicing, Feridoun mounted the empty throne, and the
crown of Iran having been placed upon his head, all the
people bowed before him, and named him Shah.

But, you may ask, where was Zohak that he perished not
at the hands of the fateful Prince? Well, from Jemshid's
sisters Feridoun now learned that the tyrant, with an immense army, had gone upon a secret mission toward Ind;
and, upon questioning further, he ascertained that in this
direction lay the country of the magicians with whom the
Serpent King was in secret conference, hoping, from a renowned enchanter there, to obtain such means as should
enable him to charm his enemy into his power. For, said
the damsels:

"Night and day the terror of thy name, O Feridoun,
oppresseth him. His heart is all on fire, and life is one
long torture to him."

But if Zohak was troubled before, imagine his surprise
and terror when he learned from Kandru, the keeper of
the talisman, the strange tidings of the fall of his capital!
Disguising his fright, however, the tyrant immediately
turned unto his army, hoping by its aid to regain his
throne. But in vain; for both soldiers and people at once
declared loyalty to the new Shah, resisting, to a man, the
offers of gold and jewels and treasure made them.

So, disappointed in the army, Zohak determined to seek
revenge alone. Stealing away secretly, therefore, he proceeded rapidly toward his capital, arriving by night at the
palace of Feridoun. There, ascending a height, himself
unobserved, he beheld the new Shah, in all the glory of his
kingly robes, seated beside the lovely Shahrnaz, sister of
Jemshid, enjoying her beauty and the charm of her con-

versation. Alas! at this sight, the fire of jealousy and revenge made blind with rage the fallen monarch, who, like a mad elephant, dashed upon Feridoun, thinking to slay him unawares.

But Feridoun, roused by the noise, started up quickly, and, meeting the charging Serpent King—who was indeed a most terrible sight—with his cow-headed mace he struck him a powerful blow upon the temple, crushing the bone. Then observing the hissing vipers, Feridoun knew his enemy, and was about to strike again, but his hand was stayed, as the Angel Serosch, swooping down, cried warningly:

"O Glorious Hero! Slay this human monster not, for his hour is not yet come. To a beetling mountain crag must he be chained, far from the haunts of men, there to die slowly and in torture, for so it is decreed."

So the cruel Serpent King was led forth unto Mount Demavend, accompanied by a hooting, mocking multitude; and there, on the edge of the precipice, over the abyss, he was bound with mighty chains and nails driven into his hands, and left to perish.

And oh, the woe of Zohak! for behold the hot sun shone down upon the barren cliffs, and there was neither tree nor shrub to shelter him; also the chains entered into his flesh, and his tongue was consumed with thirst. But he was not alone, for continually before him there passed the great procession of his victims: Jemshid, sawn asunder, mockingly performing obeisance; then for hours a mighty throng of youths and maidens, sighing as they passed along, "We are the serpents' victims"; and Iblis, too, appeared before the Serpent King, assuring him, as he rubbed his hands and laughed in fiendish glee, that he should continue to live so—on and on in torture—for a thousand years. So was the wicked Zohak punished for his evil deeds.

But as for Feridoun, for five hundred years he ruled the world gloriously, and all his days he did that which was beneficent and good, his heart being ever open unto his people. Yea so brave and just and generous was he that, writing of him many hundreds of years later, the great poet Firdusi, to whom we owe these hero tales, is able to say of his countryman

> "The work of heaven performing, Feridoun
> First purified the world of sin and crime.
> Yet Feridoun was not an angel, nor
> Composed of musk or amber. By justice
> And generosity he gained his fame.
> Do thou but exercise these princely virtues
> And thou wilt be renowned as Feridoun."

IRIJ, A GENTLE HERO

NOW it is recorded that Ormuzd the Blessed caused three sons to be born unto Feridoun the Shah, and these youths were tall and strong, and fair of mien, their mother being the lovely Shahrnaz of the house of Jemshid. But the names of the young princes were not yet known unto men, for it remained unto Feridoun to test their hearts. But before their hearts were tested, the princes were wed, and of this you shall hear.

Lo, it is chronicled in the Book of Kings that the great Shah, beholding that his sons were come unto years of strength, sent forth a messenger to search through all the world for three princesses, born of the same father and mother, and adorned with every grace and accomplishment, that should make them worthy of alliance with the line of Jemshid, in order that the princes might be wed.

So the messenger went forth, travelling far and wide over many lands, at last finding the object of his search in the three beautiful princesses of the house of Yemen. But unfortunately, Serv, the King of Yemen, did not wish to part with his three fair daughters, and so put hindrances in the way, requiring the sons of Feridoun to present themselves at his court before he would give his consent unto the alliance.

Therefore, counselled by their father as to how they should conduct themselves, the three princes set forth to win their brides. Now they were received by the King of Yemen with becoming honor, and as they came through the tests to which they were subjected successfully, the King could no longer withhold his consent unto the betrothals.

That same night, however, Serv, being a master magician, called forth biting cold and frost, thinking to freeze to death the three princes as they lay upon their perfumed couches in the rose-garden of the King. But, though the cold and frost were sharp enough to kill all the flowers in the garden, the Angel Serosch awakened the princes in time. Whereupon seeing that it was useless to fight against the inevitable, the King finally prepared a great marriage feast, after which the three brides set out with their husbands upon the long journey back to Persia.

Meanwhile the chronicles relate that when informed by couriers of the near approach of his sons with their brides, Feridoun at once determined to go forth to meet them, in order to prove their hearts. And as, above all things, he was anxious to test their courage, he took upon himself the form of a terrible dragon that foamed at the mouth with fury, and from whose jaws vomited mighty flames.

Stationing himself in a gloomy mountain pass, therefore, when the train from Yemen drew near, he fell upon it suddenly, like a whirlwind, raising a cloud of dust above the place with his writhings, and roaring so horribly as to cause even the stoutest heart to quake.

Now, as it happened, the eldest brother was in the lead, and, consequently, he was the first to see the frightful beast about to fall upon them. Being given a moment in which to think, however, he said within himself: "A wise and prudent man fighteth not with dragons." So, turning his back upon the monster, he retreated, leaving the dragon to fall upon his brothers.

So the furious beast, robbed of the first brother, quickly fell upon the second, who said unto himself: "If I must fight, what mattereth it whether it be a furious lion, or a warrior full of valor?" Placing himself upon guard, therefore, he took up his bow and stretched it, ready for the attack.

But the youngest of the princes, when he saw the danger which threatened his brother, tarried not afar, but, full of fire and fury, rushed upon the dragon, crying aloud in his rage: "Thou reptile, flee from out our presence, for it is not seemly for thee to strut in the path of lions. Thou beholdest before thee the sons of the glorious Feridoun, armed and ready for the fight. Beware, therefore, lest we plant upon thy head the crown of enmity." Speaking thus, the Prince sprang boldly forward; but, before he could strike, Feridoun, having now divined the character of the princes, vanished from their sight.

So, the enemy having disappeared, the train from Yemen proceeded upon its way; and when they were come unto the royal palace, the Shah warmly welcomed his sons and the three fair daughters of Yemen, music and rejoicing being heard everywhere in the land. But at the end of seven days, behold, Feridoun called his sons into his presence, and, having seated them upon thrones of splendor, he opened his mouth, and said unto them:

"O Princes of the house of Feridoun, give heed unto the words which I shall speak unto you. Know, then, that the raging dragon whose breath threatened destruction, was but your father who sought thus to test your hearts. And now, having proved you, I will give unto each a name fitting unto his character.

"Lo, the first-born shall be called Selim, for in the hour of danger, prudence became his guiding star.

"And the second, who showed no whit of fear when suddenly confronted by peril, but whose spirit burned ardent as a flame, him will I call Tur, the courageous, whom not even a mad elephant can daunt.

"But as to the youngest, him I find to be a man both prudent and brave, knowing both how to haste, and how to tarry. Irij, therefore, shall he be called, for first did he show gentleness, but his wisdom and bravery tarried not in the hour of danger."

And now the ceremony of naming his sons being completed, Feridoun called for the Book of the Stars wherein is written the fate of men, for he wished to divine the destiny of his sons. But alas! after searching the planets, he learned that though the signs pointed to success and renown for the two eldest, the horoscope of Irij, the youngest and best loved of his father, indicated misfortune and a tragic end, which disclosure grieved Feridoun deeply.

Howbeit, the King's programme was not yet finished, for next he proceeded to divide his vast empire, giving the three parts unto his sons in suzerainty. Now unto Selim, he gave the lands lying toward the setting sun; and unto Tur, the eastern provinces reaching even unto China. But unto Irij, he gave Iran with the throne of might, and the crown of supremacy, regarding him as the ablest to rule over the heart of the empire.

So the brothers now separated, each taking charge of the reins of government in the respective kingdoms, and for many long years they sat upon their golden thrones in happiness and peace. But alas! evil was written in the Book of Fate, and, day by day, as the leaves turned, it brought tragedy ever nearer unto the house of Feridoun.

Verily the great Shah, after a romantic and glorious youth devoted to valiant deeds, had been blessed by Ormuzd with long life, honor, and peace; but now was he grown hoary-headed and full of years, and his strength inclined toward the grave. And—sorry to relate—as their father grew weak and feeble, the two eldest brothers became jealous of their younger brother, Irij, who was destined to take precedence of them upon the death of Feridoun.

And it was the heart of Selim, particularly, that was turned toward evil, and whose soul gradually became steeped in greed and envy. Day after day, therefore, he pondered bitterly in his spirit the parting of the lands, and anger filled his soul. For Persia was a beautiful land, the garden of spring, full of freshness and perfume, while the other provinces were wild and uncultivated.

Finally, Iblis gaining full possession of the heart of Selim, he called unto him a messenger, mounted him upon a swift dromedary, and sent him unto his brother Tur with a letter, sealed with his private seal. And the letter read:

"O King of the house of Feridoun, may thy days be many and glorious! So sayeth thy brother Selim who greeteth thee from out the west, and asketh of thee, shall we, the elder brothers, remain ever satisfied to see the youngest born set high above our heads upon the throne of light? What sayeth Tur the Courageous?"

Now when Tur had read this letter, behold, his imagination became filled with wind, so that his head was raised above the stars. Calling the messenger into his presence, therefore, he said unto him:

"Thus sayeth the mighty Tur unto his brother: O Star of the house of Feridoun, verily I say unto thee that since our father took advantage of our innocence when we were young and simple of heart, with his own hands hath he planted a tree destined to bear bitter fruit for him and his loved Irij. In order, therefore, that thou and I may counsel together how this great wrong may be righted, I follow the swift feet of thy messenger."

So Selim and Tur met, and, as a result of their conclave, the following haughty message was sent unto Feridoun, their aged father:

"O thou who draweth with swift feet unto the tomb, behold, thy sons Selim and Tur ask of thee, art thou not afraid to go home unto thy God? For verily thine eldest born hast thou treated unfairly, and injustice doth cast its black shadow both before and after thee, since thou hast allotted thy realm with iniquity. We say unto thee, therefore, command the stripling Irij to step down from the throne of light, and hide him in some corner of the earth where he will be forgotten as we, and where he shall no longer offend our sight. For, are not we the elder brothers? Now art thou warned, and if thou heedest not, then shall come down upon thee from the mountains, fierce warriors filled with vengeance, who will utterly destroy thee."

Now the herald, who bare this message unto the court of Feridoun, was greatly awed by the magnificence which everywhere greeted him, and marvelled much at the audacity of the writing destined for the King. And this impression was deepened when, having been admitted into the great audience-room of kings, he beheld the mighty monarch, proud and venerable, with snow-white beard reaching unto his waist, seated majestically upon his gorgeous golden throne. But behold! the look of serenity and peace vanished from the face of Feridoun as he listened unto the cruel words of his sons—his soul becoming kindled with fury. Rising majestically, therefore, he straightway said unto the messenger:

"Return, O herald, unto your masters—these men senseless and perverse of heart—and say unto them: Truly Feridoun rejoiceth that at last his sons have laid bare their hearts before him, for now he knoweth what manner of men they really are. As for the parting of the realm, it was done in equity, according to the wisdom of many counsellors. But I ask of you, what shall be said of him who betrayeth his brother for greed? Verily, he is not worthy to be sprung from a noble race! And now, listen unto the word of warning sent unto you by an aged father. For I say unto you, if you persist in your vile threat, lo! your names shall be blotted out from the house of Feridoun, and destruction utter and sure shall be your inheritance. Pray God, therefore, that he turn your hearts from evil."

After the departure of the messenger, behold, Feridoun at once informed Irij of the intent of his brothers, advising him to prepare a great army to oppose them, should they really attempt to carry out their threat. For he said:

"Alas that it should be true, O my son, but in this world we can look for no defenders unless we are prepared to defend ourselves, and unto the evil of heart, a mighty army speaketh more loudly than the cry of justice."

But Irij, as he listened unto the words of his father, was very sorrowful, for he was gentle of heart, and loved not strife and bloodshed. Therefore he said unto Feridoun:

"O Royal Cypress, casting thy gracious shadow over the whole sun-kissed world! Good and not evil hath been thy influence throughout thy long reign for, blessed by thy protecting shade, the beauteous flower of peace hath blossomed radiantly throughout thy kingdom for more than a hundred years. Now I, too, O my father, would reign beneficently, for I care not to be a dragon of war, vomiting upon the world destruction and woe. Suffer me, therefore, to go forth alone unto my brothers that I may still the anger which they feel against me, since rather than dip my hands in fratricidal blood, gladly will I sacrifice both diadem and throne. For verily

> "I feel no resentment, I seek not for strife,
> I wish not for thrones and the glories of life;
> What is glory to man?—an illusion, a cheat;
> What did it for Jemshid, the world at his feet?
> When I go to my brothers, their anger may cease
> Though vengeance were fitter than offers of peace."

Now tears filled the eyes of the aged Feridoun as he listened unto the noble words of his son and with heart soothed and quickened as by a gentle shower, he said unto his youngest born:

"If such be thy desire, O my gentle son, go forth, and may flowers spring up in thy pathway, brightening and making glad unto thee every step of thy feet. But forget not that my life is rooted in thee, and return unto thy father with the speed of the swift-footed dromedary."

But, before Irij started upon his mission of peace, Feridoun wrote and gave unto him a letter that he should bear unto his brothers. Now the writing was signed with the royal seal, and it read:

"Thus sayeth Feridoun the Mighty unto his sons, Selim and Tur: Behold, your youngest brother hath descended from off his throne and is come unto you with peace in his heart, esteeming your friendship of more value than his crown and throne. Banishing from your hearts, therefore, all hostility, be kind unto him, for it is incumbent upon the eldest born to be indulgent and affectionate unto their younger brothers. As for me, I am now old, and desire naught so much as to see my sons united; and though your consideration for my happiness seemeth to have passed away, yet are your names still graven upon my heart."

So, armed with his father's letter, Irij hastened with his modest retinue into Turkestan, where he found the armies of his brothers already assembled. However, he was received courteously by Selim and Tur, and was lodged in the royal quarter. But alas for Irij! for it seemed as if his very good qualities were to bring about his destruction, as you shall hear.

Now it is related of this Prince of the house of Feridoun that, in addition to beauty of character, he was also extremely prepossessing personally—so much so, in fact, that in every place all eyes were fixed upon him, and wherever he moved he was followed and surrounded by the admiring soldiers, and crowds of people who, filled with wonder at his beauty and kingly presence, murmured among themselves, saying: "Surely this is the Prince worthy to bear the sceptre of Iran!" all of which exasperated the malignant spirit of the two brothers, bringing down upon Irij his fate.

For although at first Selim and Tur had intended to kill Irij, his youth and gentleness had in some degree subdued their animosity; now, however, they were glad to have this excuse for removing him from their pathway. So, retiring into their tents, all night they fanned their jealousy and hate, counselling how they might do hurt unto Irij; and as the day broke, Selim said unto Tur:

"O Courageous One, thou must put this usurper to death; then his kingdom will be thine."

So, when the curtain that hid the sun was lifted, revealing a glorious new day, Selim and Tur went forth unto the tent of their brother. And Irij greeted them joyously, for his heart was full of sunshine. But Tur, frowning darkly, said: "O Perfidious Stripling,

"Must thou have gold and treasure,
And thy heart be wrapped in pleasure,
Whilst we, thy elder born,
Of our heritage are shorn?
Must the youngest still be nursed,
And the elder branches cursed?
And condemned by stern command,
To a wild and sterile land?"

Now when Irij heard these bitter words from Tur, behold, he grew not angry, but replied gently unto him: "O my brother,

"I only seek tranquillity and peace;
I look not on the crown of sovereignty,
Nor seek a name among the Persian host;
And though the throne and diadem are mine,
I here renounce them, satisfied to lead
A private life. For what hath ever been
The end of earthly power and pomp, but darkness?
I seek not to contend against my brothers;
Why should I grieve their hearts, or give distress
To any human creature? I am young
And Heaven forbid that I should prove unkind!"

But alas! the gentle words of Irij unconsciously rebuked the greedy, self-seeking spirit of his brothers, and so they softened not the heart of Tur, which was proud and full of evil. Utterly unable to comprehend a nobility of soul so wonderful, he thought that Irij feigned, and so, springing up, furiously he seized the golden chair, but now his seat, and with it struck a violent blow upon the head of his brother, calling aloud, "Bind him! Bind him!"

Then Irij, thinking of his aged parent, and fearing his hour was come, begged piteously for mercy, saying unto his brother:

"O Cruel One, think of thy old father, and spare me! and if not of him, then have compassion upon thine own soul, and destroy me not, lest God ask vengeance for my blood. Verily, thou wouldst not crush even the tiny ant that beareth a grain of corn, for she hath life, and sweet life is a boon; therefore spare thy brother. For thy father's sake, grant that I may yet behold the sun. I ask only to live in peace and retirement."

Alas! strange to say, these words of piteous pleading but angered Tur the more, so that, drawing from his boot a poisoned dagger, he thrust it deep into the breast of gentle Irij. And behold, the Kingly Cedar fell, never again to raise his glorious head in the sunshine of the world. Alas, the pity of it!

But pity was far from the heart of Tur; for, in his vileness, he severed from the trunk the royal young head of his brother, and filling it with musk and amber, sent it unto their aged father with these cruel words:

"Behold the head of thy darling! Give unto him now the crown and the throne."

Then, their evil deed accomplished, behold, the brothers furled their tents and returned each unto his own land. But the end was not yet.

All this time the aged Feridoun kept his eyes fastened eagerly upon the road whither Irij had gone, for his heart yearned exceedingly to behold his boy again. And, as the time of his return drew near, he caused the walls of his palace to be readorned, and gave orders that musicians, dancing-women, and banquets should be in readiness to give his son a joyous welcome home. Then, when at last the day of his return was come, the aged King sent forth a host to greet him, he himself following close in the wake.

But when the joyous company had gone a little way, a strange thing happened. For Feridoun, riding at the head of his expectant army, suddenly beheld a mighty cloud of dust upon the sky, which, when it cleared, revealed a solitary dromedary looming out of the far horizon, whereupon was seated a rider clad in the garb of woe. And, the mournful figure drawing nearer, the King beheld that he bare in his arms a casket of gold which, upon reaching the retinue, he gave with sorrowful mien into the hands of the aged monarch.

Now Feridoun, suspecting not to what lengths greed and envy had driven his wicked sons, yet felt a dire presentiment in his heart as he gazed upon the case of gold. Commanding that it be opened, however, when the lid was raised, there was revealed at first naught but rich stuffs of silks; but when the silks were unrolled, lo! the hoary-headed King gazed upon the head of his loved Irij. Alas for Feridoun! horror-stricken by this grim sight and the cruel words of his sons, the world grew suddenly dark unto his eyes, and he fell from his horse in a swoon.

Then there rent the air a mighty cry of sorrow such as the world hath seldom heard. For the whole army wailed with grief, in their woe casting dust upon their heads, and tearing their garments in twain. And not only that, but the banners were rent, the drums broken, and the elephants

and cymbals hung with the colors of mourning, because that
the gentle Irij was now but a beautiful memory in the world,
and that the house of Feridoun was left unto him desolate.

As for the stricken monarch, when he recovered his
senses, he returned upon foot into the city, and all the
nobles accompanied him, trailing their steps in the dust,
and followed by the lamenting army. But Feridoun was
dumb in his sorrow until they were come unto the garden
of Irij, the spot loved best in the world by the noble young
King. Here his grief o'ercame him, and, casting black
earth upon his head, he tore his white hair, and shed bitter
tears, his cries and lamentations being so piercing that
they mounted even unto the seventh sphere. Then pressing the golden casket unto his breast, he spake unto God
in his grief, and he said:

"O Omnipotent One! Thou who art all-just! look
down, I beseech thee, upon this innocent whom his brothers have so foully slain, and grant unto me vengeance for
his blood. His murderers, O God, are my sons, but I,
their most unhappy father, beg of Thee to sear their
wicked hearts that they may never again know joy or
peace in the world. O Lord of the World, I long for the
earth to cover me, but let me not go hence until a warrior,
mighty to avenge, shall be sprung from the loins of Irij;
then will I depart with joy, for I am weary of turmoil and
strife."

Thus cried Feridoun in the bitterness of his soul, and,
refusing to quit the garden of Irij, he threw himself upon
the grass, and, his white locks wet with dew, he lay night
after night under the stars. Yea, the earth was his couch,
and he watered the garden with his tears, and lo! he
moved not from the spot until the grass had grown above

Then pressing the golden casket unto his breast, he spake unto God in his grief.

his bosom, and his eyes were stricken with blindness from much weeping. And, moaning continually, in his agony he lamented:

"O my son! My gentle Irij! Never prince died a death so pitiful as thine!"

Now all the land wept and bemoaned the death of Irij, and the sorrow which had come unto the great King, so that for many years Iran was like unto a house of mourning. And the voice of lamentation ceased not in the land until the happy day upon which they placed in the arms of Feridoun a babe, fair and strong, the hero destined to avenge the gentle Irij's death. But of this you must hear in another story.

MINUCHIR THE AVENGER

THE old Persian chronicles relate that the Princess of Yemen wedded by Irij, son of Feridoun, bare unto him an only child, a daughter fair and sweet as a garden in spring. Now the fame of her beauty travelled far, and kings became her suitors. But her grandsire, giving her the desire of her heart, wedded her unto Pescheng, a hero of Jemshid's race; and, in the course of time, there was born unto them a son who, in form and feature, resembled the lost Irij.

Now great was the rejoicing on the occasion of his birth, and, when he was yet a tender babe, they carried him unto the aged Feridoun, saying:

"O Shelter of the Universe, rejoice! for here is thy loved Irij come back unto thee a sweet and smiling babe."

Then,

> "The old man's lips, with smiles apart,
> Bespoke the gladness of his heart.
> And in his arms he took the boy
> The harbinger of future joy;
> Delighted that indulgent Heaven
> To his fond hopes the pledge had given.
> It seemed as if, to bless his reign,
> Irij had come to life again."

But alas! as Feridoun held the child in his arms, a mighty yearning took possession of him to behold the face of this babe like unto his gentle Irij. Vain, however, was his desire, for as you know, he was blind. Then in his longing he cried aloud unto the Almighty, and he said:

"O Lord of the World, in Thine infinite goodness, grant unto me the sight of my eyes, that I may behold this image of my son."

And God was good unto Feridoun; for, even as he prayed, his eyes were opened, and his sight rested upon the babe who, pleased with his grandsire's hoary locks, smiled up at him and cooed in glee; seeing which, Feridoun gave thanks unto Ormuzd, and called down blessings upon the child, naming him Minuchir. For he said, "Lo, a branch worthy of a noble stock hath borne fruit."

As for the child, he was nourished with the greatest care during his infancy, in the house of Feridoun, who bestowed upon him a mother's tenderness, suffering neither sorrow nor ill to come near unto him. So the years passed over his head, and the stars brought him naught but good. And, as he grew up, his grandfather had him carefully instructed in every art necessary to form the character, and acquire the accomplishments of a warrior. Brought up in the saddle, he could ride as no other; with his spear could he pierce all shields; with his arrow shoot farther and straighter than any in Feridoun's court; while in wrestling, he overcame the strongest. And, in addition to his prowess, he possessed all the personal charm which had so endeared Irij to the whole world, so that the army adored him as no other.

Now when the young Minuchir was come unto years of maturity, Feridoun gave unto him a throne of gold and a mace; he also decorated his brow with the crown of sovereignty, and bestowed upon him the key unto all his treasures. And when this was accomplished, he commanded his nobles that they should do homage unto him as King. Now at this important ceremony, there were

gathered about the throne, Karun, the brawny son of
Kavah; Serv, King of Yemen; the great Neriman, and
many other mighty princes and heroes of renown, more
than tongue can name. But the young King outshone
them all in strength and beauty and valor; and joy took
up her abode once more in Iran.

And, presently, tidings of the splendor and glory of the
new Shah pierced even unto the ears of Selim and Tur,
who, hearing of the intrepidity and valor of Minuchir, and
of the immense army that had flocked to his standard with
the purpose of forwarding his plans for revenge, were
filled with inexpressible terror; for they feared an immediate invasion of their kingdoms.

Thus alarmed, these slayers of their brother counselled
long together, finally determining to try the efficacy of rich
gifts and conciliatory language, hoping thus to regain the
good-will of Feridoun, and also to lure Minuchir into their
power, for they feared him greatly.

In pursuance of their plan, therefore, the two brothers
loaded a train of elephants and dromedaries with rich
treasure: gold, and silver, and jewels, and other articles
of priceless value; and a messenger was despatched with
them charged with abundant acknowledgment of guilt,
and profuse expressions of repentance.

Now when the messenger arrived at the court of Feridoun, at once he delivered the magnificent presents, the
sight of which caused the old monarch to observe unto
Minuchir, who in all his splendid robes of state was
seated upon the golden throne at his side:

"These gifts, O my son, are unto thee a prosperous
and hopeful omen; they show that thy enemy is afraid of
thee."

Then, all being in readiness, the great Shah commanded that the messenger be given audience, who, when he had performed obeisance, thus stated his mission:

"O Glorious Shah, whose throne of light illumines the world, live forever! Behold, I bear unto thee a message from thy contrite sons who, bowed low in the dust, venture not so much as to raise their eyes unto thy footstool. Contrite of heart, they pray that thou wilt pardon their evil deed, for it was Iblis who led them astray. Have pity, therefore, O King, upon these unfortunate ones whose eyes are filled with tears and their hearts with repentance. For art thou not, O Beneficent One, the ocean of mercy? Therefore thy forgiveness will cleanse their hearts and restore them unto themselves. And, as a sign of thy grace, they beseech thee to send unto them Minuchir, thy son, for they yearn to look upon his face and do him homage. And this they beg, O Noble Shah, being but the dust of thy feet."

Alas! As Feridoun listened unto the words of his sons, he knitted his brows in anger, for he knew the guile of their hearts, and trusted them not. Turning, therefore, unto the messenger, he said:

"O Foolish One, canst thou conceal the sun? Go, therefore, and say unto those wicked men, your masters, that their gifts and false-hearted words shall avail them naught, for it is vain white words to speak with tongues of blackness. And now, hear my answer: Go back and ask those fierce unnatural brothers, who talk of their affection for the Prince, where lieth the body of the gentle Irij—him they have slain so foully? And now they thirst to gain another victim! They long to gaze upon the great Minuchir! Yea, and they shall, surrounded by his soldiers, and clad in steel. And they shall feel, also, the edge of his life-destroying sword. Yes, they shall see him, never fear!"

Now, uttering this indignant speech, behold, Feridoun paused for a moment to show unto the messenger his famous warriors one by one, all men of giant stature and of admirable courage and valor in war. Then he resumed:

"Long, long hath vengeance slumbered, since it became not Feridoun to stretch forth his hand in battle against his sons. But, thanks unto Ormuzd, at last forth from that noble young cypress, uprooted so cruelly, is there sprung a branch which shall be as poison unto these enemies of his sire. And I say unto you:

> "Hence with your presents, hence, away.
> Can gold or gems turn night to day?
> Must kingly heads be bought and sold,
> And shall I barter blood for gold?
> Shall gold a father's heart entice,
> Blood to redeem beyond all price?
> Hence, hence with treachery; I have heard
> Their glozing falsehoods, every word;
> But human feelings guide my will,
> And keep my honor sacred still.
> True is the oracle we read:—
> 'Those who have sown oppression's seed
> Reap bitter fruit; their souls, perplexed,
> Joy not in this world or the next.'
> The brothers of my murdered boy,
> Who could a father's hope destroy,
> An equal punishment will reap,
> And lasting vengeance o'er them sweep.
> They rooted up my favorite tree,
> But yet a branch remains to me.
> Now the young lion comes apace,
> The glory of his glorious race;

He comes apace to punish guilt,
When brother's blood was basely spilt;
And blood alone for blood must pay;
Hence with your gold, depart, away!"

Now when the messenger heard these reproaches mingled with poison, he departed with speed; and when he was come unto Selim and Tur he had many ominous things to report unto them. And first he told of the glorious Minuchir who, with frowning brow, was only anxious for battle; of the mighty heroes bearing names that filled the world with wonder, who stood about him thick as flies; of the army so great in numbers and valor that the men of Roum and China could not hope to stand against them; and he told finally how that every heart in Persia was filled with hatred of them because of gentle Irij slain.

An ominous outlook for the two brothers, truly, and one that filled their hearts with fear. But Tur, who was naturally cool-headed and brave, said unto Selim:

"Henceforth, O my brother, we must forego pleasure, for it behooveth us to be first upon the field of battle, and not to wait until the teeth of the young lion are sharpened. Also, let us take heart, for the young Minuchir hath yet to show his valor, and it followeth not that he will prove a hero bold and victorious because he is descended from the brave!"

So in this spirit the two brothers rapidly collected from both their kingdoms an army that was past numbering. Helmet was joined unto helmet, and spear unto spear, and treasure, baggage, and elephants and camels without number went with them, so that the earth thundered beneath their tread. Now you would have thought it a host that none could withstand, for it covered the land like unto a flock of locusts. So they marched unto Iran, and the two Kings rode at the head, their black hearts filled with hate and rage, for they feared that their sun was declining.

As for Feridoun, when he learned that the hostile army had crossed the Jihun, he called unto him Minuchir and said:

"Behold! The forest game surrendereth itself voluntarily at the foot of the sportsman. This is well! And now wait quietly, for a little skill and patience will draw the lion's head into thy toils."

So Minuchir waited; but when the enemy had approached within hailing distance, they found the army of the Great Shah drawn up in magnificent battle-array. Now the glorious Minuchir rose above the rest like unto the moon, or the sun when it shineth above the mountains; while at his right rode Karun, the avenger, and his warriors, carrying ponderous clubs, each like a fierce lion girt with power. At his left, rode Saum the son of Neriman, and his men, whose bright scimetars flashed brilliantly in the eastern sunshine, while front and rear, for miles and miles, there was naught but bristling steel. And over all this mighty host waved the fair flag of Kavah, resplendent with jewels—that banner which never yet had recoiled or gone down before the foe!

Now, seeing this, the two brothers also drew up their legions in imposing array, and when dawn, the fair harbinger of day, had flushed the eastern sky with red, out from the mighty host sprang Tur the Courageous, and, with haughty gesture, thus addressed himself unto the chieftain, Saum:

"O Son of Neriman, I pray thee ask this new King, this young Minuchir, since Heaven to Irij gave but a daughter, who on him bestowed the battle-axe, the shining mail, the sword?"

Incensed at this insulting speech, Saum replied hotly:

"O Shedder of a Brother's Blood, thy message shall be given, and I will bring the answer too. Ye know right well what ye have done. Have ye not murdered him who, trusting, sought protection from ye? And verily for this atrocious deed must all mankind your memory curse even until the day of doom. Yea, if savage monsters were to flee your presence, it would not be surprising! And this is certain, those who die in this most righteous war will go to Heaven with all their sins forgiven."

Now having thus given vent unto his feelings, Saum went at once unto Minuchir and delivered the message. Smiling, then, the young King spake, and he said:

"Verily, a boaster must he be, foolish and vain, for, when engaged in battle, vigor of arm and the enduring soul are best proved by deeds, not words. Parley not with him. I ask but for vengeance for gentle Irij slain. Forward! to battle!"

And at the signal, verily, never saw you such an onslaught! For, like a hungry tiger breaking forth from the jungle to seize upon its prey, so did the army of the brave Minuchir fall upon the foe. And fierce indeed was the conflict, lasting until set of sun, multitudes on both sides being slain, until all the spacious plain became a sea of blood. Yea, red, red, became the ground, so red it seemed as if the earth were covered o'er with crimson tulips, their bright heads stilled by the luxuriance of their bloom. But the army of Minuchir was victorious, the flag of Kavah, at evening, still waving defiance to its foes.

But alas for Selim and Tur! for behold, it is related

that when the sun had sunk to rest upon this day of bloodshed, craftily they consulted together how they might seize upon Minuchir by fraud, for they saw that his arm was strong, since the day had witnessed many dauntless deeds of bravery performed by him, making them despair of ever conquering such a hero in battle.

So it came to pass that at dead of night Tur set forth at the head of a small band of picked men to surprise Minuchir in his tent. But the King's spies were not sleeping, and so straightway they carried the news of the evil plan unto his ears, and thus it happened that when courageous Tur burst upon the great Minuchir in his tent, at once he was surrounded, and when he would have fled, behold, the King, dexterously using his javelin, hurled him from his saddle to the ground. Then with his cruel dagger he severed the head of Tur, regarding not his piteous cries for mercy. Now the body he left unto the wild beasts, but the head he sent as a trophy unto Feridoun, pledging neither to rest nor tarry until the death of trusting Irij be fully avenged.

Now as for Selim, when he heard of the fate of his brother, he at once cast about for a new ally; and, at his solicitations, there came unto him the giant Kaku who was of the seed of Zohak. Then, deeming it prudent, they fell back with the army, taking refuge in an old fort. But Minuchir in hot pursuit soon came up with them, and besieged the castle.

One morning, however, the great Deev, Kaku, hideously black and ugly, sallied boldly forth from the fort, and running swiftly toward the centre of the besieging army, threw a javelin at Minuchir which, fortunately, fell harmless before it reached him. But retribution was swift and sure.

for the King, rushing quickly upon the Deev, seized him by the girdle, and, raising him high in the air, flung him from his saddle to the ground with such fury that he never moved again. Such was the strength and prowess of the great Minuchir.

But the young avenger was wise as well as strong and brave, and so, seeing that the siege threatened to last for some time, he now sent a message unto Selim, saying:

"O Slayer of thy Brother! behold, I, Minuchir, challenge thee to quit the fort, and boldly meet me here, that it may be determined unto whom God giveth the victory."

Now as Selim could not, without disgrace, refuse this invitation to single combat, he descended from the fort to meet Minuchir, and a desperate combat was the result. But though the fight was long, and Selim no unworthy foe in his desperation, yet, in the end, the superiority of Minuchir caused him to prevail, and Selim was slain, his head being severed from his body by the redoubtable sword of the King.

As for the army of Selim, when the soldiers beheld the head of their leader borne upon the lance of Minuchir, they fled swiftly unto the mountains and vanished like cattle whom the snow hath driven from their pasture. And, being thus at a safe distance, they took counsel together and chose from among them a man, prudent and gentle of speech, to go unto Minuchir and speak for them. Returning, therefore, the messenger said:

"O Conqueror of the World, we pray thee that, looking down upon us from thy glorious height, thou wilt have mercy upon us, for neither hate nor vengeance drove us forth against thee, but only this, that we obeyed the will of our masters. We ourselves long only after our homes, for we are peaceful men, tillers of the earth and keepers of cattle, and we pray thee, therefore, that we be permitted to return in safety whence we have come. We acknowledge thee our Shah, and will ever be faithful and loyal unto thee, for we perceive that not only art thou brave, but noble as well."

Now when Minuchir heard these words, he said kindly unto the messenger:

"Let every man lay down his arms and go his way, and may joy wait upon your feet. For Minuchir, like the great Feridoun, desireth naught but the good and happiness of his people, and that peace may dwell once more in the land."

So the vanquished army passed before Minuchir, each man bearing his armor and weapons of battle, and, calling down blessings upon his head, they laid them at his feet. And behold! of weapons there was reared such a mighty tower that Babel would have paled in its sight, and the polished steel, as it rose tier upon tier up into the blue, glittered dazzlingly in the sunshine, a glorious promise of peace.

And presently Minuchir, having disbanded the vanquished army, set out at the head of his warriors for the city of Feridoun, his vengeance being fully accomplished. And, being apprised of his approach, his grandsire came forth to meet him, and there accompanied him a glorious train. Now there were elephants swathed in gold and jewels, warriors arrayed in rich attire, and a large multitude clad picturesquely in garments of bright hue, while over them waved flags and banners, and about them the trumpets brayed, and the cymbals clashed, and sounds of rejoicing were heard everywhere.

Now beholding his grandsire yet some distance off, Minuchir got down from his horse, and, running to meet him, kissed the ground before him, craving his blessing. So Feridoun blessed Minuchir, and raised him from the dust. Then he bade him again mount his horse, and, amid shouts of rejoicing, they entered the city in triumph. But when they were come unto the royal palace, Feridoun, having seated Minuchir upon the throne of light, and placed with his own hands the crown upon his head, called unto him Saum, the son of Neriman, saying unto him:

"O mighty Warrior, loyal and brave, to thee specially do I commend this youth to nourish him for full sovereignty, and to support him royally with thy might and mind, both thee and thy house forever."

So saying, he placed the hand of Minuchir in that of Saum, and said:

Lo! my hour of departure is at hand. Soon shall I cumber the earth no more. God, in his goodness, hath given unto me the desire of my heart, and now I go unto him to render account. May he be merciful unto his servant, granting unto him peace in the life to come."

Then having thus spoken, Feridoun distributed gifts unto his nobles and servants, then, withdrawing into solitude, he bewailed without ceasing the evil fate of his sons, and the sorrow they had caused in the world. But daily he grew weaker, and at last the light of his life went out. Howbeit, the glory of his name liveth even unto this day, for even the children in Persia know and love this glorious Shah of Old.

But as for Minuchir, he mourned for his noble grandsire with weeping and bitter lamentation, and raised above him a stately tomb. Then when the seven days of mourning

were ended, lo, he put upon his head the crown of the
Kaianides, and girt his loins with the red sash of might
and the nation called him Shah, and he was beloved in the
land.

> "The army and the people gave him praise,
> Prayed for his happiness and length of days.
> 'Our hearts,' they said, 'are ever bound to thee,
> Our hearts, inspired by love and loyalty.'"

ZAL OF THE WHITE HAIR

A MONG all the great heroes who had such vast influence in shaping the destinies of Iran, there is no house so celebrated as that of Saum Swar, the mighty Pehliva, unto whom the aged Feridoun especially committed Minuchir. Seistan, which is to the south of Iran, was the hereditary province of this famous warrior, and here was bred a race of heroes that not only saved Persia again and again from out the hands of her foes, but whose marvellous deeds of valor have filled the world with wonder.

Now Saum was the son of the great chieftain Neriman, and on account of his intrepid bravery had been made commander-in-chief of the Persian armies. But, though a valiant hero upon the battle-field, he was particularly celebrated because, more than once, he had warred against the allied hosts of Deevs, and come off victorious. He also conquered the furious monster Soham, which was of the color and nature of fire, and, bringing it beneath obedient rein, he made it his war-horse in all his later battles with the Deevs.

So the great Pehliva, girt with might and glory, and smiled upon by the gracious Feridoun, passed his days in happiness, save for the grief that for long years he was childless. After the death of the great Shah, however, it came to pass that at last a son was born unto him, perfect in face and limb, and fair as the sun, but, by some strange misfortune, his hair was silvery white like that of an aged man. Now the poet says of this wonderful baby:

> "His hair was white as a goose's wing,
> His cheek was like the rose of spring,
> His form was straight as a cypress tree,
> But when his sire was brought to see
> That child with hair so silvery white
> His heart revolted at the sight."

Yes, strange as it may seem, such an unfortunate omen is it considered in Persia to have light hair and blue eyes, that in spite of its being well known in the Pehliva's household that he longed passionately for a son to perpetuate his line, yet the infant had gazed upon the light for seven days ere any one found courage to announce unto him the fact of the baby's birth.

On the eighth day, however, the child's nurse, bold as a lioness, went in unto the Pehliva, and, bowing herself low in the dust, craved of her lord the boon of speech. Permission being graciously granted unto her, therefore, the woman thus spake:

"Unto the sire of a noble house I bring good news. May the days of Saum the hero be happy! May he live to see the heart of his enemies rent asunder! And now rejoice, O mighty Pehliva, for God hath granted unto thee the desire of thy heart. Behind the curtain of the house of women, thou hast at last a son, a moon-faced boy who, young as he is, yet showeth the heart of a lion. Fresh from the Garden of Paradise, he is beautiful to behold, with nothing amiss except that by some ill-luck his hair is white. Fate would have it so. But in spite of this misfortune, the stars have decreed unto him a great destiny. Be content, therefore, with this gift of God as he hath sent it, nor give place in thine heart unto in gratitude."

Now, thus speaking, the woman again performed obeisance and departed. Then Saum descended from his throne and made haste unto the apartments of the women, where, when the curtain was raised, he beheld a child of extraordinary beauty, but with the head of an aged man, the like of which he had never seen or heard tell of before. Appalled at the sight, and filled with despair at this strange trick of Fate, which he feared boded misfortune unto his house; also dreading the jeers of his enemies who would now accuse him of bearing a demon child, Saum, the great Persian Pehliva, departed from the paths of wisdom. For, lifting up his eyes unto Heaven, he murmured against the Lord of Destiny, and he said:

"O God of all the World, eternally just and good! Source of all light and wisdom! incline unto me, and mercifully hear my cry. If I have done evil in thy sight, behold my repentance and pardon me, for lo! I am bowed in the dust at thy feet. O merciful Ormuzd, have pity upon me, for truly my soul is overwhelmed that unto me should be born a son who, with his black eyes and his hair as white as a lily, seemeth to be of the race of Satan. Alas! alas! the shame of it is greater than I can bear."

Thus spake Saum Swar in the turmoil of his soul, and, with heart full of anger, he hastily departed from the house of women, cursing the fate which gave unto him such a child. Not so was it, however, with the gentle young mother who gave unto her baby the name of Zal, and loved him, mother like, doubly on account of his misfortune.

But the superstitious people, when they heard of the white-haired child born unto the house of Saum the hero, straightway whispered together, saying:

> "No human being of this earth
> Could give to such a monster birth;
> He must be of the Demon race,
> Though human still in form and face.
> If not a Demon, he, at least,
> Appears a parti-colored beast."

And behold! the nobles of the court expressed much the same sentiment when they said warningly unto Saum:

"O Pehliva of the World, truly this is an ominous event which will, we fear, be productive of naught but calamity unto thee and thy house. Would it not be better if thou couldst remove him out of sight?"

Alas! with a heart overflowing with bitterness, Saum bore the sneers and reproaches which everywhere met him for some time. Then his superstitious fears getting the better of him, he resolved, though with a sorrowful heart, to carry the unfortunate babe unto Mount Alborz where, abandoned, he would fall a victim unto the beasts of prey.

And the resolve once made, in vain did the loving mother plead to be allowed to keep her babe; in vain she promised to hide him in seclusion so sacred that the sight of him should never again offend his father's eye; all was useless! In spite of tears and pleading, little Zal was taken from her loving arms, and carried away unto the lonely mountain, in the dead of night, and there left to die.

But though abandoned by his most unhappy father, poor little Zal was not forgotten by God, who knew that he would yet do great things for Persia. Therefore, he provided a safe and happy refuge for the babe.

For behold! upon an inaccessible cliff of Mount Alborz, whose head touched the stars, and upon whose crest no mortal foot hath ever stepped, the great Simurgh, the bird of marvel, had builded her nest. Far beyond the reach of man, this wondrous nest, fashioned of ebony and of sandal-wood, and twined about with aloe, was hidden among the great white cliffs, threaded thickly with veins of golden quartz. Around the base of this nest of marvel, however, there gleamed the stones of fire—the amethyst, the topaz, and the ruby, while in the rocks not far away the sunset fires had left their glow in the heart of the opal. So this bird of the golden plumage was happy, for she loved these precious stones because they flashed back unto her the fire of her eye, and warmed her heart with their gleaming beauty.

Now the Simurgh is a giant bird, so large that she carrieth elephants in her claws unto her nestlings. Yea and her feathers are of pure gold, being so luxuriant and soft as admirably to fit her for the protecting cares of a mother. Now her home being so near unto the stars, and in her swift flight soaring almost unto heaven's gate, it is not surprising that, by the people, the Simurgh is also called the Bird of God.

So at least on this fateful night she proved unto the forsaken babe of the house of Saum, who lay upon the hard ground, thorns for his pillow, the cold earth for his nurse. Now the night was dark, for great black clouds which foretold a coming storm had dimmed even the light of the stars. Then

"A voice not earthly thus addressed
    The Simurgh in her mountain nest—
To thee this mortal I resign,
Protected by the power divine.

> Let him thy fostering kindness share,
> Nourish him with maternal care;
> For, from his loins in time will spring
> The champion of the world, and bring
> Honor on earth, and make thy name
> The heir of everlasting fame."

And not in vain was the message, for the great mother bird listened unto the voice, and, peering over the edge of the cliff, she spied the helpless infant lying bereft of clothes and wherewithal to nourish it, sucking its fingers for very hunger. Now her own young nestlings were gathered safe and warm under her soft feathers, and as she thought of this human parent who could thus leave his tender offspring upon the cold, bare rocks to die, her heart beat hot with anger.

Rising quickly from her nest, therefore, the great bird poised for a moment in mid-air, listening to make sure that all was well in her nest, then the strong wings moved up and away through the darkness and the storm, and circling round and round in stately flight, she swept nearer and nearer unto the abandoned babe. Down she dropped at last, and the forlorn little one, looking with wondering, tear-wet eyes upon the great mass of soft plumage that seemed to have been borne unto him upon the wings of the storm, smiled and gurgled and cooed with delight, reaching out his baby arms toward his new-found friend.

At this the tender mother bird first caressed little Zal with her beak, as if to reassure him, then, wreathing him with a girdle of aloe, in which she fastened her talons securely, up, up, she soared over mountain streams and rocky cliffs, beyond the foot-hills and the higher peaks, until she reached the mountain nest hidden amidst the stones of fire. Here, a sweet, well-known note caused the nestlings to cling more closely together, and, in the newly made space, the forsaken child cuddled, finding a safe and happy retreat. For behold! his shelter that night from the cruel storm was the soft golden feathers of the Bird of God.

But the storm and the darkness passed, and in the morning, when the sunlight touched the white cliffs and lighted up the fires in the ruby and the opal, the great bird was aroused from slumber by a strange cry beneath her wings, reminding her of her human nestling, and the new responsibilities which it entailed. Rising, therefore, upon her strong swift wings, she flew forth to find food for the helpless stranger within her walls.

Now the Simurgh, being a wise bird, knew only too well that elephant's flesh would be quite too tough for her dainty guest, so she secured nice, tender venison for breakfast. And with due regard for courtesy and hospitality, baby Zal was fed with the very choicest morsels before her own loved brood were allowed to break their fast. And though accustomed to balmy milk instead of flesh, the baby laughed in glee as the tender bits were popped into his mouth, now by the mother bird, now by her nestlings, and thought it a fine breakfast—oh, ever so much better than sucking his own fat thumbs!

So, nourished and protected by the Simurgh, Zal flourished finely; and the nestlings were no less kind unto the little stranger than their mother, for from her they had learned the lessons of mercy and love. Soon upon tender wing, therefore, they, too, were bringing dainties unto their human playfellow. And so, the moons and the years rolled happily by for white-haired Zal, as he lived in the

Simurgh's home, or played amidst the rough jewels upon the crags around her nest.

But Zal's greatest treat, as he grew older, was going to school; for thus the wise old bird named the wonderful excursions upon which she took him. Now, of course, geology and mineralogy he could learn at home, from the jewelled rocks about their door; but as for astronomy, when it was the lesson of the day, quickly he would mount into his golden chariot, which was his foster-mother's soft back, and then, away he would be borne gently through the air, up, up, until he almost thought to touch the golden sun, and all the silver stars.

And, would you believe it? his language lessons he loved even better, for then would the glorious bird sweep majestically down to earth, near to the dwellings of men, and thus did Zal learn quite early to speak the language of the children of Ormuzd, though he thought it not nearly so beautiful as the wonderful notes of his mother. Oh, those were glorious excursions! but best of all, he loved his geography lessons. For then, upon the back of the Bird of Marvel, he sailed over the whole world, visiting all its places of interest, and storing his mind with knowledge. So, take it all in all, the education of Zal was quite complete, and his way of securing it most happy.

But though Zal was so contented and well cared for in his mountain home, even unto the time when he was grown into a glorious youth, for his own natural mother, in the stately palace of Saum, the years dragged by with muffled feet, bringing no balm unto her wounded heart. And the old warrior, his father, too, suffered, so that even the remembrance of his glorious deeds of valor, writ large in the heart of the Shah and the people, was but as dust in his nostrils. However, no word of repentance crossed his lips; the only sign of remorse was to be seen upon his head, for the raven locks of the great Pehliva had become as the silver poplar in whiteness. Night after night, too, he was haunted by strange and terrible dreams, so that sleep was driven from his pillow, and he knew neither rest nor joy.

But by° and by, as neither good nor evil can remain hidden forever, there came a day when the fame of the glorious youth of Mount Alborz, whose chariot was the Bird of Marvel, whose home its mountain nest, spread through the whole land, even unto the ears of Saum, the son of Neriman.

Then it came to pass that one night Saum dreamed a dream wherein he beheld a gallant youth of martial bearing riding toward him at the head of a troop of horsemen, with a banner flying before him, and a Mubid upon his left hand. And the Mubid said unto Saum:

"O Unfeeling Mortal, who in thy wick'edness cast out thy only son to die, disowning him because his hair was white, though thine own resembleth the silver poplar! How long must thy fair young offspring be left unto the tender mercies of a mountain bird?"

Now hearing these words, Saum awakened with a great cry, and so terrible was his distress of mind that he hastily summoned his Mubids and questioned them concerning the marvellous youth of Mount Alborz, whether this could indeed be his son, saved in some miraculous way.

Then the Mubids, seeing that the time was opportune, said unto Saum, the son of Neriman:

"O father more cruel than the lion, the tiger, and the crocodile—for even savage beasts protect their young,

while thou didst cast out thine own, because a mark was
set upon him by the Creator—arise and seek thy child, for
since he is in the guardianship of God, having a great
mission to perform in the world, surely all is well with him.
Pray Heaven, therefore, to forgive thy cruelty, and seek
thy child in the wild eyrie of the Bird of God."

Now when Saum heard these words of promise he was
truly contrite of heart, and calling about him his army, he
hastened quickly unto the mountain. And there, from the
foot of the inaccessible rock which seemed to pierce the
very skies, the white-haired old warrior beheld his son, a
youth of heroic mould, standing near unto the nest of the
Simurgh, gazing like a young King out over the world.
Now seeing this, the pride and glory of fatherhood awakened suddenly in the breast of Saum, and his desire to get
near unto his son was very great; but, alas! he strove in
vain to mount the cliff.

Then the great Pehliva, kneeling, called upon God in
his humility. And, behold! seeing that his repentance
was sincere, the All-Just One put it into the heart of the
Simurgh to look down upon the warrior, who with uplifted, longing arms cried eagerly unto his son. Consequently, as the father's cry mounted up unto the wondrous
nest amidst the stones of fire, it softened toward him the
tender heart of the great mother bird who, casting a
proud glance at her own loved offspring circling in the blue
above the nest, then looked sorrowfully down upon the
white-haired youth upon the cliffs below who shot out into
the world unpolished gems from his bow.

Presently, however, rising from her nest, the Bird of
God circled nearer and nearer unto the youth, finally set-
tling down beside him upon the cliff. Then, throwing aside

his bow and arrow, Zal stroked the golden plumage of his kind foster-mother, questioning her as to the proud warrior and his host who tarried upon the rocks below. Whereupon, first caressing him lovingly with her beak, the Simurgh then said:

"O thou my Nestling! verily, I have reared and been unto thee as a mother, but now the time is come when I must give thee back unto thy people. For lo! the warrior who gazeth at us so longingly from afar is thy father, Saum the hero, Pehliva of the World, greatest among the great; and he hath come hither to seek his son. And behold! glory and splendor await thee at his side."

Now as the youth listened unto these words, his eyes slowly filled with tears and his heart with sorrow, for he loved his mountain home, and longed not for greater splendor than that which was already his in the glorious nest of the Simurgh. Flinging his arms closely, therefore, in mute caress about the soft neck of his foster-mother, for a time Zal was silent; then suddenly raising his head, he burst forth into impassioned speech, and he said:

"O Wondrous Bird of God, art thou then weary of me? Ah, send me not forth! For truly thy nest is unto me a throne, thy sheltering wings, a mother's arms. In thy golden chariot have I beheld the glories of the world, and now I desire naught but to remain near unto thee forever. Then send me not forth, lest I die with longing for thee and my mountain home."

Now at this proof of affection, tears filled the eyes of the kind old mother bird. But, once more caressing Zal with her golden feathers, she said unto him gently:

"O Glorious Youth, verily it is not for want of love I send thee forth! Nay, if I consulted my heart, I would keep thee beside me forever. But the stars indicate for thee a great destiny, and so I must let thee go, for thy country as well as thy father shall be royally blessed through thee. Comfort thyself, therefore, and take heart. And who knoweth! It may even be that when thou hast experienced the joys of a real throne, with all its pomp and splendor, the glories of the wondrous nest will be dimmed in thine eyes. But, that thou mayest always remember with affection thy loving foster-mother who saved and reared thee among her little ones; that thou mayest still feel thyself safe under the shadow of her wings, take and bear with thee into the world this golden feather from her breast, and when thou art involved in difficulty or danger place it upon the fire. I will then come unto thee instantly to secure thy safety. And now, O my Nestling,

"Having watched thee with fondness by day and by night,
    And supplied all thy wants with a mother's delight,
Oh, forget not thy nurse—still be faithful to me,
    And my heart will be ever devoted to thee."

And now right sorrowfully the Simurgh bade the youth mount for the last time into his golden chariot; then in graceful circles she swept slowly down unto the wondering father. And behold! having reached the ground, the Bird of Marvel placed the youth in the outstretched arms of his father, saying unto Saum:

"O contrite Pehliva, receive thy son, and know that never royal youth was more worthy of diadem and throne. Let thy heart rejoice in him, therefore, for great glory shall he bring unto thy house."

Then Saum, when he beheld his son, with body like unto an elephant's for strength, and glorious in his youthful

Then in graceful circles she swept slowly down unto the wondering
father.

beauty, bowed low before the Bird of God, covering her with benison. And he said:

"O Shah of Birds, dwelling so near unto Heaven's gate, truly thou art the Bird of Marvel as well as the Bird of God! Mayest thou be ever safe from thy enemies! mayest thou be great forever!"

But even as Saum yet spake, the wondrous bird flew upward unto her nest, leaving father and son together. Then the Pehliva humbly acknowledged unto Zal his guilt, entreating forgiveness. And he said:

"O Silver-crowned Youth, whose glory is a reproach unto thy father, graciously let the waters of forgetfulness cover my sins, and I swear unto thee that never again will I harden my heart against thee, or refuse unto thee aught that is good."

Then reconciliation having been made, Saum clothed his son in rich robes worthy a king's son, and mounting him upon a superb Arab steed, he conducted him unto the army. Now when the warriors beheld the glorious youth, they shouted for joy, and the army being set in motion, the kettle-drummers, mounted upon mighty elephants, sounded their instruments, the tabors were beaten, the cymbals clashed, and great rejoicing filled the land because that Saum had found his son, and that Zal was a hero among men. And above this rejoicing host, far, far up in the blue, there floated the wondrous Bird of God, who accompanied the army even unto the gates of Seistan.

Now thus it was that Zal, the son of Saum, clad in purple, and covered with honors, returned unto the palace from which he had been cast out, a naked and wailing babe. And when clasped in the glad arms of his beautiful mother, who wept tears of joy over her handsome, white-haired boy, then, indeed, did he think less longingly of the wondrous nest amid the stones of fire. But again and again was he made to tell of his wonderful experiences in the Simurgh's nest, and the golden feather was prized by all as the greatest treasure of the house of Saum.

And behold! as the days and the weeks flew by, the wondrous story of Zal pierced even unto the ears of the great Minuchir, who bade his son Nuder go forth unto Seistan with a splendid troop of horsemen, in order to bring the great Pehliva and his newly found son unto the court to receive the royal congratulations.

So father and son made ready, and when they were arrived at the gates of the Shah, behold, Saum was first conducted into the presence of the great Minuchir. Now the King was seated in all his royal robes upon the throne of light, while upon his right hand sat Karun the Pehliva. Receiving Saum most graciously, therefore, the monarch bade him be seated upon his left hand. Then he questioned him as to the wondrous story of Zal; and Saum related everything unto the Shah, hiding not his own evil deed. Then when all was told, Minuchir commanded that Zal be brought into his presence.

So the nestling of a mountain bird, clad in robes of splendor, was conducted by the chamberlains into the great audience-room of Kings, and the Shah, amazed at his royal appearance, after welcoming the youth, said unto Saum:

"O Pehliva of the World! Verily, the heart of the Shah rejoiceth in this young hero born to be a glory unto the land of Iran. Guard him well, therefore, teaching him the arts of war and the pleasures and customs of the banquet. For how should one reared in the nest of a mountain bird be familiar with these things?"

Then, after talking pleasantly with Zal for some time, the Shah bade his Mubids cast the horoscope of this child of promise. And lo! it was found that the stars would bring naught but good unto the son of Saum; that he would outlive every warrior of the age, and be the defence of Iran for hundreds of years.

Now these prophecies so delighted Minuchir that he presented Zal with a beautiful Arabian horse and gorgeous armor, and as he left the audience-room slaves poured musk and amber before him. And unto Saum the Shah gave Indian swords in gold scabbards, rubies, a throne adorned with turquoises, a crown and girdle of gold, and finally, a charter that vested him with the sovereignty of Kabul, Zabul, and Ind. Then he bade that the Pehliva's horse be brought, and sent him rejoicing back unto his land.

But it was not to idleness that Zal returned, after his visit unto the court of the great Minuchir. For, in accordance with the wishes of the Shah, he was now placed under the care of renowned instructors, and daily he increased in wisdom and accomplishments, so that his fame filled the land. However, the Mubids were not his only teachers, for often when tired of the pomp and splendor of his father's court, his heart would fill with longing for his mountain home. Then climbing up unto his airy balcony, presently he would hear a great flapping of wings, and lo! there was his golden chariot, into which he would quickly mount, and then, away, away, wherever his fancy led. Now during these marvellous journeys so great was the sense of freedom and power which he enjoyed, that he envied not all the kings of earth; nay, not even the great Minuchir upon his throne. And this is not to be wondered at. For truly such delight is seldom accorded to mortals. It cometh, we are told, but once in a thousand years, and then only unto the white-haired wonder child of a Simurgh. Happy Zal!

But not even a wonder child can always remain young and free from responsibility, and so the time came when Zal was called upon to fight the battles of his country, and also to rule in his father's stead, when he was absent fighting against the Deevs. In all these things the son of Saum proved himself to be a real hero, being not only valiant and wise, but also beneficent in his power.

Then a thrilling experience happened unto Zal the son of Saum, for he fell deeply and irrevocably in love with fair Rudabeh, the daughter of the King of Kabul. The poet says of this princess, in describing her beauty:

> "Oh, wouldst thou make her charms appear,
> Think of the sun so bright and clear,
> And brighter far, with softer light,
> The maiden strikes the dazzled sight.
> Think of her skin, with what compare?
> Ivory was never half so fair!
> Her stature like the Sabin tree.
> Her eyes, so full of witchery,
> Glow like narcissus tenderly.
> Her arching brows their magic fling,
> Dark as the raven's glossy wing.
> Soft o'er her blooming cheek is spread
> The rich pomegranate's vivid red,
> Her musky ringlets unconfined
> In clustering meshes roll behind.
> Possessed of every sportive wile,
> 'Tis heaven, 'tis bliss, to see her smile."

Now Zal *did* see Rudabeh smile one moonlight night upon her balcony, and straightway he vowed to win her for his bride, though all the world opposed. And that there would be opposition enough Zal knew quite well, for the King of Kabul was of the hated seed of Zohak and therefore under a ban. But Zal determined to conquer in spite of this drawback, for not only did he love the princess, but she also loved him, saying stubbornly unto those who would have persuaded her of her folly:

> "My attachment is fixed, my election is made,
> And when hearts are enchained, 'tis vain to upbraid.
> Neither Kizar nor Faghfur I wish to behold,
> Nor the monarch of Persia with jewels and gold.
> All, all I despise, save the choice of my heart,
> And from his beloved image I never can part."

But alas for the lovers! When the mighty Saum heard of the folly of Zal, he was so overwhelmed with anger and dismay that in his great distress of mind he cried out bitterly:

"Ah, woe is me, for my son, whom a mountain bird hath reared, is become a prey unto wild desires, and who can foretell the end?"

But the anger of Saum was mild compared with that of Minuchir. For when he heard the ill news, at once he commanded Saum to go straight to Kabul, there to tarry until he had burned the palace of Mihrab, and utterly destroyed his whole family and all who served him, since he willed that the entire serpent brood of Zohak be wiped from the earth.

Then to complicate matters still further, Mihrab, when he learned the Shah's decree, straightway determined in his terror to slay the Princess whose folly was causing all the trouble. But Rudabeh faced her father proudly, and as the Queen interceded in her behalf, offering to go alone unto the mighty Saum to beg for mercy, the King relented and Rudabeh was saved.

But while these events were happening in Kabul, Zal was not idle. Going straight to his father, he pleaded most eloquently for his love, reminding Saum that when a helpless babe he had cast him out to die, and that now once more he threatened his happiness. He also recalled unto his father's mind his promise never to refuse his son aught that his heart desired; and so, being thus beset, Saum finally withdrew his opposition. And not only that, but he also gave unto his son a strong letter of pleading to carry unto the Shah.

So once more Zal set out for the Court, this time to besiege the great Minuchir. And here he had no easy time, for the Shah, determining to try the young hero, instructed that his Mubids should propound unto him six hard riddles, most difficult of solution, in order to test his wisdom. But Zal answered them every one, and all the Court wondered at his great intelligence. Then the King required that he give proof of his physical prowess, and in the tournament which followed, behold, Zal outstripped every competitor, arousing the greatest enthusiasm by his remarkable exhibitions of skill and strength and courage. But it was the Mubids who finally gained the day for Zal, as you shall hear, for, after consulting the stars, they said unto Minuchir:

"O Shelter of the Universe! Lo, in the Book of Fate it is written that the love of Zal and Rudabeh shall shine as the stars, for from their union shall spring a son, beside whom all the heroes of the world shall pale. Long life, courage, strength, and honor shall be his, and in the hour of peril the great Shahs of Iran will never call upon him in vain."

Now hearing this, Minuchir could not reasonably with-hold his consent, so quickly the gallant young lover speeded him back unto Kabul where a most gorgeous wedding took place. And after this great event, for days and days, naught was heard but merry sounds of rejoicing through all the land. For the people loved White-haired Zal, and their hearts were glad because of his victory.

But the happiest time for the lovers was when, the fuss and parade all over, they were allowed to settle down amid the roses and fruits of their vine-wreathed home. Yea, and here, for many, many moons, the young chieftain and his fair bride lived happy as it is ever given unto mortals to be.

But alas! One day there was darkness and gloom in the thicket of roses, where the night-bird trilled his song unto the drooping flowers. There was darkness also upon an inner-room, for the shadow of death hovered over the fair Princess, who lay ill and in terrible peril, the court physicians having given up all hope of her life.

Now for a time, after hearing this dire verdict, Zal sat stupefied with sorrow; but suddenly as he gazed blindly at the dying fire, he thought of the Simurgh's plume. Pausing not an instant, therefore, he quickly secured the beauteous golden feather, and laid it softly upon the fire. Then with bated breath he waited, listening! listening! and lo! in a moment there came the rushing sound as of a tempest, the wings of the Simurgh gleamed in the darkness, and the great, soft mother bird stood beside her foster-child.

And, oh! how Zal's eyes lighted up with joy and hope as he threw his arms about her soft golden neck, and leaned upon her gorgeous plumage! Waiting not for him to speak, however, the Bird of God said caressingly unto Zal:

"O, thou my Nestling! Wherefore art thou troubled? And why do I see the eyes of the lion wet with tears?"

Then quickly Zal told unto his foster-mother of the great joy that had come unto him, followed, alas, by the present sorrow, unto all of which the Simurgh listened attentively. And the story told, bidding him be of good cheer, the loving mother bird whispered a few directions in his ear, after which away she flew back to her mountain nest.

But Zal speeding him to carry out the directions of the Simurgh, soon joy reigned once more in the bower of roses, for Rudabeh was out of danger. Yea; and not only that, for with the Bird of God, tucked safely under her soft wing, had come a priceless gift unto Zal and Rudabeh—a splendid young son to crown their happiness. And now Rudabeh, too, loved the beautiful Simurgh, with a love almost as great as that of Zal himself, because the golden chariot had brought her babe so safely. And behold! they called the boy Rustem, which meaneth "delivered"; for, said the Mubids, while he liveth will he ever stand between Persia and her foes.

RUSTEM THE WONDER CHILD

NEVER, I suppose, in the legends of any land is there given account of so wonderful and prodigious a child as Rustem, the son of Zal.

Now he was as fair as a nosegay of lilies and tulips, we are informed, and when but a day old he was so tall and strong and vigorous that he seemed to have been born a whole year. You will not be surprised to hear, therefore, that at first he required the milk of ten nurses, so great was his hunger; and when he was weaned, his food was bread and meat, and he ate as much as five men. Now by all this you will see that the babe was a true wonder child; but then that was to be expected, since he was brought by the Simurgh from—who knows what enchanted region?

And never, I am equally sure, was there greater rejoicing over the coming of a babe! For, when the tidings sped forth that unto Zal the hero a son was born, behold, the whole land of Iran was given over to feasting and rejoicing —even the very poor sharing in the general mirth; for so great was the satisfaction of the great Shah over the coming of this child of promise, foretold by the Mubids, that thousands of dinars were given away in charity throughout the land.

But who shall describe the joy of the two grandfathers? —particularly that of King Mihrab, who became so puffed up with pride that, like a great gas-inflated balloon, he threatened any minute to fly off into space, or to burst with joy. The father of Zal, however, was away fighting the Deevs of Mazinderan at this time, so his son sent swift messengers to carry unto him the good news, and Zal sent with them a likeness of Rustem worked in silk, representing him upon a horse, armed like a warrior, and bearing in his hands a cow-headed mace. Now when the old champion beheld the image of this lion's whelp, it made him almost delirious with delight. Returning thanks unto Ormuzd for this splendid gift unto his house, therefore, the old warrior then poured mountains of gold before the messengers, and distributed munificent gifts unto all his army.

As for Rustem, he continued to grow in wonder with his years. At three, it is said, he rode upon horseback; and in his eighth year he was as tall and powerful as any hero of his time. In fact, so great was his physical perfection, that the chronicles and the poet unhesitatingly declare of him:

> "In beauty of form and vigor of limb
> No mortal was ever seen equal to him."

But though twice four years had rolled over his head, the eyes of Saum had not yet been gladdened by the sight of his wonderful grandson. Finally, however, the war was over and, at the head of a splendid retinue of warriors, the aged Prince set out for Zaboulistan, the home of Rustem and his noble father, the White-haired Zal.

And behold! when the old warrior was yet a day's journey from the city, Rustem, with a gorgeous train, went forth to meet him, for he longed to hear his grandsire tell of war and battle, which his soul loved and longed for, and in his eagerness he could not wait. So his father let him go, but not alone, for as the young Prince passed through the city gates, his body-guard, mounted upon coal-black steeds, rode in advance, their golden maces and battle-axes gleaming in the sun, while above them waved the red flag of the house of Zal. Then followed the elephants, upon whose backs, seated in gayly decked howdahs, rode the lords and nobles of the land, their waving plumes and bright ensigns making them appear like a troop of gorgeous butterflies. And following these came a multitude of young warriors, the flower of Iran, riding beautiful Arab horses, with swords at their sides, and long spears resting upon their saddle-bows; and there was music, too, for the drums beat, the cymbals clashed, and the trumpets brayed, filling the air with sounds of rejoicing. Thus rode young Rustem forth to greet and do honor unto his illustrious grandsire, Saum the son of Neriman.

And lo! when Rustem beheld the retinue of Saum yet a long way off, he commanded his own attendants to stand still, while he, dismounting from his great war elephant, went forward on foot. Then when he was come near enough to behold the face of his grandsire, he straightway touched with his eyelashes the ground before his feet, saying unto him:

"O Pehliva of the World! Greatest of the great among the defenders of Iran! Behold, I am Rustem, thy grandson, and much I have longed to see thee! And now I crave thy blessing that I may return in happiness unto Zal, my silver-crowned father."

Now, beholding the youth, Saum was struck dumb with wonder, for he saw that not half had been related unto him as to the boy's stature and grace. Filled with delight, the old warrior commanded his elephant to kneel, and having descended, he raised and blessed his grandson. Then, having seated him in the howdah beside him, the two rode side by side into Zabulistan.

And how the two enjoyed that journey! Also, how they talked, or rather Rustem did! But first, he gazed and gazed in open delight at the great warrior by his side, concealing not his admiration and pride, for though a giant in size, the heart of Rustem was that of a child. Then he said unto the old man:

"O my grandfather, now I perceive that I am sprung from thee, and I rejoice. For my desires are not after pleasure, neither do I think of play, or rest, or sleep; but ever and always I long to be a hero, fighting fierce battles and performing deeds of valor. But most of all, just now, I crave a horse of my own, and a hard saddle such as the Turanian riders use; a coat of mail, too, and a helmet like those thy warriors have. Then with my lance, and my arrows in which I delight, I will vanquish the enemies of our house and of Iran, and my courage shall be like unto thine and that of my noble father. Then thy heart will rejoice, O my grandsire, and side by side we will fight the battles of the great Shah and of Iran."

Now when Saum heard these words he was both amazed and delighted, and he blessed the boy yet again, promising him that as soon as he reached the stature of his father, he should have his heart's desire. And so great was his joy and pride in his grandson that his eyes could not cease from gazing upon the bright, eager face of the youth. And he said unto him:

"O my young Hero, valiant of heart, for more than a hundred years have I been the chief of the Princes of Iran, and great are the honors that have come unto me, yet never have my eyes been gladdened as in thee. Verily, being now full of years, I fear that my fighting days are almost over, but I rejoice that in Rustem the house of

The two rode side by side into Zabulistan.

Saum will still live and shine as the sun in glory. And to this end, it behooveth thee to grow up strong and valiant and wise like unto thy father and the other heroes of thy house. Then will the heart of thy grandsire indeed rejoice in thee, and all will be well in the land."

But alas! The home pleasures of a warrior are of short duration, and so scarcely a moon had run her course before Saum was again called unto the field of battle. During the whole of his stay, however, he insisted upon having Rustem always with him, and when finally he was obliged to go, he said unto Zal:

"Remember, O my son, that when this child's stature is equal to thine own, he is to have a horse of his own choosing, and all the trappings such as we ourselves wear in battle. Honor this, therefore, as my parting command."

Now hearing this, Rustem, leaving his grandfather's side, and placing himself near unto White-haired Zal, said, smiling:

"And see, father! I am only eight, but even now I am almost as tall as thou. Truly, I shall not have long to wait!"

Then the two warriors smiled, well pleased with the boy; and as they embraced in parting, Zal gravely promised that he would surely remember.

But time passed, and when yet two summers had rolled over the head of Rustem, behold, one night he was awakened from his slumbers by a great noise and cries of distress outside his door. Starting up quickly and listening, therefore, he distinguished the cry:

"The King's white elephant! The King's white elephant! He hath broken his chain, and is crushing and trampling the people to death. Flee! Flee, for thy life!"

Now Rustem, when he caught the import of the words, sprang quickly from his bed, seized his grandfather's great club, and commanded the guards to let him pass into the court that he might subdue the beast. But the attendants barred the way, saying harshly:

"Rash boy! What wouldst thou do? The night is dark, and the white elephant is loose. It is sure death, therefore, to venture out. Lend thyself not unto folly, nor yet give place unto rage, for how can we face the fury of thy father, if we allow thee to run into danger?"

But Rustem did give place unto both rage and disgust at such faint-heartedness. For, realizing that hundreds of lives were in danger and that he must not delay, behold, he struck the attendant who barred his path so terrible a blow that his head rolled off like a ball struck from a bat, seeing which, the others quickly made way for him. Then with his mighty arms and his strong fists he broke down the barriers of the door; and as he stood without, he beheld how all the warriors were sore afraid of the elephant, because that he was mad with rage. Then Rustem was ashamed for them in his soul, for he said within himself:

"Verily, what counteth the life of one against a hundred?"

Laying his club upon his shoulder, therefore, he hastened after the elephant; and when he was come near unto the furious beast he ran toward him with a loud cry. Then the elephant, beholding the son of Zal, rushed madly forward, roaring like the river Nile, and raising his trunk to strike. But Rustem, regarding the huge beast with a cautious and steady eye, fearlessly struck him a blow with such strength and vigor that the iron mace was bent almost double. Now at this the elephant trembled, his legs failed under him, and he fell with a crash so appalling that you had said a mountain had fallen, the noise of it being heard afar. As for Rustem, when he had done this deed, he returned unto his bed and slept sweetly until morning.

Now the next day, when Zal heard of the prowess of his son, he was delighted. Sending for him therefore, he said unto him:

"O my glorious son, Ormuzd hath been indeed gracious unto thee. In years thou art but a child, yet there is no one to match thee in courage, strength, and stature. On this account, therefore, thou shouldst accomplish great things in the world; and that thy judgment may also be cultivated, I wish to send thee forth upon an enterprise which will delight thy heart. And now listen carefully unto that which I shall relate:

"Many, many years ago, in the reign of the glorious Feridoun, thy distinguished grandfather, the aged Neriman, was sent by that monarch to take an enchanted fortress situated upon Mount Sipend. This fort, high up upon a steep eminence, was said to contain beautiful lawns of freshest verdure, delightful gardens abounding with fruits and flowers, and fair castles filled with marvellous treasure; for no caravan going that way ever returned. Yet no eye had ever beheld the beauties of the place, and no army, however strong or strategic, had ever scaled the heights, for the fort seemingly was impregnable.

"Again and again valiant warriors and mighty armies, at the command of the Shah, besieged this place of Deevs, but in vain. And alas! thy grandfather, great champion that he was, fared no better, for after a whole year's siege, with nothing accomplished, he was finally killed by a rock thrown upon his head by one of the evil Deevs, and as a consequence, again an unsuccessful army returned unto Feridoun.

"Then thy grandfather Saum, being deeply afflicted by the fate of his gallant father, himself set out against the fort. But though he wandered for months and years over the desert looking for the fortress, he could not find the way which led unto the place, for never a being was seen to enter or come out of the gates. So finally, other duties obliged him to give up the appalling enterprise, and he was forced to return without having avenged his father's death.

"And now, my son, it seemeth unto me that, since thou art yet unknown, it may be easy for thee to accomplish our purpose. But thou must go disguised, since the keepers of the fort will not then suspect thee, and thus thou mayest secure entrance unto the fortress. It occurreth unto me, also, that it might be well to disguise thyself as a camel driver, coming in from the desert with a cargo of salt, since it is said that there is nothing in that country valued higher than salt. When they hear that this is thy commodity, the gates of the fortress will surely be opened unto thee. Then destroy the wretches utterly, root and branch, for, behold, they have cumbered the earth too long.

"Now, that this is a glorious opportunity by which to test thy prowess, O my son, I need not say unto thee. But of this I am sure, if thou shalt prove thyself successful in this endeavor, surely Saum, thy grandsire, will consider that the time is ripe for thee to have thine own horse and armor, together with all the privileges and honors of a young warrior. Then go forth, O my Wonder Child, and may the desert blossom beneath thy feet, and the Blessed Ormuzd wreathe thy brow with victory."

So spake the White-haired Zal, and as Rustem listened he became so filled with delight that he scarce felt the earth beneath his feet. For his soul was that of the warrior, and he longed mightily for adventure and combat; yea, they were as honey unto his lips. So the grass grew not under his feet, but right speedily he prepared a great train of camels. And so cunningly was the train disguised that, had you seen it, you would have said:

"Why, here is a salt merchant starting with his caravan across the desert!"

But the salt merchant was Rustem, and the camel drivers his brave companions in this adventure. And besides salt, the huge packing-cases contained Rustem's great club with which he slew the white elephant, as well as all the arms of his warriors. But so well was all arranged, and so clever the disguises, that the breath of suspicion could not possibly fall upon so innocent-looking a train.

So right merrily they set forth, and, after marching many days, they at last approached the fortress. And lo! it happened even as Zal had thought, for when the keeper of the gate saw them from a distance, he ran quickly to the governor of the fort, saying:

"My Lord, a caravan with a great number of camel drivers hath arrived, and, judging by the cases, I should say they have salt to sell. What are thy commands?"

Then the governor replied unto the gate-keeper:

"Why, this is most fortunate! It was but yesterday that my chamberlain reported unto me that the Deevs were famishing for salt. Admit them by all means, for now my people can be satisfied."

So the gates were thrown open, and Rustem and his whole train entered the fortress. And behold! after cour-

teous greetings had been exchanged between the governor
and Rustem, he was allowed to repair unto the bazaar,
taking his camel drivers with him. And here the salt merchant drove a brisk trade, for thousands crowded around,
eagerly making their purchases, some giving clothes in exchange, some gold, and some jewels; and not a thought of
fear or suspicion was there in the heart of any one of them.

Howbeit, when night came on and it was dark, Rustem
impatiently drew forth his weapons from their hiding-place,
and quickly arming himself and his companions, started
to execute his plan of attack. And first, advancing toward
the governor's mansion, he raised his furious battle-cry;
then, with one blow of his mace, he shattered the great
iron door, and fell upon the guards. Now right and left
he levelled them, and none could stand before him. Indeed, so fierce and overwhelming was he that you would
have sworn that this was no mortal man, but the Great
White Deev himself, falling upon his brethren. For in his
fury, not only did he slay the mighty Deev who ruled the
fortress, but all his chiefs as well, felling some to the earth
with his club, striking others down with his sword, so that
when morning was come not a Deev was left alive in the
fortress.

And this accomplished, Rustem's next step was to storm
the governor's treasure palace. Now this was built of
stone, and the gate was of iron, but this did not deter for
a moment the mighty son of Zal. With his formidable
battle-axe he soon demolished the entrance, and then,
pressing eagerly forward, treasure, priceless treasure,
everywhere met their gaze.

But all this was as naught in comparison with what was
to come, for in the heart of the palace they finally discov-

ered a marvellous temple, constructed with infinite skill and science, beyond the power of mortal man. And well Rustem knew that here the cow-headed mace would be of no avail, for it was plain that this was the work of magic. Undaunted, however, the son of Zal drew forth from his breast, at this crisis, a beautiful golden feather, which, applying to the lock, the door immediately flew open, revealing a most gorgeous sight. For lo! there were rubies, and emeralds, and diamonds, and opals, amethysts and onyx, turquoise and pearls, to say nothing of crowns and girdles, sceptres and thrones of pure gold, inlaid with jewels. Also, there were tapestries and rugs, brocades and silks, carvings and armor, together with heaps and heaps of glittering coins. But words cannot describe it, for truly never in the world was there such a gorgeous sight as that treasure palace of the enchanted fortress.

And now a problem confronted Rustem, for he was puzzled to know what to do with such enormous and valuable spoils. He therefore sent a messenger unto Zal to announce his victory, and to receive directions as to the treasure. Then Zal, rejoicing, sent unto Rustem two thousand camels to bring away the booty, thinking this number sufficient. But alas! when these were all loaded there was still much treasure remaining, for, you see, it was the wealth of thousands of caravans. Having taken all they could, however, Rustem, following the instructions of his father, then burned the place with fire, so that naught remained of it. Then, his work being finished, lo, he departed back unto his father.

But, strange as it may seem, the chronicles yet record that all this treasure was as nothing unto Rustem in comparison with the joy in battle, the delight in conquest which he now knew for the first time outside his dreams. Again and again on the homeward journey, he lived over the blissful experience, and so engrossed in it did he finally become that the glorification which awaited him upon his arrival home—his father's words of praise, his mother's fond embrace—all passed over him but half noted, for his mind was busy with other things. After much pondering, however, he finally said unto his father:

"O my silver-crowned father, one of these days I am going to be a great warrior; of that I feel sure. For in battle my soul knoweth perfect joy. And now, having avenged my illustrious grandsire, surely I may choose my war horse and enter upon my career as a warrior, for truly I am now no longer a child."

So ended Rustem's youth, with all its exploits which seem so marvellous for a child. But then it must be remembered that he was not an ordinary, but a wonder child—which explains it all perfectly.

RUSTEM THE YOUNG WARRIOR

NOW when the news of Rustem's capture of the enchanted fortress reached the ears of the aged Saum, at once he sent a swift messenger unto Zal, his son, commanding that, as a reward for his valor, Rustem should now be allowed to choose his own horse and enter upon his career as a warrior.

Accordingly, without delay, a proclamation was sent out into all the provinces of Persia, commanding that upon the first day of the approaching Festival of Roses all the choicest horses in the land should be brought in unto Zaboulistan that Rustem might choose from among them his steed of battle. Now, to the owner of the lucky horse chosen, the reward was to be mountains of gold, but the warning was also given that should any man hold back a steed of value on the day named, the weight of the Shah's displeasure would certainly fall with blighting force upon his head.

And, oh, what a horse-fair this proclamation produced! For the fame of it spread away beyond the borders of Persia, and as a consequence, for weeks before the day appointed, great herds of horses were brought in daily until, upon the hills and plains without the walls of the city, there was an exhibition, the like of which the world hath not seen.

For, in addition to the large number of beautiful, home-bred steeds, the hill-slopes to the south of the city were white with the tents of the most famous breeders from Kabul and the Afghan pasture-lands, whose choice collec-

tions of animals were truly a joy to behold. Then on the
plain, a mile or so from the gate of the city, were tethered
a herd of heavy-built, dark-maned horses brought in by a
horde of half-wild Tartars, wearing black sheepskin caps
and carrying long spears. And near unto them was a caravan of low-browed men from the shores of the Caspian,
who rode their clean-limbed, swiftly-moving animals fresh
from the freedom of the steppes, at full speed, standing
erect upon their saddles. There were, too, a number of
superb Arab coursers, for which more than one princely
sum had been offered, but the patriarchal sheik who had
travelled with them from the distant valley of the Euphrates was looking for still greater opportunities. And besides
all these, there were also scores and scores of single horses,
each the flower of the flock and the joy of his master's life,
brought in not because of the reward, but through fear of
punishment. Now, gazing upon this wonderful collection
of beautiful horses, you would have said that surely the
world had nothing left to be desired in the shape of perfect
steeds. But we shall see!

For the morning which ushered in the great Festival of
Roses dawned at last, and at a very early hour the whole
city was astir. Now the beautiful golden throne, from
which Zal and Rustem were to inspect the horses, had
been placed just outside the western gate, and it was tow·
ard this Mecca that everybody hastened. Here also the
ladies of Zaboulistan were seated in the covered pavilion
on the top of the wall, from which, without being seen, they
could look down upon the passing show. And though still
early, every available point of view was already crowded
with a picturesque crowd of onlookers who discussed
eagerly the possible choice about to be made by Rustem.

And finally, all being now ready, at a given signal the horses, which had already been brought together at a convenient spot, were led, one by one, through the long passage of armed men, directly before Rustem, the son of Zal. And the first to pass were those of the Zaboulistan herds, strong, beautiful horses, many of them bred and reared with the one thought of their being chosen as the Prince's steed of battle.

"O Mighty One, behold this beauty!" cried the foremost keeper enthusiastically unto Rustem. "Truly, never hast thou seen his like. Why, so swift is he that the wind is outstripped and put to shame in a contest with him, and yet he is so gentle that he will eat sugar from thy hand!"

Smiling at the keeper's enthusiasm, Rustem stepped forward, replying unto him:

"A beauty he is truly, but Rustem must have strength as well as swiftness in his steed."

Now, thus speaking, the Prince placed his hand upon the horse to see if it could stand that test. But the animal shuddered beneath his grasp and sank upon its haunches from the strength of the pressure, so that, crestfallen, his master was forced to lead him away.

And alas! so fared it with horse after horse brought forward, with those from the home pastures as well as those from the steppes, the mountain valleys, and the plains of the Oxus. Verily, not one of them could stand the mighty weight of Rustem's hand.

Then came the long-bearded, venerable old sheik from the Euphrates, and he led forward the largest of his magnificent Arabs. And behold, so splendid was this courser that cries of admiration from all the spectators greeted his appearance, for seldom, even in that land of beautiful

horses, had an animal been seen which was in every way
so near perfection. Sure of success, therefore, the old
sheik, smiling with satisfied pride, said unto Rustem:

"O Seeker after Perfection, verily I perceive that naught
but a blameless steed will satisfy thee! Well, behold! here
are beauty, and strength, and swiftness, and intelligence,
combined with gentleness and affection. Step up, My
Beauty, and greet thy future master!"

Now, at this, the magnificent creature stepped proudly
forward, tossing his head and coquetting as if perfectly
conscious of the admiration he was exciting. But alas! so
high-spirited and mettlesome was he, that when Rustem
quietly subjected him unto the same test that the others had
undergone, he quailed and trembled, not so much because
he could not bear the weight, as that it fretted his proud
spirit to feel the weight of such an iron hand. So he also
was led away.

Then, last of all, the traders from Kabul brought forward a herd of ten which they had carefully selected for
their great strength, and which were the flower of all those
bred in the Afghan pastures. But not one of all the ten
could stand the test of Rustem's hand.

Alas! at this last failure, disappointment filled the heart
of Rustem, for he knew not what he should do for a steed
of battle. But letting his eye rove over the plain in one
last grand muster, behold! he suddenly spied beyond the
tents of the Kabul traders a mare and her foal feeding
quietly upon the hillside. Now the mare was gray, and
though her height was not remarkable, she appeared as
strong as a lioness. But it was the colt that held Rustem's
eye, and little wonder, for its color was that of rose leaves
scattered upon a saffron ground. And not only that, but it

also appeared as strong as an elephant, as tall as a camel, and as vigorous as a lion, while its eyes fairly beamed with the fire of intelligence. Also, its tail was long and arched and its hoofs were like unto steel, seeing which, lo, hope blazed up once more in the heart of Rustem. Turning quickly unto the traders therefore, he said:

"O Sons of Kabul, unto whom belongeth the gray mare that feeds beyond your tents? And whose is the colt that follows after her? Verily, I see no mark upon its flanks!"

Then the herdsmen, shaking their heads gravely, replied unto Rustem:

"Most Gracious Prince, now thou asketh that which we cannot answer. Only this can we say, that all the way from the Afghan valleys they have followed us, and we have been unable either to drive them back or to capture them. We have heard it said, however, that the name of the colt is Rakush, or Lightning, because that he is as light as water and as swift as fire; but we do not know his master. Men say, also, that it is now three years since the colt hath been ready for the saddle, and many nobles have desired to possess him, but in vain! For as soon as the mother seeth a man's lasso, she runneth up like a lioness to defend her young, and will suffer no one to touch him. Now what mystery is hidden under all this we know not, but of a truth it is safest to leave them alone, for so savage is the gray mare, she will tear the heart out of a lion and the skin off a leopard's back in defence of her foal."

Now no sooner had Rustem heard all this than he snatched a lariat from the hand of the nearest herdsman, ran quickly forward, and threw the noose, without warning, over the head of the startled colt. Then followed a furious battle, not so much with the colt as with its frenzied mother, who ran at Rustem like a wild elephant, and would have seized his head in her teeth. But lo! the son of Zal roared at her with so terrible a voice that the gray mare stood still in astonishment. Quickly then, Rustem, seeing his opportunity, dealt her a mighty blow upon the head with his fist, so that she rolled over and over in the dust. And not in vain was this form of persuasion, for when she got to her feet the gray mare had no desire to renew the attack, but quickly hid herself in the herd.

So the mare having retired crestfallen from the field, Rustem tightened the knot of the lasso, and then pressed one of his hands with all his might upon the colt's back. But Rakush did not bend under it; indeed, one would have said that he was unconscious of it. Then Rustem gave a great cry of joy, and caressing the beautiful creature fondly, he cried:

"O Rakush! Rakush! verily thou shalt be my throne, and seated upon thee, I shall accomplish great deeds, and now away, My Beauty, away!"

So speaking, with a great bound the young Prince leaped upon the back of Rakush, and the rose-colored steed bore him over the plains with the speed of the wind. But when thoroughly tired he turned at a word from his master, and came quietly back unto the city gates, where the vast crowd cheered mightily both Rustem and Rakush.

Then Zal, well pleased that at last the desire of his son was accomplished, said unto the men from Kabul:

"Good Herdsmen, what wish ye in exchange for this dragon? Be not afraid to speak, for I see that he pleaseth Rustem mightily."

But the herdsmen, turning quickly unto Rustem, replied gravely:

"If thou art Rustem, mount him and retrieve the sorrows of Iran, for his price is the land of Persia, and, seated upon his back, no enemy can stand before thee."

Now thus it was that Rustem won his great war-horse, Rakush, and none too soon, for it was not long before Iran had need of a champion, being plunged in war and bloodshed, as you shall hear.

And first you must know that after having flourished for twice sixty years, the good King Minuchir made ready to pass from the world. Now being informed by the astrologers that his end was near, the Great Shah called before him Nuder, the young Prince, and gave unto him wise counsel. Then when he had so spoken, he closed his eyes and sighed, and was gathered unto the tomb of his fathers. And lo! all the world mourned for the great Shah gone.

And well might Persia mourn, for Nuder, alas, was not great and noble like unto his father, whose wise counsel he soon forgot. And so it came to pass that presently so great became his injustice and tyranny that finally the nobles of the land came unto Saum the great Pehliva, and prayed that he would wrest from Nuder the crown and place it upon his own head. But Saum, being grieved at these words, replied unto them:

"Not so, O Men of Might, for it beseemeth me not in my old age to be untrue to the sovereign unto whom I have sworn loyalty—I and my house."

Then the nobles insisted, pointing out that Nuder was unworthy the throne. But the aged Saum who for so long a period had faithfully served his country was not at last to prove untrue to his duty. Sternly refusing the proffered honor, therefore, he advised the nobles to return unto their allegiance, promising to go himself before the Shah in the interests of the people.

So Saum the aged girt on his sword, and, taking with him a large retinue, he proceeded unto the Court, where he exhorted Nuder with prayers and tears to turn from the paths of evil, that he might earn for himself a glorious immortality like unto Feridoun and Minuchir, his glorious predecessors. Now so earnest and eloquent was Saum that Nuder listened unto his voice, and joy was abroad once more in the land.

But alas! The tidings of the death of the mighty Minuchir, and of the unpopularity and weakness of the new Shah, spread quickly, finally reaching even unto Turan. And there Poshang, who was of the race of Tur, heard the news with gladness, for he decided that now was the time ripe to take vengeance for the blood of his sire. Therefore he called about him his warriors, and his son Afrasiab who was next unto himself in the kingdom, and held counsel over the matter.

Now it is said of young Afrasiab the Prince that he was as strong as a lion or an elephant, and that his shadow extended for miles; that his tongue was like a bright sword, his heart as bounteous as the ocean, and his hands like the clouds when rain falleth to gladden the thirsty earth. Therefore his father found it not difficult to imbue his chivalrous and youthful spirit with the sentiments he himself cherished as, calling him into his presence, he said unto him:

"O my son, generous and brave, even as the great Minuchir in days gone by took vengeance for the blood of his sire, so ought thou now to take vengeance for thine; for I say unto thee that the grandson who refuseth to do this act of justice is unworthy a noble ancestry."

So, inspired by the thought of avenging old wrongs, and lured on by ambition as well, in the council which followed, Afrasiab gave his voice for war. But Aghriras, his younger brother, advised peace, for he said:

"Though Persia can no longer boast the prowess of Minuchir, O my father, still be not precipitate. For behold! the great warriors Saum, and Zal, and Karun yet live, and we have only to remember the result of the war in which Selim and Tur were involved to be convinced that it would be better not to begin the contest at all than to bring ruin and desolation upon our own country. Think well, therefore, before undertaking so mighty an enterprise."

To this prudent counsel, however, Poshang turned a deaf ear, for he coveted the rich provinces of Persia, even as Selim and Tur before him, and he thought the time particularly fit and inviting to carry out his ambitious schemes. So when the verdure of spring covered the plains the Tartar army set forth.

Now this event could not have happened in a more unlucky hour for Persia, since the great Pehliva Saum had just been gathered unto the dust; and Zal, his white-haired son, tarried in his house to build him a tomb; while Rustem was ill with the small-pox. Nevertheless, the grandson of Feridoun, when he learned of the coming of the Tartar horde, raised as great an army as he could, and prepared to meet the foes of his land, which covered the ground like ants and locusts.

And presently it came to pass that the two great armies had approached within two leagues of each other, whereupon, a Tartar champion, Barman, by name, rode forth challenging the Persians to single combat; and as it happened, there was no one to answer the call but the aged Kobad, the oldest warrior in the army. Now Karun and Kobad were brothers, being both sons of Kavah, and both leaders in the Persian army. Seeing how unequal would be the conflict, therefore, Karun tried to dissuade his brother from the undertaking, saying unto him:

"O my brother, go not forth to meet this giant, for should thy hoary locks be stained with blood, thy legions would be overwhelmed with grief and, in despair, decline the coming battle!"

But brave old Kobad resisted all the arguments and entreaties of Karun, replying unto him:

"This body, this frail tenement, O my brother, belongeth unto death. No living man hath ever yet gone up to heaven, for all are doomed to die—some by the sword, the dagger, or the spear, and some devoured by roaring beasts of prey; some peacefully upon their beds, and others snatched suddenly from life, endure the lot ordained by the Creator. And if I perish now, fighting against my country's foe, doth not my brother live, my noble brother, to bury me beneath a warrior's tomb, and bless my memory? And what can a soldier brave ask more?"

Now, speaking thus, brave Kobad rushed forward to the field, and the two champions met in desperate conflict, the fearful struggle lasting all day long. But at evening, as the combat was about to end for the day, behold, Barman threw a stone at his antagonist with such force that Kobad, in receiving the blow, fell lifeless from his horse.

And then was Karun furious! Bringing forward his whole army, therefore, he at once advanced in fearful

charge to avenge right speedily the death of his brother.
Then seeing this, Afrasiab himself advanced, and an encounter ensued which was fierce and terrible.

> "Loud neighed the steeds, and their resounding hoofs,
>   Shook the deep caverns of the earth; the dust
>   Rose up in clouds and hid the azure heavens—
>   Bright beamed the swords, and in that carnage wide,
>   Blood flowed like water. Night alone divided
>   The hostile armies."

But the next morning the battle was renewed, and from
dawn to set of sun the terrible conflict raged. Now the
carnage was so great that blood flowed like water, and
heads fell from their trunks like unto autumn leaves,
kissed by the soft south winds; and the clamor and confusion were so mighty that earth and sky seemed blended in
one.

However, of all the events of that dreadful day none was
more terrible than when King Nuder himself charged
from out his army to meet the valiant Afrasiab. Now not
only did the two combatants hurl javelins at each other,
and fight until their swords were hacked like unto saws,
and their spears were shivered, but they even closed with
each other like two serpents, so deadly was the struggle.
But finally, as night was coming on, Afrasiab began to prevail, and the King had hard work to escape with his life.

So when the javelins cast long shadows upon the plain
at even-tide, the Tartar host had won the day, and many
a famous Persian chief lay dead upon the battle-field.
Howbeit, King Nuder and Karun escaped, securing themselves by falling back unto the White Fort.

But, that same night, Afrasiab despatched one of his
noted chiefs with a body of horsemen unto Iran for the

purpose of intercepting and capturing the shubistan of
Nuder; and Karun, hearing of this important move, was
all on fire to pursue the enemy and frustrate their object,
wishing not to see the helpless women and children of the
King's household in the hands of the enemy. So, supported by a strong volunteer force, he set off at midnight,
and as fate would have it, it happened that at dawn he fell
in with a detachment of the enemy under Barman, who
was also pushing forward into Persia.

So, considering this unusually fortunate, straightway
Karun, in revenge for his brother Kobad, sought out the
champion and dared him to single combat. And so great
was his fury that, throwing his javelin with the might of a
Deev, he hurled Barman violently from his horse, so that
he lay upon the ground stunned. Then Karun, quickly dismounting, severed the head of the giant, and hung it at his
saddle-bow. And this being accomplished, he attacked
and defeated the whole Tartar company, being in full
possession of the field when joined by King Nuder.

But now Afrasiab came up, and so again was the battle
renewed. Now from morning until evening the conflict
raged so fiercely that the ground could not be seen for the
dead, and in the end the Persians suffered a great defeat.
But, most unfortunate of all, King Nuder again fell into
the hands of the Tartar chief, and long they fought, but
finally Afrasiab succeeded in grasping his royal opponent
by the girdle and, furious, dragged him from his foaming
horse, and carried him off a prisoner.

But worse was to come, for when Afrasiab learned of
Karun's valorous deed, and that as a consequence, not
only Barman, but many of the bravest of his warriors were
slain, in a fit of rage, he slew his royal prisoner, and also

many of the thousand brave warriors who fell into his hands with Nuder; and Persia was without a King.

And presently it came to pass that Afrasiab himself sat down upon the throne of light, proclaiming himself lord of Iran. And not only this, but he required all the people to do homage unto him, and to pour gifts before his face. But the people would not listen unto his voice, and in their distress they sent messengers unto Seistan, asking counsel of the great Pehliva. Then Zal, hearing of the sad plight of Iran, cast aside his sorrow for Saum, his father, and replied thus unto the messengers:

"O Men of Iran, verily all my days have I feared no enemy save only old age, and now it is come upon me; for my back is bowed, and I can no longer wield the sword as in former years, but, thanks unto Ormuzd, the old stump hath put forth a noble shoot, and, therefore, my son Rustem will do all that can be done to succor Iran from her foes, for he is strong and courageous, and is now ready and longing for battle. Wherefore, be of good cheer!"

Then Zal, dismissing the messengers, called before him his son and said unto him:

"O Hero of the House of Saum, verily thou art strong as an elephant, and thy courage is as that of the lion who defendeth her young. Nevertheless, O my son, thy lips still smell of milk, and thy heart should be going out after pleasure instead of battle, for thou art yet but a youth. But alas! the times are perilous, and Iran looketh unto thee for succor; so the time is come when I must send thee forth to cope with heroes, both thou and Rakush thy steed! And, armed with thy grandsire's famous club for thy mace, I mistake me if thou spreadest not consternation among the Tartar host. What sayeth the proud son of Zal?"

Now at this Rustem smiled. Then drawing near unto his father he said:

"O my noble father, with my grandsire's mighty club I slew the King's white elephant. Hast thou forgotten that? And also how I took the enchanted fortress? Verily, I know that I am young, but it would be a disgrace if I were to be afraid of Afrasiab and his warriors, and verily, I am not afraid. For, seated upon Rakush, and armed with my grandsire's mace and helmet, my heart telleth me that I shall not disgrace the house of Saum the Hero. Give me thy blessing, therefore, and send me forth. Then shall Persia be delivered from her foes."

Now Zal's heart laughed within him for very gladness when he heard these words of manhood from his son, and immediately preparations were made to take the field, a large army being raised and equipped by Rustem.

But, though Afrasiab heard of the preparations being made by Zal and Rustem to come out against him, the news disturbed him not at all, for he said:

"Verily, why should we fear? The son is but a boy, and the father is old; therefore, it will be simply play to vanquish these heroes, so let us feast and be merry!"

So they feasted, hearing not as they made merry over their wine the steady tramp, tramp of the approaching army, which daily drew nearer, and of whose might they dreamed not.

Now it was the time of roses, when Zal led forth his host against the offspring of Tur, and the meadows smiled with verdure, filling all the air with fragrance. At the head of the mighty multitude marched Rustem, the flag of Kavah floating o'er him gloriously. But White-haired Zal was not at his side, for he marched in the midst of the men, while

Mihrab and Gustahem led the two wings. Also there followed after Rustem a number like the sands of the sea, and the sounds of cymbals and drums made a noise like unto the great day of judgment. So marched they until they came near unto the Tartar camp. Then, assembling his veteran chiefs, Zal said unto them:

"O my Brave Warriors, valiant in fight! Behold, we have here a great army; we have also daring chiefs and wise counsellors; but we suffer a great disadvantage because that we have no King. But rejoice and be not dismayed, for a Mubid hath revealed unto me that at Mount Alborz there yet liveth one of the royal race of Feridoun, unto whom belongeth the throne; and that he is a youth wise and brave, and a lover of justice and truth."

Having thus spoken unto the chiefs, behold, Zal next addressed himself unto Rustem, and he said:

"My son, I pray thee depart at once for Mount Alborz, neither tarry by the way. And when thou art come unto the mountain, do homage unto Prince Kaikobad, and say unto him that lo! the army is asking for its King. We shall expect thy return with the Prince within fourteen days."

So, with great joy, Rustem leaped upon the back of Rakush, and rode off at full speed. Now he had gone but a short distance when a number of Tartars who had posted themselves upon the road, seeing the young hero galloping toward them, attacked him. But Rustem, club in hand, fell upon them with fury, striking many to the ground, and driving the rest before him, so that they returned unto Afrasiab full of terror.

Meanwhile, Rustem, tarrying not, rode on until he was come unto Mount Alborz, unto a spot where he beheld a splendid palace standing in a beautiful garden whence came the sounds of running waters. Trees of tall stature uprose therein, and under their spreading shade, beside a gurgling fountain, there was placed a throne upon which sat a youth of singular beauty. And circled round about him were nobles, girt with red sashes of might, and they paid homage unto the youth.

Now beguiled by the charm of the place, which was really a paradise as to perfume and beauty, Rustem drew rein for a moment, and when those within the garden beheld it, they came out unto him, saying courteously:

"O noble youth, thou appearest to have ridden fast and far! Descend from off thy horse, therefore, and drink a cup of wine with us, for we would greet thee as our guest."

But Rustem, thanking them, refused the courtesy, saying unto them in explanation:

"Unfortunately, O gracious Pehliva, my errand is one that demandeth haste. For lo! the borders of Iran are encircled by the enemy, and in every house there is mourning because that the throne is empty of a King. Wherefore, I may not stay to taste of wine."

Hearing this, the nobles no longer sought to detain Rustem, but said graciously unto him:

"Verily, if thou art on thy way unto Mount Alborz, brave youth, tell unto us thy mission, for we are of those who guard its sides."

Then Rustem, satisfied as to their integrity, replied unto his questioners:

"Behold! I seek upon Mount Alborz a King of the pure royal race, a youth who reareth high his head. His name is Kaikobad, and if ye know aught of him, I pray that ye give me tidings as to where I may find him."

Now at this the youth upon the throne arose, and said unto Rustem:

"Sayest thou, O Pehliva, that thou seekest Prince Kaikobad? Verily, he is well known unto me, and if thou wilt graciously enter this garden, and rejoice my soul with thy presence, surely I will give thee tidings concerning him."

So Rustem, at this promise, quickly dismounted from off the back of Rakush, and hastened to where the nobles were congregated by the fountain. Then the youth who had called unto him took his hand and led him unto the steps of the throne, and, pouring out wine, he drank to his guest, giving also unto Rustem. Then this ceremony being ended, he said:

"O Valiant One! Why seekest thou Kaikobad? At whose desire art thou thus sent forth?"

Then Rustem replied:

"O Prince, I bring unto Kaikobad good tidings, for the nobles of Iran have chosen him to be their King. And lo! my aged father, Zal, hath sent me with all speed to pray the young King to hasten unto his own, that he may lead the host against the enemies of Iran."

Now the youth listened attentively unto Rustem; then, smiling, he said:

"O Son of the White-haired Zal! Rejoice, for thy quest is ended, since thou beholdest in me Kaikobad of the race of Feridoun."

Then Rustem, bowing his head, kissed the ground before the Prince, saluting him as Shah. And Kaikobad, calling for a cup of wine, touched it with his lips in Rustem's honor. Then Rustem also drank, crying loyally:

"May the Shah live forever! May he bring destruction

unto the enemies of Iran, and reign gloriously for a thousand years!"

And now music rent the air, and shouts of joy from the nobles, because that the King was come into his own. But when silence was once more restored, the young Shah opened his mouth and said:

"O Nobles of Iran, hearken unto my dream, which is now come true, and you will know why I called upon you this day to stand in majesty about my throne. Behold, last night in my sleep, suddenly from out the blue I beheld two falcons, white of wing, flying toward me by way of Iran; and in their beaks they bore a sunny crown which they placed upon my head. And lo! here is Rustem, come out unto me this day like a white bird; and his father, the nursling of a bird, hath sent him, while the sunny diadem is the crown of Iran."

Now all marvelled at the dream, and Rustem said:

"Surely, O King, thou art chosen of Ormuzd, and blessings will be showered upon Iran while thou art seated upon the throne of light! But since there is now need for haste, I pray thee let us tarry no longer, for the enemy is at the door."

So Kaikobad swung himself upon his steed of war, and in yet the same hour they set out with their followers, toward Iran. And they rode day and night without stopping until, having left the glorious hills far behind them, they were come unto the green plains, already clad in all their spring beauty. Whereupon, being come unto the outposts of the enemy, Kaloun, the great Tartar champion, came out to attack them, and when the King saw him and his ugly-looking followers, he was for giving battle. But Rustem said:

"O Lord of Iran, truly it becometh not thy greatness to honor such a foe. And, moreover, my horse and my club, with God on my side, will be enough, I think, to settle this handful of the enemy."

Now so speaking, and waiting not for reply, Rustem gave Rakush the rein, and made a dash for the Tartars; and fearful was the onslaught! For coming up with the enemy, the hero, catching one trooper from his horse, struck another with the man as if he were a club, dashing out his brains. Then one by one he tore the riders from their saddles, dashing them to the ground with such force as to break their skulls, and necks, and backs. And finally it came the turn of the great champion also to feel the wrath of Rustem. Reaching out his hand, therefore, quickly he caught hold of Kaloun's spear, tore it from him, and with it struck him from his saddle. Then as he lay upon the ground, Rakush trampled upon him until he was naught but a mass of clay. Now when the remaining Tartars saw their chief treated in this fashion, they thought that a demon had broken his chain, and was riding about with a club and a lasso fastened unto his saddle; so being filled with terror, they turned their backs and fled.

Then, having given the enemy somewhat to report unto Afrasiab, Rustem rode back unto the King, and they continued their journey. And that night, in the darkness, Rustem led the "Hope of Iran" safely through the enemy's line within the tents of Zal. And after this, seven days they feasted and counselled together, but on the eighth day the crown of Iran was placed upon the head of Kaikobad, who mustered the army and led it forth against the Tartar host.

And then, what a conflict! Fierce and terrible it raged for days, and many were the deeds of valor performed by both

Iranian and Turk. But the men of Turan prevailed not, though Afrasiab made one terrible onslaught in which so great was the clamor and confusion that it seemed as if heaven and earth had closed in deadly conflict, the result of which would be victory for the enemy. Now the spectacle was magnificent, awe-inspiring, and terrible. For, what with the clattering of hoofs, the shrill roar of the trumpets, the rattle of the brazen drums, and the vivid glitter of spear and shield, there was produced a scene of indescribable tumult and splendor, while the neighing of the steeds of battle, the cries of dying men, and the blood which flowed like water, testified to the deadly work being done by the Tartar King, who beheld the crown of Iran just within his grasp.

But the bravery of Afrasiab upon that dreadful day was as nothing beside that of Rustem. Seemingly everywhere on the field at the same time, so terrible was the destruction which he caused that, verily, you would have said he was war incarnate. Now his power was that of a hungry lion which causeth all men to flee; neither could his strength be broken, for his shadow extended for miles, and, unaided, he performed deeds of prowess of which no hero e'er dreamed, so that from this time forth men named him Tehemten, which meaneth "the strong-limbed." But behold! when the conflict had lasted for some time, as the battle ebbed for a moment, Rustem said unto Zal:

"O my father, where think you hideth Afrasiab? What dress doth he wear, and what is his standard? for verily I see him not! Why doth he not stand forth that I may meet him in single combat?"

Then Zal, laying a detaining hand upon his son, said gravely:

"Listen, O my son, and stick not thy hand in the lion's jaws! For truly this young Tartar, Afrasiab, rageth in the conflict with the fury of the lion and the crocodile; yea, he fighteth in the saddle like a sharp-fanged dragon; and in his wrath, as he wieldeth his bright scimitar around him, he staineth the earth with blood. Beware of him, therefore, for black is his banner, black his coat of mail and the plume upon his helmet, and behold, woe followeth ever in his train."

Now, hearing this, Rustem quickly loosened his father's detaining hand, saying unto him earnestly:

"Yea, and black is his heart also, O my father, for he murdered his gentle brother. Dragon or Demon, therefore, I fear him not, for Heaven is not his friend. Let him come forth, therefore, and soon we shall see unto whom Ormuzd giveth the victory."

Then away galloped Rustem, and as he rode he shouted his terrible battle-cry which caused the enemy to flee before him like fire before the wind. Now noting the havoc caused by the youth, Afrasiab, astonished, said unto his chiefs:

"O Men of Turan, what dragon is this who scoureth the plain, causing my warriors to flee before him? Verily, his claws need trimming!"

Whereupon, the nobles, surrounding Afrasiab, said eagerly:

"What! Hast thou not then heard? Yonder roaring lion is Rustem, the mighty son of Zal, and verily, his power is that of a thousand Deevs! Seest thou not the club that he wieldeth with such deadly force? Lo, it is that of Deev-fighting Saum, his grandsire, and the youth seeketh renown, even as that illustrious Pehliva. And much we fear,

O Afrasiab, that if his power be not speedily broken he will carry all before him."

Now, having heard this report, Afrasiab galloped straight unto the front of his army where, being seen by Rustem, he was at once challenged to single combat. With a fierce cry of joy, then, the warriors closed, and long and fearful was the struggle. At last, however, Rustem deftly caught Afrasiab by the girdle, and dragged him from his saddle, intending to carry him thus captive unto Kaikobad as a trophy of his first day's fighting. But, what with the weight of the King, and Rustem's mighty arm, the leather of the girdle broke, and Afrasiab fell headlong to the ground, whereupon he was immediately surrounded and rescued by his warriors, but not before Rustem had snatched off his crown, which together with the broken girdle he bore off in triumph.

Meanwhile, Afrasiab, having been mounted by his chiefs upon a swift horse, succeeded in making his escape, owing to the great confusion, and his army was left to shift for itself. As a consequence, in the general engagement which now took place, it fared ill indeed with the enemy, for the Persians, fired by the example of Rustem, performed prodigies of valor, many a brave hero on this field fighting his last fight for Iran.

But, among them all, no one could compare with Rustem. On that tremendous day, with sword and dagger, battle-axe and noose, he cut, and tore, and broke, and bound the brave, slaying and making captive with his own hand as many as a whole army. It is even said that at one fell swoop more than a thousand fell before his life-destroying sword, and that, witnessing this feat of supernatural power, the Tartar hordes fled in dismay, their black banners trailing in the dust, and with no sound of trumpet or drum to indicate the course of their flight.

So, in this sad plight, the conquered Tartar legions pursued their noiseless retreat unto their own land. But the Persians, when they beheld the enemy vanish as the mist, fell slowly back unto the capital, where the victory was celebrated with great pomp and splendor, Kaikobad rewarding the valor of Rustem by appointing him captain-general of the armies under the title of the "Champion of the World," and also giving unto him a golden crown, carrying with it the privilege of giving audience while seated upon a golden throne.

But alas for Afrasiab! With a heavy heart he returned unto his father, in bitter humiliation communicating unto him the misfortunes which had overtaken him. And he said:

"O my father, verily we acted not wisely in provoking this war. For lo! there hath arisen in Iran, from the race of Saum the Pehliva, a youth who cannot be matched anywhere, either in strength or valor or prowess—for hath he not utterly subdued thy legions? Yet now he is but a mere weanling! I ask you, therefore, to consider what is likely to come to pass when he reacheth his full vigor?

"Now well thou knowest, O my father, that thy son is no weakling, but a hero desiring to possess the world, and of established valor; yea, the stay of thy army, and thy refuge in danger, yet before this young dragon of war his power is as nothing, as thou shalt hear.

"For behold! when in the midst of battle he beheld my standard, like a crocodile he sprang to the fight. Verily, thou wouldst have said that his breath scorched up the plain, so fiery was he! Then long we fought, but suddenly

seizing me by the girdle, he caught me from my saddle with
such mighty force that hadst thou seen him thou wouldst
have said he held no more than a fly in his grasp. Then
broke my golden girdle, and down I fell ingloriously upon
the dusty ground; and this was well, for quickly then was
I rescued by my body-guard and spirited away. But
knowing well my prowess, O my father, and how my
nerves are strung, thou canst conceive the wondrous
strength, the marvellous power which sunk me thus to
nothing.

"And now I say unto thee, haste to make peace with
Iran, else Turan is lost, for verily the hero liveth not who
can stand against this mighty man of valor."

Poshang listened unto this bitter tale with sorrow and
dismay, astonished, too, to hear the fierce and valiant
Afrasiab speak so hopelessly of the undertaking. Well he
knew, therefore, that he must sue for peace, and tears of
exceeding bitterness fell from his eyes, as, calling unto him
a scribe, he dictated unto Kaikobad the Shah a letter, in
which he said unto the great King:

"O Glorious Shelter of the Universe, in the name of
Ormuzd, the great ruler of sun and moon and earth, greeting from the meanest of thy subjects, who sayeth unto thee:
Wherefore should we seek the land of our neighbor, since
in the end each will receive in heritage a spot no larger
than his body? Let the Jihun, therefore, be the future
boundary between Turan and Iran, and lo! not one of my
people shall pass over its waters; nay, not even in their
dreams! Then shall the two nations live at peace, and all
will be well in the lands."

Now Kaikobad smiled at this wily letter; nevertheless,
he replied unto Poshang, saying:

"O Tartar King, well thou knowest that Persia sought
not this war, but Afrasiab, who thought to subdue a mas-
terless land, to satisfy his own ambitions, thus following in
the footsteps of Tur, his grandsire. For, even as he robbed Iran of gentle Irij, so Afrasiab hath taken from it
Nuder the Shah; and from thee, O King, thy noble young
son whom he so cruelly stabbed! Nevertheless, since
Kaikobad loveth peace rather than war, he agreeth to thy
proposals of peace; but see to it well that Afrasiab crosseth
not the Jihun."

So peace was made between Iran and Turan, and so
Rustem won his first laurels as a warrior.

RUSTEM'S SEVEN LABORS, OR ADVENTURES

LISTEN unto the tale of the seven adventures of Rustem, encountered while rescuing a foolish Shah from the consequences of his folly.

Now the foolish one was not the glorious Kaikobad who reigned beneficently over Iran for twice fifty years, but his son Kaikous, who, when his father exchanged the palace for the tomb, seated himself upon the throne of light, at first exercising many of the princely virtues of his illustrious predecessors. But alas! as his riches increased and his armies grew stronger, he became filled with self-admiration and pride, indulging more and more in the fascinations of the wine cup, until in the midst of his luxurious feasting with his warriors and chiefs, he, like the great Shah Jemshid, beheld no one but himself in the world.

Then it came to pass that one day as the vain Shah sat in his trellised bower in the garden of roses, drinking wine, boasting, and making merry with his friends, a Deev, disguised as a minstrel and playing sweetly upon his harp, presented himself before the King's chamberlain, desiring audience. And he said:

"Thou beholdest before thee, O Servant of the King, a singer of sweet songs, come unto thee from Mazinderan, desiring to pay homage unto the great King of Kings. Admit me, therefore, I pray thee, into the arbor of flowers, for in my throat are gay singing-birds which will make the bower a paradise of joy."

So the chamberlain, beguiled by the charm of the youth, hastened at once unto the King to beg audience for him. And he said:

"O Shelter of the Universe, at the gate is a minstrel with his harp. And lo! in his throat he hides a flock of singing-birds fresh from the gardens of paradise. He hath come hither desiring to prostrate himself before the most illustrious of all the Shahs of Iran, and he awaiteth thy commands, being naught but the dust at thy feet."

So the King, pleased with this flattery, and with no suspicion of guile, commanded that the musician be brought before him. Then the youth, being admitted, and having performed obeisance, warbled forth unto the monarch words of deep cunning, for his song was of the enchanted land of the Genii:

> "Now thus he warbled to the King—
> Mazinderan is the bower of spring,
> My native home; the balmy air
> Diffuses health and fragrance there;
> So tempered is the genial glow,
> Nor heat nor cold we ever know;
> Tulips and hyacinths abound
> On every lawn; and all around
> Blooms like a garden in its prime.
> Fostered by that delicious clime.
> The bulbul sits on every spray,
> And pours his soft melodious lay;
> Each rural spot its sweets discloses,
> Each streamlet is the dew of roses;
> The damsels, idols of the heart,
> Sustain a most bewitching part.
> And mark me, that untravelled man
> Who never saw Mazinderan,
> And all the charms its bowers possess,
> Has never tasted happiness!"

Now as the King's great desire was to drain the cup of happiness to the dregs, no sooner had he heard the minstrel's lay of this enchanting land than straightway he became inflamed with the desire to possess it for his own. Turning, therefore, unto his warriors, he at once declared that the glory of his reign should be the conquest of this wonderful country. For, he said:

"Verily it behooveth a great Shah to be a hero among men, and the world should be his footstool. Now in wealth, and power, and splendor, I, Kaikous, surpass not only the glorious Jemshid, but all my predecessors, and I say unto you that my prowess shall also be greater, for verily I mean to be master of Mazinderan which hath ever resisted the might of the greatest of the Shahs of Iran. Too long, O my nobles, have we abandoned ourselves to feasting, but now I bid you prepare for battle, for presently I will lead you into the enchanted land of the Genii, thus causing the glory of Kaikous to mount even unto the stars."

Alas! the nobles, when they heard these words of vanity and folly, grew pale with dread, for they had no desire to invade the country of the Deevs. But knowing the temper of the Shah, no one was brave enough to utter protest, though the hearts of all were full of misgivings and their mouths of sighs. But among themselves, when they could speak openly, they said one unto another:

"What folly is this! And what calamity will it bring upon us, unless, by good fortune, the King forgetteth in his cups this wild undertaking! Why, even the great Jemshid, whom the Genii and the Peri and the very birds of the air obeyed, never dreamed of trying to conquer the Deevs of Mazinderan, before whom the sword hath no power and wisdom is of no avail! And the great Feridoun, though he was the wisest of Kings, and skilled in all the arts of magic, never cherished such an enterprise! Truly, Kaikous is mad!"

So they talked in their anger and perplexity; and finally they sent forth a wind-footed dromedary and a messenger unto Zal, the Wise One of Iran, saying unto him:

"O Gracious Pehliva, once again is Iran in danger and hath sore need of thee. Therefore, though thy head be covered with dust, tarry not to cleanse it, but come quickly unto us, for verily the Evil One hath strewn mischievous seed in the heart of the Shah which threatens a bitter harvest, and we look unto thee to speak wise words of counsel unto him that this calamity may be averted."

Sore distressed by the words of the messenger, Zal shook his head sorrowfully, for he had not dreamed that this leaf on the royal tree would so soon show signs of canker. Nevertheless, he spoke words of comfort unto the messenger, saying:

"The great Kaikous is, I fear, puffed up with vanity, being not yet tried by either the cold or the heat of the world. And alas! I fear me, if what thou sayest be true, that the sun must revolve yet oft above his head ere he learneth the wisdom of the great; for unto true wisdom alone is it given to know when to strike and when to withhold the hand. Verily, he is like a child with a sword who thinketh the world and all therein must tremble, if he but upraiseth it. He will learn better with experience. I will not abandon him, therefore, to his folly, but will give him the best advice that I can. Then if he be persuaded by me, well; but if not, Rustem shall safeguard the army for the sake of the welfare of Iran."

Now having thus spoken, Zal quickly girt about him his red sash of might, took in his hand his great mace and hastened unto the court, where, being received with great honor and kindness, he proceeded to unburden his heart, entreating the Shah not to give his warriors and treasure unto the wind by undertaking the useless journey into Mazinderan.

But Kaikous, arrogant and self-willed, only smiled at the warnings of the white-haired old warrior, saying unto him:

"O Pillar of Iran, while I despise not thy counsel, yet thy words shall not divert me from my purpose, for in thy arguments, one thing thou forgettest: that I, Kaikous, am bolder of heart, and my power and wealth greater than any of the Shahs of Old. Yea, and I ask you, who among them had such warriors as thyself, and Rustem, thy glorious son? But verily, I shall not need any of the house of Zal in this war, since thy heart is not set upon glory. Thou and Rustem, therefore, can guard the kingdom while I go forth to soul-appalling conflict, which I fear not,

"For what are all the Demon-charms,
     That they excite such dread alarms?
What is a Demon-host to me,
     Their magic spells and sorcery?
One effort, and the field is won;
     Then why should I the battle shun?
Lo, when I reach the Demon fort,
     Their several heads shall be my sport!"

Thus spake the King in his pride and vanity, and Zal, seeing that words were useless, bowed his head low in the dust before the monarch, saying unto him:

"May the great Shah never have cause to recollect the

warning voice of his servant with repentance or sorrow!
May his glory shine on undimmed forever!"

Now when he had so spoken, Zal departed, and all the
people mourned for they saw that Kaikous was wholly
given over unto folly, and their hearts misgave them.

But not so was it with the King, for ere the week had run
its course, the great army of Iran was set in motion, while
at its head rode the vainglorious Kaikous, confident, self-
satisfied, merry, his magnificent retinue of richly caparisoned horses and camels making the earth tremble beneath
their tread. So they marched, each night pitching their
tents and passing the hours in revel, until at last they were
come near unto the land of enchantment. Then Kaikous,
calling before him Gew, one of the bravest of his warriors,
said unto him:

"O Valiant One, choose, I pray thee, two thousand of
the bravest men, and the boldest wielders of the battle-axe,
that ye may break down the gates of Mazinderan. In thy
progress, burn and destroy everything of value, and when
thou hast taken the city, spare no dweller of the place,
neither man, nor woman, nor child, for all are Deevs."

So Gew advanced, and when he was come unto the city,
he found it indeed arrayed in all the splendor of Paradise,
even as the minstrel had sung; for beauty, and verdure,
and fragrance filled all the senses with delight, while gold,
and jewels, and treasure of priceless value glittered and
gleamed, and massed itself everywhere. And in all the
streets, too, were beautiful maidens, richly adorned, with
faces as bright as the moon, and cheeks tinted with the hue
of the pomegranate flower by the beautiful Houri of Paradise. But Gew, knowing that all this was the work of enchantment, was not in the least beguiled. So soon clubs

rained down upon the people like hail, and the city that resembled a garden was changed into a desert, and all the dwellers therein perished at the hands of the enemy; neither was mercy shown unto any.

Meanwhile, as this terrible work of slaughter and destruction was being performed by his brave warriors, the valiant Kaikous, at a safe distance, was encamped in splendid state upon the plain, indulging in revelry and the wildest dreams of a glorious victory. When the news of the destruction of the city and of the great treasure hidden within its palaces was brought unto him, therefore, wild with elation, he sprang to his feet, and holding his wine cup high, cried exultantly:

"Hail to the glorious Kaikous, who hath overcome even the Deevs of Mazinderan! Aye, and blessings upon the sweet singer who warbled unto him of this glorious land of treasure! May his life's tree put forth many green leaves; may it blossom in the garden of Paradise!"

Thus spake Kaikous; and his warriors, too, rejoiced at the thought of the limitless treasure soon to be theirs. So on the following day the whole army pressed forward to join Gew and his warriors in Mazinderan, and for seven days they ceased not from plundering, neither was there an end to the gold and jewels which they found. And in their greed they sorrowed not for the beauty laid waste, or the woe which they had caused, but, like madmen, they spent their days in plundering and their nights in revelry.

But retribution was at hand, for now the news of the havoc being wrought by the Persians pierced even unto the ears of the distant King of Mazinderan, who at once despatched a messenger unto the Great White Deev, the most powerful and dreadful of all the master magicians of

the East, entreating him to come at once unto the rescue,
lest the whole land perish under the feet of Iran. Then the
dreadful White Deev uprose in his wrath until he appeared
like unto a snow-capped mountain in his fury, roaring like
the River Nile, until all the earth trembled, and he said:

"Thinks this puny, childish Shah to pit himself against
the master magicians of the East, that he thus invadeth
our land? Verily, the imbecile shall pay dearly for his
folly!"

So it came to pass that on this same day, when the night
was fallen, a wonderful cloud, heavy and dark, spread itself
over Kaikous and his army, wrapping them in a tent of
blackness. Then from out the pitch-black sky the wrath-
ful Deev caused it to rain stones and javelins, causing a
terror and confusion like unto the great day of judgment.
Nor could the men of Iran protect themselves against this
strange attack, since all was the work of magic. So the
dead piled up, and the cries of the wounded swelled into
a horrible dirge, while the horror of it all drove many to
madness. And not only this, for behold, when the day
dawned after this night of horror, lo! the King, and all
those who had not fled, or been killed by the hailstones
and javelins, were stone-blind.

Then followed for the sightless monarch and his followers seven terrible days of anguish as, moaning and lamenting, they sat helpess among the ruins of Mazinderan.
Yea, the great Kaikous wept bitterly in his terror, and the
army with him, until so awful became the cry that it
reached even unto the Seven Mountains where dwelt the
great White Deev, arousing him from his mid-day slumber. Then suddenly his voice, loud as a clap of thunder,
fell upon the ear of the wretched Kaikous. And he said:

"Vain Monarch! Thou thoughtest in thy folly to conquer the land of the Great White Deev, who from the gorgeous vault of heaven can charm the stars. Thou fool! Now there thou liest, struck down like a rotten trunk, and upon thine own head alone resteth this destruction. Verily, thou hast attained unto Mazinderan, which was thy heart's desire, wherefore be now content!"

But alas! The Shah and his unfortunate companions were not soon to know content, since they were now turned over into the charge of twelve thousand Genii whose duty it was to keep them in prison, withholding from them wine and all good cheer, but giving unto them each day just enough food to keep them alive, that their suffering might be prolonged, for they gloried in their wretchedness.

Now thus dwelt Kaikous in the land after which his heart had yearned, until the eyes of his soul being opened, in genuine repentance, he bowed himself in the dust, casting black earth upon his head and acknowledging his fault. Then, casting about in his mind how they might obtain release, finally, after many weary moons, the King succeeded in sending a messenger unto Zal of the white hair. And he said:

"O my Great Pehliva, hearken unto the voice of thy sovereign who crieth unto thee in penitence and woe! Verily, I have sought what the foolish seek, and found what they find, and I deserve not thy help, since I turned a deaf ear unto thy words of wisdom; yet for my companions' sake, I beseech thee to gird thy loins and come quickly unto us, or we perish in our misery."

Thus humbled himself the great Shah, but Zal, when he received the message, was cut to the heart that the pride of Iran should be thus trailed in the dust; and he wrung his hands bitterly, crying out against the folly which was to cost the land so dear. Nevertheless, he quickly sent for Rustem, saying unto him:

"O my glorious son, word hath just reached me that the King is held with his companions blind and captive in the dragon's den. As for me, I am old and feeble, a warrior bowed with the weight of two centuries, no longer able to fight against the Deevs. But thou art young and thy soul rejoiceth in battle. Gird about thee, therefore, thy leopard's skin, saddle Rakush, and deliver the King from out the hands of the Genii, thus winning for thyself immortal fame."

Now Rustem smiled as he heard his father's words, saying unto him:

"O my silver-crowned father, verily thou knowest that Rakush and I are spoiling for battle, and though of old the mighty went not forth to fight the powers of darkness, being not so weary of the world as to walk willingly into the mouth of a hungry lion, yet with God's help will I overcome these wicked Deevs, and gird our army anew with the red sash of might, since the glory of Iran demandeth it."

Then Zal blessed his son, speaking unto him long and earnestly as to the arduous task before him. And he said:

"I understand, O my son, that two roads lead into this land of enchantment, both of them difficult and dangerous. The King went by the longer way. It is the safest, but since it behooveth vengeance to be fleet, choose it not. But the other way, though by far the shorter, is beset by baleful evils, and is surrounded by darkness. Still it will be wisest, I think, to go by this road, for though difficult, it will have an end, and Rakush will carry thee quicker than a bird can fly. Go, therefore, my son, and may Ormuzd return thee safe unto my arms. If, however, it be the will of Heaven that thou shouldst perish by the hand of the great White Deev, why, who can escape his destiny? Verily, soon or late Death's door swings wide for every child of Ormuzd, and thrice blessed is he who leaveth behind him in the world a trail of glory."

When Rustem had drunk in the noble words of his father, he embraced him tenderly, feeling his strength to be sufficient even for the Great White Deev. Then he commanded that Rakush, the fleet of foot, be brought unto him. But alas! when he would have departed, Rudabeh uttered bitter cries that her boy should be sent to fight alone and unaided the wicked Deevs, and in her sorrow she would have hindered him. But Rustem suffered it not, making light of her fears and comforting her with his voice and arms. So finally, embracing him, Rudabeh let him depart, but her heart yearned after him, and her eyes were wet with tears yet many days after his departure, and she prayed continually unto Ormuzd, that Serosch the Angel of Pity keep nightly watch over his slumbers.

So, with only his faithful steed for company, but brave of heart, Rustem set out upon his perilous journey; and, as if recognizing the urgent need for haste, Rakush caused the ground to vanish under his feet, his speed being so great that he accomplished two days' journey in one. But at last, evening having fallen, the young hero of the world, finding himself weary and hungry, decided to stop for the night.

Now the plain upon which Rustem chose his camping-ground was filled with herds of gor, which made it easy for him to secure his evening meal, since there was no escape for the swiftest beast when Rustem was mounted upon Rakush. Soon, therefore, with his lasso, he succeeded in snaring a wild ass, which he quickly roasted and ate. Then, his hunger appeased, the young warrior prepared for himself a couch among the reeds, and, his mace by his side, he lay down to sleep, fearing neither wild beast nor Deev, while Rakush grazed contentedly near by.

But, unfortunately, in the rushes near the young hero's couch was hidden the lair of a fierce lion, and after Rustem had fallen asleep the hungry beast, attracted by the odor of the gor's flesh, returned unto his haunt; and then a pair of fiery eyeballs moved stealthily nearer and nearer unto the dying fire. But when at last within the circle of light, what was the lion's astonishment to behold, lying peacefully asleep upon the rushes, a man as tall as an elephant watched over by a noble charger!

Now the king of the forest was hungry, not having been successful in his hunting, so as he gazed his heart rejoiced at the thought of the fat meal in store for him. But, being a sagacious beast, he said unto himself:

"Since I am very, very hungry, I must take no chance of allowing this delicious morsel to escape my lips. Consequently, first I will subdue this gentle-looking steed; then I can feast upon the rider at my leisure."

So, suddenly the huge beast bounded from the underbrush, falling upon Rakush with great violence. But the faithful steed was not caught napping, for while apparently unconscious of the approach of danger, he had at once scented the foe, and was ready for the attack. What was the lion's astonishment, therefore, to find himself received with a terrific and well-aimed kick that sent him back into the bushes more quickly than he had come forth! And not only that, but before he could recover from his amazement, like a flash of light Rakush was upon him, striking him on the head with his fore-feet, tearing him with his sharp teeth, and battering and trampling him like a Demon. Yea, so furious was his rage, that he was still stamping upon the lifeless mass when Rustem awoke!

Then the Hero, seeing the dead lion, which was truly of a monstrous size, knew at once what had happened, and calling Rakush, he rebuked even while he caressed him. And he said:

> "Ah, Rakush, why so thoughtless grown,
> To fight a lion thus alone?
> For had it been thy fate to bleed,
> And not thy foe, my gallant steed!
> How could thy master have conveyed
> His helm, and battle-axe, and blade,
> Unaided to Mazinderan?
> Why didst thou fail to give the alarm,
> And save thyself from chance of harm,
> By neighing loudly in my ear;
> But though thy bold heart knows no fear,
> From such unwise exploits refrain,
> Nor try a lion's strength again."

Now having thus exhorted Rakush, Rustem again composed himself to slumber, and rested undisturbed until the morning light had tinted the distant mountain peaks with rose and amber. Then having broken his fast, he saddled Rakush, and pursued his perilous journey, thanking God that, owing to the faithfulness and bravery of his steed, the first adventure had terminated happily.

But alas! he had now to accomplish the most difficult part of his journey, for the way led across a waterless

desert so hot that not even the birds could fly over it.
Now the morning hours were endurable, but when the
noon-tide sun poured down upon their heads its pitiless
rays, making of the sand living fire, then horse and rider
became tortured with the most maddening thirst, and nowhere could water be found.

At this crisis Rustem dismounted, since he was no longer
able to keep his place upon the back of his brave steed,
but, nevertheless, for some time longer he continued to
struggle forward, supported by his spear. Finally, however, his strength became broken and, utterly exhausted,
he sank upon the earth, his body prostrate upon the burning sand, his tongue and throat parched with thirst. Then
in his agony, his soul lifted itself up in a mighty cry unto the
Almighty for protection against the evils which surrounded
him, for he feared that his hour was come. But not so,
for behold! even as he prayed, there passed before him
a well-nourished ram, which was at once hailed by the
hero as a harbinger of good. For he said:

"Surely an oasis must be somewhere near, or how could
this sheep so bear upon it the impress of the drinking-
place!"

Rising up quickly, therefore, Rustem followed the ram's
footsteps, holding the bridle of Rakush in one hand and
his sword in the other, and behold! it led him unto a fountain of water, clear and cool, in the shade of a clump of
trees. Stooping down, therefore, Rustem drank greedily
until his thirst was quenched, giving also unto Rakush,
and bathing him in the waters. Then being refreshed,
he looked about for the ram, but lo! it had vanished.
So then Rustem knew that Ormuzd had wrought a
wonder for his sake, and falling upon the ground, he

gave thanks unto the All-Merciful One. And so full was
his heart of thanksgiving that he also blessed the ram,
saying:

"O Beast of God, wherever thou art, may no harm come
unto thee forever! May the grass of the valleys and of the
desert be always green for thee! May the spear-point be
blunted and the bow be broken of him who would hunt
thee, or do thee harm! For verily, without thy guidance,
Rustem would have perished in the desert, and the heroes
of Iran would have been left without succor in the hands of
the cruel Deevs."

And now the Mighty One, being hungry, killed another
gor, of which he ate almost the whole. Then having
bathed in the fountain, as the shades of night were
coming on he gladly sought a resting-place among the
stunted herbage. But before lying down he said unto
Rakush:

> "Beware, my steed, of future strife,
> Again thou must not risk thy life;
> But should an enemy appear,
> Ring loud thy warning in my ear."

Now having thus spoken, with a sigh of thankfulness
that his second adventure had terminated thus happily,
Rustem threw himself down upon his warrior's couch,
and being fatigued, soon sleep wrapped him about, holding him fast until the bright constellations in the tropical
sky pointed to the hour of midnight.

Then he was awakened unto a new horror, for you must
know that in this part of the desert there lived a monstrous
dragon, eighty yards in length, and so fierce that neither
elephant, nor demon, nor lion ever ventured to pass by its

lair. Yea, so terrible was it that not even the birds dared fly across that part of the desert, for with its poisonous breath it could bring down even the eagle from the sky. Imagine, then, how this scourge of the desert opened wide his snaky eyes with astonishment when, emerging from the forest at the turn of the night, he beheld a man slumbering softly beside his lair!

But, as usual, Rakush was on the alert. Consequently, as he caught the gleam of beady eyes, and scented the poisoned breath of the dragon, he quickly stepped nearer to his unconscious master, stamping with his hoofs upon the ground, beating the air with his tail, and neighing loudly. Now all this noise so startled the dragon that he quickly drew back into the forest, and as a consequence, when Rustem awoke he could see nothing disquieting, for of course the monster had vanished. Seeing no cause for alarm, therefore, he was angry at being needlessly disturbed, and rebuked Rakush for his nervousness, saying:

"Rakush, thou thunderer! I fear me the sun hath turned thy brain. Quiet now, quiet! for to-morrow will bring for us another hard day's journey."

So, having thus somewhat calmed his excited steed, once more Rustem gave himself up to slumber, but not for long! For, though the darkness became thicker and more impenetrable, in a short time the watchful horse once more caught the gleam of baleful eyes, and again he ran with all speed unto his master, tearing up the ground and neighing angrily. So a second time was Rustem awakened and a second time also did the dragon vanish ere the eyes of the hero beheld him. Then was Rustem angry, and in his impatience he spake sharply unto Rakush, chiding him

for thus disturbing his slumbers by causeless alarms.
And he said unto his brave steed:

> "Why thus again disturb my rest,
> When sleep had softly soothed my breast?
> I told thee if thou chanced to see
> Another dangerous enemy
> To sound the alarm; but not to keep
> Depriving me of needful sleep,
> When nothing meets the eye nor ear,
> Nothing to cause a moment's fear!
> Now if again my rest is broke,
> On thee shall fall the fatal stroke,
> And I myself will drag this load
> Of ponderous arms along the road;
> Yea, I will go, a lonely man,
> Without thee to Mazinderan."

Alas, poor Rakush! grieved and wounded by the unjust
reproaches of his master, with drooping head he drew
quickly back; but as Rustem wrapped his leopard's skin
about him, and a third time slept, softly he drew near once
more, standing a tireless watcher by his side. Then the
dragon, seeing that the hero slept, once more came forth,
prepared to fall upon him, and Rakush was sore distressed, for he knew not how to act. But as his love for his
master was great, taking courage, once more he stamped
the earth and woke him.

Then Rustem sprang up in a rage, but Ormuzd who
watcheth ever over his children, at this moment caused the
eastern sky to flush with a rosy glow, in the light of which
the hero beheld the prodigious cause of alarm. Pausing
not, therefore, he quickly drew about him his armor, and,
unsheathing his sword, rushed forward to meet the ugly

monster. But to his surprise, as he advanced, the dragon spoke, and he said:

"Vain creature, what doest thou here? Verily, the mother that bare thee shall weep, for I will tear thy soul from out thy body, and thy name, if thou hast one, shall be blotted from the book of life, for no man hath ever yet saved himself from my claws."

Uttering this terrible threat, the dragon belched forth fire and roared horribly, but Rustem, no whit deterred, continued to advance, saying proudly:

"Hideous monster! Thinkest thou to terrify me with thy smoke and noisy words? If so, thou errest. For behold! I am Rustem, son of the white-haired Zal, and there is naught upon earth that I fear, for I come of a race of heroes."

Now hearing these bold words, the dragon laughed, for he held them to be the vain boasts of a stripling; and again he vomited forth fire and poison. Then he fell upon Rustem, and dreadful was the shock, and perilous unto the hero, for the vile creature wound himself around and about his body, threatening to crush him with his writhings, and you would have said that the end of the valiant one was at hand, so dreadful was the dragon's embrace.

But at this perilous moment, Rakush, beholding the contest to be doubtful, laid back his ears and proceeded to take a hand in the battle. And being wise, he fell upon the enemy from the rear, with his keen teeth, furiously biting and tearing away the dragon's scaly hide, just as he had torn the lion. Now this gave unto the pinioned hero his opportunity, and, quick as thought, he severed the ghastly head, deluging all the plain with horrid blood. And lo! as the hideous coils unclasped, the amazement of

Rustem was truly great as he gazed at the monstrous form which extended endlessly before him; and he wondered not that for centuries it should have been known unto men as the scourge of the desert.

Giving thanks unto the Omnipotent, therefore, that it had been vouchsafed unto him to rid the world of so great a pest, after bathing Rakush at the fountain, he sprang into the saddle and started out upon his fourth adventure.

Now all that day Rustem travelled across the plain, arriving at sunset in the land of the magicians, and as here all was enchantment, everything was most beautiful. The feathered palms along the way nodded their heads lazily, coquetting with the soft south wind, while the bananas flaunted their silken flags around the ripening fruit, and on the ground, in rich profusion, lay, temptingly, rose-apples and citrons. A crystal stream flowed along between sloping banks of luxurious foliage, and in the woods the glorious nightingale chanted joyously unto the nodding flowers.

And lo! in this beautiful wilderness, upon the sight of the hungry adventurer there suddenly appeared a daintily-spread table, where the richest tropical fruits and sweets lay beside a roast of venison, while the cups were filled with purple wine. Now seeing, thus unexpectedly, in the green and shady vale, all this good cheer awaiting him, Rustem's heart sang with delight, for he suspected not that it was the evening meal of certain magicians who had made themselves invisible at his approach.

So, hastily dismounting, the weary warrior unsaddled Rakush, bidding him graze and drink. Then seating himself at the table, he partook freely of the dainty fare, his spirit laughing with pleasure at finding in the wildwood

such an excellently-appointed table. Indeed, so gay in
spirit was he that, his hunger being satisfied, he took up
the lyre which he saw lying by the flagon of wine, and
chanted a lively ditty about his own wanderings and the
exploits which he most loved; and ever and again there
echoed the refrain:

> "Oh, the scourge of the wicked am I,
> And my days still in battle go by;
> Not for me is the red wine that glows
> In the reveller's cup, nor the rose
> That blooms in the land of delight;
> But with monsters and demons to fight."

Alas! though Rustem dreamed it not, as he sang his
voice reached the ears of a famous enchantress, who quickly
changed herself into a beautiful maiden with a face of
spring, lovely as only enchantment could make her, as you
shall hear. For her complexion was like shell-tinted ivory;
her lips like the pomegranate and her cheek like its flower;
her soft, dark eyes were curtained with long, sweeping
lashes, and her eyebrows were arched like a fringed bow;
her lovely form, scarcely concealed by the misty, oriental
robes which she wore, was a joy to behold, and so sweet
was she that, at her coming, all the air was perfumed with
the delicate fragrance of a spring garden.

But though conscious of a new sensation of delight, at
first Rustem did not realize that he was no longer alone.
As the bewitching maiden drew nearer, however, singing
softly Rustem's refrain, and holding out her beautiful
hands in greeting, then indeed did his heart pulse strangely,
for never had he beheld such dazzling loveliness. And,
moreover, resting herself at his side, and turning her radiant eyes upon him, his charming guest now crooned into

his ear a strange song of enchantment which disturbed while it yet delighted the hero.

Remembering the duties of hospitality, however, as the music ceased, the enraptured warrior extended unto his beautiful companion a glass of wine in welcome, bidding her drink in the name of Ormuzd. But behold! as the hero named the name of God, suddenly the wicked sorceress changed color, becoming in the twinkling of an eye as black as charcoal. Then Rustem knew her for a witch, and quick as the wind he snared her in his lasso, crying unto her:

"Thou wicked creature, show thyself at once in thy true shape, for I would not destroy the innocent."

Now at these words of the Hero, immediately the witch was changed into a decrepit, leering old creature whose whole being showed her wickedness of heart. Therefore, with a single blow of his sword, Rustem severed her in twain. But behold! as he would have swept the vile clay from his path, it vanished, and the low, mocking laugh of the fiend was heard in the distance, showing that not even the sword had power to hurt her. And gone, too, was the dainty table with its tempting viands and poisoned wine; for the magicians, when they beheld the valor of Rustem and realized that he was under the protection of God, dared not come forth to contend with him. So in this fourth adventure, also, was the son of Zal victorious. Nevertheless, he tarried not longer in this spot, for it had become hateful unto him.

Continuing his journey, therefore, Rustem pressed rapidly forward until the following morning, when lo! he was come unto the land of darkness, where the sun never shone, neither did moon nor star ever lighten up the awful, im-

penetrable gloom. Now here he paused, not knowing
what new trial the darkess might conceal. But presently,
lifting up his heart unto Ormuzd for protection and guidance, he gave unto Rakush the rein, and plunged boldly
forward into the gloom. But ah, the horror of it! for
there was no path, and so for many long hours they stum-
bled about in the pitch blackness, constantly on the alert
against unknown danger, and not knowing whither their
steps might lead them. But finally, thanks unto the All-
Merciful One, the intense darkness lightened, and they
emerged into a most beautiful country where the sun was
shining brightly and the earth was covered with waving
grain.

And here, being tired after the long, hard travel, Rustem
dismounted, took off his cuirass of tiger-skin and his helmet, and bidding Rakush find pasture where he would
in the fertile fields, he himself lay down to sleep, his shield
beneath his head and his sword and mace by his side.

Yea, and while the tired Rustem slept, his faithful horse
grazed upon the growing corn, storing up strength for
future prowess. But alas! a disturbing element soon entered upon this scene of peace and contentment. For the
keeper of the pasture returning unto the field, and beholding a strange horse destroying and devouring his corn,
became filled with rage, so that running unto the spot
where the weary warrior was couched, he flung at him reproaches and evil words, at the same time beating the soles
of his feet with a stick. Then, having roused him, he said:

"Son of Satan! Why allowest thou thy demon steed to
rifle our corn-fields? Verily, if thou wouldst keep thy
soul in thy hulking body, up and away, both thee and thy
beast, else it will be the worse for thee!"

Now for just one second, after being thus rudely awakened, Rustem gazed quietly at the keeper. Then, without uttering a single syllable, good or bad, he sprang up, seized him by the ears, and wrenched them from his head. And lo! the mutilated wretch, surprised and dismayed at this treatment, gathered up the severed members and fled howling unto his master, Aulad, who was the ruler of all this fertile country. Bursting into his presence, therefore, his ears in his hand, the keeper bawled:

"Master, Master! Behold, out in the fields there is a great black demon and his steed, a veritable son of Satan, clad in a tiger-skin cuirass, and an iron helmet! And alas! alas! not recognizing him as a demon, thy faithful servant attempted gently to remonstrate with him because that his horse was trampling and devouring the corn, when, wouldst thou believe it? without a word, suddenly he leaped upon me, tore my ears from my head, and then calmly lay down to sleep again. And lo! here are my ears in my hands."

Now as it happened, when the keeper burst upon Aulad with his shocking tale, the great warrior was about to go hunting with his chiefs; but being informed of this most surprising deed of violence, he became so filled with wrath that at once he called together his fighting men, and hastened unto the place indicated by the keeper, swearing vengeance upon the perpetrator of the evil deed, be he man or demon.

But Rustem was prepared for the invaders, since, seeing the approach of Aulad and his warriors, he had donned his armor, mounted upon Rakush, and now rode boldly forward, his soul filled with joy at the thought of battle, even though it was to be one against a hundred. And, indeed, so gigantic and fearsome looked he, with the spirit of the fight upon him, that Aulad himself questioned, as he drew near, whether his antagonist was man or demon. Nevertheless, he shouted unto him angrily:

"Son of Perdition, what is thy name? And why comest thou here to disturb our peace? Verily, thou shalt pay dearly for lopping off my keeper's ears, and thy demon steed also for trampling my crops."

Then Rustem, heeding not the puny threats of Aulad, thundered forth disdainfully, his words striking like cannon-balls:

"Thou Worm! Verily, if thou shouldst hear my name, it would freeze the blood in thy veins, causing thy heart to stand still with terror. And though thou art come out against me with a host, behold how I shall scatter them! Yea, they shall fall beneath my sword like unto leaves in an autumn gale, and the earth shall be watered with their blood."

And this was no idle threat, for, having thus spoken, Rustem drew his sword, and fastening his lasso securely to his saddle-bow, dashed at the foe as a lion into the midst of a herd of oxen, and dreadful was the havoc! Now, with every blow of his sword he cut off a warrior's head, his arm working as by magic, until he had beaten down or scattered the whole company. And lo! as Aulad saw what was come to pass, he wept and fled in dismay. But he was not to escape, for Rustem, pursuing him, threw his lasso about his neck, so that the world became dark unto Aulad. Then, having bound him, the hero said unto his captive:

"O Pinioned One, listen unto the voice of a wise counsellor who sayeth unto thee: Verily, if thou wilt faithfully point out unto me the caves of the White Deev and his warrior chiefs, and wilt guide me to where the Shah and his men are imprisoned, saying unto me how I can deliver them from their bondage, then, as I live, thy reward shall be the kingdom of Mazinderan, for I myself will place thee upon that throne. But beware, if thou deceivest me, for in that moment thy worthless blood shall dye the earth."

Now having listened unto the voice of Rustem, Aulad was glad, and he said:

"Stay, O Mighty Warrior, and be not wroth, for verily thy desires shall be fulfilled! Behold, a hundred farsangs from this spot is where Kaikous groaneth in bondage, but it is yet another hundred farsangs unto the mountain pass where dwelleth the Great White Deev. Here, between two dark and lofty mountains, in two hundred caves, immeasurably deep, his people dwell. But dangerous is the way, for the passes are guarded by lions and magicians, and a stormy desert lieth full before thee, which not even the nimble deer hath ever passed. Then a broad stream two farsangs wide will obstruct thy path, and upon its banks thou wilt behold a mighty host of demon warriors who ever guard the passage unto Mazinderan.

"O Mighty One, verily thou art terrible in battle; but for all thy strong arms and hands, thy keen, life-destroying sword and thy giant club, I fear me thou wilt find the White Deev a terrible enemy. For lo! like unto a reed the mountains tremble, if the Terrible One but raiseth his voice. And moreover, even if by the help of Ormuzd thou shouldst conquer this mighty chief of all the master magicians, behold, in the city of Mazinderan thou wilt be pitted against thousands of demon warriors, and not a coward among them all. War-elephants have they, too, by the hundreds, and they rage in battle with the fury of the crocodile, while every demon chief fighteth in his saddle like sharp-fanged dragons.

"And now, I ask thee, O valorous chief, canst thou, alone and unaided, yet hope to overcome these fearful sons of Satan and all the obstacles that block the way?"

Now hearing all this, Rustem answered simply unto Aulad, and he said:

"O Timorous One, show me but the way and thou shalt see what a single man, who putteth his trust in God, can do, even though pitted against the powers of darkness."

So Rustem mounted once more upon Rakush and rode forward upon his sixth adventure; and Aulad, having been loosened from his bonds, ran in front of him to show the way. Now for a whole day and a night they sped like the wind, neither did they halt until they were come near unto the spot where Kaikous had fallen into the power of the evil Deevs. And here, about midnight, suddenly they heard a great beating of drums and saw many fires blaze up. Then Rustem said unto Aulad:

"I pray thee, good Aulad, what meaneth this piercing clamor, and the watch-fires blazing up to right and left of us?"

Then the guide, starting up, replied unto Rustem:

"O Mighty One, behold, yonder is Mazinderan! And verily it seemeth unto me that Arzang, the most powerful chief of the Great White Deev, must have arrived to-night, else why these sounds of greeting!"

Being satisfied, therefore, as to the cause of the disturbance, Rustem lay calmly down once more and slept soundly until dawn. Then having bound his guide unto a tree to keep him safe, the hero donned his helmet, and also the magic tiger-skin to defend his broad chest, and with his grandfather's club hanging safe at his saddle-bow, he rode boldly forward unto the city of Deevs. And behold! when he was come near unto the camp of Arzang, he uttered a cry that rent the mountains—that terrible battle-cry which from this time forth was to strike terror to the heart of many a valiant foe!

Now upon hearing this mighty cry of a human voice, surprised, the great Arzang issued hastily from his tent, ready and anxious to attack this bold invader of his camp. But Rustem, setting spurs unto Rakush, galloped forward like the wind, seized the mighty chief, and dangling him in his grasp like a puny worm, behold, in the twinkling of an eye he had wrenched off the ugly black head and cast it, all gory, far into the ranks of the shuddering Deevs, who, beholding the fate of their chief, and dismayed at the sight of Rustem's mighty club, now fled in the wildest confusion, fathers trampling their sons in their eagerness to escape. But as by a hungry lion they were pursued, hundreds of them being put to the sword. And lo! the fear of Rustem was great in the land.

But the hero of this mighty adventure, having ceased from pursuing the scattered Deevs, paused not. Quickly returning unto his guide, therefore, he commanded that he now lead the way unto the prison-house where Kaikous and his companions pined in bondage. So Aulad led on as before, and behold! when they were come unto Mazinderan, Rakush neighed, and neighed so joyously that the sound of it pierced even unto the ears of the captive monarch who, hearing it, exclaimed rapturously unto his companions:

"Dance! Dance for joy, O my comrades! for surely our evil days are ended. Listen! Hear ye not the voice of Rakush? Yea, it is the voice of Rakush, for so neighed he in the days of old when he and his master first tasted the joys of battle in the war against Afrasiab."

Alas! the Persians, when they heard the words of the King, shook their heads sorrowfully, thinking that grief had distraught his wits, for they heard not the neighing of Rakush, neither could the monarch convince them. Imagine their delight, therefore, when Rustem presently appeared! Verily, so wild with joy were these poor blind warriors at the prospect of release, that Rustem himself shed tears of gladness, giving thanks anew unto Ormuzd for protecting and guiding him hither. Then having related unto them the story of his wonderful progress and adventures, the King, embracing him, said:

"O Beloved of Ormuzd! Truly there is none like unto thee for prowess; nay, not even the great Saum, thy glorious grandsire, ever equalled thee! But enough of sweet words! for, if we are to be delivered from our bondage, not a moment must be wasted.

"Behold, it is borne in upon me, O my Pehliva, that when the Great White Deev shall hear of the fall of Arzang, his favorite chief, he will surely come forth from out his mountain fastness, bringing with him such a multitude of evil ones that not even thy great might will enable thee to stand before them. Go, therefore, at once unto the Seven Mountains and conquer the hideous monster before he heareth of thy coming.

"And alas! I must send thee forth alone upon this dangerous adventure, for we cannot help thee—being all of us blind; yet is this new enterprise far more difficult than any thou hast had to encounter, and the odds are tremendous against thee. For the way lieth over the Seven Mountains,

all of them guarded by troops of Genii, and if thou art successful in passing over them, then thou wilt see before thee
a deep, dark cavern, more terrible, I have heard, than the
pit of eternal darkness. Now the entrance is guarded by
horrible monsters, and in its depths dwelleth the Great
White Deev who is both the terror and the hope of his
army. And alas! our hope is he, too. For a Mubid hath
revealed unto me that the only remedy for our blindness is
to drop into our eyes three drops of the White Deev's
blood.

"Go forth, therefore, O Hero of Might, slay the Deev,
and bring back unto us the blood of his heart. Then shall
the tree of gladness blossom once more in Iran, and the
name of Rustem be blazoned among the stars."

Now thus exhorted, once more the son of Zal vaulted
into the saddle, Rakush carrying him like the wind, while
Aulad showed unto him the way. So they sped, and when
they were come unto the Seven Mountains, having passed
through difficulties many and sore, behold, not only the
summits, but all the caverns, were crowded with myriads
of companies of Deevs, fierce, black, and horrible beyond
belief, seeing which, Rustem said unto Aulad:

"Behold, the time of conflict hath come! Say unto me,
therefore, how I may vanquish this innumerable host of
evil ones."

Then Aulad, shaking his head doubtfully, replied unto
Rustem:

"O Mighty One! Verily thou hast one hope, and but
one. I counsel thee, therefore, that thou tarry here until
the sun be high in the heavens, for at noonday, when it
beateth fierce upon the earth, the Deevs are wont to slumber. Then when they are drunk with sleep, fall suddenly

upon them, for thus victory may be thine, if so the stars decree."

So Rustem, taking Aulad's advice, halted by the roadside until the sun was at its highest. Then binding his guide securely, he drew forth his sword, and uttering his thunderous battle-cry, he rushed upon the hordes of evil Deevs, slaying first the few waking sentinels, and then rapidly destroying the slumbering fiends. Nor was there noise or confusion, for as each black one awoke, so suddenly he received his death blow that he had no time to give the alarm; and so swift and terrible was Rustem in his work of slaughter that few escaped his fury. And harmless were those who did, for at once they fled screaming into the deepest caves of the mountain, leaving the champion victorious. Then Rustem, having thus dispersed the guards, advanced fearlessly unto the lair of the Great White Deev.

But alas! alas! Never in all his imaginings had the hero dreamed of a place so gloomy, and foul, and awesome. And as he stood at the mouth of the cave, looking down, down into the black recesses, dismal as the pit of eternal darkness, for a time he doubted as to what he should do. But as he was void of fear, presently he decided to go forward.

Now the air of the cavern was murky and heavy with evil odors, and as Rustem advanced he could not see his path. But, though he knew that danger lurked on every side, and that at any moment he might have to encounter the evil genius of the place, as well as the powers of magic, his heart quaked not. Nay; not even when at last there loomed up before him from out the darkness a monstrous shape which filled the whole breadth of the huge cavern, did he tremble or draw back. Yet well he knew by the thunderous snoring that this was no huge, snow-capped mountain, but the Great White Deev taking his noonday nap.

Bold as a lion, therefore, Rustem advanced, shouting his piercing battle-cry, for he scorned to take advantage of his adversary while he slept. But verily he knew not what he did, for upon being thus suddenly aroused from slumber, the wrath of the Great White Deev was terrible. Uttering a hideous shriek that made the blood run cold, quickly he caught up from the ground in his mammoth hand a stone as big as a small mountain, and pausing not, with flaming eyes and foaming lips he advanced, hurling it with all the force of his powerful arm straight at the head of Rustem. But in vain; for quick as light it was dodged by the hero. Nevertheless, now for the first time Rustem felt a thrill of fear, so malignantly awful appeared the Deev.

Nevertheless, summoning all his strength for a mighty effort, in return for the stone the son of Zal dealt the oncoming monster such a powerful stroke with his sword as to cut off one of his feet. Now this so infuriated the Deev that, mad with pain, he sprang at Rustem like a wild elephant, and they grappled in a struggle the shock of which caused the very mountains to tremble. And though having but one foot, the monster wrestled hot and sore, tearing from Rustem's body great morsels of flesh, so that all the earth was crimsoned with his blood. Indeed, so terrible was the struggle that the hero said within himself:

"Verily, if I escape to-day, I shall live forever!"

Howbeit, in spite of his doubts, Rustem defended himself mightily, inflicting such terrible injuries upon his antagonist that his mad fury became as that of the raging croco-

Mad with pain, he sprang at Rustem like a wild elephant.

dile; while the mutual havoc wrought caused rivers of sweat
and blood to run down from the bodies of both combatants. So cool-headed was Rustem, however, and so telling
every blow, that the Great White Deev said unto himself:
"Alas! Alas! Even if I succeed in delivering myself
from out the claws of this sharp-toothed dragon, verily,
I greatly fear that never again shall I see Mazinderan!"

Now this thought nerved anew the arm of the mighty
Deev, imparting unto him such furious strength and courage that Rustem could not stand before it. Then feared
he that his hour was come, but lifting up his heart unto
Ormuzd, and putting forth all his strength, suddenly he
caught the huge, gasping Deev in his arms, and by a supreme effort hurled him over the face of the cliff into the
yawning chasm below. Yea, and so fearful was the force of
the fall that straightway his soul was driven from out his
body, the life-blood oozing from his crushed and mangled
form, which had made of the valley a plain. Stooping
down, therefore, Rustem severed the ugly head, fastening
it unto his saddle-bow. Then he also tore out the pulse-
less heart which was destined to restore sight unto the
King and his helpless warriors, and this being done,
quickly he returned unto Mazinderan.

So,

> "The champion brought the Demon's heart
> And squeezed the blood from every part,
> Which dropped upon the injured sight,
> Made all things visible and bright;
> One moment broke that magic gloom,
> Which seemed more dreadful than the tomb."

Now thus was the foolish Kaikous saved from perpetual
blindness, and as he beheld once more the glories of the

world, so great was his joy, as well as that of his warriors, that verily they shouted and danced like children, being unable to contain themselves for happiness. Yea, seven days the Shah and his warriors feasted together in thanksgiving, and continually they exalted Rustem, mighty slayer of the Great White Deev.

But the days of feasting having passed, behold, there came unto the tent of Rustem, Aulad the guide, and he said:

"O Champion of the World! Verily, I behold upon thy brow the crown of victory; but my body, alas, beareth the marks of thy bonds. Respect, therefore, I pray thee, the promise of reward made unto me. For a hero should ever be bound by his word."

Then Rustem, smiling, replied unto the suppliant:

"A faithful guide hast thou proven thyself, O Aulad, well worthy of reward; and verily thou shalt have it. But first, this country must be thoroughly purged of the magicians that encumber it, else uneasy will be thy seat upon the throne of Mazinderan, where surely one day I will place thee. Wherefore, be of good cheer!"

So now it came to pass that Kaikous, after consulting with Rustem, dictated unto the King of Mazinderan, the last of the great magicians, a letter. And he made not many words, but said:

"O King of Mazinderan! Where is now the great chief Arzang? Where the Great White Deev? Enviest thou them their fate? If not, then it behooveth thee, O King, to appear right speedily before the Great Shah Kaikous, to pay homage and tribute unto him, else shalt thy life be even as theirs."

Now the King, when he received this communication, was both angry and troubled, for he feared that the sun of

his glory was about to set. Nevertheless, he concealed his
distress from the messenger, showing unto him his vast
resources, and sending by him an arrogant answer unto
the Shah. And he said:

"O vain Monarch, famed for thy folly, thinkest thou
that I am one unto whom the foolish can say, 'Come down
from off thy throne, and do homage unto me'? Verily,
my hundred war-elephants say unto thee, nay! Prepare,
therefore, for battle, for surely I will bring such destruction
upon Iran as shall cause to pale the havoc wrought by
Rustem and thy warriors at Mazinderan."

Thus in his pride wrote the King of the magicians unto
Kaikous who, losing no whit of the insolence of the message, became very angry indeed. As for Rustem, when it
was told unto him he was so indignant that every hair
upon his head started up like a spear, and he said:

"O Lord of the World, if it please thee, graciously permit thy Pehliva to go forth with yet another writing which
shall be as keen as a sword and as threatening as the
giant club of Saum the Mighty. Perchance the King may
then give ear unto reason."

So once more the Shah wrote:

"O King of Mazinderan! Verily, I say unto thee that if
within three days thou changest not thy robe of arrogance
for one of humility, then truly it shall be changed for thee
into a shroud. Yea, and the ghost of the Great White
Deev shall call the vultures to feast upon thy severed head,
hung from the walls of thine own Mazinderan."

Alas! when the King of the magicians learned that
Kaikous was sending unto him yet another messenger, he
bade the flower of his army go forth to meet him. Then
Rustem, when he beheld them draw nigh, laid hold of a

huge tree with great spreading branches that grew by the
wayside, and twisting it mightily,. tore it from the earth,
roots and all, brandishing it in his hands like a javelin.
Now all who witnessed this amazing feat of strength were
filled with wonder, and Rustem, beholding their awe,
laughing, flung the tree among them, saying:

"Greetings from the great Shah of Iran!"

Then forth from the great host of the King there stepped
one of the giants of Mazinderan, and he begged to grasp
the hand of the mighty one in congratulation. So Rustem
extended his hand, and the giant pressed it mightily, hoping thus to wring off the valorous member. But so feeble
was his grasp that the champion could but smile, for well
he knew his purpose. When, however, it came his turn,
he caught the giant's hand in his with a grip so mighty
that all the bones and sinews cracked, and in agony he fell
fainting from his horse.

Now beholding the fate of the giant, quickly one of the
nobles hastened unto the King to report what had befallen
his champion. Then, mortified and angry, at once the
monarch summoned into his presence his most valiant
and renowned chieftain, Kalour by name, and directed
him to punish, signally, the warrior who had thus presumed
to triumph over his heroes. And he said:

"Go, O Mighty One, and show unto this insolent Persian thy prowess. Cover his face with shame, and return
not unto me until thou hast retrieved the honor of the
magicians."

Then Kalour, who was the strongest Deev of his tribe,
said proudly unto the King:

"Lord of the World, I go. And verily I will force the
tears of pain from out the eyes of this upstart!"

So Kalour rode quickly forth, and when he was come unto Rustem, he stretched unto him his mighty hand, wringing that of the hero with the strength of a dragon. Now the hand turned blue in the cruel grasp, but Rustem neither flinched nor gave sign of pain. But when, presently, he wrung the hand of Kalour, behold, blood issued from the veins, and the nails fell off, dropping unto the ground like withered autumn leaves.

Alas for Kalour! Bowed with shame, and his sight clouded by bitter tears, slowly he turned and rode back unto the King, showing unto him his hand. And he said:

"O Glorious King, truly the path of humiliation is not pleasant to tread! Nevertheless, it seemeth unto me wiser to make peace than to attempt to fight with this elephant-of-war whose strength is such that neither man nor Deev can stand against him. Pay the tribute, therefore, and accept their terms; otherwise, this sharp-toothed dragon will utterly destroy our land and people."

Now the King was loath to sue for peace. Nevertheless, when the Elephant-bodied arrived at the gates the monarch received him graciously. But alas! having read the letter of Kaikous, his face became black with anger, and verily his voice was like rattling thunder as he said unto Rustem:

"Mad! Stark mad! is this prating monarch; else never would he dare address such words unto me. But verily he forgetteth that if he is master of Iran, I am lord of Mazinderan, and never will I submit unto so petty a monarch, whose only weapon seemeth to be haughty words. Go, therefore, and say unto thy master that the King of Mazinderan scorneth to accept peace at the hands of a monarch whose only crown should be the cap and bells of a trick elephant. Verily, war shall it be between us now—war to the finish!"

So Rustem returned with this dire message unto Kaikous, and soon both monarchs were preparing for battle, the King of Mazinderan gathering about him an army of horsemen and foot-soldiers and war-elephants which caused the earth to groan as they marched forth unto the meeting-place. And behold! when the two armies were drawn up in battle array, immediately there stepped forth from out the ranks of the magicians a champion who challenged the men of Iran to single combat. Huge, black, and ugly, he advanced arrogantly, brandishing a great club in his hands, and he cried in a voice of thunder:

"Ho, dogs of Iran! Pray, slink not so together, but come forth and show whether there be any prowess among you!"

Now at first, this insolent challenge remained unanswered; for the Persians, being unaccustomed to fighting with Deevs, feared the giant magician's power of sorcery. Then Rustem, seeing this, gave unto Rakush the rein, and galloping up to the King, he said:

"O Lord of the World, graciously permit me to meet this arrogant magician that I may show unto thy army how little availeth the power of sorcery when brought to bear against the strong arm and the stout heart of a true child of Ormuzd."

So, being given permission, Rustem rode boldly forth, and meeting the champion in full sight of both armies, he thundered forth:

"O Son of Satan! Behold, thy tomb yawneth at thy feet! For thy folly maketh it necessary that I quickly blot thy name from out the book of the living."

But the champion, brandishing his mighty club, replied fearlessly:

"Vain Boaster, flee, for behold, my club maketh mothers childless!"

Howbeit, Rustem fled not. Instead, he advanced quickly, shouting in a voice which rivalled that of the Great White Deev:

"Tremble, thou Son of Perdition! For behold, thou hast now to do with Rustem the Mighty!"

Now when the magician heard this dread name, at once he turned to flee, for he had no desire to fight the champion of the world. But his cowardice availed him naught, for Rustem, raising his lance, pierced him through and through his coat of mail, lifting him thus from his saddle. Then holding him poised in the air for a moment, even as a bird which a man hath run through with a spit, suddenly he dashed him with contempt lifeless to the ground. And, this being done, slowly he turned, and rode quietly back unto the army, leaving the Deevs thunderstruck at the sight of so much strength and prowess.

But now Kaikous gave the signal, and there began a battle the like of which hath seldom been fought. For seven long days it lasted, and what with the screams of the Deevs and the shouts of the warriors, the clanging of trumpets and the beating of drums, the groans of the dying and the screams of the elephants-of-war, earth was turned into a pandemonium as hideous as war could make it. But still victory leaned unto neither side.

Then Kaikous, fearing defeat, on the eighth day clothed himself in the robes of humility and prostrated himself before Ormuzd, beseeching that the kingdom of light might triumph over the kingdom of darkness. And not in

vain; for behold! when evening was come, the army of
Mazinderan was a power no longer to be dreaded. For lo!
Death had waved his magic sceptre over the field, and thousands of Deevs lay, as if enchanted, taking their last long
sleep.

And now at last Rustem, who all day had been trying
to pierce unto the King of Mazinderan, spied the monarch, surrounded by his few remaining chiefs and a great
host of war-elephants. Immediately, therefore, he challenged him to single combat. So the King consenting, with
a cry like a lion's roar, Rustem charged him with his spear,
dealing him such a mighty blow that at once he fell heavily
to the ground. Quick as light, however, he regained his
feet, and fiercely they fought together, both with sword
and javelin. But presently once more Rustem gained the
advantage. Then raising his lance to strike, he cried:

"Perish, Thou Wicked Magician! for little will thy
sorcery help thee now."

Then it came to pass that Rustem dealt a stroke of tremendous power which would certainly have slain the
King; but behold, in the twinkling of an eye, he had
changed himself, before the eyes of the whole Persian
army, into a great mass of rock! And now was it Rustem's
turn to marvel, for never in all his battles with the Deevs
had he witnessed the like. But at this moment Kaikous
came up, and beholding Rustem, he said:

"O Glory of the Battle-field, why standest thou thus
spellbound, gazing at this rock?"

Then Rustem, awakening from his astonishment, replied unto the King:

"What! Sawest thou not, O Lord of Iran, the feat of
magic but now performed before our eyes? Alas! this

mighty rock is the King of Mazinderan who, fearing
the sword of Rustem, hath thus put himself out of our
power. But verily he shall not so escape me."

Now in this predicament Kaikous thought a moment;
then he commanded that the rock be taken up and placed
before his throne. So the mighty warriors of the King who
were most noted for their strength meshed the mass of
rock with strong cords, being unable to raise it from the
ground, and tried to draw it forward. But even so, not all
the combined strength of the heroes could move it a jot.
Then Rustem, the elephant-limbed, determined that his
prey should not escape him, bent his sturdy back, and
grasping the rock in his mighty arms, swung it lightly
unto his head, where, poising it easily, without difficulty,
he bore it across the plain. There, throwing it down
before the King's tent, he cried:

"O cowardly Magician! Verily, if thou comest not
immediately forth, with my mace will I grind this stone
into powder, and scatter in unto the four winds!"

Then the King of Mazinderan, seeing that his trick was
useless, quickly made himself visible, frowning as black
as a thunder cloud. But Rustem, smiling, led his captive
at once unto the Shah, saying unto him:

"O Lord of Iran! Behold, I bring unto thee this piece
of rock whom fear of my mace hath brought unto
reason."

Now the King wasted not many words with the magician,
for when he saw how wicked of aspect he was, with the
neck and tusks of a wild boar, he knew him to be unworthy a throne. Therefore, calling unto him the executioner, he bade him slay the evil Deev, cutting his body
into a thousand pieces.

And behold, the magicians being destroyed, Kaikous, after making haste to secure their wealth, which was very great, distributed honors and rewards upon every warrior for his heroic services, giving unto Aulad the throne of Mazinderan. But unto Rustem the Shah gave gifts the like of which you have never dreamed. Now there was gold and jewels, brocades and silks, horses and camels, youths and maidens, perfumes beyond price, and carvings of ivory. And last of all, there was a letter, written upon pages of silk, in ink made of wine and aloes and amber and the black of lamps, naming Rustem the Champion of the World, and giving unto him anew the kingdom of the south.

But the praise and gifts of the Shah were as nothing unto Rustem in comparison with the welcome home which he received. Now the whole city turned out to meet him, and when he arrived at the palace such an ovation was given him as seldom awaiteth a returning hero. And sweeter than all unto Rustem, was the wonderful love and pride which beamed upon him from the eyes of Silver-crowned Zal as he related unto him the amazing adventures of that mavellous march into Mazinderan.

RUSTEM THE PEHLIVA

BEHOLD, it is chronicled in the Book of the Shahs, that Kaikous and his folly parted them not company, even after his chastening experience at Mazinderan. Consequently, almost immediately after having wrought his seven great labors, once more Rustem was called upon to perform the services of a Pehliva. And of this you shall hear.

Now it came to pass that Kaikous, appropriating unto himself the glory which resulted from the marvellous conquest of Mazinderan, became so inflated with pride that the day came when he found his capital too small for him. Therefore, he decided to bless the eyes of his people by a triumphal journey through his dominions. So with a magnificent train of warriors, nobles, and slaves, and with the music of trumpets and cymbals and drums, he travelled through the land. And behold! wherever the great Shah passed, men did homage unto him. For, verily, the lamb cannot wage battle with the lion.

But since in the Book of Fate it is written that not even unto a gorgeous Eastern potentate, with the world for his footstool, can life remain forever one long, bright fête day, so soon there sprang forth thorns in the Shah's fair garden of roses. For lo! the King of Hamaveran, desiring to throw off the yoke of Persia, took this opportunity to stir up a powerful revolt in Syria, which suddenly brought unto an end the vainglorious parade of the Shah.

Returning unto his capital, therefore, Kaikous quickly mustered his army, leading them forth against the rebels, who, after an obstinate resistance, were overpowered and obliged to ask for quarter. Now foremost in laying down his arms, and asking pardon of the Shah, was the King of Hamaveran, unto whom Kaikous granted it joyously. For behold! it had become known unto him that behind his curtains this King had hidden a daughter of rare loveliness. As a condition of peace, therefore, the Shah demanded this Moon of Beauty for his wife.

Alas! when the King of Hamaveran learned of the desire of the Shah, his heart was filled with bitterness, and he murmured exceedingly that Kaikous, who had the world at his feet, should have the power to take from him his one treasure. Nevertheless, he called before him Sudaveh, his fair daughter, and unburdening his heart, bade her counsel him how he should reply unto the Lord of the World, who desired her for his wife. And he said:

"Fair Pomegranate Flower, well thou knowest that thou art my heart's solace and delight, since I have but thee. In the garden of the Shah, however, bloom many fair flowers. There thou wilt be but one, while here thou hast no rival. Now losing thee, I lose the light of my eyes. Yet how can I stand against the great King of Kings?"

Now unto this touching appeal, Sudaveh, who was ambitious, and unto whom the thought of becoming the queen of the most powerful sovereign in the world was not at all unpleasant, replied coldly:

"If there be no remedy, O my father, why not smile in the face of destiny?"

But alas! though the King assented to what he now saw were the wishes of his daughter, he could not smile, for his heart was smitten with sorrow. Nevertheless, an alliance was soon concluded according to the forms of the land, and after seven days of feasting, Sudaveh was sent unto the tents of the Shah, robed in garbs of splendor, and accompanied by a magnificent train. Now the Princess was borne upon a litter, and was attended by six hundred slaves, while as to her dowry—it required two thousand horses and camels to carry it.

So went Sudaveh unto the King, and as she descended from her litter, glowing with beauty, Kaikous, beholding her, was struck dumb with admiration and rapture. And so impatient was he to possess this rare loveliness, that the marriage rites were performed at once, after which he raised Sudaveh unto the throne as his Queen. Then were they glad in each other, and wist not that sorrow knocked at the door.

But though this royal bridal pair were happy, the King of Hamaveran, brooding day by day over his wrongs in his lonely palace, became more and more miserable, until finally he determined to try to regain his daughter unto himself, since thus only would there be for him any joy in living. And since he knew that only by stratagem could he hope to accomplish his design, behold, when Sudaveh had been gone but seven days, the King sent forth an invitation unto his new son-in-law, entreating him to make glad the heart of his father by feasting within his gates.

Now when Sudaveh was informed of this message, at once she urged her royal bridegroom to decline the invitation, for she divined that her father meant no good by the proposal. But Kaikous, who on account of his easy victory had formed a poor opinion of the courage of the

Syrians, would not give ear unto the warnings and counsels of Sudaveh, for his soul loved feasting and homage,
and he did not dream that the King would dare, anew, to
attack the Persians.

Wherefore, the King and his nobles rode gaily forth
unto the court of Hamaveran, where they were received
most graciously. And verily the heart of Kaikous was
glad, for the banquet was a royal one, and behold, they
feasted and made merry without ceasing for many days.
And not only did they banquet, but in his desire to do
honor unto his guest, the King caused priceless gifts to be
rained down continuously upon Kaikous, flattering him
with sweet words, and cozening his vanity. Nor was his
generosity less great unto the nobles, for unto them also
he gave gifts, praising their courage and darkening their
wits with sweet wine.

But when at last the wily King saw that all suspicion
and distrust had been lulled to sleep by the bounteousness
of his hospitality, then, like a flash of light out of a clear
sky, came the reckoning. For suddenly, as Kaikous
reached forth his hands to grasp yet richer gifts, in the
twinkling of an eye, he and his chief warriors were seized
from behind, bound with strong chains, and thrown into
the dark dungeon of a fortress, whose head touched the
sky and whose foot was planted in the ocean, there to
repent at leisure this second disastrous plunge into folly.

And now was the King of Hamaveran glad as, having
seen his captives safely hidden away in the fortress, he at
once sent forth a strong force of warriors unto the camp
of Kaikous, charging them, with the speed of the swift
dromedary, to return his heart's delight unto his arms.
But alas for the King's hopes! For beholding the ap-

proach of the warriors, and the veiled women who accompanied them, at once Sudaveh surmised what had happened, and so great was her distress that she tore her hair in anguish, crying aloud against the treachery of her father. Yea, and not only that, for when she was led into his presence, she reproached him bitterly, swearing that not even he should part her from her lord, though the path to him led but unto a tomb.

Now as the King listened unto the scathing words of his daughter, he shed bitter tears of disappointment and anger. Then, furious that she should prefer the glory of the Shah to the love of a father who lived but to serve her, angrily he drove her from his presence, commanding that she be placed in the same prison as her foolish lord. But this distressed not Sudaveh, who went to the dungeon with a light heart, for she loved her husband, and seated by his side, she served and comforted him, thus lightening the weight of his captivity.

But alas for Iran! For once more the King's folly left an empty throne, which immediately attracted the avaricious eyes of her foes. And of these, not only was there the angry King of Hamaveran, but also Afrasiab who, hearing that Kaikous was once more paying the penalty of his follies by being enchained in a Syrian dungeon, straightway forgot hunger and sleep in his fierce desire to be first upon the ground. Bursting over the borders, therefore, with an immense Tartar horde at his back, he defeated the Syrians, and took possession of the land, men, women, and children falling into bondage at his hands. Then Iran, the kingdom of light, became under his sway, the kingdom of darkness, and terror and distress reigned throughout the land.

And now as ever, in their troubles, did the Persians appeal for counsel and aid unto the great house at Seistan; and not in vain. For, though Rustem was angered at the Shah whose folly had thus once again endangered the throne, yet was he also grieved for the vanished glory of Iran and for the distress of the people. So, for his country's sake, and because of the oath which his grandsire, Saum the hero, sware unto Feridoun, that he and his house would support and uphold the glory of the Shahs forever, he put aside his anger, and forthwith sent a secret messenger, a man subtle and wise, unto Kaikous, bidding him be of good cheer, since his Pehliva would surely deliver him from out the claws of the Syrian lion.

But in addition to this, Rustem sent forth yet another messenger unto the King of Hamaveran, summoning him to yield up the royal prisoner he had won by treachery, or prepare for the destruction that awaited him when Rustem the Mighty should appear at the head of an invincible host, to wreak vengeance upon his head. Now this threat troubled the King of Hamaveran, for he knew somewhat of Rustem's power. Nevertheless, he sent back reply that never again should Kaikous step forth from his dungeon. Yea, and he threatened Rustem with the same fate, if he came forth against him, which answer caused Rustem to smile and say:

"Verily, either this King is in his dotage, or else the Evil One hath filled his head with smoke. On, my men! On to Hamaveran!"

So the army of Seistan set forth, and behold, so mighty of mien was Rustem, with his strong arms and his lion's chest, his great mace and his redoubtable charger, that when the army of Hamaveran caught sight of him, lo, their hearts quickly departed from out their bodies, and they fled from before his face in terror, returning unto the King without having struck a blow.

Then was the King filled with dismay, and in his terror of defeat, at once he sent swift runners unto his neighbors, the Kings of Egypt and Berber, soliciting their aid—which being gladly given, it came to pass that three kings and their immense armies were drawn up against the power and resources of one man. Indeed so great was the combined forces that they stretched for two leagues in length, and you would have said that the handful of Rustem had no chance against them.

But the hero was not dismayed. On the contrary, his soul was full of courage, the great numbers dismaying him not, for he said:

"What mattereth it even though there be a hundred thousand men pitted against us? With Heaven our friend, soon will the foe be mingled with the dust."

Now having thus inspired his men, Rustem caused the trumpets to sound, and with a great shout he fell upon the armies of the Kings, like unto a flame that darteth hungrily, driven by a fierce wind. And verily so great was the havoc wrought by Rakush and his master that the ground quickly became a crimson stream, while everywhere rolled horrid heads, severed from the bodies of the enemy.

But of all the chiefs, the King of Hamaveran was the first to fall back with his legions before the sword of Rustem. Quickly, however, the King of Berber advanced to fill his place, for he was ashamed of his colleague's cowardice. But alas! receiving a slight blow from Rustem's mighty hand, terrified, he turned to flee, hoping thus to escape his fury. But in vain, for quickly throwing his

noose, the champion caught and dragged him from his
horse, making him prisoner. And this being accomplished,
it now became the turn of the King of Egypt to feel the
power of Rustem. Before his charge like that of an
angry dragon down went this last of the Kings, and with
him forty of his principal chiefs, for verily against such
battle fury only the lion-hearted could hope to stand.

So ended this day of ill-fortune for the King of Hamaveran, who beholding at sunset the overthrow of his
allies, and all the horrible carnage wrought by the champion, knew that as well might the lamb contend with the
lion as he with this sharp-fanged dragon-of-war. Quickly,
therefore, he sent a swift messenger unto the great Pehliva,
soliciting a suspension of the fight, and offering to deliver
up Kaikous, and all the men and treasure that were his,
if clemency were shown him.

Now to this acknowledgment of defeat, Rustem replied:

> "Kaikous to liberty restore,
> With all his chiefs, I ask no more;
> For him alone I conquering came;
> Than him no other prize I claim."

So Kaikous was liberated from his prison, and Sudaveh
with him, together with all the illustrious heroes imprisoned with them in the mountain fortress. And so great
was their joy that continually they sang the praises of
Rustem, the King's Pehliva, who so quickly had caused
light to shine upon a dark place and hope to spring up
where despair had been. And not alone were the Persians
in extolling their hero, for behold! the three Kings were
so impressed with the mighty prowess of Rustem that
gladly they sware a new allegiance unto the Shah, march-

ing with the army upon its return journey into Iran, in
order to go out against Afrasiab.

And the army, thus made strong, behold, when the
Shah was come safe home again unto his land, he sent
a message unto Afrasiab, commanding him to quit the
country he had so unjustly invaded. Yea, and he twitted
the King upon his previous adventure with Rustem, saying unto him:

"Hast thou forgotten Rustem's power,
    When thou wert in that perilous hour
By him o'erthrown? Thy girdle broke,
    Or thou hadst felt the conqueror's yoke.
Thy crowding warriors proved thy shield,
    They saved and dragged thee from the field;
By them unrescued then, wouldst thou
    Have lived to boast thy prowess now?"

Alas! thus reminded of past humiliations, Afrasiab replied scathingly unto the King, and he said:

"O thou, whose folly hath become a proverb, verily
the words which thou hast written are not becoming unto
a monarch such as thou, who didst covet Mazinderan, and
whose lightness of head hath twice endangered thy life and
throne. But truly thou doest well to boast of thy Pehliva,
since without the Elephant-limbed the boasted power of
Kaikous would cause little alarm unto his foes. As for
Rustem, Afrasiab feareth him not, neither that the sceptre
of Iran will be wrested from his grasp, for behold! the
great Pehliva hath no time to fight with heroes, being fully
employed in extricating his glorious sovereign, the mighty
Kaikous, from the predicaments into which his folly ever
leadeth him."

Now the Shah's reply unto this insolent message was an instant call to war. And, as it had been with the Syrians, so now was it with this new foe, for the havoc wrought by Rustem in his battle fury caused such terror and consternation that all the Tartar chiefs fled before him in dismay—upon seeing which, the spirit of Afrasiab boiled over like unto new wine. Riding along the lines, therefore, he tried to rally his chiefs for yet another charge by fair promises, saying unto them:

"O my brave Tartars, whosoever shall deliver into my hands, alive, Rustem the Pehliva, him will I reward with a kingdom and an umbrella. Yea, and the hand of my daughter will I also bestow upon him, and he shall sit upon a throne of splendor!"

So, inspired by these alluring promises, once more the men of Turan girded themselves for resistance. But alas! it availed them naught, for soon Rustem watered the earth with their blood. Then Afrasiab, beholding how the breath of this fierce dragon-of-war snuffed out the life of his heroes, himself dashed forward to cope with the champion. But even his bravery was unavailing, and soon he was glad to retreat, the remnant of his army following forlornly after him, leaving Rustem in full possession of the field.

Then was the Shah glad, and gave thanks unto his Pehliva, through whose prowess once more he was safely seated upon the throne of light. And, turning his back upon folly, for many moons he busied himself as a builder, erecting mighty towers and palaces, so that the whole land was made fair at his hands.

But alas! in the midst of his useful activities, one day there appeared before Kaikous a beautiful youth about whose head was twined a wreath of roses., And behold! after presenting unto the Lord of the World the fair flowers, and extolling the glory of his achievements, the youth, concluding, said:

"O Monarch of the earth and sea,
Thou art great as king can be,
Boundless in thy majesty;
What is all this earth to thee,
All beneath the sky?
Peris, mortals, demons, hear
Thy commanding voice with fear;
Thou art lord of all things here,
But—thou canst not fly!

"That remains for thee; to know
Things above, as things below,
How the planets roll;
How the sun his light displays,
How the moon darts forth her rays;
How the nights succeed the days;
What the secret cause betrays,
And who directs the whole!"

Now when Kaikous heard these words of guile, immediately his mind became filled with smoke, even as Iblis had designed, and forgetting that it is not given unto man to mount unto the skies, from this time forth he pondered without ceasing how, without wings, he might ascend unto the stars to inquire into their secrets. And finally, in his perplexity, he consulted his astrologers, who, after much thought, suggested a possible way of accomplishing his desires.

So it came to pass that presently an eagle's nest was robbed of its young, the eaglets being reared with great care, until they became large and strong of wing. Then

a framework of aloe-wood was prepared, at each of the
four corners of which was fixed, perpendicularly, a javelin,
surmounted upon the point with the flesh of a goat. And
this being done, the four young eagles, who longed for the
sun, were bound unto the corners of this cunningly-devised
chariot, and Kaikous, with great pomp, seated himself in
the midst thereof, a goblet of wine in his hand, while all the
people shouted, "Bah! Bah!" in admiration.

And behold! the eagles, excited by the smell of the flesh
so pleasing unto them, desired after it exceedingly, being
hungry, so, with a mighty flapping of wings, away they flew
upward, bearing the aloe-wood chariot and the graciously-
smiling Kaikous up, far up, into the glorious blue, away
from the sight of his wondering subjects. But alas for the
eagles! for though they struggled sore, the meat was
always just beyond their grasp. Nevertheless, being continually urged to new effort by the whip of hunger, on
they swept, ascending higher and higher into the clouds,
and conveying the astonished King far beyond the borders
of Iran.

But though the Shah now became filled with terror, he
knew not how to guide his novel steeds, and so, breathless,
he sat, all desire for new worlds to conquer forever quenched
in his quaking breast. And finally the climax came, for,
after long and fruitless exertions, the strength of the eagles
being spent, they ceased to struggle. And lo! as they
rested on quiet wing, down from the sky, like a pricked
balloon, tumbled the chariot of the glorious Kaikous, and
great was the shock thereof as it kissed the earth.

And now, indeed, was the plight of the presumptuous
Shah a sorry one, for, battered and bruised, he awoke from
unconsciousness to find that the eagles had borne him unto

And finally, in his perplexity, he consulted his astrologers.

the desert of Cathay, where there was no man to succor him and no tender hands to minister unto his needs. So he suffered hunger and thirst, loneliness and despair; yea, and mortification of soul, that yet again in his folly he had become a laughing-stock unto his enemies and a source of shame unto Iran. Then in his trouble he prayed unto Ormuzd, confessing himself unworthy his throne and people, and continually for many days he watered the desert with his tears of penitence.

Meanwhile, when the news of this new calamity in which Kaikous had wantonly involved himself was made known unto Rustem, at once he set out with an army to seek him, but he was angry and shamed in his soul. So when the Shah was brought safely back, indignantly he upbraided him, sparing neither words nor reproaches. And he said:

"Verily, never hath the world seen the like of Kaikous for foolishness! One would say, from his actions, that his head was void of all save wind, and that a mad-house were fitter for his occupancy than a throne. Now all her days will it be a reproach unto Iran that a King once sat upon her throne, so puffed up with vanity and pride that in his folly he mounted into the sky, thinking to visit the sun and moon and stars, thus wresting from the heavens the secrets of the Almighty. Truly such mad adventures are unworthy the great King of Kings, whose forefathers ruled so gloriously and added such lustre unto the crown of Iran!"

And behold! of all the faithful service rendered unto the great Shah by his loyal Pehliva, these scathing words were far from the least. For, listening unto them with chastened spirit, the vanity of Kaikous all evaporated, leaving him humble and ashamed. Yea, so true was his penitence that when Rustem left him, for forty days and nights did he lie in the dust before God, shut away from the eyes of men. And when finally he seated himself once more upon the throne of light, verily he ruled the land with wisdom, liberality, and justice, for Kaikous and his folly had parted company.

RUSTEM'S ROMANCE

Listen, my children, and you shall hear,
Of the wondrous love of a maiden dear,
For a mighty warrior, the pride of his day,
Who loved, and married, and rode away,
For this is the romance of Rustem.

BEHOLD, it is written, that never in the Garden of
Kings bloomed there a fairer flower than Tamineh,
only Princess of the house of Samengan. Fresh
and sweet as a nosegay of lilies and pinks, this beauteous
pomegranate flower, with her laughing dark eyes, her blue-
black curls, and her soft, velvety voice was indeed a joy to
behold, and many there were who loved her.

But alas! the Princess was wilful, as well as fair, and
so, though she had many suitors from far and near, she
was attracted by none of them. For lo! her eye was fixed
and her heart was set upon a bright, particular star, blazing away with more than heavenly splendor, in far, far-off
Persia. So, when her father would have married her unto
this or that great Prince, half laughing, half earnest, she
would say:

"Nay, nay, my father! One man only will I marry,
and that is Rustem, the hero whose mighty prowess is ex-
ceeded only by his grandeur of soul."

Now as it happened, the King of Samengan was feuda-
tory unto Afrasiab, the deadly enemy of Iran, and though
the two countries were now at peace, the probability that

Rustem, the great Persian Pehliva, would ever visit the small kingdom of Samengan, or even so much as hear of the beautiful Tartar Princess, seemed most unlikely; therefore, when Tamineh thus spoke of Rustem, the King chided, saying unto her:

"Foolish child! Verily, as well mightst thou cry for the moon as to set thy heart upon so distant and so bright a star. For lo! the southern palm stretcheth forth not its arms unto the northern pine; neither doth the lion mate with the gazelle. Cast, therefore, O Pearl of my Heart, this hero from thy thoughts, since only grief and pain can it bring unto thee, forever to dream of the unattainable."

But this Tamineh could not do, for Rustem had become a part of her life, both waking and dreaming, as you shall hear. For it happened that the Princess had for her nurse a Persian woman, Fatima by name, who loved nothing so well as to talk of the great champion of her country, so that from childhood up had the Tartar maiden heard the wonder tales of her hero. Yea, the most beautiful part of every day unto her, as far back as she could remember, was the twilight hour, when, seated at her nurse's feet, her head pillowed in her soft lap, for hours she would sit spellbound, listening eagerly unto Fatima as she related the mighty deeds of Rustem: How, when only eight years old, he slew the King's white elephant; of the capture of the magic fortress; of his wonderful march into Mazinderan; of Rakush; and of all his daring deeds as a warrior.

And behold! Fatima had also other things to relate of her hero: tales illustrating his beautiful tenderness, loyalty, and greatness of soul. And as the Princess grew older, these stories appealed more to her than the wonder tales or the deeds of prowess; but all was listened to with eagerness and delight by the infatuated Tamineh, who, thus fed upon romance, grew into a tall, beautiful maiden with never a thought for any man save Rustem the Mighty.

But though it seemed most unlikely that the Princess would ever behold her hero, lo! it was written in the stars to the contrary. And that which is written, shall it not surely come to pass? So, at least, believe the Persians, and so happened it unto Rustem and Tamineh.

For presently it came to pass that upon a certain morning Rustem, in far-away Persia, awoke from his slumbers unrefreshed, after a restless night of dreaming. Concluding, therefore, that his muscles were in need of exercise, there being no enemies to fight, the hero resolved to go off upon a long hunting trip. So, filling his quiver with arrows, he saddled Rakush, and set out for the beautiful wilds that border upon Turan.

Now, arrived at the hunting-ground, Rustem found good sport, for the plain was covered with great herds of wild asses that roamed at will from the sullen grandeur of the uplands to the fairer vales below. Setting spurs to Rakush, therefore, gaily the hero pursued them through wood and glen, and often did his quivering darts pierce the glossy skin of the dangerous game. Yea, and oft too, did his lengthy lasso unfurl, ring upon ring, snaring the wily beasts for his club. So long he hunted, until finally, night drawing on, he said unto Rakush:

"Enough, My Beauty, enough! for to-morrow will be another day."

So, his hunting done, straightway the hero proceeded to light a great fire. Then, making a young tree serve as a spit, he ran it through the body of a nice fat gor, hung it over the fire, and roasted it for his meal. And behold, being deliciously done, hungrily he tore it joint from joint, ate of it his fill, and broke the bones for the marrow. Then, tired with his long day's sport, the weary hunter sought the shade of a thicket, and lay down to sleep, fanned by the plumes of the glorious palms above his head, and lulled to rest by the cooing doves and sunbirds that fluttered through their swinging crowns. Yea, and watched over by faithful Rakush who wandered never far from his sleeping master.

Now while Rustem peacefully slept, the hand of Fate was busy weaving into the pattern of his life some new threads. For, on this eventful day, a traveller on his way to Samengan had beheld the Mighty One hunting. So it came to pass that having arrived at the court, he told the astonishing news, which spread until it reached the ears of Fatima, who at once rushed to inform her young mistress. Now at first, Tamineh, upon hearing this story, was incredulous, but having summoned the traveller into her presence, her doubts were soon dispelled, for he said:

"Gracious Princess! Behold, as I crossed the great salt plains upon the border of the kingdom this day, I encountered a solitary huntsman, mounted upon a magnificent charger, and towering in his saddle like a giant among men. More like unto a god than mortal man, surely this could have been no other than Rustem, the Champion of the World, and his famous war-horse Rakush; for verily there exist not two such mighty heroes in the world! —of that I am certain."

Thus spake the traveller, and being dismissed, Fatima, all excitement, cried eagerly unto her mistress:

"O Rose of the World, rejoice! for behold, thy hero draweth near, and yet thine eyes may be gladdened by his coming! For surely no man could see the Mighty Rustem and mistake him for another, since as the traveller sayeth, in all the world there are no two such; nay, nor methinks in heaven either!"

Now hearing these words, the heart of Tamineh leaped and rejoiced like unto that of a gay singing-bird, as, embracing Fatima, she exclaimed joyously, her soft, dark eyes shining like stars:

"Fatima, Old Dragon! Listen and admire. For, behold, thy Bright Pomegranate Flower hath determined to gaze upon this glorious Persian Sun, and if it withereth all her gay petals! and the stars decree that thou must help her."

But Fatima, hearing these words, quickly repented of her impetuosity, for right well she knew the wilfulness of her mistress, and she feared unto what it might lead. Therefore she replied unto Tamineh:

"Pearl of my Heart! be not foolish; for how is it possible for thee to accomplish the desire of thy heart? The great Rustem is travelling north, and it is not probable, either that he will visit our Court, or delay his journey. How then canst thou hope to see him?"

Now thus questioned, for a time Tamineh was silent. But, being a young woman of some resource, she was not to be dismayed by obstacles which might have deterred smaller souls, for had she not all her life been hoping against hope for just this opportunity? And now that it had come, was she to sit quietly down, allowing it to pass by unimproved? Verily, nay! For some minutes, however, the Princess did sit down, thinking hard. But pres-

ently, springing gaily to her feet, a mischievous light
sparkling and dancing in her wonderful dark eyes, she
cried:

"Kiss me, Fatima, kiss me! for verily thou beholdest
before thee the happiest Princess in the whole, wide world.
Soon I shall see, and perhaps win the hero of my dreams,
and thou, too, methinks will rejoice once more to behold
thy country's champion. Now let not thine eyes pop out
of thy head, Old Dragon; neither be thou dismayed, for
I shall not go forth unto the great Rustem, but he shall
come unto me. For, look you! the plan is quite simple,
since we have only to take captive Rakush, when the
hero will come quickly enough to recover his glorious
steed."

Alas! the proposition of stealing Rakush was unto
Fatima as daring and awful an idea as the thought of
stealing Rustem himself, but realizing that it was useless
to oppose her young mistress, she replied not, save by a
deep groan.

Ignoring the groan, however, the Princess continued:

"Listen now, my dear old Fatima, for verily the plot
is a famous one! But it must be carried out to-night, before Rustem hath departed, else will it be too late. Now
methinks that not by strength but by stratagem must
Rakush the terrible be captured. Therefore, when darkness covereth the land to-night, we will send forth six wily
herdsmen, mounted upon light, swift horses, spurring them
on to the enterprise by offering them princely rewards if
successful. They must be, of course, men expert with the
lasso, and they must entrap, without harming, Rakush
while Rustem sleeps, returning with him unto the royal
stables before dawn."

Thus elaborated Tamineh her plan unto Fatima, who, relieved that it threatened no danger to the Princess, nevertheless protested loudly, tearing her hair and clothes, weeping and lamenting bitterly. But of course she ended by doing the will of her mistress, as did also the men chosen, for well they knew that any service faithfully performed would be liberally rewarded by the Princess Tamineh.

Meanwhile, little dreamed the mighty Rustem, as he soundly slept on his bed of moss that night, after his famous day's hunting, of the filmy web that this bright-eyed Princess was securely weaving about him. Yea, and even intelligent Rakush, though he slept not, little suspected that for long seven dark figures had stealthily stalked him through the night. For the Tartar warriors who followed him, knowing quite well that no easy task was involved in carrying out the commands of their Princess, proceeded most cautiously.

Finally, however, advancing stealthily, the seven clever ones tried to take their prize, unawares, by throwing a lasso over his head. But in vain; for the noise of the uncoiling lariat piercing unto the ear of Rakush, dexterously he avoided the cruel cord, standing with ears alert and pawing feet of anger. Now for a second thus he stood; then having located his enemy, like a lion he sprang upon them, striking two of the foe dead with a single stroke of his forefeet, and savagely biting off the head of a third. Thus three of the company were safely disposed of, and the brave Rakush was not yet taken. Nor would he have been; for never yet had man or Demon entrapped or overcome the glorious steed; but for the sake of the beautiful Princess, the stars decreed it. So presently, after a hard fight, the four succeeded in entangling him with their lassos, and thus it came to pass that just before the day dawned the proud war-horse of Rustem was led, gagged and blindfolded, into the stables of the King of Samengan.

And behold, when the Princess Tamineh from her balcony at last beheld the famous war-horse loom up along the shadowy road, so great was her joy that, regardless of the fact that Rakush was tossing his head, stamping his hoofs, and snorting protests like an angry dragon, she would have flown down to welcome him with soft caress, had not the faithful Fatima urged that such a step might undo all that had been accomplished.

But though the dawn brought joy unto Tamineh, its message unto Rustem was that of sorrow. For behold! when he called unto Rakush no answering neigh rang out the glad reply. Thinking, however, that his steed had perhaps but strayed beyond the sound of his first gentle call, the hero quickly came out into the open, calling unto Rakush in a voice of thunder; but still there came no answer. Then was the heart of the Mighty One troubled, for well he knew that his faithful steed had not willingly strayed away. Now in his dismay he said unto himself:

"What a dilemma! for now must I go on foot, carrying my quiver and my great club, this heavy helmet and coat of mail, and my life-destroying sword. And seeing me thus, how the Tartars will scoff, saying among themselves: 'Behold the Mighty Rustem! While he slept, some one must have stolen his horse!' Now thus shall I be put to shame before my enemies, that which never yet hath happened unto Rustem."

Thus communing with himself, busily the hero searched for some trace of his missing steed, and not in vain,

for at last he detected the footprints of a scuffle down
by the stream that murmured at the foot of the shady
glen. Here great hoof-marks pointed out the field of
battle, the ground being ploughed up upon all sides, indi-
cating how desperately the mighty steed had resisted his
wily captors. Then farther on could be traced the steps
of Rakush between two other horses, closely followed by
a third, which plainly said unto Rustem that his faithful
companion had been stolen.

And now, boiling over with rage and sorrow, the heart
of Rustem beat to but one refrain: Vengeance! Vengeance
upon the captors of Rakush! Pausing not, however,
quickly he followed the traces of his horse's hoofs, and lo!
they led him unto the gates of Samengan. Then Rustem,
perceiving whither the footprints led, sware unto Heaven
a great oath, and he said:

"By the sun and moon and stars, I swear that if aught
of harm hath come unto Rakush through this King or his
people, verily the thief shall pay for it with his head!"

Meanwhile, knowing naught of the capture of Rakush, as
Rustem approached the shining turrets of the city, great
was the astonishment of the King and those about him
when they beheld the manner of his coming. Nevertheless,
they hurried forth to greet their distinguished guest, the
King saying unto him:

"O glorious Pehliva, never hath Samengan been so
honored in a guest, and lo! her King sayeth unto thee,
'Welcome.' But how happeneth it that the mighty Rustem
cometh unto us afoot and unattended? If misfortune
hath befallen, behold! we are all at thy service!"

But unto this courteous greeting Rustem replied coldly,
relating briefly unto the King all that had come to pass.

Then becoming more angry as he talked, once more the hero sware that many heads should quit their trunks if his charger were not returned unto him right speedily, void of harm.

Then the King, seeing that Rustem was beside himself with anger, spake words of comfort unto the hero, for he knew how dear unto him was his glorious steed. And he said:

"O Hero of Heroes! Be not so disturbed in thy spirit, for verily anger profiteth nothing. It is by charming that one lureth the serpent from his hole. As for Rakush,

> If still within the limits of my reign,
> The well-known courser shall be thine again.
> For Rakush never can remain concealed
> No more than Rustem on the battle-field.

"Take courage, therefore, and be of good cheer, for soon thy glorious other self shall be restored unto thee, and all will be well. As for the thief, when detected he shall be placed in thy hands, to slay or to spare, according to thy good pleasure. But as for Rustem!—for this one night, at least, he must tarry at Samengan as our honored guest."

So, being satisfied with these promises, Rustem put away all suspicion from his mind, and became the King's guest. Then all day they feasted and made merry, beguiling the hours with wine and sweet words. Nor could the King sufficiently honor his guest, though he encompassed him with music and song, and waited upon him with his own hands, as though he were his slave. And behold! when night was fallen the monarch himself led Rustem unto a couch perfumed with musk and roses, bidding him slumber peacefully until morning, when he should again be made glad in Rakush, his steed.

Now thus delightfully couched, Rustem slept dreamlessly until the star of morning stood high in the arch of heaven. Then suddenly there fell upon his ear the murmur of soft womanly voices which caused the hero to start up in confused amazement. Seeing nothing, however, he closed his eyes again, for he thought that he had dreamed.

But though his conclusion was natural, the hero dreamed not, for presently the heavy curtains were drawn softly aside, and there stepped within the chamber a slave bearing a lamp perfumed with amber. And following after, her veil but half concealing her lovely face, Rustem beheld the fairest maiden his eyes had ever gazed upon. Now for a moment the lovely vision lingered upon the threshold, poised like a frightened bird for hasty flight, the rich color suffusing her olive cheek, her dark eyes beaming beneath their splendid lashes, and her pomegranate mouth, flower-soft and sensitive, slightly parted. Then gaining courage, slowly she advanced toward the hero, and as she moved, fragrance was scattered from her robes, and her long black ringlets, musk-perfumed, seemed unto Rustem as fateful as the warrior's kamund. Yet, though enchanted, the warrior sighed, for again he thought he but dreamed.

But even as he would have settled himself once more unto slumber, behold, like music upon his ear fell the soft voice of Tamineh, bidding Fatima retire to the distant window. Now this fully awoke the young warrior, who, springing quickly from his couch, gazed in astonished delight at his enchanting visitor. Then Tamineh spoke in the soft, velvety tones she could use so effectively when she chose. And she said:

"My Lord Rustem, thou beholdest before thee the Princess Tamineh, daughter of the King, and she hath come thus into thy presence because the need is urgent. For she would crave thy pardon for a great wrong which she hath done unto thee, and which, she heareth, carrieth with it a fearful penalty."

Now amazed at this most surprising confession poured forth from tempting lips, moulded for love's recompense alone, for a second the valiant Rustem was silenced by the wonder and unexpectedness of it all. Quickly recovering himself, however, he replied unto the maiden:

"Thou, Fair Princess! Thou hast done me a wrong? Truly, I know not what wrong thou canst have done me, unless it be the mischief wrought by thy bright eyes since they have shone so radiantly upon me. It is true, my heart whispers unto me that thy wondrous beauty hath caught me in its snare, but if that be thy sin, it carrieth with it a delightful penalty—one which thou needst not fear."

Now this reply, so unlike that of a mighty warrior, caused a roguish smile to play about the fascinating lips of the Princess Tamineh, who, casting upon the speaker one bright, admiring glance from her sparkling eyes, then modestly dropped them, replying demurely unto this gallant speech:

"Who knoweth, My Lord, but that, perchance, I would gladly add that theft unto the other! But greatly I fear that thou wilt consider my first offence the greater. For it was I, and none other, who had stolen from thee Rakush, thy steed of battle, who even now slumbereth peacefully in the royal stables."

So spake Tamineh, and though, as we know, her words were true, yet was it long before she could persuade the

master of Rakush that she did not jest. When she finally
convinced him, however, so great was his joy in knowing
Rakush safe and unharmed, that, behold, he forgot to be
angry with the thief. But, after all, who could blame him?
for the thief was very fair, and she confessed with a voice
that rivalled the magic notes of the bulbul chanting unto
his mate. And besides, the master of Rakush had it in his
heart to ask a great boon of the Princess, and this time he
remembered that not by anger, but by charming, one
lureth a bird from the bush. So, smiling, he said unto
Tamineh:

"Fair Princess, behold, thou standest before thy judge,
convicted of two serious crimes. Two conditions must
thou fulfil, therefore, if thou wouldst obtain thy pardon.
First, the judge must be allowed to gaze upon the face of
the fair culprit, else how can he administer suitable punishment? And second, he must be informed as to the
motive of the theft, for that puzzle hath yet to be unrav-
elled."

Now at this embarrassing sentence, the lovely Tamineh
stood silent before her judge, looking indeed like a culprit
fostering half a desire to flee. But presently, rallying her
forces, she replied bravely unto the Mighty One, though
her soft voice trembled and she looked not up:

"My Lord Rustem, though news unto thee—since thou
art a mighty warrior—I suppose it is yet true that every
maiden hath her hero. Now it is owing to Fatima, there,
who is a Persian, that I have mine: a hero of whose fame
and valorous deeds I have dreamed my life long, whose
like ne'er was and ne'er will be again, whose glory reacheth even unto the stars. And thou must know also, O
Mighty One, that every maiden longeth to gaze upon the

face of the only hero in the world for her. That is why I stole thy horse. And now, since thou knowest my utmost guilt, findest thou my crime too great for pardon?"

But unto this plea, for some minutes, Rustem replied not, for persistently his heart kept singing: "The only hero in the world for her! The only hero in the world for her!" Now praise was no new thing unto the Champion of the World, but never before had it been offered with such subtle charm. And besides, with joy the warrior recognized that here was a spirit akin unto his own in its dauntlessness and longings after the best. Drawing near unto the Princess, therefore, "The Only Hero in the World" said unto her softly:

"Fair Pomegranate Flower, one of the conditions, truly, thou hast fulfilled; but the other must be met also; for verily my eyes are hungry for full sight of lips that can murmur words so sweet to hear!"

But the Princess, drawing closer the long white veil which half concealed her face, stepped quickly back, saying proudly unto the eager Rustem:

"Nay, nay, my Lord! That is a privilege I grant only unto the man who weddeth me."

Now saying this, slowly the Princess moved toward the curtains, as though she would go. But Rustem, detaining her, cried out impetuously:

"O Pearl among Women, stay! for verily my heart hath wakened and calleth unto thee for its mate. Only consent, therefore, and to-morrow will we be wed."

But, though these words sounded unto Tamineh like a pæan of victory, she received them coldly; for well she knew that no man—least of all a warrior—careth for what he can win too easily. And then it was that Rustem, in whom contradiction ever roused a fiery purpose to obtain his will, vowed again and yet again that he could not live without her; that he would wed but her, and that before the morrow's sun had set; that from henceforth honor and praise and glory would be as ashes unto his lips, unless shared with his Moon of Beauty.

So now, having thus aroused desire, softly the Princess drew aside her veil. Then before the enraptured Rustem had wakened to the danger, like a gay humming-bird, swiftly away she flew, leaving in his hands her veil, which he in his eagerness had seized lest she hide that lovely face again too soon. And as she fled, like chimes of bells there floated back the sound of merry laughter, which but fanned the flame glowing already so brightly in the awakened heart of the hero left gazing so ruefully upon love's only token—the dainty, fragrant, cruel film of lace. Now regarding it tenderly, the warrior smiled and said:

"Behold, the gay young Singing-bird hath flown, leaving her pretty wing in the too rough hand of her captor! But, by the sun and moon and stars, I swear that yet shall she be mine, for mighty in love shall Rustem be as well as in deeds of valor."

Consequently, when morning dawned, and the hero once more beheld the King, ceremoniously he asked Tamineh's hand in marriage. Yea, and the monarch of Samengan listened unto him gladly, for was it not Rustem the Mighty who sued! And did he not know but too well the heart of his Moon of Beauty! So that very day was the marriage bower crowned with roses and decked with white lilies, while the royal abode was flooded with music and sunshine to grace the glad wedding of the Princess Tamineh. And when all was over, verily it seemed unto Rustem and his pretty Singing-bird as if the world, like some vast tidal wave, had rolled away, leaving them alone with their happiness upon the golden shores of the Land of Delight.

Now thus it was that Tamineh, Princess of Samengan, obtained her heart's desire. And behold! for one bright summer month she tasted such happiness as is seldom vouchsafed, even unto the children of Ormuzd. Wandering in the myrtle groves, or strolling together in the shady forest, the Princess now heard from the hero's own lips marvellous tales of adventure, and, the days passed for both like a happy dream. But alas! In the Book of Fate it is written that pure happiness is not for mortals, and so, when one bright moon had run her course, relentlessly sorrow—joy's sombre twin—invaded this Land of Delight.

And behold! not suddenly, but with stealth, the invader drew nigh, attacking first the hero of battles. For gradually Rustem became restless, and impatient with his life of inactivity, longing intensely for the excitement of warfare and adventure to which he was accustomed and for which he was formed. For alas! Nature, in giving unto him his giant frame and mighty muscles, his valorous heart, and his soul that joyed, above all else, in battle, had planned and destined the mighty son of Zal to shine through all the ages—not as a lover, but as the type of the perfect warrior.

Now slowly this truth was brought home unto Tamineh, as she noted the ever-increasing restlessness of her hero, which even she could not always still, though she knew that he loved her tenderly. And though she spake not of it, her heart became burdened with sorrow, for she knew that the time was now not far off when Rustem would go

The days passed for both like a happy dream.

back unto his own people and life, perhaps forgetting her in the more powerful attractions of war, while she must needs love him forever.

And alas! Tamineh was right in her surmise, for it needed only the rumor that war had again broken out in Persia to cause Rustem to buckle on his sword and armor with joy at the prospect of battle. Then hastily seeking the King, he said unto him:

"O Royal Cypress, long have I rested in the shade of thy glorious land, but now I must say unto it farewell. For behold! duty calleth me back unto Iran, and it is well, for verily my sword hath rusted too long in its scabbard, and Rakush neigheth with longing to bear me once more in the thick of the fight."

Now having thus spoken, the hero opened his arms and took unto his heart Tamineh, the Peri-faced, bathing her cheeks with tears and covering her hair and eyes with kisses; also he whispered unto his Singing-bird sweet words of enchantment. But alas for Tamineh! Clinging unto the neck of her hero, bitterly she wept, crying unto her beloved:

"O Light of my Life! I fear that thou goest from me forever, and how shall I live without thee?"

But, kissing away her tears, Rustem spake unto Tamineh brave words of comfort, telling her that he would surely return unto her when his fighting was over, laden with fresh laurels to lay at her feet. And he bade her be strong and dauntless of spirit, as was seemly for a warrior's bride, since even for this was it that he loved her. And last of all, taking from off his arm an onyx bracelet, upon which was engraved the image of a Simurgh, he gave it unto Tamineh, saying:

"Pearl of my Heart, listen! If while I am away, God should send unto us a daughter, fasten this amulet under her curls. If, however, a son should be sent to gladden our hearts, then let him wear it upon his arm, as his father hath worn it, for it will protect him from the powers of evil, being the badge of Rustem and of Zal."

Now having thus spoken, hastily Rustem threw himself upon the back of Rakush, and the wind-footed bare him swiftly away from out the sight of Tamineh, unto whom the world suddenly became dark, so blinded were her eyes with tears.

Then with leaden feet passed the days for the Princess Tamineh. Howbeit, as time passed on, news came from the Mighty Rustem of fresh victories, together with a present of three great rubies of priceless value and three wedges of finest gold. But alas! the letter said •no word of the hero's return, only of more battles and victories to come. And Tamineh, reading between the lines, sighed bitterly, taking no pleasure in the rubies and gold.

But a great joy was in store for Tamineh, for one night as she sat sorrowfully upon her balcony, suddenly she heard a flutter of mighty wings, and behold, there was dropped into her lap a priceless treasure—a babe whose mouth was filled with smiles, and who in feature resembled his glorious sire. Then was Tamineh comforted, and because of his smiles she called her babe Sohrab, which meaneth Sunshine.

SOHRAB THE YOUTH

NOW if we are to believe what the old chronicles tell us, never, I suppose, since the world began was there born a more lovable babe than Sohrab, the son of Rustem. When he came unto his mother, behold, his eyes and mouth were still alight with the sunshine of Paradise, and, instead of crying, he kicked and crowed with delight, trying thus to say unto Tamineh that he was glad to leave even the Garden of the Blessed to come unto her.

And truly the babe was a joy to behold! for in addition to all the gay loveliness of Rustem's bright Singing-bird, from his illustrious father he had inherited the splendid physique of the noble house of Zal. Following after Rustem, too, he grew so rapidly that when he was a month old he had the limbs of a yearling child; at three years he learned exercises of arms; at five he was bold as a lion; and at ten there was not a hero in the whole country who dared wrestle with him.

So, practising all the exercises of an athlete and a warrior, the boy grew up tall, dark, and straight as a young cypress, with limbs like unto an elephant, heart bold as a lion's, and his foot as swift as that of the wild stag; yet withal, so simple, gay, generous, and lovable, that from his proud grandsire, the King of Samengan, down to the meanest subject in the realm, he was admired and adored by all—while as for his mother, unto her he was the very breath of life, filling every sleeping and waking thought.

Now Sohrab had inherited from Tamineh one trait which drew them very close together. For behold! whatever the day's occupation, and no matter what else tempted, at the evening hour the boy always sought his mother upon the balcony, where, seated at her feet, his bright head pillowed in her lap, he spent the happiest hour of his day listening unto the marvellous hero tales that poured like magic from her lips. For Tamineh, wishing her boy to be steeped in the legends of his father's land, gladly related unto him the wonder tales of the Persians, all of which found an answering echo in the eager young soul of her listener. For verily Sohrab could not have been the son of Rustem without longing for battle and adventure.

And of course in all these stories the Hero of Heroes was Rustem the Mighty, unto whom the fair narrator did full justice. For Tamineh loved "The Only Hero in the World for her!" still, though he had never returned unto her; and so, as her hand strayed in mute caress through the thick, dark locks of Sohrab—who was, alas, love's only legacy unto her!—she told of all the Champion's wondrous deeds of valor with such fire and passion that the cheeks of both glowed with the tremendous stress of it. Yea, and Sohrab never wearied of these tales, begging to have them repeated again and again; and, as a consequence, he grew up with the thought that never had the world known such a mighty Pehliva as Rustem the Persian.

And Rakush, too, delighted the boy's soul—Rakush the dauntless who carried the great hero of his country so gallantly through the thickest of the fight; Rakush the lion-slayer; Rakush who neighed for joy at the battle's roar; Rakush who feared neither man, nor dragon, nor

Deev; Rakush the gentle, who loved to eat sugar from his master's hand.

Now listening unto all these inspiring tales, Sohrab determined deep in his soul that one day he, too, would be a great hero—yea, even the Champion of the World, as Rustem, leading his armies on to victory, and performing such deeds of valor as should bring fame and glory unto Turan, his land, and pride unto the heart of his mother, whose cheek—he promised himself—should flush one day as she related his brave deeds, even as now when she spoke of Rustem, the Hero of Heroes. For did he not intend that the name "Sohrab" should go ringing down the ages as the symbol of courage, generosity, loyalty, high endeavor, and chivalrous deeds? Yea, he would try hard; then, perhaps, one day the great Rustem might hear of him, and it might even happen that he would meet him face to face.

Thus the lad dreamed, not knowing that Rustem was his sire, for Tamineh had not revealed unto him his lineage. And alas! neither was it known unto Rustem that God had blessed him with a noble son. For, at the birth of Sohrab, the gentle mother, fearing that if the truth became known unto the great Persian chieftain, at once he would send and take the boy from her to train him up as a soldier to fight against her country, had sent word by a messenger who travelled unto Persia that a little daughter had been born unto him in Samengan. And behold! so little were daughters prized in the East at that time that Rustem never asked to see the child, and so remained in ignorance as to Sohrab.

For, although the years passed, Rustem was so busy fighting, that he never came back unto Samengan. But for Sohrab, therefore, the whole episode would have seemed unto Tamineh as naught but a blissful dream. In her beautiful, high-spirited boy, however, the Princess was consoled, for she knew that in him she possessed forever the best of Rustem—the hero's heart, the dauntless spirit, the enduring soul—that which she had most loved in her hero. So gradually the warm, living presence of dreamy-eyed Sohrab, whose arms loved to linger round his mother's neck, caused Tamineh to think of Rustem as a glorious warrior, but also as quite apart from her life.

Nevertheless, the Great Pehliva was the tie that bound this mother and son so closely together—for was he not the ideal of each? And often—yea, very often!—the wish sprang up in the heart of Tamineh that Rustem might behold his glorious son. But alas! when she remembered that as a consequence, her boy might be taken from her, her heart grew weak and she held her peace.

So the years passed by, bringing naught but joy unto Sohrab, until he was grown into a strong, manly, courageous youth of seventeen, who could ride, joust, tilt, hunt, and use both sword and spear better than any warrior in the whole kingdom of Samengan. Then one day he sought his mother, saying unto her:

"Mother, think it not strange, but I care not for a wonder-tale to-night; for much I have been thinking lately, and this once I would question thee of other things. And first, thou must know that but to-day Piran-Wisa hath told unto me that in the arts of war and of prowess he can teach me no more. So now I would hear of my race and lineage. Now of course I know that I am nobly born, for I feel it in all my being; but what shall I say unto men when they ask me the name of my sire? for verily I know it not."

Now hearing these words of spirit, Tamineh smiled, because that his fire and pride were like unto that of his father; but she sighed also, for she scented in these words of manhood the loss of her boy. Nevertheless, disguising her sorrow, she replied gaily unto Sohrab and she said:

"So thou art tired of thy mother's wonder stories, art thou? And desirest to speak of other things! Ah, but one more tale must thou hear, my Stately Young Cypress —one that I have been saving for thee right jealously for many days; one that will be unto thine ears sweeter than the song of yonder bulbul as he chanteth so entrancingly unto his mate. Nay, do not kiss me now, but cuddle down close to my side, and listen unto thy mother's love song. It will not detain thee long!

"Well, once upon a time in the glorious spring-time of the world, Ormuzd the Blessed, in the fair gardens of Paradise, conceived in his heart the thought of fashioning and sending forth into the world a hero who should be mightier and more illustrious than any of the sons of men. So, long he thought, and shaped, and wrought, for he planned a perfect hero, and his task was not easy. But finally, the beautiful Peri of Paradise having kissed dimples into the soft skin of the babe, curl into his hair, and the pomegranate bloom into his cheeks,—even as they must have done unto thee, O Beauteous One, before they sent thee forth unto me—all was pronounced finished, and the Blessed One smiled at his work, pronouncing it good, for behold, in this wondrous creation, not a thing was there that marred, all bearing the stamp of perfection.

"Now they loved this babe in Paradise, and so it lingered there awhile. But, since not for this was it created, at last, reluctantly, the Blessed Ormuzd, summoning unto him the Wondrous Bird of God, tucked the laughing little one safely under her golden feathers, and sent it forth, bidding the tender mother-bird carry her treasure safely unto the house of White-haired Zal, in Persia.

"Ah, now my Young Cypress raiseth high his head, and I perceive that he hath guessed the name of my hero! But listen, for my tale is but just begun!

"And alas! it runneth not now so pleasantly, for Iblis, who hateth perfection, even as he hateth Ormuzd the Blessed, beholding this wondrous babe, in its cradle murmured over it vile words of magic. And having wrought his spell, maliciously he smiled, and said:

"'Behold, now art thou perfect no longer, though thou appearest the same. And though a mighty warrior thou shalt be, truly, a heavy price shalt thou pay. For behold! all the days of thy life the tender joys of the heart shall be little known unto thee, though thy deeds shall be glorious!'

"Now this explaineth perfectly, doth it not? why thy great hero, Rustem, joyeth above all else in the roar and tumult of battle. It may also whisper unto thy heart other things, even as it hath unto thy mother, whose hero is also thy hero, and whose deeds of valor thrilled her maiden heart even as they now call forth such responsive echo in thine own.

"But though thine ear hath been delighted with many an adventure of Rustem, thou hast yet to hear, methinks, of a certain great hunting expedition upon which the hero lost his horse, but won a bride. For, be it known unto thee, my Sun-kissed Cypress, that a certain wicked Princess of Samengan, Tamineh by name, in order to behold the face of her hero, audaciously caused the redoubtable Rakush to be stolen, thus luring the mighty Rustem unto

the Court, where for one happy month the love of his
lady succeeded in blotting out from his heart all desire for
battle and bloodshed. Then, alas, War, the true mistress
of his life, once more regained her dominion! And so,
seventeen long years ago, he bade good-by to his gay
young Singing-bird, and never again hath he returned
unto Samengan.

"But though her hero returned not, behold, the Princess
was not left comfortless. For Ormuzd the Blessed, who
ever keepeth a watchful eye upon his own, beholding the
sad heart of the forsaken one, unperceived of Iblis, once
more fashioned a perfect hero and sent him forth, this
time unto the house of Tamineh. Now this beautiful
babe seemed made of the essence of sunshine, and so, soon
it came to pass that unto the lonely Princess he became
the very light of her eyes and the joy of her life; yea, the
very breath of her heart! for whom had she beside?

"And so the wonder tale revealeth that the proud
Young Cypress, who gazeth with such shining eyes into
those of his mother, is the noble shoot of a mighty tree
whose shadow extendeth over the earth, and whose fame
shall be sung by the Children of Ormuzd as long as the
world lasts.

"And now, the tale being finished, if the promising Hero
of Noble Race will graciously raise his fair head, not unto
the stars, but unto his mother's lips, much she would like
to greet him!—ere the word is of other things."

Now thus it was that Tamineh told unto Sohrab the
story of her love, and having revealed unto him all things
concerning his father, she charged him to keep secret
what he had heard, lest Afrasiab, the enemy of Rustem,
should slay the son because of the father, or lest Rustem

should send for his son, thus bringing grief unto the heart of his mother.

But Sohrab, in the pride of his youth, with flashing eyes and uplifted head, replied proudly unto his mother. And he said:

"O Pearl among Mothers, verily my heart telleth me that this is a secret that cannot long remain known unto but two! For doth not the fame of Rustem, my noble father, even now fill the whole world with glory? And am not I his son? And shall not the son of Rustem also be glorious? Verily, thou mayest not think it, since as yet I am only a youth, but, mother, there is that within me which whispereth that one day I, too, shall do valiant deeds! Yea, and the day is not now far distant. For listen, O my mother!——

"Soon will I put myself at the head of an innumerable army of Tartars, and with them to aid me it will not take long to deprive that foolish Kaikous of his head and throne; for verily he is not fit to rule over a great country like Persia! Then will I place upon the throne of light the true monarch of Iran, even Rustem the Mighty. And behold! this being done, my father and I will, together, make war against Afrasiab, and I will possess myself of his throne. For, since Rustem is my father and I am his son, verily I will not suffer that there be any Kings in the world but him and me! For unto us belong the crowns of might. And dost thou know what thou wilt be then, O my Glorious Mother? Why, Queen of the whole world! And when that day shall come, as it surely will, then thy cheek shall flush with pride not only for the Mighty Rustem, but also for Sohrab, thy son. For, having subdued the wicked and the foolish, with wisdom and gentleness will we reign, so that all the world shall be glad because of the house of Zal."

Now taking the ardent young speaker in her arms, Tamineh kissed his flushed cheeks and bright eyes again and again for answer, realizing with sorrow that the time was nigh when she must let her bold young eaglet go forth to try his wings. But though her heart was heavy, she spake brave words of wisdom unto Sohrab, promising that when the time came for him to go forth, she herself would buckle on his sword.

So all was yet well in the house of Tamineh. But lo! that night the Angel Serosch, in her sevenfold flight around the world, beheld Sohrab's youth vanish from him forever, leaving in its place an aspiring hero, whose one desire was to behold the face of his glorious sire and to perform brave deeds like unto his.

SOHRAB AND THE WARRIOR
MAIDEN

BEHOLD! among the many legends of Sohrab, the son of Rustem, it is chronicled that with no one was he a greater favorite than with the famous Tartar general, old Piran-Wisa. And his interest in the child manifested itself in a practical way, for whenever he came unto Samengan, he put the lad through military exercises, teaching him thus the tactics of war.

Now at the time when Sohrab learned of his lineage the Kurds and Tartars were carrying on a fierce war against the Persians, and so eager was he now to acquire experience in battle, that finally he persuaded Piran-Wisa to secure him a command in the army of Afrasiab. And this was not difficult of accomplishment, for already had the fame of the great strength, and skill, and bravery of Sohrab pierced unto the ears of the King, who gladly accepted his services, scenting in him a mighty champion, later on, for his army.

So, having received his commission, Sohrab knelt before his grandfather, the King of Samengan, promising to keep untarnished the sword and shield which that monarch had presented unto his grandson, as his first gift of manhood. And the King blessed the youth, giving unto him also the noblest charger in the royal stables. Then Tamineh buckled on his sword, and bound about his wrist the amu-

let of the house of Zal, speaking naught but brave words
unto her son. And so, proud and happy, they sent him forth.

After this, it is recorded that brave Sohrab fought in
many battles, conducting himself with so much wisdom and
valor that all men spake his praise. But notwithstanding
his victories and growing.fame, the youth was not content.
For, in the thick of battle, as in his quiet hours of dreaming, one great wish ever possessed his soul—to meet his
father, the Mighty Rustem, face to face, and win his word
of praise.

So, pondering ever his great desire, Sohrab knew no
peace until finally he decided to go in search of his father;
and having arrived at this decision, straightway he sought
out his grandsire, beseeching his counsel and aid. Now
the King of Samengan, rejoicing in the courage and prowess of Sohrab, having listened unto his desire, quickly
opened unto him the doors of his treasury, pouring forth
gold without stint, for he loved the boy tenderly. And as
a sign of his good pleasure, he also, at this time, invested
his grandson with all the honors of a King.

As for Tamineh, beholding that her son's charger now
quivered beneath his weight, quickly she commanded the
guardians of the herd that they lead forth all the royal
horses before Sohrab that he might choose him a war-
steed worthy this glorious enterprise. But alas! one and
all bowed themselves beneath his weight, even as they had
when tested by the Mighty Rustem, when he chose his
steed of battle. But presently there came before Sohrab
one who told of a beautiful foal—sprung from Rustem's
glorious Rakush—clean-limbed, strong, and beautiful,
which, having tested, Sohrab declared perfect. In his
joy, therefore, he cried out gaily unto his mother:

"Fair Queen of the World! Behold, the brave sons of Rustem and of Rakush crave thy blessing ere they go forth in search of laurels and a sunny crown to grace thy glorious tresses—one of which thy hero craveth that he may seem in truth to carry thee ever near his heart."

Alas! Tamineh, as she gazed at her splendid son, longed neither for laurels nor a crown, but only to joy in his glorious presence forever—for such is the way of mothers. Nevertheless, meeting banter with banter, graciously she allowed that one dark lock be severed from her abundant tresses, and she smiled as she noted the admiration and love exhibited by the nobles and warriors who flocked so gladly to Sohrab's standard. Yea, and deep in her heart she longed to be a youth that she, too, might follow this glorious young leader, watching over his safety in the capacity of devoted body-guard.

And well if this might have been! for, though Tamineh suspected it not, on this expedition, much Sohrab was to need the offices of a wise, devoted, and loyal companion, since he had enemies who, even as he recruited his army, were plotting his destruction. Indeed yes, and of these Afrasiab was the instigator, for upon hearing the news of Sohrab's intention, straightway he called unto him Human and Barman, two of his most doughty chieftains, and said unto them:

"O my Pehliva, listen unto my voice, for verily I have a plan which shall rid us of all our enemies. For behold! it is known unto me that Sohrab is sprung from that great disturber of our progress, Rustem the Mighty, who suspecteth not that he hath a son. It must be hidden from him, therefore, who it is that cometh out against him, for these two champions will surely meet in battle, and it may

be that the young lion will kill the old one. Now if that
shall come to pass, behold, Iran, devoid of Rustem, will
fall an easy prey into our hands; and when that shall have
happened, it will be an easy matter to take Sohrab by
stratagem and slay him. If, on the other hand, however,
Rustem should slay his son, then would his heart be devoured with grief, so that he would trouble his enemies no
more."

So spake Afrasiab unto his chiefs, and having poured
out all his guile, he bade them quickly gather together
a great army to join the ranks of Sohrab, and depart unto
Samengan. And behold, they bare with them gifts of
great price to set before the face of Sohrab, and they
carried unto him also a letter from the King, filled with
words of honey. And the letter said:

"O Glorious Stripling, whose equal existeth not in all
the world, behold, the King laudeth thy valorous resolve
to bring Iran unto thy feet, and he sendeth unto thee
a mighty army that right speedily Turan, Iran, and Samengan may be one land, and all the world at peace."

So Sohrab, thus encouraged by the King, and unsuspicious of his guile, caused the cymbals of departure to be
sounded, and the army set forth upon its tour of conquest.
Now the track of this youthful conqueror was marked by
desolation and destruction, but behold, he marched on
unstayed until he was come unto the White Fortress,
which was the key to the heart of Persia.

Now the governor of this stronghold was Gustahem the
brave, an old and famous warrior, but now, alas, so feeble
that he could assist in the defence of the fort only by his
counsel. He had under him, however, a young captain,
Hujir by name, who was known unto the enemy as a very

brave and powerful champion, so the White Castle was considered impregnable. Believing themselves to be secure, therefore, when Hujir beheld from afar a dark cloud of armed men, with gallant Sohrab at their head, immediately he donned his armor and rushed forward to challenge him, crying arrogantly:

"Halt, thou Stripling! for if thou venturest one step nearer, verily I will lop off that towering head of thine, and give thy soft, baby flesh unto yon hungry vultures for food."

But behold! this fierce menace deterred not for a single second the onward course of Sohrab, who, hesitating not, boldly charged the champion, quickly o'ercoming him. For, though Hujir fought bravely, in the hands of Rustem's mighty son he was naught but an infant. Seeing himself at the mercy of the invader, therefore, humbly the vanquished hero begged for quarter, and Sohrab, who was young and tender of heart, granted unto his adversary his life, binding him with cords and sending him captive unto Human.

Howbeit, though successful in this encounter, Sohrab was to face another adversary upon this eventful day—one powerful in a fashion of which he dreamed not. For behold, it is chronicled that in the Fort there also dwelt the lovely daughter of Gustahem, a war-like maid, skilled in athletic sports, and famed for her exploits in many a battle. Now the name of the maiden was Gurdafrid, and beholding the overthrow of Hujir, her heart was filled with anger and shame.

So, filled with fury, quickly the warrior-maiden clothed herself in burnished mail, hiding her glorious tresses under an iron helmet. Then, mounting her fiery steed, she rode boldly forth from out the gates of the White Castle, fiercely challenging the enemy to produce a champion worthy to meet her in combat, that thus the fate of the Fort might be decided.

But behold! none answered the challenge, for all thought that they gazed upon a mighty warrior, not knowing that the burnished steel hid naught but a woman with quickly-beating heart. Seeing that none of his warriors desired to take up the challenge, therefore, once more gallant Sohrab stepped gayly forth, crying:

"Methinks I see before me another wild ass for my lasso. Come forward, Puny One, for verily Hujir is lonely in his captivity."

Now having thus spoken, with a smile of exultation Sohrab rode forward to his second encounter; and the maid, at his approach, let fly a storm of arrows, attacking him first from one side, then from the other. Yea, the missiles fell thick like hail, whizzing about the hero's head so that he could not defend himself, and behold, he was angry and ashamed, for was not the whole army gazing upon his discomfiture?

Nevertheless, it was a pretty sight to watch the maid! For, as she rapidly wheeled her horse from side to side, now retiring and now advancing, smiting her shield with her spear to frighten the hero's horse, and raining her shower of arrows, verily she seemed the personification of dexterity and skill, and it looked as if the overthrow of Sohrab was at hand.

But, though for a time the contest was doubtful, the advantage was not to be always upon the side of the maiden. For Sohrab, mortified and enraged, advanced with fury, regarding not the arrows. But think not that he dismayed Gurdafrid a whit! Nay, for when she saw him approach, dexterously she threw her bow over her shoulder, put her spear in rest, and galloped to meet him. Then Sohrab, drawing his spear back until the point was almost level with his body, delivered it with all his force, striking Gurdafrid upon the girdle. Now the force of the blow was so great that it burst the fastenings of her coat of mail and hurled her from her saddle like a ball struck by a racquet, and you would have said that now the contest was ended. But not so, for, quick as a flash, the maiden twisted herself under her saddle, drew a sword from out her girdle, and cut Sohrab's spear in half. Then, having performed this feat, quickly she sprang again into her saddle and turned to go, for she was weary from the fierceness of the combat, and she saw that the day was hers.

But Sohrab, perceiving her intent, slackening the reins of his horse, galloped after the fleeing one at full speed, and, having come up with her, boldly grasped the helmet from her head; for he desired to look upon the face of the hero who could thus withstand the son of Rustem. Imagine his surprise, therefore, when from out the iron helm there rolled coil upon coil of beautiful dusky hair! For this informed him that his valiant adversary was no battle-tried warrior, but only a fair young maid. Now confounded at this most astonishing discovery, Sohrab cried:

"O Valiant One, truly thou confoundest me! For if all the daughters of Iran are like unto thee, then not even the mightiest hero can conquer thy land."

But though overwhelmed with astonishment, Sohrab neglected not to make captive his fair prisoner, though he dreamed not that as he bound her with his lasso, even so was she snaring him with her bright eyes. For continually he gazed at Gurdafrid with ever-increasing admiration, and he said:

"O Moon of Beauty, I understand it not, but verily thy soft radiance delighteth my heart more than thy brilliant splendor in battle. Seek not to escape me, therefore, for surely never captive like unto thee hath fallen into the hands of hero."

Then Gurdafrid, beholding the spell which her beauty wrought in the heart of the hero, turned unto him her fair face that was unveiled, for she perceived no other means of safety. Nevertheless, she spake derisively unto Sohrab, and she said:

"O Hero without Flaw! verily I envy thee not. For will not thy army laugh and jibe when they learn that the brave Sohrab was all but o'ercome by a woman? Let us hide this adventure, therefore, lest thy cheek have cause to blush because of me; and let us conclude a peace between us. For verily the Fort with all its soldiers and treasure now belongeth unto thee; thou hast only to follow and take possession of thine own."

Alas! Sohrab was too young and ardent not to be affected by the beauty and witchery of the maid, as well as by the fear of derision, so he was easily beguiled into following his fair captive unto the Fort. And he said:

"Verily, thou doest well to make peace with me, Fair Warrior-Maid, for though the walls of thy fortress were as high as the vaults of heaven, my club would easily level them unto the ground."

Now so speaking, the gallant Sohrab and his captive came unto the entrance of the Fort. And behold, Gustahem, when he saw their approach, opened unto them the portal, and the warrior-maid stepped leisurely over the threshold. But alas! when Sohrab would have followed after her, he was not able, for the door had swung quickly to, leaving him upon the outside. Then Sohrab knew that he had been duped, and his fury knew no bounds. And—would you believe it?—as he yet lingered, overcome with surprise and shame, lo, the beautiful warrior-maiden came out upon the battlements, and there floated down unto the hero, from her smiling lips, words of poison coated o'er with honey. And she said;

"Why, I wonder, doth the Mighty Lord of the Tartars —the Invincible Sohrab—weary himself with waiting? Surely, since he cannot stand before a mere woman, he will fall an easy prey unto the great Rustem, when the Pehliva learneth that vile robbers from Turan have broken into the land, hoping to subdue it unto black-hearted Afrasiab."

So spake the triumphant maiden, and as the mocking words floated down unto Sohrab, verily he raged with all the fury of a wild elephant. And he cried:

"Treacherous One, well mayest thou mock! but I swear, by Ormuzd and all the Peri of Paradise, that yet will I bring thee into subjection. And upon that day, verily thou shalt pay dearly for thy guile and thy double-faced words."

But the maiden, beholding how the Hero raged, laughed tormentingly, giving no heed unto his words. Then, leaning far over the battlements, so that her bewitching face was once more plainly visible to the discomfited Sohrab, again she mocked. And she said:

"Such noble stature! Such arms, and such a chest! What a pity that it should become food for jackals! Such strength, and such softness of heart! And yet, I fear me the stupid cow will soon be ruminating upon the grass which covers thy grave.   Ah, woe is me!"

Now Sohrab was covered with shame that he must hear such derisive words.   Nevertheless, the dauntless spirit of the maiden delighted him, while the soft, mocking lips, the fair, flushed cheeks, and the laughing, dark eyes exercised a strange fascination over him, causing his heart to beat with more than shame and anger.   Realizing, however, that he could not hope to compete with his fair adversary in a battle of words, he now replied proudly unto her:

"Fair Mocker! I go; but if the Fort be not surrendered by dawn to-morrow, then shall it be levelled to the dust!"

And, having thus hurled at the Warrior-maid this telling bomb, the hero gave rein unto his horse, and galloped back unto the army, followed by the sweet, mocking laugh of Gurdafrid, which rang in his ears like beautiful, tantalizing music.

True to his word, however, at dawn Sohrab marched with his army against the Fort.   But as they drew near they beheld not a single soldier upon the walls, and upon advancing unto the gates, they were found to be open, while there remained not a single armed man in the place.   You see, the truth was that the governor of the Fort, well knowing the fate that awaited them if they tarried until Sohrab stormed its walls, had escaped with all his people, in the darkness of the night, by a secret passage known only unto the Persians.

So thus was Sohrab again outwitted, and thus also vanished the Warrior-maid, so beautiful and so brave, from the sight and grasp of the bold eaglet who had flown so gayly and confidently forth from the heights of Samengan to conquer the world.

THE WRATH OF RUSTEM

NOW although Sohrab, the son of Rustem, was known throughout the length and breadth of Turan as a valiant young warrior, yet up to the time of his adventure with the Warrior-maid his fame had not spread unto Iran.

But this was now to be changed. For behold, the governor of the White Fort, when forced to give into the hands of Sohrab this key to the heart of the empire, hastily sent forth a swift messenger bearing a letter unto Kaikous the Shah. And the letter told how that an army, like unto locusts for multitude, had flown forth from Turan, at whose head rode a chief whose head towered above the stars, and whose prowess, though he was still but a child in years—shamed that of the lion, the dragon, and the fierce crocodile. Yea, and he told how that Hujir had been overcome and taken prisoner by this great champion, and how he now threatened to overrun and conquer all Persia, unless the great Shah right speedily opposed his progress.

Now Kaikous, when he had read the letter of Gustahem, was greatly troubled. So he called about him his nobles to take counsel, and behold, with one accord they cried:

"Verily, Rustem alone can deliver us from this great peril!"

So the Shah hastily summoned a scribe, dictating unto him a letter. And he said:

"O mighty Pehliva, whose glorious deeds have ever caused the throne of light to shine with splendor greater than the sun, behold, once more thy country calleth thee unto her aid! For lo! among the Tartar host there hath appeared a mighty champion whose like hath never been seen save in the house of Saum and Neriman. Already hath he demolished the White Fort, and only Rustem can bar the path that leadeth to the throne. Come quickly, then, to Iran's aid, rivalling the wind-footed dromedary in thy speed. Be it night or day, tarry not e'en to speak the word that hangeth upon thy lips, and if thou bearest roses in thy hands, stop not to smell them, lest Sohrab conquering come and all be lost."

Now having finished the letter, the Shah gave it unto a warrior named Gew to carry unto Rustem. And he said:

"O my Pehliva, truly my soul suffereth an agony of fear! Haste thou, therefore, unto the great Champion, pausing for neither rest nor food. And when thou art come unto thy journey's end, do not linger there for even an hour, for my heart crieth, haste! haste! and truly the need is great."

So Gew departed, pausing for naught until he set foot within the gates of Rustem. And so great was his speed that the watchman upon the tower at Zaboulistan, noting his approach, marvelled greatly, hastening quickly unto Rustem with the news. And he said:

"O Mighty One, the watch-tower revealeth a warrior coming by the way of Persia, riding like the wind. I fear me that he bringeth bad news."

Now being thus informed, at once Rustem and his chiefs rode out to meet the messenger, as was the Oriental custom. And when he beheld that it was Gew, he greeted him cordially, for they were old comrades in arms. Being informed of his mission, however, and of the strength and courage of the gallant young Tartar, who was causing the Shah such agony of soul, Rustem marvelled greatly. And he said:

"Verily, I should not have been surprised if such a hero as thou namest had arisen in Iran; but that a warrior of such renown should spring forth from amidst the Tartar horde is certainly past belief. Yet thou sayest—dost thou? —that the lineage of this Pehliva, so like unto Saum and the great heroes of my house, is Turanian? Strange! Now I myself have a child whom the daughter of a Tartar King bare unto me; but the child is a girl. And even if it were a son, it is yet but an infant, while that which thou sayest hath been done, surely it is not the work of a babe! But enter, I pray thee, into my house, and we will then confer further as to this matter."

Then Rustem, seeing that his guest was fatigued, commanded that a great banquet be made ready, and he feasted his comrade so royally that he caused him to forget both care and time. But when morn was come, Gew remembered the commands of his Shah, and he spake thereof unto his host, who replied unto him:

"O my brave comrade! Behold, we must all die some day. Let us, therefore, bask in the sunshine of the present! As for this Tartar, disquiet not thyself concerning him, for though he be a hero, the like of which the world hath not seen, verily he shall fall into my hands! But all in good time! To-day, however, we will feast, for I perceive that thy lips are yet parched with the speed of thy journey."

So Rustem made ready another banquet, and for three days the comrades feasted and made merry without ceasing. But on the fourth day Gew, who feared the anger of the Shah, uprose with resolve, appearing before his host girt for departure. And he said:

"O Glory of Iran, generous hath been thy hospitality, and long will it warm the heart of Gew! It behooveth us now, however, to return unto the Shah. For behold! the fear of Sohrab weigheth upon his soul like a nightmare, and he burneth with impatience, since sleep and rest have deserted his pillow, and hunger and thirst are exercising their dominion over him! Let us make haste, therefore, for well thou knowest that Kaikous is a man senseless and easily aroused to wrath."

But Rustem, smiling, replied with easy courtesy unto Gew:

"Really, comrade, there is no need for such haste! It is true that thou art right about Kaikous, but as for his anger, let it give thee not a moment's anxiety! For verily the man liveth not who dareth to be wroth with Rustem."

Nevertheless, his army being now recruited, the great Pehliva commanded that Rakush be saddled, and they set forth unto the Court; and great was the train that followed after them. And behold, when they were come near unto the King's palace, a great company of nobles rode out to meet them to do honor unto the Glory of Iran, and to conduct him into the presence of the Shah.

So, presently, Rustem entered the great audience-room of kings and, advancing unto the throne, performed obeisance unto the Lord of the World. But alas! Kaikous was black with rage, and so, opening the doors of his mouth, words of folly escaped his lips. And he said:

"So thou art come at last, O Insolent Pehliva! Verily, it is well. And now I should like to ask, 'Who is Rustem, indeed, that he dareth to defy my power and disobey my commands?' Truly, if I had a sword in my hand at this moment, like an orange would I split his head, half in half, and throw it unto the jackals! As I have not—Guards, seize him!—for I will that he be hanged alive upon the nearest gallows, and that his name be blotted out from the list of my heroes."

Now Gew, when he heard these words of anger, was confounded, and in his sore dismay he cried unto the King:

"O Lord of the World, wilt thou really lay hands upon Rustem? I pray thee, forget not that he alone is the bulwark of the throne—yea, e'en as he and his house have ever been through long generations!"

But alas! Gew's words of wisdom but fanned the blaze of the King's anger. Beside himself with fury, therefore, he raged in his wrath like unto a mad elephant, shouting with a roar that made the very throne tremble:

. "Guards! Seize yon barking dog also, and hang him alive with the other. Haste! Out of my presence!"

Now at this, Tus, who feared that Kaikous in his mad rage might do unto the Mighty One an injury, laid his hand gently upon that of Rustem, to lead him from the audience-chamber; but the Pehliva would not suffer it. Breaking away from his grasp, therefore, he stood boldly before Kaikous, his anger rivalling that of the King. And he said:

"Petty Monarch, darest thou really to rage at me—Rustem? Verily thou shalt bitterly rue thy temerity! And now, in turn I ask of thee, 'Who, after all, is Kaikous

that he ventureth to talk of the gallows unto me—Rustem?'
Listen, and I will tell it unto thee:

"Verily, Kaikous is that madman who led his brave
army into Mazinderan and Hamaveran, and who also
winged his foolish flight, once upon a time, into heaven;
Kaikous is that Shah who hath ever in his folly brought
derision and shame unto Iran and sorrow and woe unto
his subjects; Kaikous is the monarch who ever sendeth
for his Pehliva when danger threateneth, instead of going
boldly forth himself to meet his foes—aye Kaikous is a
brave fellow! for, hath he not the heart of a mouse and
the head of that stubborn creature who flappeth his long
ears and brayeth unto the moon?

"And now, having disposed of the glorious Kous, I will
answer unto thee as to Rustem:

"Verily, Rustem is the son of Zal and Saum and Neriman, heroes who have ever supported the throne of light,
and but for whom Kaikous would never have sat upon its
seat; Rustem is a free man, being slave unto none and
servant alone unto God, who hath given unto him his
glorious strength and courage; Rustem is the Pehliva
whose deeds shine as the sun in a dark world, and who
again and again hath been entreated to take his true place
upon the throne of Iran; Rustem is the Champion who
hath the world at his feet, and yet who hath desired no
throne except Rakush, no crown but his helmet, and no
sceptre but his grandsire's mighty club; yea, Rustem is
the Pehliva who, times without number, hath risked his
life to save the illustrious Kous from the penalty of his
foolish deeds.

"But at last, O Senseless One, hath Rustem reached the
end of his patience. And now he sayeth unto thee, be-

hold, when the brave Tartar chieftain cometh, go thyself
out to meet him—thou who art brave, and wise, and full of
strength and valor like unto the Shahs of Old! Perchance
thou canst then use thy boasted gallows for him. But as
for Rustem, verily thou shalt see him no more in the land
of Persia, for he is sick unto death of thy follies."

Thus spake the Great Rustem in his wrath, and having
finished, fearlessly he turned him, and strode unhindered
from out the presence-chamber. And having mounted
upon Rakush, lo, he vanished, ere the dumfounded Kaikous had rallied from his astonishment.

Now the nobles and chiefs of Iran were greatly troubled
by the wrath of Rustem, for they were sheep and the
Great Pehliva was their shepherd. So they murmured
against Kaikous, saying:

"Truly the Shah, in his anger, hath forgotten all gratitude and decency! else how dare he threaten the Great
Rustem, to whom he oweth his life and his throne, with
the vile gallows? Verily, the wrath of the Mighty One is
righteous! But what, alas, is to become of Iran, if her
only invincible Champion forsaketh her now that so great
a peril threateneth?"

So talked the nobles of Iran, and finally in their dilemma
they decided to choose a mediator, Gudarz the Aged, who
should stand before the King; and, though the mission was
fraught with danger, Gudarz quailed not, but spake long
and without fear unto the Shah, counting over, as a string
of pearls, each glorious deed of Rustem. And having so
spoken, then fearlessly he reproached the weak monarch
with ingratitude. And he said:

"O King of Kings, can it really be possible that so soon
thou hast blotted out from thy book of remembrance all

that Rustem hath done for thee and this land? How he conquered Mazinderan and the Great White Deev; and how he gave back unto thee the sight of thy eyes? Yet now as his reward thou commandest that he be hanged alive upon a gallows, thou who art King only by his grace! Now I ask thee to answer me truly—is this the justice of a great and wise Monarch, or that worthy of the great King of Kings?

Alas! beholding his acts, spread out thus naked before him, Kaikous was ashamed of that which he had said in his anger. So, humbling himself before Gudarz, he said:

"O white-haired Pehliva, verily thou speakest well! The words of a mighty monarch should be those of wisdom and not such as provoke wrath. Go, therefore, unto Rustem and say unto him that Kaikous repenteth him of his bitter words and calleth him back to be his most honored Pehliva."

So, thus armed, swiftly Gudarz rode forth in search of the angry Rustem, and behold, all the mighty chiefs of Iran joined themselves unto him, so that there was a great company. Now they rode fast and far before they overtook the anger-spurred hero, but when they were finally come up with him, lo, the entire company prostrated themselves in the dust before him. And Gudarz said:

"O Hero of Heroes! Listen, I pray thee, unto the words of an aged warrior who loveth both thee and Iran well. Now truly thy wrath is just, and so have I said unto Kaikous, whose thoughts in his anger o'erflow like unto new wine that fermenteth, being sour and bitter unto the taste. But, though hasty, the Shah soon repenteth him of his anger, and behold, already is he both ashamed and sorry for his ingratitude unto the Pehliva, who is the light of his eyes and the support of his throne!

"Now as for Kaikous—alas! For yet oft must the sun revolve above his head ere he learneth the wisdom of the great—even as hath been so aptly said by Zal, thy silver-crowned father. But behold, the whole world knoweth that Rustem is noble of mind as well as wise, and brave, and strong of limb! And though he be justly angered against the Shah, yet hath Iran done no wrong that it should be left to fall into the hands of black-hearted Afrasiab."

So spake the aged Gudarz in his wisdom. But alas! though so aptly spoken, the words fell upon deaf ears, for Rustem was still in a towering rage. Turning unto the old man, therefore, he said:

"Speak not unto me of Kaikous, Brave Gudarz—either of his anger or his repentance—for what is he unto me but a grain of vile dust? Behold, Rustem feareth only his Creator, and from henceforth Him alone will he serve. As for Kaikous, let him do his worst, for verily I am not only sick, but ashamed in my soul of his weakness and follies, and I will fight no more of his battles."

Now when the nobles heard these words, they wailed in sorrow, and cast dust upon their heads. But Gudarz despaired not, for he had not grown old at the Court without learning much of human nature, which he knew to be the same in a great hero as in ordinary mortals. So, in his wisdom, he still held in reserve a barbed arrow, sharp enough to pierce even the armor of the invincible Rustem; and this he now shot forth, saying gently unto the hero:

"O Glorious One, all that thou sayest, verily it is just and true! But it appeareth unto me that there remaineth

somewhat still to be considered. For, when it shall be
learned throughout the land that the Mighty Rustem—
undisputed Champion of the Whole World—hath fled
before the face of a much-heralded Tartar chief, young
and full of prowess, will not all the warriors say:

"'Alas! alas! We had not thought it, but truly Rustem
is getting past his prime. What a pity that a hero's glory
vanisheth so quickly, when he beginneth to grow old!
Now soon will Rustem also be heard of no more, for since
he feareth this valiant young Tartar, surely he must be
a mighty hero, who will soon supplant the Elephant-
limbed as Champion of the World.'

"Yea, greatly I fear, O mighty One, that not only this,
but much more bitter unto the taste will be said. Therefore I, Gudarz the Aged, ask thee: Is it wise, at this hour,
to turn from thy allegiance unto the Shah, thus tarnishing
thy glory and causing the downfall of Iran to rest upon
thy head? Verily, nay; for thy retreat would be the path
of folly, which thy soul hateth. Put from thee, therefore,
the empty words of Kaikous, and lead us forth unto battle
against this Tartar. For verily it must not be said that
Rustem feared to fight a beardless boy!"

Thus sharp was the poison-tipped arrow of Gudarz,
and not fruitlessly did it speed unto its mark. For behold!
Rustem stood confounded by this view of the matter, such
thoughts being new unto him. Rallying from his surprise, however, he said proudly unto the Shah's messenger:

"Verily, if by searching, Rustem could find one atom of
fear in his heart, quickly would he tear his soul from his
body in shame! But the slayer of the Great White Deev
needeth not to vindicate his courage, for it is known unto
all the world."

So spake Rustem. Nevertheless, he continued to ponder the words of Gudarz, for he knew them to be the message of an old man grown wise in the thoughts of men. And so, the current of his anger being changed, soon he decided to do for the sake of Iran, what he knew to be right. For, though he really feared not for his glory, yet well he knew that none but Rustem could meet this crisis in the history of his country. And besides, deep in his soul was the longing to meet this vaunted Tartar champion and joy once more in battle.

Therefore, great were the shouts of joy when, in obedience to his master's hand, Rakush faced once more toward Persia. But verily it was with proud step and uplifted head that the hero appeared once more before the Shah. When Kaikous beheld Rustem, however, so great was his relief that he stepped down from off his throne to welcome him, saying unto him in deep humility of spirit:

"O glorious Pehliva! Verily, I am foolish of soul, as thou sayest, and not worthy to sit upon the throne of light. But must not a man be as Ormuzd hath made him? Now thou art brave, but alas! my heart was full of fear because of this mighty Tartar, and I looked unto thee for safety, for art thou not the bulwark of my throne? But, though haste is my birthright, long thou wert in coming, and so in my wrath I spake unto thee foolish words, though now my mouth is full of dust."

So spake the contrite Shah, and Rustem, beholding his humility, replied unto Him:

"O King of Kings! Verily the world is thy footstool, and all its inhabitants thy slaves, for such is the prerogative of the Shahs. As for Rustem, ever hath his loins been girt in fealty unto Iran, and so may it ever be while he liveth."

So, peace being once more restored, Kaikous made a great feast, inviting unto it all his heroes. But of all the mighty ones present, none were lauded save only Rustem, the Champion of the World, before whom rich gifts were poured—yea, until mountain high rose the enormous pile! Then, and not until then, did Kaikous say unto the slaves "enough!" for Rustem would have no more. And now all was well again within the gates of the Shah, for lo! the wrath of Rustem had been appeased.

RUSTEM THE SPY

BEHOLD! on the morning following the reconciling feast of Kaikous and Rustem, the Shah caused the clarions of war to be sounded throughout the city, calling the loyal sons of Iran to go forth to meet the Tartar host. Now over one hundred thousand horsemen in glittering mail responded unto the call, so that the earth was covered with warriors like unto blades of grass, and all the air was darkened with their spears. A troop of ponderous war-elephants also accompanied the legions, making the ground tremble beneath their mighty tread.

Thus marched the army, and so imposing was it that when at evening they pitched their tents, and the torches gleamed in the canvas streets, the camp seemed like unto a great city. So, marching by day and resting at night, the legions finally drew near unto the White Castle, where Sohrab still remained, preparing his forces for an advance upon the capital. When they were come unto the plains where stood the great fortress, however, they set up their tents silently in the dead of night, planning a surprise for the Tartars.

Now thus it happened that, the black veil of night being lifted, behold, the watchman upon the high towers of the White Fortress saw spread out on the plains before him an immense white city, set up as by magic. Surprised and dismayed, therefore, he set up a great shout, which at once brought Sohrab and Human, the two great Tartar chiefs, out upon the ramparts.

And behold! when Human saw upon every side the mighty Persian legions, looking so brave and formidable, he grew suddenly pale, and trembled like unto an aspen. But Sohrab, demanding a cup of wine, drank unto their destruction, speaking words of cheer unto his companion. And he said:

"Look, Brave Human! There are many men in this hostile army, it is true, but within its ranks I see no hero with mighty mace who can stand against the fearless son of Rustem. When that mighty champion himself appeareth, then will it be time indeed for us to rally our courage. But as for these others—why, they are but dogs! And see, I spit upon them! for without Rustem to inspire them, they have neither courage nor heart."

So saying, Sohrab went down from the ramparts, and proceeding unto his pavilion, which was pitched upon the plain in front of the Fort, he invited his great warriors and chiefs unto a banquet. Yea, gayly he issued his invitations, saying unto his guests:

> "To-day let us feast; let us banquet to-day,
> For to-morrow to battle we'll hasten away."

But behold! at Sohrab's banquet there was to be one uninvited guest. For when night had swathed the earth in darkness, Rustem the Mighty went boldly unto the King, demanding permission to go forth unarmed to spy out the forces of the enemy, and to learn the character of the chieftains opposed unto him—particularly of Sohrab, whose renown had aroused such dread in the heart of Kaikous.

So, permission being granted, the dauntless Rustem clad himself in the dress of a Tartar, and thus disguised, under the cover of darkness, he stole forth like a lion which stalketh a herd of antelopes, penetrating into the very presence of the great Sohrab and his warriors as they sat at their feast. Now so stealthy had been his advance that none dreamed of his presence as they feasted and made merry around the festal board—nay, not even the valiant Sohrab, as he sat relating unto his warriors some of the mighty deeds of the heroes of old.

Wherefore, as Rustem stood by the door watching, he beheld that the young Champion was like unto a tall cypress of good sap, while round about him were seated more than a hundred brave warriors, scarcely equalled in the Persian army—so fiery and courageous appeared they as they listened unto the inspiring tales of Sohrab. And it was indeed a festive scene! For torches gave back the flash of arms, and the gleam of eyes eager for the morrow's battle, even as they were now bright with the red wine which slaves poured from golden bugles into the crystal glasses before them. And behold, not only was there glorious fare to delight the palate, but music to charm the ear! So gayety and merriment ruled the hour; neither did they dream of coming sorrow.

But as Rustem watched the scene from the shadow of the door, presently it came to pass that Zendeh, one of the warriors, having occasion to go forth, came nigh unto the spot where the Hero was concealed. Now Zendeh was brother unto the Princess Tamineh, who had sent him forth with her son that he might point out unto him his father, whom he alone knew of all the army. And the Princess did this that harm might not befall should the two champions meet in battle. But alas! as Zendeh retired from the banquet, it chanced that he perceived the shadow of some one in ambush. So, advancing unto the place where Rustem was hidden, he said quietly:

"Vile Persian! Come forth into the light that I may see thy face. For well I know, by thy stature, that thou belongest unto Iran."

Now unto this Rustem answered never a word. But ere Zendeh had ceased from speaking, he struck him so fierce a blow upon the nape of the neck that he laid him dead at his feet. So, though there was to be no more feasting and fighting for Zendeh, yet so swift and silent had been Death's messenger, that the revellers within dreamed not that the Dark Angel still hovered at the door.

But presently Sohrab, beholding his uncle's place at the table still vacant, asked wherefore he tarried; and, attention being thus called to his long absence, one of the chiefs went forth to seek him. Now in so doing he found the body of the unfortunate warrior cold upon the pavement. Quickly returning unto Sohrab, therefore, he related unto him in an awed voice the fatal happening. But Sohrab would not believe that, almost within their midst, without a struggle or cry, death could have so suddenly o'ertaken his uncle. So, commanding that torches be brought, he ran quickly unto the spot of the tragedy, followed by all the warriors and bright singing-girls. But alas! here Sohrab found that the bad news was indeed true; and being sore grieved, he said unto his nobles:

"Woe! Woe unto Turan! For behold! the wolf hath stolen into the fold and, in spite of the shepherds and the dogs, hath taken the best of the flock. But verily, God helping me, I will be fully avenged for the death of Zendeh!"

Now having thus spoken, Sohrab came back unto his place at the table and continued the feast. For, though his own heart was heavy with sorrow, he wished not the spirits of his warriors to be dampened by pity, or fear of this terrible, silent, unknown foe. Raising his glass unto his lips, therefore, he cried lustily:

"Drink, my brave comrades, drink! Death to the slayer of Zendeh, and destruction, utter and sure, unto the Persian host."

So the warriors and chiefs all drank, standing upon their feet; and as the hours passed by, Sohrab continued to fan into a yet more glowing flame the lust of battle which slumbered in each warrior's soul, so that finally one and all desired naught but death unto the Persians, and a glorious victory for Sohrab, their gallant young leader, whom they toasted with such mighty shouts of pride and joy that it was heard even within the lines of Iran.

As for Rustem, having accomplished his purpose, after silencing Zendeh, he returned quickly and silently unto the Persian camp, knowing not that his victim was the loved brother of Tamineh, who was to have stood between Sohrab and his fate.

But behold, as Rustem would have entered the Persian lines he encountered Gew, who was acting that night as sentry. Now as this doughty warrior suddenly perceived— looming up mountain-high out of the darkness—a warrior clad in the garb of a Tartar, his heart quaked with fear, for he thought that surely he had to do with Sohrab, the terrible Tartar Champion. Nevertheless, he quickly drew his sword ready for combat, challenging the invader to give his name and errand.

Now this demand was greeted by a burst of mighty laughter, for Rustem, surmising from the quaver in Gews' voice what his thought had been, could not but enjoy the situation. Still laughing, therefore, he said unto Gew:

"Brave comrade! tremble not so. For lo! thou beholdest before thee a most harmless creature—Rustem the Spy—who returneth from the banquet of Sohrab and his chiefs. Now Sohrab presenteth his compliments unto Gew, the brave warrior of the Persians, saying that he will be unable to meet him until to-morrow, when he will hurl forth unto him his challenge to combat."

So spake the Mighty Rustem unto Gew, twitting him yet again upon his lion's roar and his great disappointment at being deprived of his much-longed-for combat with Sohrab. Then when they had laughed together, Rustem described unto Gew his adventure, ceasing not to sing the praise of Sohrab, who, he said, had not his equal in the world.

Whereupon, having thus spoken, the Great Champion said good-night unto his comrade, bidding him roar gently in case of danger. And so with merry jest ended the adventure of Rustem the Spy.

THE COMBAT OF SOHRAB AGAINST RUSTEM

G IVE ear unto the combat of Sohrab against Rustem, though it be a tale replete with tears. So runneth the legend as told by Firdusi. But upon the morning after the night of feasting in his pavilion, tears were far from the eyes of brave Sohrab. For was he not bent upon the accomplishment of great deeds? Yea, and did he not hope soon to behold the face of his illustrious father?

But alas! a bitter disappointment awaited the hero in the early morning, for in vain did he try to learn from Hujir, the defeated champion of the White Fort, which of the mighty warriors encamped upon the plains before them was Rustem, the great hero of the Persians. For that brave patriot, fearing for the safety of Iran, refused utterly to discover the identity of the Great Champion unto his enemy, even though Sohrab strongly suspected a certain great warrior in a green tent, who was, indeed, Rustem.

Defeated in this endeavor, therefore, Sohrab returned unto the Fort, where, donning his chain mail and arming himself, he and his band of sturdy warriors sallied forth unto the plain. Now so sudden and swift was the onset that the Persians were taken unawares, so that Sohrab in hurling the army of Turan against the intrenched camp of the Shah, was able to penetrate almost at once unto its very centre. And truly it was a magnificent sight to behold the irresistible charge of this stripling, who, though but a mere youth, yet appeared a very god of war.

But, though taken by surprise, the Persians soon rallied, and then so fearful was the contest that the very earth seemed to shake beneath the shock, and the carnage was fearful. For, though from end to end the plain glittered with bright steel armor, it covered, alas, the forms of fallen heroes as often as it shielded the daring hearts of living riders, since as the tide of battle ebbed and flowed, thousands fell upon either side, night alone putting an end to the fearful conflict.

Now through all the long hours of battle, although Sohrab seemed to be everywhere upon the field, never once did he catch a glimpse of the owner of the green tent, and much he wondered. Nay; not even when he thundered forth words of pride in the very face of the Shah, telling him he had sworn to hang him alive upon a gallows, to avenge the death of Zendeh, and challenging him to combat, did he—or any other champion—stand forth. So great was the terror that his valor had aroused in the hearts of his foes!

But in spite of the day's successes, that night Sohrab lay wakeful in his tent, restlessly tossing upon his bed of skins, while busy thoughts surged through his brain. Finally, however, when the first faint streak of dawn had crimsoned the eastern sky, behold, the Hero arose, passing through the silent line of tents, until he reached the one set apart for Piran-Wisa, the old chief who had but reached the scene of battle the by-gone eve. Here, lifting the heavy curtain, Sohrab entered silently, but seeing that his old friend was also awake, he said:

"O glorious chief, whose wisdom hath ever been my guiding star, behold, once more I come to seek thy counsel and to make known unto thee a plan which hath kept me wakeful upon my bed.

"Now it is indeed well to fight valiantly and win success upon the field of battle as we did to-day, but for me, Sohrab, that is not enough; for I long without ceasing to perform some mighty deed that shall reach the ears of Rustem, my father, whom I seem destined never to find. So now I have reached a conclusion: I would have thee challenge the bravest of the Persian Pehliva to meet me, man to man, in single combat. If I prevail, Rustem will surely learn of it; while if I fail, no man need hear of me again."

So spake impetuous Sohrab, and Piran-Wisa listened quietly. When he had finished, however, he said unto him:

"My son, much I love thy valorous spirit, which hath ever striven and longed for the noblest and best. Nevertheless, in this matter I counsel thee to think of thy mother, and be content to share the common risk of battle which falleth unto all alike. Or if thou wouldst seek that loved father whom thou hast never seen, seek him where men say he now dwelleth, in far-off Seistan with his aged father Zal."

But to this wise advice Sohrab replied passionately:

"Alas, good old Piran! Canst thou not understand that I wish not to go unto my father empty-handed? I am so proud of him, and with reason I must make him proud of his son also. For are we not of the same noble blood? And see! am I not tall, and strong, and brave, like unto my father? Fear not, therefore, for truly I will overcome the bravest of the warriors sent out by the Persians to meet me. Then surely the great Rustem will hear of it and I shall perhaps meet him."

Now though Piran-Wisa liked not the plan, yet could he not withstand Sohrab's eloquent pleading. For verily who can restrain the eagle in his flight toward the sun?

Having given his consent unto the challenge, therefore, the old general summoned unto him his herald, and taking his ruler's staff in his hand, he went forth, marshalling the whole Tartar army upon the plain. Then the Persians, noting this move of the enemy, also formed into battle array opposite, bright in burnished steel and splendid in rank upon rank of brave warriors.

And presently, all being in readiness, Piran-Wisa advanced unto the front, while the herald blew a blast upon his trumpet to make known that he had something to say. Then silence, deep and thrilling, reigned in both great armies as Piran, in ringing tones, offered Sohrab's challenge.

And when the Tartar host heard called the name of their champion, behold, they rent the air with their shouts, cheering long and loud for Sohrab. No Persian, they felt sure, could match their gallant young leader, who now, in all the pride of his youth and strength, advanced and stood by Piran-Wisa's side.

But alas! unexpected was this call unto the Persians, and as a consequence deep silence reigned within the lines of Iran. For so great was the fear of Sohrab that no man dared take up the challenge. After the first shock, however, from mouth to mouth there was breathed the one word: Rustem! Rustem! So quickly Kaikous sent a messenger unto the Great Pehliva, saying:

"O Mighty One! Come quickly, for behold, the faces of my warriors grow pale before this young Tartar, and only thy sword can cause the sun to weep."

Now when Gudarz, the messenger, entered the tent of Rustem, the hero rose and greeted him joyfully, both hands outstretched in welcome. "These eyes could see no better sight," he cried; and added quickly, "What news?"

Then Gudarz delivered his message, hearing which, Rustem frowned, for he remembered the bravery of the Shahs of Old, and the cowardice of Kaikous made him sick with shame. Nevertheless, he said nothing, being too angry for words. Whereupon, Gudarz continued:

"Truly, this young hero is marvellous! and this time, Kaikous is not to be condemned for his terror. For, as I live, the Champion existeth not who can match Sohrab —save only Rustem the Mighty, unto whom all eyes turn."

But Rustem, who was once more angered at Kaikous, replied bitterly unto Gudarz:

"If the Shah himself feareth to meet this young lion, let him send forth any one of the young striplings whom he, in these days, delighteth to honor. When other Shahs have called me, it hath been sometimes unto battle and sometimes unto the banquet, but behold, Kaikous never calleth me except to fight for him. Therefore, I say, let one of the King's favorites meet Sohrab to-day; I will fight him to-morrow."

Gudarz, however, would not listen unto Rustem when he spoke thus of delay, but urged him even as he had upon another great occasion, saying unto him:

"Take heed, O Mighty One, lest men say that thou fearest to peril thy fame with younger men!"

Then Rustem, frowning with displeasure, consented to
meet the Champion, but only upon condition that he fight
unknown and in plain arms. So, his consent being won,
the hero was allowed neither to linger nor to waste time
in words; for quickly the nobles buckled upon him his
armor, threw his leopard-skin around him, saddled Rakush and made him ready for the strife. Now when he appeared among the Persians they greeted him with mighty
shouts of pride and joy, causing the Tartars to wonder
much as to the identity of this stalwart Champion fighting
in plain armor and giving no name.

But behold! the combatants being now ready, at a
signal the Persian and the Tartar hosts formed themselves
into two long lines, down which the two great Champions
advanced to meet each other.

Now as Rustem moved forward, once more he eyed
with wonder the slender youth who dared thus to defy all
the most valiant chiefs of the army. Who could he be?
Where was he reared? What was there about him so
strangely familiar? As he gazed, therefore, suddenly a
great pity filled his soul that this noble-spirited youth, so
full of life and manly beauty, must shortly be lying upon
the sand, his life-blood paying the penalty for his temerity.
Verily, never had Rustem, the fierce warrior, felt moved
like this before, and so he spake gently unto his adversary,
saying:

"O Young Man, the air of heaven is soft and warm, but
the grave is damp and cold. Wherefore, then, wilt thou
rush upon death? Truly pity filleth my soul at the thought,
and I would not take from thee the boon of life. Yet if we
combat together, surely wilt thou fall by my hands, for
behold! I am vast and clad in iron, and tried, and none

have been able to withstand my power—neither man, nor
Deev, nor dragon. Desist, therefore, from this perilous
enterprise, and come over unto Iran. Then shalt thou be
as a son unto me, and fight beneath my banner while I live,
winning both honor and fame."

So spake Rustem, and Sohrab, listening unto his voice,
and gazing upon his mighty form, planted like a great
tower upon the plain, felt his heart go out unto him
strangely. And, a sudden hope filling his soul, eagerly he
ran forward, knelt before the hero, and gazing up at him
wistfully, said:

"O Glory of the World, verily my heart leapeth forth to
greet thee as unto a loved kinsman! Tell unto me, therefore, thy name, for it seemeth unto me that thou must be
Rustem, the mighty son of White-haired Zal. For surely
unto none other is it given to be so gloriously perfect as
thou!"

But Rustem, misunderstanding Sohrab's ardor, replied
coldly unto him, saying:

"Rash Boy! Men look upon Rustem's face and flee.
And well I know that if that mighty hero stood here to-
day, then would there be no further talk of fighting. But,
unfortunately for thy pride, thou hast now to do with no
noble Pehliva, but with a comman man, possessing neither
throne, nor palace, nor crown."

Now Rustem spake thus sternly unto the youth that he
might be afraid when he beheld his prowess, and think
that still greater might was hidden in the camp of the
Persians.

But Sohrab, when he heard the words of Rustem, was
sad, and his hopes, that had risen so high as he beheld his
mighty antagonist, were shattered. Yea, and the day that

had looked so bright was made dark unto his eyes. Howbeit, hiding his disappointment, with flashing eyes he replied unto Rustem:

"Fierce Warrior! Thinkest thou to terrify me by thy proud words? If so, verily thou errest. Now it is true that thou art more vast and tried than I, but unto whom will be the victory only the event will teach us in its hour. Yet in one thing, I give thee right: Did Rustem stand where thou art standing now, then, indeed, would there be no combat here to-day. But come! Let us not parley words."

So the two Champions chose a narrow place, marked out the lists, and mounted upon their powerful steeds, ready for the combat. Now they began the attack by hurling their javelins; and when they were blunted against the steel bucklers they drew their long Indian swords and fell to work again. And behold, when their swords were broken, then they used their clubs. Terrible blows they dealt each other with these implements of war and great was the skill and agility with which they fought, calling forth many a shout of admiration from the breathlessly-watching armies.

Nevertheless, they seemed to be about equally matched in wariness, skill, and strength. For, though Rustem's eye shot fire as he raised high his spear and hurled it down with swift, unerring aim, quick as a flash Sohrab sprang to one side, and the spear buried itself deep in the sand, doing naught of harm. In return for this, however, Sohrab struck full upon Rustem's shield, so that the iron rang and rang again. Then Rustem, furious, seized his gigantic club, which no one but himself could wield, and with one mighty stroke would have felled Sohrab to the earth, had he not again been too quick for him in springing aside. But alas! the club came thundering down with such prodigious force that it caused Rustem himself to fall forward and loose his hold upon it. And behold! in an instant, Sohrab could have pierced the fallen hero where he lay. But instead he drew back, without even unsheathing his sword, saying unto his unknown foe:

"O Mighty One! Thou sayest thou art not Rustem. Well, be it so! But who art thou, then, that thou canst so touch my soul? I pray thee, let the fight end here, and let there be peace twixt thee and me."

But Rustem, trembling with rage and fury, would not hearken unto the words of Sohrab; rather, they increased his wrath and shame. For it was, indeed, bitter for the old Champion to think that he owed his life unto this slight, sunny youth. So, again seizing his spear, with taunting, bitter words he rushed upon Sohrab, attacking him with renewed vigor. Then Sohrab saw that this fight must be to the death, and he, too, allowed the lust of conquest to take full possession of his soul.

Falling to again, therefore, behold, the heroes fought until their spears were shivered, and their swords hacked like unto saws, and all their weapons were bent and broken. Even then, however, they did not desist, but wrestled with each other until the sweat and blood ran down from their bodies and their throats were parched and dry like unto parchment. But at last so weary were they that neither the warriors nor their horses could move more, yet to neither was given the victory. So, with mail shattered and torn, and with bruised and wounded bodies, the exhausted heroes stayed them awhile to rest. Then Rustem said unto himself:

They drew their long Indian swords and fell to work again.

"Verily, never in all my long life of battle have I seen man or demon with such strength and activity as is possessed by this redoubtable Sohrab! Why, even my great battle with the White Deev was but as child's play unto this, and though never yet have I been conquered, alas, now my heart faileth me before this youth without a name!"

But Sohrab, when he had rested for a few minutes, thus gaily addressed his antagonist:

"Ho, Angry One! when thou art rested, come and try if thou canst fight with bow and arrow."

So presently the Champions fell to again, fighting with arrows; but still one could not surpass the other, though they rained from their bows like hail. Then, in desperation, Rustem seized Sohrab by the belt, hoping to drag him from his saddle, as he had done unto many a hero in battle. But alas! it availed him naught. For as soon could a mountain be moved from its base as Sohrab from his saddle. And neither could Sohrab lift his antagonist, though mightily he strove to perform this feat of strength.

So, being thus unsuccessful both with arrows and in wrestling, once more the champions betook themselves to clubs, and after a time Sohrab succeeded in dealing Rustem a mighty blow that bruised his shoulder. Now so great was the agony that Rustem writhed under it, though he was strong enough to stifle any cry of pain. Nevertheless, Sohrab saw that he had struck a telling blow, and, smiling, he taunted the wounded one, saying:

"O Smitten Lion! Truly thou art brave, but how canst thou hope to stand against the blows of the strong? But alas! it is thy age that disableth thee. Go, therefore, and measure thy strength with thy equals, for verily it is folly for the aged to try to match themselves with the young and strong."

Now so furious was Rustem at the taunts of Sohrab that, in his frenzy, he turned suddenly upon the army of the Tartars, charging its ranks even as a tiger rusheth upon his prey. And behold! when Sohrab saw this, he in his turn, fell upon the Persians, scattering them like a flock of sheep before him. Whereupon, Rustem, beholding the flight of his countrymen, turned quickly from pursuing the Tartars, crying fiercely unto Sohrab:

"O Man of Blood! Why hast thou fallen upon the Persians like a wolf upon the fold?"

Turning in astonishment, therefore, at this most surprising question, Sohrab said:

"Thou Mad Elephant! Didst not thou, thyself, first charge the Tartar host, though they had not joined in battle? Wherefore, then, reproach me?"

Now Sohrab was still gay and unruffled, and Rustem's heart sank as he beheld how fresh and full of vigor was this laughing stripling, for all the hard day's fight. So he said:

"Behold! night descendeth upon the plain. It is too late, therefore, to renew the combat to-day. If thou art still for war, however, we will fight again to-morrow, and God shall decide who is the better man."

So, by mutual consent, the heroes now separated, each riding back to his own army, where they were received with shouts of admiration, which rang and rang again. But, strange to say, it was Sohrab's gay farewell that rang longest in Rustem's ears, for his soul was filled with wonder and admiration at the lightness and strength of this mavellous youth. Seeking Kaikous, therefore, who was all unnerved by the day's conflict, in reply to his eager questions Rustem said:

"O Lord of the World, truly my heart misgiveth me, for never during my long life have I witnessed such overwhelming valor as hath been exhibited this day by yon laughing boy, whose body, I should say, was formed of iron, were it not for his remarkable lightness. For behold! I have fought him with sword, and spear, and arrow, and mace—not only once, but again and again—and yet remaineth he alive and merry. In the warrior's art he appeareth to be my superior, and Ormuzd alone knoweth what will be the outcome of the conflict to-morrow. May he grant unto his servant sufficient strength and courage for the hour!"

Now after his conference with the Shah, Rustem returned unto his tent, where he held serious converse with Zuara, his young brother, saying unto him:

"O my brother! Behold, it hath been given unto me to fight this day with a champion, the power of whose arm is prodigious! I say unto thee, therefore, that should anything untoward happen upon the morrow when the conflict is renewed, verily it will fall unto thee to see that my army is returned in safety unto Zabulistan. And thou must also console my mother in her sorrow, bidding her not to bind her heart forever unto the dead, since her son hath no cause to complain of fate. And say unto Zal, my silver-crowned father, that since old and young must die, what mattereth it if it be written in the stars that only another sun shall shine for Rustem, since he hath lived long and fought gloriously for Iran!"

Meanwhile, in the camp of the Tartars, Sohrab, also,

lauded the might of his unknown antagonist, saying unto Human:

"Alas, Brave Human! Though I understand it not, truly my heart is strangely drawn unto the mighty warrior with whom I have fought this day. I seem to see in him, too, all the signs by which my mother told me I was to recognize my father, and my heart is filled with misgivings. Verily, I must not fight against my father!"

But Human, following the directions of the King, replied unto Sohrab:

"O Glory of the World! Naught but the longings of thine own heart give credence unto thy words. Now oft have I looked upon the face of Rustem in battle, and mine eyes have beheld his deeds of valor, but alas! this man in nowise resembleth him, save in bulk alone. Neither is his horse the famous Rakush; nor is his manner of wielding his club the same. In fostering this thought, thy imagination carrieth thee away."

Now though Sohrab suspected not the plot which Afrasiab had formed for his destruction, yet was he not wholly satisfied with Human's words. Howbeit, as he could not refute them, he held his peace. And that night, also, feasted he gaily with his chiefs.

Nevertheless, when the harbinger of a new day had lightened the sky and cleared away the shadows, behold, Sohrab donned his cuirass and his helmet and, arming himself, mounted his horse and rode into the space between the two armies. Then Rustem, beholding his antagonist, also rode out from among the Persians.

So once more the champions met, and behold, as Sohrab greeted Rustem his mouth was full of smiles, for how could it be otherwise when his heart was as full of sunshine as the new Eastern day with light? Gaily, therefore, he said unto the Pehliva:

"Ah, let us not fight to-day, Old Dragon! for as soon would I combat with my own father as with thee. Rather, let us sit together upon the ground, and thou shalt relate unto me thy deeds of valor. For verily my soul delighteth in heroic tales—as my mother could say unto thee—and thy life hath been full of them, I know. Yea, if I mistake not, even the great Rustem, thy countryman, canst thou rival in thy thrilling adventures and conquests, and much I should like to hear them. As for combat, there are plenty of other brave men with whom thou canst do battle, but with me, I pray thee, make a covenant of friendship, for my heart sayeth unto me that we were not meant to be foes.

But Rustem, who still thought that Sohrab spake in guile, replied unto him:

"O Hero of Tender Age! Behold, we are met here to fight, and not to blow forth empty wind upon the air. Save thy words of lure, therefore, for "other brave men," if perchance thou livest to meet them in battle; for verily my ears are sealed against them. As for me, I am an old man, and thou art young, but forget not that it is the Master of the World who holdeth the balance in his hands."

Then Sohrab, rising lightly unto his feet, said:

"Old Champion, I see I have spoken in vain, and it grieveth me. Now I would have had thee die upon thy bed, when thy time should come, but behold! thou art brave enough to prefer a hero's death. Well, so be it! at least thou shalt die gloriously, after the fight of thy life— and what can even the beloved of Ormuzd ask more?"

So once more the two champions prepared for combat. And—this time we are informed—the place of contest was in the centre of a lonely, treeless plain, through which coursed a deep, winding river. Yea, and gloomy gray mountains skirted the distant horizon, so that, in spite of the brilliant Eastern sunshine, it was a scene of dreariness and mystic solitude. For, to prevent the two armies from falling upon each other in the excitement of the conflict, the chiefs had removed them to a distance of several miles from the scene of battle, so that the two champions were the only living figures upon the plain.

Now as the combat was to be renewed upon foot, the two heroes fastened their steeds unto the rocks, and then, clad in complete mail, they approached each other stealthily, and in diminishing circles, each watching for the chance to pounce like a lion upon his foe. And behold! when the two champions met, so terrific was the crash of their encounter that it was heard, like thunder, from end to end of the standing hosts. And then, so terrible was the fight that even the sun refused to shine upon so unnatural a conflict; and the heavens, too, grew dark and lowering, as though in sore displeasure; and the wind rose, moaning and sweeping the plain in anger.

But still the heroes fought on—unconscious of the frown of nature—from morning until noonday. Yea, and from noonday until it was time for the shadows to lengthen upon the plain. Yet unto neither was given the advantage.

Presently, however, Sohrab's shield was almost cloven by a terrific stroke from Rustem's sword. The iron plating flew, but, fortunately, the good steel yet resisted. Then Sohrab, with his sword, smote off the proudly-waving crest of Rustem's helm—that plume which never yet had bowed

unto the dust; seeing which, Rustem clenched his teeth
—and still they fought on!

And now the gloom grew blacker, angry storm clouds
rumbling overhead; but the fierce combatants heard it not.
Then, quite suddenly, Rakush the intelligent put forth
a fearful cry—a cry so unearthly, so full of woe, that a
shiver ran through all the Persian lines. But it troubled
not the combatants, for, unconscious of it, still they fought
on!

Howbeit, presently leaping like a lion, Sohrab seized Rustem by the girdle, lifted him from the ground, and hurled
him down, his face and mouth buried deep in the dust.
Then he couched upon him—yea, even as a beast of the
jungle coucheth upon its prey! Yea, and he drew his
sword, thinking to sever his enemy's head—even as was
the Oriental custom. But at this crisis, Rustem, gifted
with the wisdom and cunning of long experience, realizing
his peril, opened his mouth and said unto Sohrab:

"Stay, thou Wild Elephant! Knowest thou not the
customs of chivalrous warfare? Now it is written in the
laws of honor that he who overthroweth a brave man for
the first time shall not destroy him, but wait until the
second throw when usage entitleth the victor honorably
to take the life of the vanquished. Behold! this is our
custom though it appeareth not to be thine."

Alas! Sohrab, who was as generous of heart as he was
brave, hearing the words of Rustem, immediately removed his grasp from the Hero, and permitting him to rise,
agreed to a short truce.

As for Rustem, scarcely believing himself alive after
such a narrow escape, gratefully he returned thanks unto
Ormuzd, looking upon it as nothing short of a miracle.

Then, having bathed his limbs, covered with dust and blood, in the river, he readjusted his torn armor, and sat him down to rest, wondering how this desperate duel would finally end.

But no such misgivings troubled Sohrab as he rested. Nor was he alone; for Human, beholding the truce, came out unto the Hero to ask of the adventures of the day. When Sohrab related unto him of the fight, however, and of how he had spared Rustem, Human reproached him for his folly, saying:

"Alas, O Sohrab! The lion whom thou so unwisely released from thy toils hath caught thee in a yet more cunning snare. Beware, therefore, when the combat is renewed, for Fortune rarely giveth us twice the opportunity to overcome our foes. And only think what an enemy is this!"

Now Sohrab was abashed when he learned how that Rustem had duped him. But, hiding his chagrin, he said lightly unto Human:

"Brave Human, be not troubled, for in an hour we meet again in battle, and though twice I have shown mercy unto this old warrior, a third time shall it not happen, for now all the demands of honor have been met."

Now while Sohrab and the Tartar chief thus spake of Rustem, behold, the Hero himself had gone aside, and kneeling beside the running brook, he prayed unto Ormuzd, entreating that such strength be granted unto him that victory should crown his final efforts. Yea, and the All-Merciful One heard the cry of his troubled child, granting unto him such increased strength that lo! the rock whereon he knelt gave way beneath him, because it had not power to bear his weight. Then Rustem, feeling that too much strength might prove his undoing, prayed yet again asking that part thereof be taken away. And again Ormuzd listened unto his voice.

So, rested and reinspired, when the hour was ended, once more the champions turned them unto the place of combat, determined to bring the awful struggle to a close ere another night set in. Now Rustem's heart, in spite of his increased strength, was full of care; but Sohrab came forth like a giant refreshed. Running at Rustem like a mad elephant, therefore, he shouted in a voice of thunder:

"Ho, Wily One! Prepare to meet thy end. For this time thy words of guile shall avail thee naught."

Now Rustem, when he saw the rage of the hitherto laughing young stripling, learned at last to know fear, and in his heart he quickly prayed unto Ormuzd, asking that the strength withdrawn be restored unto him. Then, imbued with all his new-found might, Rustem raised high his head, his eyes glaring with the wild light of battle, his sword brandished on high. So for a second he stood, after which, with a terrible roar, he advanced upon Sohrab, instinctively shouting his old, thunderous battle-cry: "Rustem! Rustem!"

Alas for Sohrab! Stopped midway in his charge by the sound of that much-loved name, for one fateful second, he gazed, bewildered, then instinctively he recoiled, dropping his shield, thus leaving himself uncovered. Quick as a flash, therefore, Rustem drew his blade, and drove it with mighty force through the breast of the youthful hero who, staggering back, sank heavily to the ground. And now, the awful din of arms being hushed, behold, the sun shone forth once more from between the parted thunder-clouds, revealing a fierce warrior standing triumphant over his fallen foe!

And alas that it must be said! but as Rustem gazed upon the prostrate young hero, not one drop of pity filled his heart; for the black shadow of defeat and humiliation yet hovered too near unto him to allow aught but bitterness and anger to rule his soul. Wrathfully, therefore, he said unto Sohrab:

"Foolish boy! In thy pride thou thoughtest to slay a Persian hero this day and boast thy trophy in Afrasiab's land. Now here thou liest, slain by an unknown man."

Now Rustem spake thus because, having been so nearly o'ercome by this valorous youth, after all his proud years of triumph, in his bitter mortification he fain would have deprived him of the satisfaction of knowing by whose hand he had fallen. Alas! a small feeling was this to find its way into the heart of so great a hero, and bitterly was Rustem to repent it.

For, though wounded unto death, behold, Sohrab was still unconquered. Looking up fearlessly into the eyes of his foe, therefore, he said proudly:

"Vain boaster! Vaunt not thy mighty prowess, for not *thy* puny strength hath slain me. Nay; *Rustem* slays me! For that loved name it was unnerved my arm, and so thy boasted spear pierced an unarmed foe. But hear me now, fierce man, and tremble. For behold! Rustem, my father, whom I seek through all the world, will surely avenge my death—though I, alas, shall never see him now! When he learneth of my doom, however, beware! For if thou shouldst become a fish and lose thyself in the depths of the sea, or a star to hide thyself in the highest heaven, verily my father would draw thee forth from thy hiding-place to wreak vengeance upon thy head. Ah, how his heart will be filled with wrath and sorrow when it shall be told unto him that Sohrab, his son, perished in the quest after his face!"

Now Rustem listened unto the words of Sohrab coldly, gazing upon him with scornful, unbelieving eyes. And he said:

"O vanquished youth! Verily, thou wanderest in thy talk. The mighty Rustem never had a son. Now of this I am sure, for am I not a Persian?"

But Sohrab answered still proudly, though his voice had grown faint and hoarse. And he said:

"Stubborn Crocodile! The son of Rustem am I, and none other, and when one day the news of my death shall reach him, it will pierce him like a stab. And alas, my poor mother! what will be her grief when she shall learn that never again shall Sohrab return unto his native land! For well she knoweth that her son sped not for empty glory forth from far Samengan, but to seek his father, lest he perish with longing after him. And now it is all in vain!"

Now, though still unbelieving, Rustem could not but be touched by Sohrab's grief. For, as he gazed at the youthful hero, so full of strength and manly beauty, slain, alas, by his hand in the morning of life, he could not but regret this waste of precious life. So, very gently he spake unto Sohrab. And he said:

"O Valiant One! Well might Rustem be proud of such a son. Nevertheless, men have told thee false. For well I know that the Great Pehliva never had but one child—and that a girl, who dwelleth afar with her mother, and dreameth not of war and its cruelties."

Alas! the anguish of Sohrab's wound was growing great, so that he longed to pull out the sword and end his pain.

But Rustem's unbelief angered him, and he resolved first to convince his stubborn foe. So he said wrathfully:

"Thou Great Persian Ox! Who are thou that thou darest to deny my words? Knowest thou not that truth sitteth upon the lips of dying men? I tell thee that bound upon this arm I bear the amulet of the house of Zal, which Rustem gave my mother. Men may have told *thee* false, but surely my mother knoweth whereof she speaketh, and the story had I from her own lips."

Alas for the Great Rustem! When he heard these words he was shaken with dismay. Nevertheless, he said quietly unto Sohrab:

"Bare thy arm, Stripling, for if thou canst show this token, that were proof, indeed, that thou art Rustem's son."

So, with trembling fingers, Sohrab bared his shoulder, and there upon his arm Rustem beheld the amulet which he had given unto Tamineh so long ago. Now as he gazed, lo, there broke from the heart of the Hero a terrible cry of anguish, after which, suddenly, the earth became dark unto his eyes, and he fell in a swoon beside his valiant son.

And behold! hearing this groan of horrible heart-break, Sohrab knew at last that the unknown warrior was none other than his long-sought father, Rustem the Mighty. So, though fierce was the pain of his wound, Sohrab managed finally to reach the place where Rustem lay, pillowing his head upon his knee. Yea, and he bathed his face with tears, whispering unto him fond words of endearment, trying thus to coax him back to life.

But alas! When Rustem opened his eyes once more, it was upon a world of woe and anguish. In his agony of spirit, therefore, he rent his clothes, and tore his hair, and beat upon his breast, moaning and crying in his terrible sorrow:

"O my son whom I have slain! My son so young and brave and beautiful! Would that my name had been struck from the lists of men ere I had done this cruel deed. But behold! one grave shall suffice for father and son, for no longer will I cumber the earth."

Now so speaking, Rustem clutched his sword, and would have slain himself had not Sohrab stayed his hand, saying:

"Father, forbear! For truly, not thou, but Fate is responsible for this woful happening. Ah, how our hearts cried out one unto the other! and how we should have joyed together! But alas! it hath been decreed otherwise by Him who changeth not. Weep not, therefore, and do thyself no harm, for what is written in the stars, shall it not come to pass? And listen! In spite of all, a great joy hath come unto Sohrab—for doth he not behold thy face? O my father, so brave and splendid, how I have longed to see thee! Come, sit beside me on the sand, therefore, and hold me fast. Yea, take my head between thy hands, and kiss me on the cheek, murmuring, just once, the tender words: 'My son! My valiant son!' Quick! for my life is ebbing fast."

Then Rustem, weeping, cast his arms about his son, murmuring unto him broken words of praise and anguish. And Sohrab was content, for had he not his heart's desire? So, still he lay, and naught disturbed the oppressive silence save only Rustem's heart-breaking cries of woe.

But behold! The father's sad lament reached and caused distress unto other ears than those of quiet Sohrab. For Rakush, hearing his master's plaintive voice,

whinnied back unto him distressfully, knowing not what
to think.   Then, as Rustem came not unto him, presently,
after many brave tugs, he tore up the rock unto which he
was fastened, and hastened, as fast as his burden would
allow, unto his master's side.   But alas! in his terrible
grief, stricken Rustem had only words of chiding for his
devoted steed, saying unto him:

"O Rakush! Rakush! Verily, thy feet should have
rotted in thy joints before ever they bare thy master to
this field."

Now at this outburst, Sohrab raised his head, gazing
with bright eyes at the great charger, whose joys and sorrows were so closely bound up with those of his master.
And much he wondered to see the big, warm tears roll
down from the soft, compassionate eyes of drooping Rakush. Smiling gently, therefore, he said unto him:

"So thou art really Rakush! Ah, how oft have I heard
my mother tell of thee, thou faithful, loving steed! And
how I envy thee! For thou hast been where I shall never
go—even unto far-off Seistan, my father's sunny home.
There White-haired Zal himself hath stroked thy arching
neck, and given thee food, and bidden thee bear thy master well. But alas! Sohrab will never see his grandsire's
charming home, nor hear his voice in greeting."

Thus spake the dying Sohrab, and Rustem, hearing his
sorrowful plaint, brake forth afresh in woe, refusing to be
comforted. And he cried:

"Oh, that I were dead, and the waves of yon dark river
rolling peacefully over me! For never shall I know happiness more in the world."

But again Sohrab spake words of comfort unto his
father, bidding him live for Iran—thus reaping in his old

age a second glory of great deeds. Yea, and he also prayed
Rustem to ensure that his followers be allowed to cross
the Oxus back in peace, and that brave Hujir be granted
his liberty. And he said:

"As for me, O my father, carry me back with thee unto
Seistan, and bury me with the heroes of my house, for I
shall sleep more peacefully there."

So Rustem, stifling his tears, promised that Sohrab's
every wish should be fulfilled. And he said:

"O my glorious son! Never shalt thou be forgotten.
For behold! I will build thee a stately tomb, with a tall
pillar rising unto the skies. And so imposing shall it be
that all men shall see it from afar, and point to it as Valiant
Sohrab's tomb. Yea, and all thy brave deeds shall be
recorded there, cut so deep in the marble that not even
Time shall be able to erase them. So shalt thou live forever, thy glory rivalling that of all the heroes of Iran. For,
generous hast thou been, as well as mighty and valiant!"

Now hearing these wonderful words, Sohrab smiled
radiantly upon his father, caressing his mighty hand.
Then sinking back into his arms, he murmured:

"Ah, the world is so beautiful! So beautiful! And I am
young to die. Nevertheless, I am content. For, O my
father! that was a glorious fight. . . . And I am not
ashamed. Only, my poor young mother!"

So, with his mother's name upon his lips, Brave Sohrab
sighed gently, his head drooped, and then, white and mo-
tionless, the fair young body lay forever quiet in his father's
arms. But behold, the smile upon his lips still spake of
content, for it said that the beautiful spirit had soared once
more unto the sunny Gardens of the Blessed.

But alas! In departing, Sohrab took all the sunshine of

the world with him. For now night came down, heavy and dark, upon the plain, and a chill fog rose up from the rushing river. By and by, however, the moon came out, shining solitary through the mist, and its rays fell softly upon Sohrab, lying with radiant, upturned face, so still upon the sand. But alas! The Queen of the Night could not lighten the dark figure that—with horseman's cloak drawn low over bowed head—sat silent and immovable by the side of the sleeping youth. Nay; not even Rakush could rouse his master now, though he caressed and whinnied and coaxed for long hours.

Alas! so it was that the warriors, sent out by the two great chiefs, found the morning's gay champions. But so great was their awe that none dared draw near to question. So, silently they rode back, and gave the news unto their leaders. But not even the Shah dared disturb the Great Pehliva in his grief, when it was learned that Rustem had slain his son. In the morning, however, the gentle hands of many brave warriors lifted the sleeping Sohrab and bare him in a litter, sorrowfully unto the Persian camp, amid such wailing as the earth ne'er heard before. For the mighty hosts of both great armies mourned for the brave young Hero gone.

Yea, and after this, Rustem, having built a great fire, flung into it his tent of emerald and his trappings of Roum, his saddle and his leopard-skin, his armor well tried in battle, and all the appurtenances of his throne. Now thus was the pride of the mighty warrior laid low. Yea; and without regret saw he his heart's treasures burn, for his soul was sick of war. And he cried:

"O Sohrab! Sohrab! Not even for thee will I fight more. For what availeth glory unto me now?"

And having thus sacrificed his pride, behold, Rustem commanded that Sohrab be swathed in rich brocades of gold, worthy his fair young body; and when they had thus enfolded him, he made ready his army to return unto Seistan. But for one night, Brave Sohrab lay in state, watched over by his own gallant chiefs, who had feasted with him so merrily in his tent, and who now, alas, mourned for him with a bitterness that filled the night with woe.

When morning dawned, however, the sorrowful procession set forth unto Seistan. Now all the nobles of Iran marched before the bier, their heads covered with ashes and their garments rent and tattered. And behold! Rustem heaped black earth upon his head, and tore his hair, and wrung his hands; but his cries could not be heard for the mighty wailing of the army. And not only this, but lo! the drums of the war-elephants were also shattered, and the cymbals broken, and the tails of the horses torn to the roots, for thus did the Persians mourn their mighty dead.

Now when the mournful train drew near unto Seistan, Zal marvelled to see the host returning thus in sorrow. For, as he beheld Rustem at their head, he knew that the wailing was not for him, and he could think of no other worthy such martial honors. When they drew near, however, Rustem led him unto the bier, and showed unto him the youthful Sohrab, so like in feature and might unto Saum, the son of Neriman. Then he told unto him all that had come to pass, and behold! Zal, too, tore his white hair and wept at this dire misfortune and loss that had come unto his house, and for brave, laughing Sohrab gone.

And lo! the days of mourning being ended, the Mighty Ones built for the sleeping hero a tomb like unto a horse's hoof; and therein they laid him to rest, in a chamber of gold, perfumed with amber. Yea, and they covered him with soft brocades, and placed his arms beside him, so that right royally he took his rest. And when it was done, behold, the house of Rustem grew like unto a grave, and its courts were filled with the voice of sorrow. So they mourned for Sohrab in the home of his fathers, and it seemed as if joy could never again take up her abode in the anguish-smitten heart of Rustem.

But alas! not alone in the home of his fathers was Sohrab mourned. There at least his passing left no gap. But in far Samengan, how different! For, though so brave about letting her nestling fly forth, well Tamineh knew that until he winged his glad flight back unto the home nest there would be no more sunshine in her life. Now gladly would she have laid herself down and slept, even as the Princess of old, until the glad day when her brave young Prince should, by his kiss, call her back once more unto the joy of life. But behold! even slumber was denied her.

So, night after night, too restless and anxious to sleep, Tamineh sat upon her balcony, gazing down the moonlit road by which one day her brave young warrior must return. For at first she dreamed not of ill. But alas! one night as she gazed with longing that would not be stilled, suddenly she fell to shivering. For behold! no longer did she see the long dusty road, but in its stead there flowed a great silent river, which shone in the moonlight like molten silver. And alas! upon its surface floated Sohrab, a radiant smile upon his lips, and in his hands a bunch of blood-red flowers, which silently he offered her.

Now Tamineh knew that she had but dreamed, and yet a vague foreboding took possession of her heart, causing her more anxiously still, from this time forth, to watch for her boy's return. And alas! one night as she sat soothed and entranced by the magic beauty of the moonlit world, suddenly she saw loom up from out the shadows, upon the white gleaming road, a great riderless horse, led by a man upon horseback, whose figure seemed strangely familiar, seeing which, Tamineh thought that again she dreamed. But alas! this time she dreamed not. For slowly the riderless horse, with shorn tail and saddle reversed, advanced unto the palace gates, and then there floated up unto the waiting mother a terrible cry, which was taken up and echoed through every corner of the palace, and it ran:

"Sohrab is dead! Sohrab is dead! The brave young Prince will return no more unto his native land."

And now, indeed, was there grief and lamentation throughout the Court. For not only did the nobles and warriors wail and throw dust upon their heads, but the women also tore their long white veils, and wrung their hands as they clustered around the bereaved Tamineh, who at the first sight of the face of Piran-Wisa, before ever his sad errand was told, knew what had befallen, and with a terrible cry had swooned at the feet of her maidens.

And alas! long Tamineh lay as one dead, but, when consciousness finally returned, from the lips of aged Piran she heard the whole sad story of her boy's untimely death. And behold! as the white-haired general recounted how Sohrab had borne himself in that last mighty conflict, the mother's eyes flashed and dilated, while the soul looking out from behind them seemed to cry aloud with pride, and joy, and woe, and despair, in turn. To be slain by Rustem, and slain in equal combat. was a hero's death, truly. But ah, the woe of it!

Yea, the woe of it!   For all Turan mourned for the child of prowess that was fallen in his bloom; but never was there grief like unto that of Sohrab's mother.   Night and day she grieved for her son, her only comfort being the horse and cloak which once had been his.   Weeping, she would kiss the horse's mane and cling about his neck, while at night she held his cloak in her arms, pressing its empty folds unto her bosom.   So she mourned, neither eating nor sleeping till her love for her dead son drew her spirit like a strong cord—away from the weary body—away from the sunless earth which no longer held her heart's dearest.

But behold!   Tamineh's mourning lasted but the accustomed time, for, seven days after Piran-Wisa's return with the riderless horse, she also floated away upon the silent river, and the beautiful smile upon her lips, as she lay, surrounded by her weeping maidens, said plainly that Rustem's Bright Singing-bird had flown also unto the Gardens of Paradise—she and her brave nestling happy forever in the smile of Ormuzd the Blessed.

SIAWUSH THE PERSIAN SIR GALAHAD

BEHOLD! it is recorded that upon a certain day, while the great Shah, Kaikous, was still seated upon the throne of light, Tus, Gew, Gudarz, and other brave Pehliva of Iran departed from the stately court upon a hunting excursion. Now it was in all a goodly company, for the warriors were accompanied by numerous retainers and falconers, and also by leopards such as are trained to hunt the gazelle and the wild ass of the desert.

So they went forth, and after a merry day's hunting, at evening they came unto a vast wood, reaching many leagues. And behold! as the huntsmen entered its dark recesses, what was their surprise to discover there a maiden of marvellous beauty, her hair and neck spangled with costly jewels. And, strange as it may seem, with the exception of the horse which nibbled the grass near by, this beautiful maiden was entirely alone in the green solitude.

Now much the huntsman wondered at this most unusual sight, and Tus, who first discovered the maiden, advancing courteously, said: "O Maiden Fair, by the sun, and moon, and all the silvery stars, I swear that——

"Never was seen so sweet a flower,
In garden, vale, or fairy bower;
The moon is on thy lovely face,
Thy cypress-form is full of grace;
But why, with charms so soft and meek,
Dost thou the lonely forest seek?"

Then the Princess—for she was a princess of the house of Feridoun—told unto the Pehliva how that she had fled from her home to escape the wrath of her father who was angry with her because she had refused to wed Poshang, the ugly, bad-tempered old ruler of Turan.   And she said: "Alas! my father is quick——

> "But when his angry mood is o'er,
>   He'll love his daughter as before;
> And send his horsemen far and near,
>   To take me to my mother dear.
> Therefore, I would not further stray,
>   But here, without a murmur, stay."

Now the maiden was so beautiful that the impressionable hearts of both Tus and Gew warmed toward her, each desiring her for his wife.   And alas! so great was their ardor, that almost the two heroes came to blows, in their hot discussion as to the possession of the Princess.   However, misfortune was finally averted by wise old Gudarz, who persuaded the rivals to refer the matter unto the King.

So behold! they led the Peri-faced maiden before Kaikous who, when he gazed upon her blooming cheeks, her smiling lips, and fascinating mien, smiled, and bit his lip, saying unto Tus and Gew:

"O my Pehliva, I perceive that ye have brought back from the hunt but a single gazelle—one, however, which, unless I mistake me, belongeth unto a King's garden.   As Queen of the moon-faced beauties of my palace, therefore, shall she reign, for I perceive she is worthy to recline upon cushions of silver broidered with gold."

Now, this unlooked-for decision of the King was as the essence of wormwood unto Tus and Gew.   However, the Lord of the World sweetened the bitter cup by presenting

At evening they came unto a vast wood, reaching many leagues.

unto each brave warrior a diadem, and ten superb horses. But upon the Princess he showered rubies and pearls, and in his heart she reigned as Queen of Queens.

And behold! in the course of time there came to take up his abode in the King's palace a splendid son, tall and fair and strong of limb. And the name that was given unto him was Siawush.

Now Kaikous rejoiced greatly in this son of his race, and offered grateful thanks unto Ormuzd the Blessed. But he was grieved, also, because of the message of the stars concerning him. For alas! the astrologers foretold for the infant a career of great vicissitude, ending in sorrow. Neither would his virtues avail him aught, for these, above all, would bring destruction upon him.

But Kaikous, who was of a sanguine disposition, soon allowed hope to delude him into forgetting the inevitable, and so he thought of Siawush only as a child of promise; while unto his beautiful young mother he was the very joy of life.

Yea, and also unto another brave heart did Siawush cause joy. For behold! when the news that a son had been born unto the Shah spread unto far-away Seistan, Rustem the Mighty, aroused him from his sorrow for Sohrab, and going up unto the Court, he asked for the babe that he might rear it for the glory of Iran. And Kaikous suffered it, feeling that a great honor had been done unto the child. So joyously Rustem bare Siawush back unto his kingdom.

And fortunately for Iran, as time passed by, so absorbed became the Great Pehliva in this child of his care, that once more he experienced the joys of living. For, anxious that justice should be done unto the surprising virtues of Siawush, Rustem himself taught his charge horsemanship and archery; the use of arms, and how to hunt with the falcon and the leopard; how to conduct himself at a banquet, and in fact, all the manners, duties and accomplishments of Kings, and the hardy chivalry of the age. His progress, too, in the attainment of every species of knowledge and science was surprising, for in this his soul delighted. So, as the years passed by, this King's Son grew to be a youth of such noble proportions, possessing a face so radiant with winsomeness and intelligence that verily you would have said that the world held not his like.

Now when Siawush had become skilled and strong so that he could easily ensnare a lion or a tiger, behold, one day he came unto Rustem bearing high his head. And he said:

"O Glorious Pehliva! single-handed have I this day ensnared and slain a mighty king of the forest. Is it not time, therefore, that we go up unto the Shah, my father, that he may perceive what manner of man thou hast made of me? Now truly I love Seistan, and thee, and thy dear father—the White-haired Zal. But now I am no longer a child, and it appeareth unto me that out in the world there must be work for me to do."

Then Rustem smiled, for the lad's words pleased him well. And, as his wishes accorded with his own plans for the Prince, almost at once they marched with a mighty host unto Iran. Now when they were come unto the Court, a royal welcome was accorded them, and so pleased was Kaikous with his son that he rained upon Rustem jewels, and gold, and precious things past the telling, and all the land rejoiced and gloried in Siawush, the noble heir unto the throne. Yea, and to celebrate his return, there was given a banquet such as the world hath not seen the like, and behold! none were toasted save Siawush alone.

But unto the Prince, his return home brought no joy so great as that of being reunited with the beautiful young mother whom he not only resembled but also adored. But alas! his happiness was of short duration. For, in the midst of the festivities which celebrated his home-coming, the fair young Queen fell suddenly ill and died.

Alas! no words can describe the sorrow of the noble young Prince for his mother. For, unto the impressionable lad, who had lived his life thus far principally as a warrior among men, the gentle presence of this lovely spirit exercised a wonderful charm. So, quickly had mother and son become inseparable, and this congenial companionship did much, though unconsciously, to develop that strength and beauty of character which was the Queen's most precious legacy unto her son, and which causes his name still to be loved and revered by all the Children of Ormuzd.

But not long was Siawush allowed to indulge his grief, for after the days of mourning were over, for seven years longer was his education continued, under the tutorship of the wisest men in the land. Howbeit, in the eighth year, after that Kaikous had proved his spirit, he gave unto his son a throne and a crown. So all was well, and men forgot the evil message of the stars concerning Siawush. But alas! the day of ill fortune was now not far distant from the noble son of Kaikous.

For behold! Sudaveh, the wife of the Shah, having no son of her own, became jealous of Siawush, the noble heir to the throne. And, finding that she could not by wile lure him into the paths of evil and destruction, lo, she hated him—though she tried to win his liking. But Siawush would not make friends with Sudaveh because he perceived that her thoughts were evil, and because enshrined in his heart was the memory of his own fair mother who had taught him to value honor, and purity, and truth above all things in the world.

Seeing, therefore, that she could neither win Siawush unto herself, nor yet make him love the wrong, behold, Sudaveh was very wroth, and unscrupulously she plotted his ruin. At first she complained unto the King of Siawush, slandering his fair fame, thus trying to prejudice him against his son. Then she caused the most evil reports to be circulated throughout the land damaging to the honor of the Prince. And finally, when the time was ripe, this wicked woman devised a plot against Siawush so deep and cunning that it was impossible for the King to decide as to the guilt or innocence of his son. In his perplexity, therefore, after consulting his Mubids, Kaikous decided to put Siawush to the ordeal of fire, in order to test his innocence.

So now it came to pass that the King caused dromedaries to be sent forth, even unto the borders of the land, to bring cords and cords of wood from the forests. And behold! when it was brought, there was reared a mighty heap of logs, so that the eye could perceive it at a distance of two farsangs, and it was piled so that a narrow path ran through its midst. And this being accomplished, the Shah next commanded that naphtha be poured upon the wood and that it be lighted. And alas! so great was the pyre in width and height that two hundred men were needed to kindle it, and lo! the flames and smoke overspread all the heavens, so that men shuddered with fear when they beheld the tongues of fire; and so great was the heat thereof that it was felt in the far corners of the land.

And presently, the preparations being all completed, Kaikous commanded Siawush, his son, that he ride into the midst of the burning pyres. So, attired in his golden helmet and white robe, and mounted upon a coal-black charger, Siawush advanced unto Kaikous, saluting him. Then fearlessly he rode forward, commending his soul unto the Almighty. Now as he entered upon the fiery path, a great cry of sorrow arose from all the people, for they loved their brave young Prince, and they dreamed not that any man could come forth alive from such a fiery furnace. Therefore they murmured against Kaikous, as did all his nobles, for their hearts were filled with wrath against the King for permitting this wicked deed. So, for long minutes, naught was heard but the angry murmur of the people and the fierce cackle of the hungry flames.

But, though all of Iran grieved, one there was of the King's own household who exulted in this terrible scene. For, when the wicked Sudaveh saw from her windows the fierce flames that struggled to mount unto heaven, she came forth upon the roof of her house. And alas! so given over unto evil was she, that when she beheld Siawush leap so bravely into the fiery depths, she danced and clapped her hands, praying unto the Wicked One, and whispering fierce incantations and charms that should cause destruction unto the Hero.

But behold! with soul uplifted unto Ormuzd, undaunted, Siawush rode boldly through the fiery flames, his white robes and ebon steed being plainly visible unto all. Yea, fearlessly he rode, hasting not at all, but pressing steadily forward, until he was come unto the end of the pathway. And having come forth, lo, there was not singed so much as a hair of his head, neither had the smoke blackened his garments.

Then, realizing that it had been vouchsafed unto him to come through the test safely, involuntarily Siawush raised his eyes unto the starry sky in thanksgiving unto Ormuzd the Blessed. And lo! floating above the great burning pyres, which were now throwing out a tremendous heat, he beheld two white-robed figures. And lo, one was Serosch, the Angel of Pity, and the other his fair young mother. Now beholding this vision, yearningly the young Prince stretched forth his arms, for suddenly the earth had grown hateful unto him. But even as he gazed, the figures vanished, and the world seemed chill and cold in spite of the blazing fire.

The heart of Siawush was soon warmed, however, for when the people beheld that their noble young Prince was come forth alive, they rent the air with their shouts of joy. And Kaikous, seeing that the fire had not touched his son, knew indeed that Siawush was pure of heart. So he raised him from the ground, placing him beside him upon the throne, and asking forgiveness for his evil doubts. Then in his joy Kaikous feasted Siawush for three days. On the fourth day, however, the King mounted upon the throne of light, commanding that Sudaveh, his much-loved wife, be brought before him. And behold! when she was come into his presence, Kaikous reproached her for her evil deeds, bidding her make ready to depart the world, since death was to be the penalty of her misdeeds.

But Sudaveh, who knew her power over the King, pleaded eloquently for her life, asserting that Siawush had escaped, not because of his innocence, but by the power of magic.

Nevertheless, the King, hardening his heart, gave orders that she be led forth unto death; and all the nobles approved the decision, for they knew that the woman was powerful for evil. But now Siawush, being chivalrous and generous of heart, pleaded for Sudaveh's life, for he knew that her death would be a great sorrow unto the King. So, the boon being granted, once more this wicked woman was in a position to work mischief, and this she did right speedily.

For lo, it is chronicled that about this time Afrasiab again invaded Persia with a mighty host, thinking to gain possession of the land. Whereupon, Kaikous, greatly angered because the Tartar had broken his covenant, quickly made ready his army to oppose him. Then Siawush, hearing that the King himself expected to lead forth the men of Iran, having sought audience with his father, asked it as his right that he be permitted to lead forth the host.

So, permission being granted, Siawush set about preparing himself and his men for the coming campaign. But, as he was inexperienced in war, and his foe was wily and powerful, swift messengers were sent unto Rustem, bidding him go forth to battle with his charge, to guard and aid him with his experience. And Rustem, whose heart leaped once more at the thought of battle, answering, said:

"O King of Kings! Verily thy noble son Siawush is unto me the light of my eyes and the joy of my soul, for it seemeth unto me that in him Sohrab yet liveth. Therefore will I go forth once more unto battle."

So the trumpets of war were sounded, and the two Mighty Ones led forth the host to meet the enemy. And behold! when the two armies encountered each other upon the field of battle, Siawush fought so bravely that even Rustem was amazed, for his had seemed to be the gentler and nobler virtues. Yea, and inspired by their noble young leader, so valiantly did the men of Iran fight, that after three fiercely-contested battles, the Persians finally succeeded in shutting up the enemy in Balkh, the capital of Afrasiab.

Now when the news of this calamity was carried unto the King of the Tartars, he was seized with the utmost terror, which was increased by a frightful dream which visited his slumbers. Yea, so terrible was it, that Gersiwaz, the King's brother, found the brave Afrasiab lying upon the floor of his chamber, roaring in agony of spirit, and shouting like a man bereft of reason. And alas! even when he finally recovered his wits, still did he continue to tremble with terror and fright, for he feared that his hour was come. Nor did the Mubids give him comfort, for they revealed unto the King that Siawush would bring destruction upon Turan, hearing which, Afrasiab said unto Gersiwaz:

"O my brother! Never shall I recover from the horror of my dream. But surely if I cease from warring against Siawush, disaster will be avoided. It behooveth me, therefore, to send unto this powerful young Prince, silver, and jewels, and rich gifts, that thus we may bind up with gold the eye of war."

So the King bade his brother take from the royal treasury, gold and jewels of price to bear unto the camp of Siawush, together with a message, saying:

"O Prince of a Noble House! Verily, since the days of Selim and Tus, when Irij was slain unjustly, hath the world been disturbed by our wars. Now, once for all, let us forget these things, that peace may reign once more in the world."

Behold, upon the receipt of this message, a secret council was held as to the answer that should be given, for Rustem trusted not the words of Afrasiab. After long deliberation, therefore, Siawush replied unto the messenger:

"O Prince of the Land of Turan! Behold, we have pondered thy message well, and have decided to grant unto Afrasiab his desire. Yet, since it behooveth us to know that poison be not hidden under the words of thy brother, we demand: First, one hundred distinguished heroes, allied unto Afrasiab by blood, that we may guard them as a pledge of the royal words; and second, the restoration of all the provinces which the Turanians have taken from Iran."

Alas! though Afrasiab was loath to send the hostages, yet dared he not refuse, fearing that in that case the evil foretold would surely fall upon him. So choosing out from among the army the required number of his kinsmen, he sent them unto Siawush. And the negotiations being thus concluded, Rustem hastened to bear the tidings unto Kaikous.

But behold! when the King of Kings learned that a treaty of peace had been concluded, he was angry, for already had rumor informed him of Afrasiab's dream, and of the interpretation put upon it, by the astrologers. In his wrath, therefore, he declared that Siawush had behaved like an infant, and he also heaped reproaches upon Rustem, whose counsels, he said, were those of an old man who had lost his courage. And finally he commanded Rustem that he return right speedily unto Balkh, bearing unto Siawush the message that he should destroy the hostages of Turan utterly; that he should again fall upon Afrasiab; nor cease from fighting until he had wiped from the earth both the King and his army.

Now unto these foolish words, Rustem replied:

"O King of Iran! Beware how thou sowest the seeds of evil, lest they bring forth fruit bitter unto thy taste. For, verily I say unto thee that Siawush will not break his oath unto Afrasiab; neither will he destroy the men of Turan delivered into his hands—for so is he not made! Nay, sooner would he die a thousand deaths of torture than so dishonor his manhood."

But alas! This noble tribute unto his son only fanned the fierce flame of anger that burned in the heart of Kaikous. So he upbraided Rustem yet more, saying unto him that but for his evil counsel the young Prince would not have swerved from the path of victory. Yea, and he taunted Rustem for his loss of vigor, bidding him go back unto Seistan, that refuge for old men, since Tus the Valiant should go forth as Pehliva in his stead.

Now at these unjust reproaches, Rustem's anger burst forth, so that once more he threw into the teeth of the Shah his deeds of folly, telling him not to send for him when again he put his hand into the lion's mouth. And so saying, he turned his back upon the Court, thinking never to visit it again.

So thus it came to pass that Tus went forth unto the army in place of Rustem, and behold! he carried with him strict orders unto Siawush that the hostages should be bound and sent unto Kaikous for execution. But Siawush, being a Prince of the highest purity and honor, could not be a party unto any such disgraceful deed. For he said:

"How, alas, can I appear before Ormuzd the Blessed if I depart from mine oath? even if it be at the command of my father who is the Lord of the World."

Yet well Siawush knew that if he disobeyed the royal mandate of his father it was well-nigh certain that his life would pay the penalty; for he needed not to be told whose tongue it was that had poisoned the King's ear and instigated him in his evil course. After much thought, therefore, the Prince finally decided that he himself would return the hostages safe unto Afrasiab, and then abandon his country and the prospects of a throne, since only thus could he preserve his honor, and prevent his father from becoming a murderer.

So, having reached this decision, Siawush sent Zengueh unto Afrasiab with the hostages and all the gold and jewels that had been sent unto him, together with a letter wherein was written how that discord had sprouted out of their peace, and how that he was resolved to remain true unto their treaty, in spite of his father's commands to the contrary. And finally he petitioned that Afrasiab would allow him to pass through his dominions that he might hide himself wheresoever God desired. For he said:

"Verily, I shall seek out a spot far distant where my name shall be lost unto Kaikous, and where I may not hear of his woful deeds."

Now when Afraisab received this letter he was amazed, for such nobility of soul was unknown unto the wily Tartar. But he was also troubled in his spirit, for he knew not what to do. Therefore, he called unto him his great general, aged Piran-Wisa, taking counsel how he should act. And Piran said:

"O Mighty King! Truly there is but one course open unto thee. Now, I am an old man, and have drunk deep at the fountain of life, but I say unto thee that never yet have I witnessed such honor and nobility in a Prince.

Wherefore, I counsel thee, receive him within thy courts, and give unto him thy daughter in marriage, and let him be unto thee as a son. For, verily when Kaikous is gathered unto his fathers, then will Siawush mount unto the throne of Iran, and thus may the old hate be quenched in love."

So spake good, old Piran, and Afrasiab, knowing that wisdom lurked in his words, at once sent unto Siawush, offering him a home in his land. And he said:

"O noble Prince! Since I perceive that the windows of thy soul are ever open unto the sun, if thou comest to dwell among us never will I demand of thee aught that is evil; neither shall suspicion against thee ever enter my breast. Come, then, and if thy choice be retirement and tranquillity, thou shalt have allotted unto thee a peaceful and independent province."

Now Siawush, when he read Afrasiab's letter, was relieved, and yet was he also troubled. For his heart was sore because that he was forced to make a friend of the foe of his country. But alas! he saw no way by which it could be altered.

So, after despatching a touching letter unto his father, Siawush set out with his cortege, and rode until he reached the frontier. Now there he found chieftains and warriors and servants ready to escort him; and when he was well over the boundary, the great Piran-Wisa himself came forth to greet him. And lo! there followed after him a train of white elephants, richly caparisoned, and laden with gifts, which the great general poured before Siawush to give him welcome. Yea; and every town upon the road to the capital was decorated, and the people hailed Siawush as if he were their own Prince returned unto them victorious.

And behold! when they were finally come unto the capital, Afrasiab himself stepped down from off his throne to give welcome unto Siawush, and much he marvelled at the beauty and strength of the Prince, his heart going out unto him in real admiration and love. So, embracing him, and calling down blessings upon his head, Afrasiab seated him at his side upon the throne. Then, turning unto Piran-Wisa, he said:

"Truly Kaikous is a man devoid of sense, else never would he suffer a son like unto this to depart from out his sight."

Now Afrasiab could not cease from gazing upon Siawush, so truly noble and winning was he, and in his delight he showered upon him gold and jewels and precious treasure past the counting. And he gave unto him, too, a beautiful palace, and horses and servants such as only a Prince could have. And not only this, but he also prepared for his guest a royal feast which lasted many days. And lo! Siawush was exalted above even the nobles of the land. And in the great tournament which ended the welcoming festivities, in all the games of skill Siawush showed a prowess that was great beyond all the warriors of Turan. Yet were they not jealous, but only admiring.

But though Siawush won admiration and love from all sources, unto Afrasiab, even in this short time, he had become the light of his eyes and the joy of his soul. So the Prince abode in the court of the King many days, for in gladness or sorrow, in gayety or sadness, the infatuated monarch would have none other about him. And in this wise there rolled twelve moons over their heads. Then Piran-Wisa said unto Siawush:

"O noble Prince! Behold, thy home is now in Turan,

and if Afrasiab be made now thy father in truth as he is really in affection, then can no hurt come unto thee. Ask of him, therefore, the hand of his daughter in marriage, for thus canst thou secure thyself, and if peradventure, a son be born unto thee, then will he bind up forever the enmity between the two lands."

So Siawush asked the hand of Ferangis of her father, and Afrasiab gave it unto him with great joy. Now he also prepared a mighty feast for the bridal, pouring upon his new son gifts past the telling. Yea, and he also bestowed upon him a kingdom and a throne. And alas! when at last the King suffered his favorite to go forth unto his realm, the sunshine of the Court seemed to go with him, so gray were the days unto Afrasiab.

But Siawush was happy in his new life, for though so gallant and brave when occasion demanded, yet at heart was he not really a warrior, but one of the heroes of progress, as he now proceeded to show. For behold! in the midst of his province he builded himself a city, making of it a place of beauty such as the world hath not seen.

Now it was builded upon a mountain, and was surrounded by scenery of exquisite richness and variety. The trees were thick, and ever fresh and green; birds warbled upon every spray; and transparent rivulets murmured through the meadows; while the air was neither oppressively hot in summer nor cold in winter, for every breeze was laden with invigorating freshness and with perfume such as could only have been wafted from the fair Gardens of Paradise. Now it was in the midst of all this natural beauty that the followers of Siawush builded them homes, while he erected for himself a glorious palace, and garden temples, in which he had painted portraits of all the heroes and kings of his age. Yea, and he caused to be constructed a great open space wherein men might rejoice in the game of ball.

And Siawush was glad in his city, as were all those around him, and the earth was happier for his presence. Yea, and not a cloud was there in the heaven of his life. But when the gallant young Prince, happy in his lovely young wife and his beautiful home, inquired of the astrologers whether this city was destined to add to his happiness, they replied that it would bring unto him ill fortune and sorrow. Now Siawush was saddened by this reply, but as time passed by and no evil befell, like a wise man he put away the thought and rejoiced in the time that was.

But alas! Not long was Siawush to rejoice in a happy present; and behold! his evil nemesis was Gersiwaz, the King's brother, who was jealous of the love which Afrasiab bare unto the Prince, and of the power and glory that were his. So pondering in his heart how he might destroy this mote in his sunshine, one day Gersiwaz presented himself before Afrasiab, praying the King that he would suffer him to go forth and visit the city that Siawush had builded, whereof the mouths of men ran over in praises. And Afrasiab granted his request, bidding him bear gifts and words of love unto Siawush his son.

So Gersiwaz sped him forth, and Siawush, who suspected no evil, received him graciously, feasting him many days in his palace. And in order that due honor should be paid unto the brother of the King, a series of athletic games were arranged for. But alas! the amazing strength and skill displayed by Siawush on these occasions, together with the splendor by which he was surrounded, fanned

into a devouring flame the smouldering envy and hate of
the King's brother.

Upon his return to the Court, therefore, Gersiwaz insidi-
ously poisoned the mind of Afrasiab by false tales, in which
he actually accused Siawush of plotting to bring a Persian
army into Turan. Yea, and he reminded the King of his
dream, thus working upon his fear. And alas! though at
first receiving these stories with hesitation, Afrasiab finally
became furious against his gentle guest, proceeding against
him with an army.

Now a terrible dream had forewarned Siawush that his
doom was at hand. Nevertheless, he entertained not the
slightest thought of trying to resist the King. When informed of his approach, therefore, after bidding a touching farewell unto his lovely young wife Ferangis, Siawush
went forth to welcome Afrasiab unto the cool bowers of
his charming city.

But alas! So infuriated had Afrasiab become by the in-
sinuations of his brother, that without waiting to confer
and learn the truth, also without warning, he hurled his
army upon the escort of Siawush, and all were cut to
pieces. But not even then did Siawush deign to defend
himself. For had he not taken oath never to raise his
sword against Afrasiab or Turan? Conscious of his innocence, therefore, he preferred to die rather than give color
unto the slander of his enemies by raising his hand against
his royal host and the father of his bride.

Seized by a thousand cruel hands, therefore, the noble
Prince was bound and thrown into a dungeon of his own
palace. Then, by Afrasiab's orders, he was dragged from
thence by the hair of his head unto a desert place, where
the sword of Gersiwaz was planted in his breast. And

alas! quickly then the executioner severed the royal head, taking care that the blood stain not the earth, lest it cry aloud for vengeance, for so had commanded fear-stricken Afrasiab.

But alas! in spite of the care taken, a drop of blood escaped the golden bowl and was spilt upon the ground. And lo! from the spot, as though by magic, there sprouted and sprang up a wondrous tree, whose bright red berries each appeared like unto a miniature sword. Now all were amazed and affrighted when they beheld this wonder, and quickly they hastened from the spot. For they feared the vengeance of Heaven, knowing their deed to be evil.

Now when the news of this atrocious deed was spread abroad, behold, a mighty clamor arose in the house of Siawush, the cries of Ferangis piercing even unto the ears of Afrasiab in his far-away pavilion. Then the King, angry that his child should sorrow thus for her lord, commanded that she, too, be slain.

And alas! this certainly would have happened but for the timely intervention of good old Piran-Wisa, who, hearing of the tragic end of Siawush, and of the fate that awaited Ferangis, quickly saddled his swiftest steed with his own hands, and dashed madly over hill and valley, pausing neither to eat nor sleep until he drew rein before the pavilion of King Afrasiab.

Then with noble courage the old man strode into the presence of the cruel King, and, upbraiding him for his perfidy, foretold a certain retribution when Kaikous and Rustem should learn of the treatment awarded unto the pure and high-minded Siawush. Yea, and he pleaded in lofty terms also for the life of Ferangis, saying:

"O thou who art more heartless than the fierce beasts of prey, wouldst thou really lift up thine hand against thine own offspring? Hast thou not done enough that is evil? Shed not, therefore, the blood of yet another innocent, for truly the day will come when thou shalt pay with thine own heart's blood. Now, if Ferangis be hateful unto thee because of Siawush, I pray thee confide her unto me, that she may be unto me a daughter in my house, and I will guard her well from sorrow."

Now hearing these words of warning, Afrasiab was filled with remorse for his evil deed. So, releasing his daughter from her chains, he gave her into the care of Piran, who bore her unto his home beyond the mountains.

Then Afrasiab returned speedily unto the Court, for the city of Siawush, in spite of its entrancing beauty, had become hateful unto him. And behold! from this time forth, a great fear gnawed persistently at his vitals, allowing him neither rest nor sleep, and ever before him he saw the pure face of the cruelly murdered Siawush.

So lived and died this noble Prince of the land of Iran whose tragic fate yet moveth the Children of Ormuzd to tears, even unto this day. But of the vengeance that was accorded him you must hear in another story.

RUSTEM THE AVENGER

L O, in the Book of the Shahs it is written, that when the tidings of the cruel death of Siawush pierced unto the land of Iran, behold, throughout the length and breadth of the King's dominions there was raised unto heaven such a mighty wailing that even the nightingale in the cypress was silent of her song, and the leaves of the pomegranate-trees in the forest were withered for sorrow.

As for the mighty Rustem, when he learned of the tragic fate of the Prince so dear unto him, he was bowed to the earth with agony, so that for seven days he stirred not from the ground, neither would have aught of food or comfort. But on the eighth day he roused himself from the earth, causing the trumpets of brass to be sounded in the air. And behold! when he had assembled all his brave warriors, he marched with them unto Iran, where, appearing before the Shah, he demanded audience.

Now when Rustem was come into the presence-chamber, he beheld the King of Kings seated upon his throne, and lo! he was clothed in dust from his head unto his feet, because of his grief. Yea; and all the heroes that stood about the throne were clad in garbs of woe, bearing dust upon their heads instead of helmets. But Rustem was not moved by the grief of the Shah, for he remembered but too well who had driven Siawush forth unto his doom. So pitilessly he said unto Kaikous:

"O King of Evil Nature! Verily it must be bitter unto thee to know that with thine own hand thou hast felled the noble young cypress of thy house, which might have grown and cast a glorious shadow over Iran. Alas for Siawush, so noble and yet so treacherously slain! But dearly shall his murderers pay; and lo! vengeance beginneth at the King's palace. Nay, tremble not, for, being the King, thou art safe from my sword. But as for that wicked sorceress who poisoned thy mind with her charms, now she must die; and verily all Iran will glory in her death. And now hear me, O King, and ye heroes of Iran, for I swear unto thee that henceforth I will know neither rest nor joy until the atrocious death of Siawush be fully avenged. Let his murderers beware, therefore, for behold! Rustem is upon their track."

Now having thus unveiled his heart, Rustem strode disdainfully from out the presence of the King, hastening at once unto the palace of Sudaveh, who had given over Siawush unto death. And behold! the Hero found this charming sorceress sitting upon a golden throne, in a bower that rivalled paradise in beauty, with a coronet upon her head and her hair floating around her in long musky ringlets.

But as Rustem beheld all this luxury and splendor, and thought of Siawush abandoned unto the foes of his land, because of this wicked woman, all compunction left him. Tearing her from her gorgeous throne, therefore, quickly did he rid the world of this source of evil; nor did he feel pity or regret when he saw her dead at his feet. For he remembered how Siawush had pleaded for her life and how his generosity and nobility had been rewarded.

And behold! having thus purged the earth of a part of

its wickedness, Rustem strode forth into the pure air of heaven, fearing naught. For though well he knew that the heart of Kaikous would be torn with anguish when he learned of the death of Sudaveh, yet would he not dare to oppose himself unto his great Pehliva in his wrath.

So, the hand of vengeance being stretched forth, Rustem now directed his course toward Turan, saying unto his heroes:

"Verily, this accursed land shall tremble before my mace as the earth upon the day of judgment, and Afrasiab, the black-hearted, shall cry for the rocks to hide him from my anger, which burneth ever fiercer."

Thus spake Rustem, and paused not in his forced march until he was come face to face with the forces of Afrasiab. Now the King having learned that a great army was coming out of Iran to avenge the death of Siawush, had sent forth Sarkha, the best-beloved, and the bravest of his sons, to oppose the invaders, begging him, however, to have a care that Rustem, the son of Zal, put not his life in danger.

Now when the two armies beheld one another, lo, their hate burst forth, and the battle raged sore. And alas for Afrasiab! for in the midst of the conflict Sarkha fell into the hands of Rustem, who spared him not, but delivered him over unto the same death as that of Siawush, knowing that thus would the heart of Afrasiab be torn with anguish.

And now the frenzied King of Turan, having received the golden dish containing the blood of his son, and beheld his severed head suspended from the gates of his palace, hastened himself to resist the conquering career of the enemy. And behold! this new force having come nigh unto Rustem, it came to pass that Pilsam, that was brother unto Piran-Wisa, a warrior valiant and true, begged permission to oppose his single arm against the Mighty Rustem. To which Afrasiab said:

"O Valiant One, subdue Rustem, and thy reward shall be my daughter and half my kingdom."

So, though Piran tried to dissuade Pilsam from the unequal contest, yet went he forth and summoned Rustem to fight. But behold! hearing the call, Gew accepted the challenge himself, Rustem being at a distance. Then long they fought, but so superior was the activity and skill of the Tartar that almost Gew was thrown from his horse. Luckily, however, Feramurz saw him at the perilous moment, and darting forward, with one stroke of his sword he shattered Pilsam's javelin to pieces. So now Pilsam and Feramurz fought together with such desperation that presently both Heroes were exhausted. But at this moment Rustem, perceiving the combat, pushed Rakush forward, calling aloud unto Pilsam:

"Ho, Puny Tartar! I am told that thou desirest to try thy strength with Rustem. Behold! he hath come in answer to thy call."

Now when Pilsam gazed upon the mighty warrior, wrapped about with anger, he was afraid. Nevertheless, he proceeded to encounter him, striking with all his might at the head of the champion. But though the sword of the Hero was broken by the blow, not a hair of Rustem's head was disordered. Waiting not for a renewal of the attack, however, Rustem now fell upon the Tartar with fury, lifting him lightly and easily from the saddle. Then taking him by the girdle, he flung him, as a thing contemptible, into the Tartar camp, shouting in a voice of thunder:

"Ho, black-hearted King! Here cometh thy glorious conqueror. Pray, wrap him in robes of gold, for I fear that my mace hath made him blue. And give unto him now thy daughter and thy treasure, thy kingdom and thy soldiers, for is he not, indeed, a bright jewel in thy crown of sovereignty? And hath he not added lustre unto Turan, the land of mighty heroes?

So spake Rustem in his anger, and so terrible was he that suddenly the courage of the Tartars all departed from out them. Neither could Afrasiab incite them to fresh endeavor, though he strove mightily; for lo! the fear of Rustem the Avenger had taken full possession of their hearts.

Then Afrasiab, shamed by Rustem's taunts, himself appeared in arms against the champion, and fiercely they fought for hours. Finally, however, Rustem struck the head of Afrasiab's horse which, floundering, fell, over-turning his rider. Then, quick as a flash, the great Persian sprang to seize his royal prize and wreak a perfect vengeance. But alas! the Tartar, Human, rushed between and saved his master, who, vaulting upon another horse, fled, murmuring unto himself:

"Alas! alas! The good fortune which hitherto hath watched over me is asleep."

Now thus it was that Afrasiab became a wretched wanderer upon the face of the earth. For behold! not only did Rustem utterly demolish his capital, but he paused not in his work of destruction until the whole land was laid waste. And yet was the vengeance of Siawush not complete.

HOW GEW HELPED A HERO-PRINCE
UNTO A THRONE

BEHOLD! it is chronicled that after the death of Siawush there was born unto Ferangis, in the house of Piran-Wisa, a son so attractive of mien that already in his cradle he was like unto a King.

Now evil counsellors bade Afrasiab destroy this Prince, who, according to the astrologers, was destined to bring destruction upon Turan. But the King, whose heart had been softened by his sorrow for Siawush and by the eloquent pleading of Piran-Wisa for the life of the child, shut his ears unto them, saying:

"Verily, I repent me of my evil deed unto Siawush, and though it be written that much evil shall come unto me from this offspring of his race, yet will I not again stain my hands with the blood of any of his house. Let the babe live, therefore, but let him be brought up among shepherds in the mountains, far from the haunts of men, and let his birth be hidden from him, that he may never seek to avenge the cruel death of his sire. So may all yet be well."

So, rejoicing that the Prince was to be spared, quickly Piran hastened to hide him in the mountains, before Afrasiab should repent him of his clemency, for well he knew the King's fickleness of humor. Now the old man gave the little Prince unto shepherds of the flock, bound unto him by ties of gratitude, saying:

"O Men of Peace! Behold, I give unto you a glorious charge, and I say unto you, guard this child even as your own souls, letting neither rain nor dust come nigh unto him, for verily he is precious in the sight of Ormuzd the Blessed."

Thus it came to pass that no man knew of the whereabouts of the young Prince—nay, not even Ferangis, his mother, for thus only could he be safe from Afrasiab. But alas! the thought of his charge caused Piran many an anxious hour, for greatly he feared that strife and disaster would come unto Turan through him, yet on account of the promise of protection given unto Siawush, his friend, whom he had led to put his trust in Afrasiab, he felt bound in honor to preserve the child at any cost.

Now when some time had passed, the shepherds came unto their patron, the great Piran-Wisa, saying:

"Verily, Sire, no longer can we restrain the bold young eagle that thou hast placed in our mountain eyrie, for behold! he ever seeketh to fly unto the sun."

So, hearing this report, Piran returned with the shepherds to visit KaiKhosrau, for so was the young Prince named. And lo! when he looked upon him, beholding his beauty, and strength, and winsomeness, his heart went out to him as unto a son, and he pressed him unto his bosom with tenderness. Then was KaiKhosrau surprised, and he said unto the white-haired, stately old warrior:

"O Stately Poplar, that bearest high thy head! Art thou not ashamed to press unto thee the son of a shepherd?"

Then Piran, who was carried out of himself by the wondrous promise of the boy, stopping not to ponder his words, cried out in admiration:

"O Heir of Kings! Would that thy father could see thee now! How his heart would rejoice in a son so truly royal!"

Thus spake Piran in his admiration, and having betrayed in part the secret, he now related unto KaiKhosrau the story of Siawush his sire, and, having done so, he bare him back with him unto his mother. Then was the Prince clad in robes befitting his station, and from this time forth he was reared in the bosom of Piran, and of Ferangis, his mother, the days rolling above their heads in happiness and peace.

But alas! so could it not ever be, for again was Afrasiab having bad dreams. So shortly it came to pass that a messenger was sent in great haste to summon Piran-Wisa unto the Court. Then Afrasiab said:

"O venerable Chieftain, I have called thee into my presence because of the disquiet of my heart on account of KaiKhosrau, the child of Siawush. For lo! in my dreams I have beheld that he will do much evil unto Turan, on account of which, I repent me of my weakness which kept him alive. Bring him before me, therefore, that I may avert by his death the avalanche of calamity which threateneth."

Now when Piran heard these words he was filled with dismay. But, smiling, he said unto Afrasiab:

"O Mighty King! Verily it grieveth me that thou shouldst have been caused one minute's pain on account of this Prince, who, though blessed with a face like unto that of a Peri, yet carrieth upon his shoulders a head ill-fitted to bear a crown, since it is empty of reason. Commit, therefore, no violence, but suffer that this innocent one, devoid of wit, continue to dwell harmlessly among the flocks."

So spake the great Piran, and Afrasiab felt the burden of his heart lighten as he listened unto these reassuring words. Yet he said:

"O Venerable One! Truly thy words are as a comforting shadow in the burning desert. Nevertheless, I say unto thee, bring this KaiKhosrau before me that I may behold with my own eyes his simplicity."

And behold! Piran assented unto the King's request, for he dared not do otherwise. So, returning unto his house, he sought out the young Prince, instructing him how he should act. Then, arrayed in princely garb, Kai-Khosrau was conducted unto the Court, mounted upon a goodly charger, and surrounded by his retinue.

Now all the people shouted with delight when they beheld the beauty and kingly mien of the young Prince, even Afrasiab being struck with wonder, as he gazed at his limbs of power. Yea, so fearful was he that he found it hard, indeed, to remember the promise he had given unto Piran—that no hair of the boy's head should be harmed. But relief was at hand. For when the King began to question, so well did KaiKhosrau act his part, that once again was he reassured. Now Afrasiab said:

"Young Shepherd! How knowest thou the day from the night? What doest thou with thy flocks? And how countest thou thy sheep and thy goats?"

Then KaiKhosrau, smiling simply into the face of the King, replied:

"The forests are void of game, and I have neither bow nor arrows. But behold my sunny crown and my golden girdle!—only, they are not for thee!"

Now the King smiled at this reply, and once more he questioned, this time as to the milk given by the flocks.

But KaiKhosrau, shaking his head sadly, replied:
"The tiger-cats are black—black as thy beard! and verily they are not good for playmates, for they have prickly paws."

Then Afrasiab put yet a third question, saying:
"O noble youth! What is the name of thy father?"

But KaiKhosrau, frowning, said:
"The dog ventureth not to bark when a lion threateneth. But alas! there are no lions now."

Then Afrasiab, questioning yet again, said:
"O Valorous Youth, desirest thou not to go forth unto the land of Iran that thou mayest be avenged of thy foes?"

But KaiKhosrau, winking drolly at the King, replied:
"When the leopard danceth, then a strange piper playeth the tune: 'Ha! Ha! Ho! Ho! Prince KaiKhosrau hath no foe.'"

Thus spake the cunning Prince, and Afrasiab, satisfied with his answers, questioned him no more, but said unto Piran-Wisa:

"O Mighty One! Restore this boy unto his mother, and let him be reared with kindness in the city that Siawush hath builded, for I perceive that from him can no harm alight upon Turan."

So, permission being given, quickly Piran hastened to remove KaiKhosrau from the Court, thanking God for the danger safely passed through. And behold! in the city of Siawush, Ferangis spake often unto her son of his noble sire, and of the heroes of Iran, his father's land; so that finally his heart burned, not only with the desire for the vengeance due unto Siawush from his son, but also that he might perform deeds worthy his glorious ancestry.

So the days and the moons rolled by until the army of Rustem invaded Turan. Then, by the advice of Piran-Wisa, the young Prince and his mother were led forth and securely hidden in the land of far Cathay, where they remained for seven long years, while Turan was given over unto the ravages of its foes. But behold! in the eighth year Rustem and his heroes were summoned by the Shah to return unto Iran, thus giving unto that cunning fox, Afrasiab, a chance to creep forth from his hiding-place.

Now the King wept sore when he beheld the havoc wrought upon Turan by Rustem and his heroes, and, gathering together a mighty army, he fell upon Iran with such fury that none could stand before him. Yea, so bitter was his hate that he suffered not repose to seal his eyelids until he had shattered the Persian host and scathed the land with fire and sword. For alas! good fortune now turned her face away from Iran; neither would Rustem come forth unto her aid, since Kaikous the foolish had again aroused his anger.

But behold! at this crisis, it came to pass that Gudarz, who was descended from Kavah the smith, dreamed a dream. Now in this vision he beheld a cloud of rainbow hues, and seated upon it was Serosch the Blessed. And lo! the Angel of Pity said unto Gudarz:

"O Hero of Iran, unto thy house is it granted, even as unto Kavah of old, to deliver thy land from anguish and from the tyranny of Afrasiab the Turk, wherefore, open thine ears unto my words. For lo! it hath been made known unto me by Ormuzd the Omnipotent that there abideth in Turan a son sprung from the loins of Siawush, who is brave and worthy the throne of light, and from whom alone can come deliverance unto Iran. Suffer.

therefore, that Gew, thy brave son, go forth to search for
KaiKhosrau, bidding that he remain glued unto his saddle until he shall have found this youth. For such is the
will of Him who changeth not, even Ormuzd the God of
the Persians."

Now when Gudarz awoke he thanked God for his
dream, touching the ground with his beard. Then,
quickly calling unto him his valiant son, he related unto
him his dream, bidding him go forth even as commanded
by the guardian of the children of Ormuzd:

Then Gew, when he heard the words of his father, replied unto him:

"O Glorious Sire! Verily my heart leapeth forth unto
this adventure, even as a flame darteth hungrily unto the
sun. Give me, therefore, thy blessing, and lo! I will depart this very hour."

But Gudarz, smiling at the ardor of his son, said:

"What about thy companions, O Impetuous One?"

To which Gew replied:

"My horse and my cord, O my father, will suffice unto
me for company. For behold! if I lead out a host unto
Turan, men will ask who I am, and why I have come
forth, while if I go alone, these doubts will surely slumber."

Then Gudarz, well pleased at the discretion of valiant
Gew, said:

"Go, my son, and may all the hosts of Heaven accom-
pany thee, strengthening thine arm and directing thy
way."

So Gew set forth, but no easy task was his, as he soon
found. For, though he wandered through the length and
breadth of Turan, he could learn naught of KaiKhosrau.
Now seven years rolled thus above the head of Gew, until

he grew lean and sorrowful; yea, even like unto a man distraught. For lo, in all this time, naught had he for a house save only his saddle; for food and clothing but the flesh and skin of the wild ass; and in place of wine, naught but bad water had he to drink. So finally the Hero began to lose heart, fearing that his father's dream had been sent unto him by a wicked Deev.

But arriving one day in a desert, the Valiant One happened to fall in with several persons who, upon being questioned, said that they had been sent by Piran-Wisa in search of the great Shah Kaikous. Now Gew doubted their story, and so took care to ascertain from them the direction in which they were travelling, passing himself off unto them as a huntsman, interested only in the amusement of snaring the wild ass.

Now during the night the parties separated, Gew proceeding like lightning upon the route described by the strangers. And behold! as morning dawned, he entered a forest, in the midst of which he suddenly beheld a fountain, and seated beside it a youth like unto a royal cypress. Now the Glorious One held in his hand a cup, and upon his head was a golden crown; noting which, Gew said unto himself:

"Verily my search is ended, for in this youth surely I behold the face of noble Siawush."

Great was his surprise, however, when, as he advanced, the stripling, greeting him, said:

"Ho, Valiant Gew! Truly thou art a joy unto my eyes, since thou art come hither at the behest of God."

Then Gew, falling at the feet of KaiKhosrau, said:

"O Hope of Iran! at last, after seven long years of search, do I find thee. But pray, reveal unto me how thou knewest my face and mission, for behold! I am lost in amazement."

Then, smiling, KaiKhosrau replied unto Gew:

"O Son of Gudarz! Verily all the great warriors and heroes of Iran are well known unto me, for oft have I gazed upon the portraits of Rustem and Tus and Gudarz—yea, and of Valiant Gew,—in my father's gallery, while from my mother's lips have I heard again and again of all the glorious deeds wrought by the Pehliva of the Shahs. And alas! before he entered upon death—his cruel death!—my father foretold unto Ferangis, my mother, how that in due time the mighty Gew would come forth from Iran to lead me unto the throne."

Then Gew, delighted with the fire of the youth, and being thus assured of his identity, fell down upon the ground and did homage before him. But KaiKhosrau quickly raised and embraced him, asking a thousand questions of Iran and its heroes.

But Gew, knowing the need of haste, quickly mounted the young Prince upon his charger, while he walked before him; and so they journeyed until they came unto the city of Siawush, and behold Ferangis received them joyfully, her quick spirit divining that the prophecy of her lord had come to pass. But she also counselled haste, for she said:

"Verily, Afrasiab will be as a raging crocodile when he learneth of thy coming. Let us flee quickly, therefore, before he heareth of thy mission. And now give heed unto my words. Lo! upon the crest of yonder mountain, whose head riseth unto the clouds, there smileth in the sunshine a meadow green as paradise, and browsing upon it are the flocks of Siawush. Now in their midst, my son, roameth Beezah, thy father's steed of battle. Go forth, therefore,

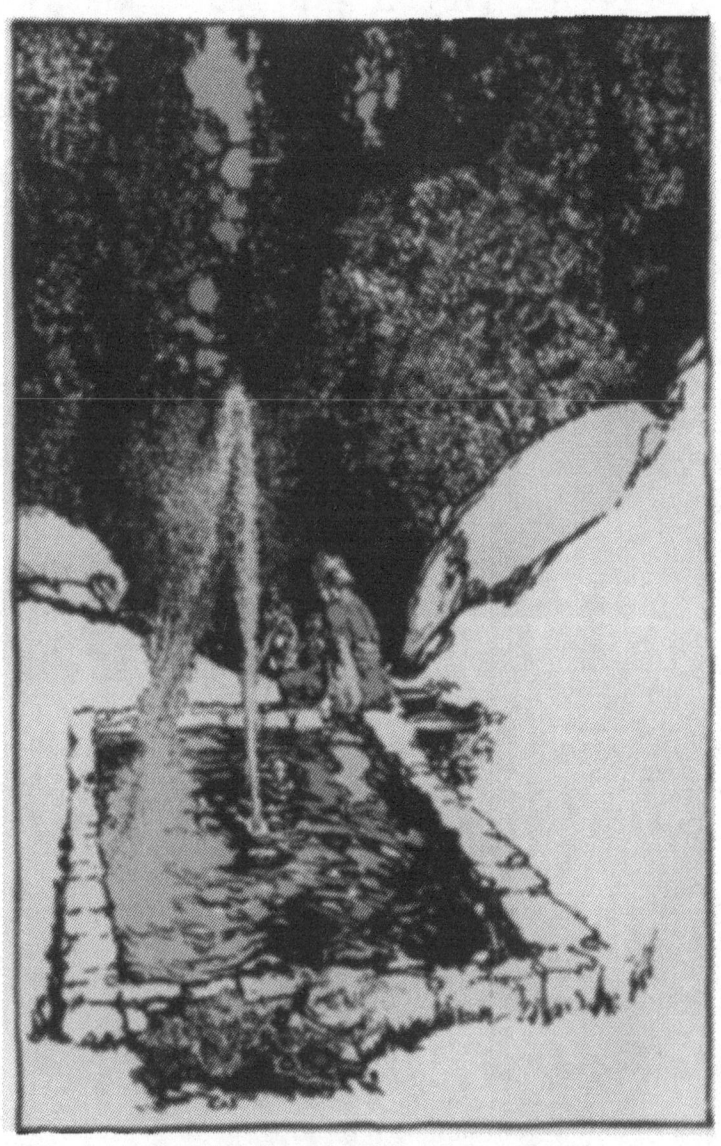

Seated beside it a youth like unto a royal cypress.

and when thou hast come nigh unto him, whisper thy
father's name unto his ear, for so will he suffer thee to
mount him. And, seated upon his back, thou shalt escape
from the slayers of thy father."

So, following the directions of Ferangis, quickly Gew
and KaiKhosrau hastened unto the meadow, where they
found the steed of Siawush towering like a king above his
fellows. And lo! when Beezah beheld his master's saddle, and the leopard-skin that he had worn, he whinnied
mournfully, his bright eyes softening with sudden dew.
Unresisting, he suffered KaiKhosrau to mount him, and
behold! when they were come again unto Ferangis, she
chose from among her treasures the armor of Siawush, in
which to gird her son, while she herself donned a suit of
mail like unto a warrior. Now, thus equipped, they
mounted their chargers and set forth. And none too soon,
for almost at once their flight was discovered.

Then, when the messengers sent for KaiKhosrau reported unto Piran-Wisa that the youth had been carried
off by a Persian horseman, behold, he was filled with dismay, saying unto himself:

"Alas! now will be accomplished the fears of Afrasiab,
and mine honor will be tarnished in his eyes."

So quickly he commanded Kelbad and three hundred
valiant warriors that they pursue KaiKhosrau, bind him,
and bring him back in chains. And behold! so rapid were
the movements of Kelbad that he overtook the fugitives
in the vicinity of Bulgaria.

Now as the great chieftain and his party came in sight,
Ferangis and her son slept for weariness by the roadside.
But Gew, perceiving an armed force evidently in pursuit of
his party, hastily donned his armor, mounted Beezah, and

advanced single-handed to the charge, attacking the horsemen furiously with sword and mace. For, having heard the prophecy which declared that KaiKhosrau was destined to become the great King of Kings, he braved the direst peril with confidence and the certainty of success. And it was this feeling, no doubt, that enabled Gew to perform such prodigies of valor. For, in a very short time it came to pass that Kelbad and his three hundred were utterly routed. Then this marvellous victory achieved, quickly Gew returned unto the halting-place, where, awakening his companions, he urged them to haste.

But alas for the defeated three hundred! For their return excited the greatest indignation in the breast of Piran-Wisa, who said angrily:

"What! Three hundred soldiers to fly from the valor of one man! Why, had Gew possessed the might and activity of Rustem himself, such a defeat could scarcely have happened. Truly such faint-heartedness maketh my soul sick with shame."

So saying, Piran and the thousand brave warriors under his command started at once to overtake the fugitives, and so swift was their march that they soon overtook the Valiant Gew and his little party. And now KaiKhosrau insisted upon being allowed to act his part, instead of remaining ignominiously idle; but Gew, determined to preserve the Prince from all risk, even at the peril of his own life, replied unto him:

"Nay! Nay! Thou art our Prince, and therefore thy life is too precious to be risked. As for me, if I fall, what mattereth it? My father loveth me well, it is true, but hath he not seventy-and-eight other sons like unto me?

Get thee upon yonder high eminence, therefore, and witness how one man shall put a thousand to flight.

So, though reluctantly, the Prince did as Gew desired, and presently he heard the mighty son of Gudarz challenge Piran to single combat. Now the contest that followed was terrible, for though the Tartar general was old, he was both experienced and skilful. Therefore, wrapped about with his anger, and the fear of Afrasiab, he was no mean antagonist. But verily not even Rustem himself could have stood against Gew upon this eventful day, for, realizing that his opportunity had come, he, too, meant to have his name writ large on the page of his country's story. So presently, after much courage and persistency, it came to pass that the Hero caught Piran in the meshes of his cord, and brought him bound unto KaiKhosrau, in spite of the shower of arrows that rained upon him like hail from the bows of Piran's brave warriors.

And behold! this deed of prowess accomplished, back again sped triumphant Gew to fight against the Tartar braves. Yea, and so great was his prowess that soon the plain was covered with the vanquished dead, while living warriors, dismayed at the sight of such mighty valor, ignominiously fled in all directions, as though pursued by Rustem, or the Great White Deev. So, the enemy being put to flight, once more Gew returned unto his companions. But great was his surprise to behold Piran-Wisa still alive. In explanation, however, Ferangis, whose eyes were full of tears, said:

"O Mighty Gew, marvel not that the sword of Siawush refuseth to take the life of this good old man, whose tenderness hath ever been an asylum unto our sorrows. Again and again hath he saved the life of the Prince, as well as my own, and had he been ever at Afrasiab's right hand, then verily would Siawush still be in the land of the living, for Piran was ever his friend. And lo! now is the time come for us to remember the benefits that we have received at his hands."

But Gew, filled with consternation, replied unto the pleadings of Ferangis:

"O Queen of the World, I pray thee speak not thus. For alas! I have sworn a great oath that I would crimson the earth with Piran's blood, and how can I depart from my vow?"

Now hearing this, Ferangis was very sorrowful, but KaiKhosrau said:

"O Hero like unto a mountain lion, verily thou shalt not break thy oath; neither shalt thou slay this good old man. I say unto thee, therefore, pierce with thy dagger the lobes of Piran's ears, and let the blood stain the earth. Thus may thy oath and my clemency both be satisfied."

So Gew did as KaiKhosrau desired, and lo! when he had crimsoned the earth with Piran's blood, they mounted him upon his charger, and, after binding him thereon, they caused him to swear unto them that none other than Gulshehr, his wife, should release him from his bonds. And Piran sware it, for he had not hoped to escape from the terrible Gew.

But behold! while these things were happening unto Piran, Afrasiab, growing impatient as he heard not of the capture of the Prince, set forth himself at the head of a great army that he might lend his assistance. But alas! when he learned that the armies had been beaten at the hands of one man, his cheeks grew pale with fear. Nevertheless, he pressed on, but only to be met in a short time by Piran, his Pehliva, tied helpless upon his charger.

Now at this sight the King's anger passed all bounds. Reviling the old man, therefore, he commanded him that he depart from out his presence forever. Then, urging rapidly forward his army, he sware a great oath that he himself would destroy this Gew, and utterly lay low the head of KaiKhosrau and of Ferangis, his mother. And that the fugitives might not escape him, at once he sent instructions unto all the ferrymen of the Jihun that they allow not the three travellers to pass over the river, as he himself was in pursuit of them. But alas! even this thoughtfulness availed him naught, for ere they came nigh unto the fleeing ones, behold, they were already come unto the banks of the river.

And lo! on the brink of the rushing stream their glad eyes perceived a boat lying ready, with a ferryman slumbering beside it. Now quickly Gew aroused the sleeping one, asking that he bear them across the river. But the man, having received the King's instructions, parleyed with Gew, saying:

"Ho, Imperious One! Thy business demandeth haste? Well, then, give unto me thy coat of mail, thy black horse, yon woman, or the crown of gold worn by the young warrior, as my fee, and quickly shalt thou be borne across."

But Gew, angry at the effrontery of the boatmen, also suspecting his intentions, whispered unto the Prince:

"Behold, yonder cloud of dust seemeth to speak of pursuers and to warn against delay; also, I trust not this ferryman. Now when Kavah, my brave ancestor, rescued the glorious Feridoun, he passed over the stream in his armor without hurt. Why should not we, then, in a cause of equal glory, do the same?"

But alas! the river was swollen by the rains, its current

being swift and treacherous. Nevertheless, the young Prince, confiding in the protection of the Almighty, fearlessly urged his foaming steed into the boiling surges. And behold! Ferangis followed with equal intrepidity, while after her came Gew the bold. Now the passage was rough and perilous, but nevertheless, after a hard fight, they all succeeded in gaining the opposite shore, much to the amazement of the ferryman, who had thought, as a matter of course, that they would all be drowned. Feeling the soil of Iran beneath their feet, however, KaiKhosrau, dismounting, kissed the earth in gratitude and joy, giving thanks unto Ormuzd for allowing him to escape in safety unto his father's land.

Yet scarce had they escaped. For behold! even as they touched the shore, Afrasiab and his army were come unto the river. Now great was the mortification of the King when he beheld the fugitives beyond his reach. Nevertheless, his wonder was equal to his disappointment; nor could he withhold his admiration as he gazed, saying:

"What spirits must they have to brave
The terrors of that boiling wave—
With steed and harness, riding o'er
The billows to the farther shore.
—It was a cheering sight, they say,
To see how well they kept their way,
How Ferangis impelled her horse
Across that awful torrent's course,
Guiding him with heroic hand,
To reach unhurt the friendly stand."

Howbeit, when Afrasiab recovered from his astonishment, in his anger and chagrin, he ordered the ferrymen to get ready their boats to pass him over the river; but

Human finally dissuaded him from this foolish measure. So, devoured with wrath and fear, Afrasiab retraced his steps unto his capital, knowing that now his dream would surely be fulfilled.

As for Valiant Gew, at once he sent swift messengers unto the Court to bear unto the Shah the news of the coming of the Prince. Whereupon, Kaikous rejoiced exceedingly, sending forth an honorary deputation to escort his grandson into his presence. Now the city was decked to give him welcome, and all the nobles received him joyfully as the heir unto the throne—all excepting Tus, the son of King Nuder, who gave his fealty unto Friburz, the son of Kaikous. Nor was his opposition passive. For, when invitations were issued unto a banquet in honor of Kai-Khosrau, at which all the great heroes and leaders were expected publicly to declare their loyalty unto the new Prince, Tus refused to go. However, his refusal was not accepted, Gew being deputed to repeat the invitation. But alas! unto all Gew's arguments, Tus stubbornly replied:

"Verily, unto Friburz shall I pay homage, and unto none other."

Now when Gew reported unto Gudarz, his father, what had occurred, the old man was aroused to great wrath. Rising up, therefore, at once he took twelve thousand men, and his seventy-eight kinsmen, together with Gew, and proceeded unto the palace of Tus to bring him to reason. So, almost was there civil war in Persia; but finally Tus, who disliked the thought of such a calamity, sent an envoy unto Gudarz, suggesting that the matter be referred unto the King. So one wise in speech appeared before Kaikous, begging that he would settle the strife among the nobles. For he said:

"Alas, O King! If we are divided among ourselves, surely we shall fall a prey unto Afrasiab. Let the Shah, therefore, bind up this quarrel which already is serious, and let us once more have peace."

Then Kaikous, realizing the seriousness of the matter, said gravely unto the envoy:

"Verily, ye ask of me that which is hard, for both my sons are dear unto me. Nevertheless, I will bethink me of a means to quiet this discussion and restore peace."

Now Kaikous pondered deeply over this troublesome question, but finally, calling his nobles together, he said:

"O Heroes of Iran, give heed unto my words, for verily I have thought of a plan which shall settle this strife. Behold! upon the borders of my dominion there is a demon-fortress which no hero hath yet conquered. Let KaiKhosrau and Friburz go forth, therefore, and let them take with them an army, and lo! I will bestow the crown and treasure upon the Prince at whose hands the castle shall be subdued."

Thus spake Kaikous, and the plan being agreed upon, Friburz begged of his father that he be sent forth first upon the expedition. So, permission being given, gaily he and Tus set out, promising to return triumphant within a few days.

But alas! when the army reached the demon fort, lo! the ground seemed all in flames—one universal fire raging round and round, while the withering wind which blew from thence was like unto the scorching breath of red-hot furnaces. And behold! though they searched and searched, these warriors brave could find neither gate nor door of entrance, though many a valiant one perished in the search, consumed to ashes by the awful heat, which seemed to be the poisoned breath of raging demons. So at length, after a fruitless week, Friburz and Tus returned, worn out, scorched, and half-dead with watching, care, and toil—and still the fortress stood.

So, it being now KaiKhosrau's turn, bravely he set forth with Gew and Gudarz, his faithful friends, and when he saw the blazing fort, reddening all the earth and sky, full well he knew that this could only be the work of sorcery. And so, since in a heavenly dream he had been taught how to destroy the charms of fell magicians, he wrote a letter, amber-perfumed, in which he named the name of God. Then piously he bound it unto his javelin's point, and when he was come nigh unto the demon fort, behold, Gew the Valiant, flung it far beyond the walls within the magic citadel.

And lo! the missile safely lodged, a noise like thunder rent the air, and all the world grew dark, as when the sun hath gone to rest. Yea, and long it so remained, but when at last once more the light appeared, behold, the magic tower had vanished from the earth.

Now thus it was that KaiKhosrau vanquished the demons, and thus it was also that at last he came into his own. For, shortly after this wondrous victory, the coronation ceremony took place with great pomp and splendor, Kai-Khosrau the Prince becoming KaiKhosrau the Shah, of whom the poet says:

> "Justice he spread with equal hand,
> Rooting oppression from the land;
> And every desert, wood, and wild,
> With early cultivation smiled;
> And every plain with verdure clad,
> And every Persian heart was glad."

LATER FEATS OF RUSTEM

NOW in the Book of the Kings it is written that when KaiKhosrau ascended the throne, Kaikous required him to swear a great oath that the waters of forgetfulness should never quench the flame of vengeance in his heart until Afrasiab, the murderer of Siawush, be utterly destroyed.

So, when he was well settled upon his throne, KaiKhosrau sent forth a great army under the leadership of Tus to begin his work of vengeance. But alas! Tus, though brave, was hot-headed and touchy; yea, and disobedient, thereby bringing unto death Firoud, the valiant half-brother of KaiKhosrau. When brought face to face with the enemy, however, he and his men fought bravely, but all to no purpose.

For lo! Afrasiab had sent Baru, a magician perfect in his art, upon the neighboring mountains to involve them in darkness, and to produce, by his conjuring, fearful downfalls of snow and hail. Accordingly, when Tus and his army advanced, they were deluged by a fearful downpour of rain and sleet, so that not even the fierce conflict with Piran's brave warriors warmed their blood, which seemed frozen in their veins. So the army of Iran suffered a great defeat, and so terrible was their suffering from the mighty cold, that the living envied their dead comrades.

Now in this extremity Tus and Gudarz prayed earnestly unto Ormuzd, when lo! the Angel Serosch appeared unto them, pointing unto the mountain from whence the tempest descended. Quickly, then, brave Gudarz galloped unto the summit, where he discovered the magician deeply engaged in incantation and witchcraft. Hesitating not, therefore, he hastily drew his sword and cut off the wizard's arms. Then suddenly a great whirlwind arose, sweeping away the darkness that prevailed, and then nothing remained of the snow, the hail, or the cold. And now, the armies being upon a more equal footing, behold, the heroes of Iran fought so valiantly that soon they won a glorious victory.

Then Tus was glad, and to celebrate the victory he made a great feast, darkening the heads of his warriors with wine. But presently when the revelry was at its height, and when Gudarz alone was master of his fate, behold, Afrasiab was upon them, and then fearful was the slaughter and utter the defeat of Iran. And thus ended the campaign of Tus, for when KaiKhosrau learned of his folly he bade Friburz, the son of Kaikous, take unto him the flag of Kavah, and the golden boots, and lead the army in place of Tus.

So Friburz, after he had reorganized and reinforced the army, once again offered battle unto Piran-Wisa, and there was waged a conflict such as the sun hath ne'er looked upon. But alas! the heroes of Iran were utterly routed; and as the handful of survivors appeared before the Shah, lo, they carried their hands crossed upon their breasts, and they were humble as slaves. Then was Kai-Khossau sick with shame when he beheld this sorry lot of heroes, and in his sore displeasure he withdrew from his courts, letting not the light of his countenance shine upon his people.

So, in their sorrow and desperation, once more the nobles hastened unto Seistan, beseeching Rustem to come
unto their aid. And the Mighty One, tarrying not for
rest, quickly came forth, mustering and putting the army
into battle order. And behold! when again the two opposing forces were met in conflict, the day belonged unto
Iran.

Then Afrasiab, hearing of the arrival of Rustem, immediately called unto his aid three distinguished champions:
Shinkul, Khakan, and Kamus. Now all these warriors
had wondrous records—Kamus particularly:

> "For when he frowned, the air grew freezing cold;
> And when he smiled, the genial spring smiled down
> Roses and hyacinths, and all was brightness!"

Now upon the arrival of the three champions, it was to
the great Kamus that Piran first paid his respects, describing unto him, in glowing colors, the strength and prowess
of Rustem. But Kamus, in nowise disturbed, replied
coolly unto Piran:

> "Is praise like this to Rustem due?
> And what if all thou sayest be true?
> Are his large limbs of iron made?
> Will they resist my trenchant blade?
> His head may now his shoulders grace,
> But will it long retain its place?
> Let me but meet him in the fight,
> And thou shalt see Kamus's might!"

But alas! when Kamus the confident challenged Rustem, quickly the Hero despatched him. Yea, and not only
him, but Shinkul and Khakan as well. Then was Afrasiab terrified, and quickly he sent Piran-Wisa forth to sue

He discovered the magician deeply engaged in incantation and witchcraft.

for peace. And Rustem spake graciously unto the old general, giving unto him greeting from KaiKhosrau, and lauding him for his good deeds unto Siawush, and unto Sohrab, his son. And he said:

"O Grand Old Hero, truly thou art worthy a better master than black-hearted Afrasiab. Come over unto Iran, therefore, and thou shalt have honor, and happiness, and riches while thou livest, for nightly KaiKhosrau and his mother behold thy face in their dreams, and much they long to see thee."

But Piran, with tears in his eyes, said unto Rustem:

"O Hero of Heroes! For five hundred years have I served Turan, my native land, and though my heart goeth out unto KaiKhosrau, my son, yet can I not prove unfaithful unto those who rely upon my good faith. So did not brave Siawush; and Turan, too, hath her heroes, O Mighty One, even as Iran the land of light."

Now Rustem's heart went out in admiration unto this splendid old hero, and he said:

"O noble Pehliva! verily I give thee honor for thy loyalty and faith, even while I grieve that Iran cannot possess thee. As for the terms of peace, KaiKhosrau desireth naught but that the murderers of Siawush be delivered into his hands."

Then Piran said sadly unto Rustem:

"O gracious Pehliva, that which thou asketh, verily it can never be. For the slayers of Siawush are near kinsfolk unto Afrasiab, who will never give them up."

So, as naught could be done, the Heroes parted sadly, but in friendship, even though they knew that battle must rage between them. And behold! once more the opposing forces were drawn up for conflict.

> "Now 'twas mid-day when the strife began,
> With steed to steed and man to man;
> And clouds of dust that rolled on high,
> Threw darkness o'er the earth and sky.
> Each soldier on the other rushed,
> And every blade with crimson blushed,
> And valiant hearts were trod upon,
>   Like sand beneath the horse's feet.
> And when the warrior's life was gone,
>   His mail became his winding sheet."

And alas! for forty days the battle raged thus, until the plains were so strewn with the bodies of the slain that an ant could not have found a road to pass between them. Now blood flowed upon all sides, and heads without bodies, and bodies without heads, covered the ground. For neither the claws of the leopard nor the trunk of the elephant, neither the high mountains nor the waters of the earth, could prevail against Rustem when he fought at the head of his hosts.

Now he slew the mightiest of the Tartars, and only good old Piran was he mindful to spare; yea, and when the remnant of the host finally fled before his wrath, he pursued them even unto the mountains, where Afrasiab and his kinsfolk, in their terror, had hidden themselves, and he destroyed his courts utterly with fire, after which he turned him back unto Iran. Then the heart of KaiKhosrau rejoiced like unto a paradise, and for a month Rustem abode in his presence, feasted and lauded continually, after which he returned once more unto Seistan.

> "And now we come to Akwan Dew,
> Whom Rustem next in combat slew."

For it is related that one day shortly after Rustem's return unto Seistan, as KaiKhosrau was sitting in his beautiful garden abounding in roses and the balmy luxuriance of spring, surrounded by his heroes, and enjoying the pleasures of the banquet, lo, a shepherd came unto the Court demanding audience, and when it was granted he said:

"O King of Kings! Behold, a wild ass is broken in among my horses, and he doeth great mischief, for his ferocity is that of a lion or a demon. Send forth, therefore, I entreat thee, one of thy heroes that he may slay him, else am I ruined."

Now the Shah knew right well that this was no wild ass, but the evil Deev, Akwan Dew, who had taken upon him this disguise. And knowing that none but Rustem would be equal to this adventure, a swift messenger was at once sent unto Seistan to summon him forth. And the Mighty One obeyed the voice of the Shah, for he was weary of inactivity, and this promised to be an exciting adventure.

So presently, guided by the shepherds, Rustem set forth, but it was not until the fourth day of his search that he fell in with the Deev. Now being anxious to take this wicked one alive in order to send him as a trophy unto KaiKhosrau, the Hero tried to throw his cord about him. But behold! in a moment the wild ass vanished under his hand. Whereupon, Rustem knew that it was really Akwan Dew with whom he had to deal, and that he must fight against the powers of magic. Yet was he not dismayed.

And now, the wild ass again appearing, lo, Rustem pursued him with his drawn sword. When he would have run him through, however, behold! the weapon cut naught but the empty air, for again the Deev had vanished under his hands. Then, disappointed with his sword, the Hero tried both spear and arrow, but still to no purpose, for again and yet again the wicked one escaped his blows by vanishing. And alas! thus for three days and nights Rustem fought, as it were, against a shadow. Wearied at last, with his fruitless exertions, however, presently he dismounted, and leading Rakush unto a green spot near a limpid fountain, he allowed him to graze, while he himself went to sleep.

But lo! when the Deev saw that Rustem slept, he rushed toward him like a whirlwind, and, rapidly digging up the ground on every side, took up the plot of ground and the Champion together, placed them upon his head, and deliberately walked away with them. Howbeit, at this critical moment Rakush, beholding the peril of his master, neighed loudly, thus awaking Rustem. And lo! when the Hero saw what had befallen, he feared his hour was come, yet he did not despair. The Deev, however, seeing that his captive was awake, said unto him:

> "Warrior! now no longer free!
> Tell me what thy wish may be;
> Shall I plunge thee in the sea,
> Or leave thee on the mountain drear,
> None to give thee succor near?
> Tell thy wish to me!"

Now Rustem, knowing that the Deevs act ever by the rule of contraries, and realizing that if thrown into the sea his chance for escape would be better, quickly said unto the Deev:

> "O, plunge me not in the roaring sea,
> The maw of a fish is no home for me;
> But cast me forth on the mountain; there
> Is the lion's haunt and the tiger's lair;

And for them I shall be a morsel of food,
They will eat my flesh and drink my blood;
But my bones will be left to show the place
Where this form was devoured by the feline race;
Yes, something will then remain of me,
Whilst nothing escapes from the roaring sea!"

Thus spake Rustem in his guile, and well for him was it that his mind was so fertile in invention. For behold! the wicked Akwan Dew, having learned the particular desire of the Hero, quickly raised him up with his hands and flung him from his lofty height headlong into the deep and roaring ocean, at a spot where hungry crocodiles would devour him.

And alas! scarcely had the Champion touched the water, when one of these horrible creatures speedily darted upon him with the eager intention of devouring him alive. But in the twinkling of an eye Rustem drew his sword and severed the monster's head. Then quickly another came, and was put to death in the same manner, and the water was crimsoned with blood. And while the Hero fought the crocodiles with his right hand, with his left he swam toward the shore, and though long was the struggle and sore, yet finally, when night was fallen, he at last succeeded in putting his foot upon the dry land. Then, when he had given thanks unto Ormuzd, and rested him, he returned unto the spot by the fountain.

But here a most unpleasant surprise awaited him, for Rakush, his steed, was not there. Then fear fell upon Rustem, and eagerly he wandered about seeking his matchless charger; but in vain, until at last, coming unto a green meadow, he spied him among the horses of Afrasiab. For alas! while the Champion was fighting the crocodiles and the mighty surges of the ocean, the keepers had succeeded in ensnaring Rakush.

When the mighty war-horse heard the soft whistle of his master, however, he neighed joyously, and brake from the keepers, running with swift foot unto Rustem, rubbing his nose gently against his shoulder, as if to make sure it was really he. But no sooner had the Hero mounted, than horse and rider of one accord made a swift dash for the keepers, right speedily running them down, and despatching them. Then Rustem took the herds, together with four white elephants, unto himself.

But presently, as the Hero tarried in the midst of the herds, Afrasiab whose heart yearned to look upon his favorite steeds, came forth from his hiding-place, dreaming not that his enemy was near. When he beheld Rustem, therefore, he was dismayed, for he thought that the Champion had discovered his hiding-place and was come forth to take him. So, quickly he offered battle unto the Pehliva, supported by those who were with him. But alas for Afrasiab! for again Rustem fought with such might that he quickly overcame the whole force, slaying sixty with his sword and forty with his mace. Then the King, terrified, fled swiftly and silently away unto a new hiding-place, lamenting anew his bitter fate.

Now Rustem longed to pursue Afrasiab, but at this moment Akwan Dew came forth once more, thinking that after such a strenuous fight the Hero would fall an easy prey into his hands. But Rustem, springing quickly upon him, struck such a mighty blow with his sword that lo! the Deev's head rolled off, before that he could vanish by magic, as before. Then triumphantly Rustem returned unto the Court, bearing with him, as trophies of his adventure, Afrasiab's favorite steeds, and the hideous head of the wicked Akwan Dew, who would trouble the world no more with his wickedness and tricks of sorcery.

So ended Rustem's adventure with the Deev, but behold! another was soon to follow, and this was nothing less than his conflict with the Champion Barzu. Yea, and almost was this the Hero's last combat—so mighty was the prowess of this giant, especially trained by Afrasiab to cause the world to become dark unto Rustem.

Now when KaiKhosrau learned that Afrasiab had put into the field against him ten thousand experienced horsemen, under Barzu, his mighty champion, he was amazed; for he had not dreamed that so soon after his overwhelming defeat he could place another large army in commission. However, he ordered Tus and Friburz, with twelve thousand horsemen, to go forth at once, while he prepared to follow later with a still larger force. Yea, and he sent for Rustem also, for this time he hoped to exterminate utterly, not only Afrasiab, but all his kin.

But alas! before KaiKhosrau arrived at the front Barzu and Tus had engaged in a terrible battle, which resulted in a glorious victory for the men of Turan. Yea, and worse! for so terrible was the might of Barzu, that in the end, all the Persians fled, leaving Tus and Friburz to fall into the hands of the Tartars. Quickly, however, Rustem hastened to the rescue of the two heroes, taking with him Gustahem, the brother of Tus.

Now the two warriors stole softly into the enemy's camp, and by chance they came unto the tent of the King, wherein they found what they sought. For behold! Afrasiab was seated upon his throne, with Barzu upon his right hand, and Piran-Wisa upon his left, while Tus and Friburz stood in chains before them. And, listening, the two warriors heard the King say unto the captive Princes:

"Sleep well, O Persian Dogs! for to-morrow shall ye behold the sun rise for the last time, since ye are sentenced to die the death of Siawush."

Thus spake black-hearted Afrasiab, and departed, leaving the prisoners in the hands of the guards. Then Rustem, requesting Gustahem to follow cautiously, drew near and waited until the watchmen were off their guard. Then silently they overpowered and killed them, stealing softly away with their prisoners, without being discovered, and behold! great was the rejoicing when they were come safely unto the Persian camp.

But alas! when Afrasiab learned that Rustem had stolen into his camp and liberated the prisoners, he fairly writhed with anger and mortification. And at once he sent forth Barzu to challenge Rustem to single combat.

So the Champion of the World went forth, and behold, Barzu was his equal in size, and apparently also in strength and skill. For though they fought long, first with one weapon, then with another, Rustem prevailed not. Then they tried wrestling, and terrible were the wrenches and grasps they gave and received, but Barzu, noting that this also was vain, once more grasped his mace, and, raising it high, struck Rustem such a blow upon the head that the Champion thought a whole mountain had fallen upon him. But, though one arm was completely disabled, no sign thereof did Rustem give—to the great amazement of Barzu, who cried:

"Truly, thou art a most surprising warrior, and seemingly invulnerable. Now if I had struck such a blow upon a mountain, quickly would it have been broken into a thousand fragments; and yet upon thee it seemeth no more than the prick of a flea."

Yea, and he said unto himself, shaking his head thoughtfully:

"Heaven forbid that I should ever receive so bewildering a blow upon my own head!"

But Rustem, having successfully concealed the anguish of his wound, now artfully suggested that, as it was late, perhaps it would be better to finish the combat on the following day, to which Barzu readily agreed, as he, too, was exhausted by the long struggle. So the two champions retired, and Rustem, showing his lacerated arm unto the Shah, said:

"O Glorious One! Behold, I have escaped from yon raging dragon, but I bring back with me the marks of his teeth. And now, alas! who will finish the struggle on the morrow?"

But behold! though Rustem spent a night of pain and grief, morning brought unto him glad news, for Feramurz, his glorious son, arrived unexpectedly in camp.

So, a few hours later, when both armies were drawn up, and Barzu, like a mad elephant, rode forward to resume the combat, he was met, apparently, by his old antagonist. For lo! Rustem had attired Feramurz in his own armor, supplied him with his own weapons, and mounted him upon Rakush, telling him to represent himself unto Barzu as the warrior who had engaged him the day before.

Now as Feramurz rode forward he shot an arrow at Barzu, crying:

"O Youthful Giant! Behold thine adversary come forth once more to try thy strength. Advance, therefore, and beware!"

But Barzu, amazed at such lightness of spirit, cried:
"O Mighty One! Why this hilarity? Art thou, then, so reckless of thy life?"

And Feramurz, laughing, said:

"Knowest thou not, O Sober One, that the field of fight is, unto the warrior, the mansion of pleasure? Wherefore, then, should I not be gay?"

But Barzu, who began to suspect that he had to do with a new antagonist, said tauntingly:

"O Light O' Heart! Is the champion whom I encountered yesterday perhaps wounded or dead, that thou hast attired thyself in his mail and mounted his charger?"

Now to this challenge Feramurz replied still gayly:

"Perhaps thou hast lost thy wits, O Giant, since thou knowest not thy adversary. Now almost I extinguished thee yesterday, and to-day I mean to finish thee; so once more I say unto thee, beware!"

Thus saying, Feramurz rushed valiantly upon his adversary, struck him blow upon blow with his battle-axe, and drawing his noose from the saddle-strap, with the quickness of lightning he secured his prize. Then might he speedily have put an end to Barzu's existence, but he preferred taking him alive to exhibit unto the army.

But not without a struggle was Feramurz to carry off his prize, for Afrasiab, seeing the perilous condition of his Champion, quickly pressed forward his whole army to the rescue. But KaiKhosrau and Rustem, equally on the alert, quickly supported Feramurz—Rustem throwing another noose around the already captured Barzu, to prevent the possibility of his escape. And now, so great was the grief of Afrasiab for the loss of Barzu, that he immediately retreated across the Jihun, quitting Persia with all his troops.

As for Barzu, beholding in the youthful giant great possibilities, Rustem begged KaiKhossau that his life might be spared, and carried him back with him unto Seistan. Yea, and here he assisted Rustem greatly in his next adventure, which was with Susen, a wicked sorceress, as you shall hear.

For behold! shortly after his return unto Seistan, Rustem invited unto his courts a large number of the most celebrated heroes of the kingdom, since he proposed to give a most magnificent banquet. But alas that it must be recorded! before the feast had even begun, some of the heroes fell out—as even heroes will—and dire were the consequences.

For you must know that among the honored guests were Tus and Gudarz, who were ever hostile unto each other, and, sad to relate, shortly after their arrival at Seistan, as usual, a dispute took place between them—this time it being a question of precedence. As a consequence, therefore, Tus, who ever boasted of his ancestry, reviled Gudarz in his anger, saying unto the old warrior:

"Old Man! How canst thou put thyself upon a footing with me? For verily I am the son of Nuder, and the grandson of Feridoun, whilst thou art but the son of Kavah the smith."

Now this naturally angered Gudarz, who replied unto Tus:

"Vain Boaster, though thy ancestors were wise and mighty, greatly I fear that their robe of merit reacheth not unto thee. As for the ancestry of Gudarz, hear me this once, then put a chain upon the door of thy lips forever. For think you I need blush to be the kinsman of the glorious Kavah? Verily, nay; rather, I glory in him. For was he not the man who, when the world could boast of little valor, tore wrathfully up the infamous name-roll of Zohak, giving unto the Persians freedom from the fangs of the devouring serpents? Was it not he, I say, who raised the first banner, proclaiming aloud freedom for Iran? Verily unto Kavah the empire oweth its greatest blessing, so well may Gudarz glory to be his son!"

Unto this, however, Tus, beside himself with wrath, rejoined:

"Old Man, thine arrow may pierce an anvil, but mine can pierce the heart of the Kaf mountain!"

But Gudarz, smiling, softly said:

"Verily, if words were deeds, then would the Mighty Tus rival his glorious ancestors!"

And alas! this so aroused the anger of Tus, that swiftly he drew forth his dagger to punish the offender. But Rehham interfered in behalf of Gudarz, which so increased the rage of Tus that in high dudgeon the Hero retired from the company and set out upon his return unto Iran.

Now Rustem was not present when the dispute took place, but when he heard of it he was displeased saying that Gudarz was a relation of the family, and Tus his guest, and therefore wrong had been done, since a guest ought always to be honored. And he said:

"Verily a guest should be held as sacred as a king, and it is ever the custom of heroes to treat a guest as the king of the feast."

And having thus spoken, Rustem requested Gudarz to go after Tus, and by fair words and proper excuses bring him back unto the festal board. So Gudarz departed, but scarcely was he gone when Gew rose up and said:

"Tus, in his anger is little better than a madman, and my father also hath a hasty temper where he is concerned. I should like, therefore, O Mighty One, to follow after them to prevent further disagreement."

So, consent being given by Rustem, behold, Gew went forth taking with him Byzun, who was also anxious to go. But when the three heroes had departed, lo, Rustem became apprehensive, so he sent Feramurz forth also to preserve the peace. Then finally Zal, fearing that Tus might not be easily prevailed upon to return, either by Gudarz, Gew, Byzun, or Feramurz, resolved to go forth himself to soothe the temper so unwisely ruffled at the banquet.

Now it happened that Tus was obliged, on his return journey, to pass by the abode of Susen the sorceress. And alas! though he suspected it not, this was a trap which Afrasiab had set to ensnare the heroes of Iran—particularly Rustem, whom the King greatly desired to secure, and whom the sorceress had promised to destroy, together with his whole family. For she said unto the King:

"Fighting disappointment brings,
Sword and mace are useless things;
If thou wouldst a conqueror be,
Monarch! put thy trust in me;
Soon the mighty chief shall bleed,—
Spells and charms will do the deed!"

So, the snare being set, lo, as Tus approached this enchanted abode, he beheld cooks and confectioners on all sides, preparing many and rare dishes of food, together with every species of sweetmeat. And alas! disappointed of Rustem's banquet, also hungry and curious, Tus dismounted and, leaving his horse with an attendant, entered

the great dining-hall, where he was met by the charming
sorceress herself, who, escorting him unto a table bounte-
ously supplied with charmed viands, and goblets of rich
wine, spake unto him gay words, waiting upon him with
her own fair hands.

But behold! after Tus had eaten a few mouthfuls, he
began to feel very strange, and presently, his armor bursting asunder, he gazed in horror at himself, for he perceived
sharp quills sticking out from his body in all directions,
and happening to glance in a mirror, he beheld, not Tus,
the descendant of Kings, but a great, ugly wild boar.
And lo! as he would have cried out in his dismay, he could
do naught but grunt. Then the enchantress, laughing
wickedly, drove him out into a yard, from which there was
no escape, and prepared for her next victim.

And as it happened unto Tus, so chanced it with all the
heroes sent after him, save only White-haired Zal—him
could they not entice, for he would neither enter the enchanted dwelling, nor taste of the charmed food and wine.
For lo! Serosch the Blessed had whispered into his ear
that the howling wild boars in the yard were the heroes
who had preceded him.

And when Zal realized what had befallen, quickly he
sent word unto Rustem. Then, single-handed, he attacked
the sorceress, who, perceiving that she was discovered,
quickly fled into the strong-room of the palace, securely
bolting the door. But tirelessly Zal battered the iron until
it could resist his blows no more, whereupon, out rushed
a mighty Deev, who at once began a furious battle with
Zal, in which he was nearly victorious. But fortunately
Feramurz, who had been delayed by the way, now came
up, and bidding the venerable Zal stand aside, he took his

place, fighting fiercely with the wicked one until Rustem and Barzu arrived upon the scene.

And behold! learning what had happened, Rustem was struck with horror, for seldom was an enchanter so bold as to change the form of his victim. Leaving giant Barzu to combat with the Deev, therefore, in spite of the forces of magic that opposed him, Rustem succeeded in piercing unto the innermost hiding-place of the sorceress, and though again and again she changed her shape in her efforts to escape, he dragged her pitilessly forth into the yard where the heroes, in the shape of wild boars, were making the night hideous with their howls and growls. And here the Champion said unto his victim:

"O Wicked One, quickly restore these heroes unto their proper shape, else shall my life-destroying sword quickly make an end of thee, even as happened unto Akwan Dew."

Now the sorceress, beholding herself in the power of Deev-destroying Rustem, quickly restored the heroes unto themselves. But alas for Susen! for so thankful were her victims to escape from her power, that instinctively they exclaimed with one accord: "Thank God!" at which the wicked sorceress at once vanished from both sight and hearing.

Then quickly Rustem returned unto Barzu, but he also had vanquished his foe, though the Deev had evaded the stroke of his sword many times by vanishing. So, the wicked ones being both destroyed, Rustem set fire unto the enchanted mansion, after which the heroes all rode back unto Seistan, where they feasted gaily for a whole week.

And behold! from this time forth, Tus and Gudarz disputed no more, for when they were tempted, they quickly remembered those dreadful hours spent as snapping, snarling beasts, and so they refrained, realizing that such conduct was unworthy of heroes.

After this it came to pass that yet again Afrasiab raised a mighty army to go forth in vengeance against Iran, and behold! this time their progress was stayed by Gudarz the wise, who, at the head of the heroes of Iran, disputed their advance. Now the contest waged was long and bitter, and the slaughter fearful, for not only did the two great hosts fight *en masse*, but after this, lo, the flower of the armies met, one couple after the other, in single combat. And alas! in this mighty hero-contest, brave Piran-Wisa met a glorious death.

Then, in his anger and despair at brave Piran's loss, Afrasiab sent forth his dearly-loved son Scheideh, bidding him challenge the Shah of Iran to combat and utterly to lay him low. But behold! Rustem answered the summons, and soon the son of the King lay lifeless upon the plain. Yea, and now the Champion routed the army of Turan utterly, and once more the King was forced to become a wanderer, together with his few remaining kinsfolk.

But not long did Afrasiab escape the hands of justice. For presently Hum, a hermit of the race of Feridoun, discovered and brought the wretched monarch unto Kai-Khosrau, who caused both the King and wicked Gersiwaz to perish even as they had caused death to come upon Siawush the Prince.

And now a strange thing happened in Iran. For Kai-Khosrau, fearing to become uplifted in pride like unto Jemshed, because that all the people loved and praised him, determined, after much prayer unto Ormuzd, to quit the world before this evil should come to pass. And alas!

though Zal and Rustem came purposely up from Seistan
to try to influence KaiKhosrau against this strange deter-
mination, yet was it vain.

So, after having appointed Lohurasp as his successor,
and arranged all things for his departure, KaiKhosrau got
him upon his horse to go forth unto the mountains. And
behold! there went with him Zal and Rustem, Gudarz also,
and Gustahem and Gew, Byzun the Valiant, Friburz, the
son of Kaikous, and Tus the Pehliva.

Now these heroes followed after KaiKhosrau from the
plain even unto the crest of the mountains, and they ceased
not from mourning that which was done of their King,
striving to change his purpose. But KaiKhosrau, at peace
with himself and the world, gave not ear unto their sup-
plications.

So disconsolately the little company followed the King,
who was guided in his path by a flock of wondrous pheas-
ants, until they were come unto a place where there
seemed to be no farther path. Then KaiKhosrau said unto
the heroes:

"O my Pehliva, here must we part, for almost have I
reached the fountain shown unto me by the Angel of God;
and from here on I enter upon a path where there is
neither herb nor water. Return, therefore, upon the road
that ye have come, for lo! my hour is at hand.

So Zal and Rustem and Gudarz bade KaiKhosrau a tender farewell, and with tear-blinded eyes returned unto the
plain, lamenting that one upon whom Heaven had bestowed
a mind so great, and a heart so brave, could not await his
hour in patience.

But alas! Gew, and Tus, and Byzun, and Friburz, being
unwilling to go back, followed after the King yet another

day. But so rough was the way that their strength was spent when evening was come. However, KaiKhosrau cheered them, and soon were they come unto the Fountain of Rest. And now, once again, the Shah bade that his heroes leave him, saying:

"O Valiant Ones! Return quickly upon your path when I am gone, neither linger in this place, though it should rain diamonds and pearls, musk and amber. For presently, out of the mountains a mighty storm will arise, and there will come a fall of snow, which shall prove the winding-sheet of all who linger. Farewell, then, O my Brave Heroes, and forget not to give heed unto my words of warning."

Now, so speaking, KaiKhosrau stepped into the fountain, immediately vanishing.

> "And not a trace was left behind,
>   And not a dimple on the wave;
>   All sought, but sought in vain, to find
>   The spot which proved KaiKhosrau's grave!"

And alas for his brave heroes! For in their grief and weariness, heedlessly they laid themselves down by the fountain to sleep, and presently, even as predicted by the vanished King, a mighty wind arose, and the snow fell thick and soft, awakening not the tired ones who slumbered so fatally beside the Pool of Rest. Yea, and their sleep was long, for when, many days after, Zal and Rustem went forth to seek the missing ones, behold, they found them slumbering still, covered o'er by soft, white blankets of snow. But alas! so complete was the passing of Kai-Khosrau that his body they found not, though they dragged the fatal fountain in their search. Sorrowfully, however, they bare the snow-covered heroes back unto the plain, amidst the wailing of the whole army. And well might they weep, for thus perished the flower of the heroes of Iran, and thus also ended the old régime, so glorious in its record of brave deeds.

ISFENDIYAR'S SEVEN LABORS, OR HEFTKHAN

"Rustem had seven great labors, wondrous power
Nerved his strong arm in danger's needful hour;
And now Firdusi's legend strains declare
The seven great labors of Isfendiyar."

NOW of all the heroes of Persia, none so nearly rivalled Rustem as the brave Isfendiyar, son of Gushtasp the Shah. Young, valiant, and possessed of great ability and promise, his father gave unto him the command of his armies, promising unto him the throne of Iran, if he should conquer Arjasp the demon king, who threatened to bring the Persians beneath his yoke. Now thus it is that we hear of Isfendiyar first. And short work, indeed, did he make of his campaign with the Deevs, for though so fierce was the fight that the heroes closed not their eyes in slumber, neither ceased from conflict for the space of twice seven days, yet in the end did the valor and might of Isfendiyar prevail, and Arjasp was forced to flee before the face of the valorous youth and his brave warriors.

So, having won this glorious victory, joyously Isfendiyar returned unto his father, craving his blessing. But Gushtasp said:

"O my brave son, truly thy deeds have been glorious, but before thou mountest the throne of thy father I must send thee forth yet again, that thou mayest win the whole world unto Zerdusht, the Great Prophet, for so will thy reign be blessed."

So again Isfendiyar went forth as warrior-crusader, and lo! he travelled not only through all the provinces of Persia, but even unto foreign lands. And, so successful was he that—

"Where'er he went he was received
With welcome, all the world believed,
And all with grateful feelings took
The Holy Zendavesta-book,
Proud their new worship to declare,
The worship of Isfendiyar."

And now, having won the world unto Zerdusht, the young crusader again returned unto his father. But alas! one who hated Isfendiyar because of his valor and triumphs had succeeded in poisoning the mind of Gushtasp against his son, telling him that Isfendiyar, being ambitious, was plotting the overthrow of his father. So it came to pass that when the Hero presented himself before his sire, Gushtasp greeted him not, but, turning unto his courtiers, said:

"O Nobles of Iran! What think you should be done with that son who in the lifetime of his father usurps his authority and meditates his death?"

Then with one accord the nobles answered, saying: "O Lord of the World,

"Such a son should either be
Broken on the felon-tree,
Or in prison bound with chains,
Whilst his wicked life remains,
Else thyself, thy kingdom, all
Will be ruined by his thrall."

Alas! when Gushtasp heard the words of his nobles, quickly he turned him unto his guards, saying:

"Verily, Isfendiyar is such a son. Bind him, therefore, and let him be buried from my sight in the deepest dungeon of the palace."

So, in spite of the remonstrances and pleadings of many who loved and grieved for the injustice done unto their Prince, behold, he was imprisoned in a dreary dungeon, where chains of weight were hung upon him. Yea, and thus was he shut away from the glad sunshine of the world for many long years. And alas! the iron entered into his soul as well as into his body, for he remembered that, though innocent himself, his father had done unto Lohurasp, his sire, even as he had accused him; yet was he free and exalted.

But retribution was at hand. For, when Arjasp, the demon king, learned that Isfendiyar was fettered, and that Gushtasp was given over unto pleasure, behold, he gathered together a great army, and in a moment when he knew the kingdom to be unguarded, and unprepared for resistance, suddenly he fell upon Iran's capital, putting to death Lohurasp, the aged Shah, and taking captive the two fair daughters of Gushtasp. Yea, and he also threw fire into the temple of Zerdusht, causing much destruction and loss of life.

Now at this time Gushtasp was at Seistan, enjoying a hunting trip with Rustem; and thither hastened a messenger to inform the Shah of the great disaster that had befallen. So quickly Gushtasp called together his army, putting himself at its head, but in the first engagement Arjasp routed him utterly. Overwhelmed with dismay, therefore, the Shah quickly called together his counsellors, for he knew not what to do in the sore straits so suddenly come upon him. But neither did his nobles, and for a time their hearts were filled with despair. Then one, wise above the others, said:

"O King of Kings! Verily, Isfendiyar alone can deliver Iran from the woe which threateneth. I counsel thee, therefore, release him, for he alone can conquer this Demon King."

Then Gushtasp, remembering how the Prince had conquered Arjasp before, took heart, saying:

"Verily, if Isfendiyar shall succeed in delivering us from this foe, then I call ye all to witness that my oath is given to abandon unto him the throne and crown."

So right speedily the Shah sent messengers unto Isfendiyar, that they should unbind his chains, and with them he sent a letter, begging forgiveness for his cruelty, and promising that his enemies should be put to death in his presence; yea, and that surely the crown should be his when he again overcame Arjasp.

But too long had Isfendiyar languished in prison to be easily moved by his father's tardy, though opportune, repentance. So he said:

"Wherefore should I weary myself in my father's cause? Verily, I might have rotted in my prison, forgotten of my sire, had not his enemies forced him to remember that perchance the valiant Isfendiyar yet lived."

Then the nobles, seeing that appeal on his father's account was useless, said unto him:

"Verily, O Prince, thy father hath treated thee ill, but perhaps thou knowest not that thy two fair sisters are in bonds unto Arjasp? Surely it behooveth thee to deliver them from their living death!"

Now when Isfendiyar heard this dire news, at once he sprang to his feet, commanding that his chains be struck from off his limbs, and as the men were slow, behold, he stretched himself mightily, thus bursting his chains so that they fell clanking at his feet. Then he made haste to go before his father, for he thirsted to be revenged for the indignity done unto his sisters.

So, peace being made between Isfendiyar and his sire, soon there rallied about the Prince a great multitude that tarried not, but went forth like a mighty whirlwind. And behold! so great was their force and fury that naught could stand before them; nay, not even the great Arjasp, who fled before the face of Isfendiyar in terror of his life. For never had he seen such fury in battle, though he had fought with many heroes.

And behold! the enemy being once more vanquished, Isfendiyar returned unto his father, craving the fulfilment of his vow. But Gushtasp, when he beheld himself freed from danger, repented him of his promise, for he had no desire to give the reins of government unto another. Therefore he spake angrily unto Isfendiyar, saying:

"Verily, my son, I marvel that while thy sisters languish in the bondage of Arjasp thou canst consider thyself victorious! Now it hath been revealed unto me that they are hidden in Arjasp's brazen fortress, and that the great chief and all his demon warriors are gone in behind its walls. I say unto thee, therefore, storm this terrible fortress and deliver thy sisters who pine. Then, when thou returnest them safe unto my arms, by Ormuzd the Blessed, I swear that thy name shall be exalted as Shah throughout the land.

> "'Then go!' the smiling monarch said,
> Invoking blessings on his head,
> 'And may kind Heaven thy refuge be,
> Leading thee on to victory.'"

Now as Isfendiyar knew not the way unto the retreat of
Arjasp, behold, he called before him Karugsar, a demon
champion whom he had conquered and still held captive,
saying unto him:

"O Mighty One, reveal unto me, I pray thee, the road
unto the Brazen Fortress, for behold! we go forth presently to conquer the kingdom of Arjasp, and to restore my
fair sisters unto liberty."

Then Karugsar, surprised that any hero should think of
entering upon so hazardous an enterprise, replied unto
Isfendiyar:

"O Hero of Heroes! Behold, there are three different
routes which lead unto the fortress of brass. One there is
that occupieth three months, the way leading through
a beautiful country, adorned with cities and gardens and
pastures; a second, less attractive, but perfectly safe, employing only two months; and a third, by which the journey may be accomplished in seven days—called on this
account the Heft-Khan, or seven stages. But, mark you,
my Lord! at every stage upon this route some monster
or terrible difficulty must be overcome. Yea; and so
truly fearful is it that no monarch, even supported
by a large army, hath ever yet ventured to proceed by
this route, for assuredly any one attempting it would be
lost."

Alas! at this description of the terrors of the Heft-Khan,
Isfendiyar became thoughtful, but he said:

"Verily, no man can die before his time, and I have
heard it said that a man of valor should ever choose the
shortest route; therefore, we go by way of the Heft-
Khan."

So spake brave Isfendiyar and having selected a force of

twelve thousand chosen horsemen, together with an abundance of treasure, behold, he set forth upon the perilous way.

Now the first day passed without danger, and almost Isfendiyar thought that his guide had deceived him as to the perils of the way. But as evening fell, behold, the retinue came unto a forest and a murmuring stream, when suddenly two enormous wolves appeared and charged the legions of Isfendiyar. But soon they were laid low, for, seeing them advance, the whole host poured forth upon them showers of arrows from their bows. And while Isfendiyar attacked one of them, Bashutan, his brother, fell upon the other, so that, what with the arrows and the vigorous attack of the heroes, in a few seconds the two great monsters lay lifeless in the dust.

So, the first stage of the journey successfully passed, blithely Isfendiyar entered upon the second. But again the party travelled peacefully all day, their progress remaining undisputed until toward sunset, when a lion and a lioness stalked boldly forth, snarling and angry. Now Bashutan would have divided the labor, even as with the wolves, but Isfendiyar, seeing how ferocious were the beasts, preferred to attack them alone.

Hesitating not, therefore, the hero first sallied forth against the lion, and so watchful and dexterous was he, that with one mighty stroke he put an end to his life. And this done, behold, he approached the lioness, who pounced upon him with great fury because of her mate, and almost you would have said that Isfendiyar's hour was come. But though sore pressed, the hero lost not his coolness, holding his own against the furious beast until an opening was given him, when, rapidly wielding his sword, in a moment the head of the great lioness went bounding o'er the plain like a ball shot from a racket, and her life of hunting was ended, even as that of her mate.

But alas! though two stages of the great Heft-Khan were thus successfully passed, Karugsar informed Isfendiyar that upon the following day he would be called upon to encounter a monstrous dragon, whose roar made the very mountains tremble, and whose hideous jaws shot forth poisonous foam. So, thus warned, after some thinking, Isfendiyar ordered to be constructed a curious apparatus on wheels. Now the hero's invention was something like a carriage, unto which were fastened a large quantity of pointed instruments sharp as razors. And to this machine of death horses were fastened to drag it on the road.

So the next day the retinue again set forth, and after they had gone some distance Karugsar suddenly exclaimed:

"Surely I smell the stench of the dragon, for nothing else could so pollute the air!"

Now hearing this, Isfendiyar dismounted hastily from his charger, ascended into the new machine, and, shutting fast the doors, took his seat and drove off. But alas! when Bashutan and all the warriors saw the intention of the hero, lo, they began to lament and weep, begging him to come out of the machine, and not to rush upon certain death. But Isfendiyar bade them be of good cheer, and, taking up the reins, he drove forward with great velocity until he was come in the vicinity of the awful beast. Then alas!

> "The dragon from a distance heard
>   The rumbling of the wain,
> And sniffing every breeze that stirred
>   Across the neighboring plain,

Smelt something human in his power,
   A welcome scent to him;
For he was eager to devour
   Hot, reeking blood or limb.

And darkness now is spread around,
   No pathway can be traced;
The fiery horses plunge and bound
   Amid the dismal waste.

And now the dragon stretches far
   His cavern throat, and soon
Licks in the horses and the car,
   And tries to gulp them down.

But sword and javelin, sharp and keen,
   Wound deep each sinewy jaw;
Midway remains the huge machine,
   And chokes the monster's maw.

In agony he breathes, a dire
   Convulsion fires his blood,
And struggling, ready to expire,
   Ejects a poison-flood!

And then disgorges wain and steed,
   And swords and javelins bright;
Then, as the dreadful dragon bleeds,
   Up starts the warrior-knight,

And from his place of ambush leaps,
   And brandishing his blade,
The weapon in the brain he steeps,
   And splits the monster's head.

But the foul venom issuing thence,
   Is so o'erpowering found,
Isfendiyar, deprived of sense,
   Falls staggering to the ground!"

Howbeit, though o'ercome by the horrible stench, Isfendiyar was soon upon his feet asking Karugsar as to his next adventure, and being informed that upon the following day he would be called upon to combat the powers of magic, he was no whit dismayed. Nay; on the contrary, he set out upon the fourth stage of the Heft-Khan with increased confidence, feeling himself under the protection of the Almighty.

And behold! upon this day his trial was delayed not long, for in the early morning, as the party refreshed themselves in a pleasant meadow, a beautiful enchantress appeared, representing herself as a king's daughter in great distress on account of a hideous ghoul who had stolen her from her home and now held her in bondage. Now Isfendiyar feigned sympathy, but when the wicked one drew near, before she could weave her spells about him, lo, the hero threw his cord, quickly snaring her in its meshes. Nor was she permitted to escape, although in her extremity the fair one successively assumed the shape of a cat, a wolf, and a decrepit old man, for, vexed at her efforts to cheat him, the Hero soon made an end of her with his sword.

But behold! no sooner had this happened than a thick, dark cloud of vapor arose, and when it subsided, lo, there burst forth the black apparition of a demon with flames issuing from his mouth. Now the ghoul was indeed frightful, but, nevertheless, Isfendiyar rushed bravely forward, sword in hand, and, though the flames burnt his cloth armor and dress, finally, after a terrible fight, he succeeded in cutting off the threatening monster's head. Then the hero said unto Karugsar:

"Lo! by the favor of Heaven, both enchantress and

ghoul are exterminated, as well as the wolves, the lions, and the dragon. Now what awaiteth me next?"

Then Karugsar, who had been truly amazed at the valor of Isfendiyar, said:

"O Matchless One, truly thy success hath been marvellous, but to-morrow thou wilt be subjected to a test never before experienced by mortal man, for thy antagonist will be a mighty Simurgh. Now if thou overcomest this giant bird, fierce because of her young, thou wilt have performed a feat not dreamed of by even Rustem the Mighty, and thy name will go ringing down the ages as the hero who conquered a Simurgh. But alas! much I fear that the fifth stage of the Heft-Khan will be thy last."

But, undismayed, Isfendiyar continued his journey, coming presently unto the mountain where the Simurgh had builded her nest. And here a curious thing happened, for the giant bird, beholding with surprise an immense vehicle drawn by two horses approach at a furious rate, immediately descended from the mountain, and endeavored to take up the whole apparatus in her claws to carry it unto her nest. But alas! the swords and javelins cruelly lacerated both claws and beak, so that after a time the great bird became extremely weakened by the loss of blood. Then Isfendiyar, seizing this favorable moment, sprang out of the carriage, and with his sword cleft the mighty bird in twain. Now never had the Hero beheld a Simurgh, and much he marvelled at the colossal size and wondrous beauty of the giant Bird of God.

Tarrying not, however, the retinue moved rapidly forward, for Karugsar informed them that upon the sixth stage their fight would be with the elements, and they hoped to reach, by hard travel, a place of shelter. And

fortunate was their haste, for as they arrived upon the
skirts of a mountain there suddenly swept down upon them
a furious storm of wind and heavy snow which covered all
the ground; yea, and biting cold, which almost froze the
heroes where they stood. Now to escape the wrath of the
elements, Isfendiyar and his men took shelter in a huge
cavern, and there three lingering days they spent, while
the snow still fell, and still the chill winds blew, and
man and beast grew faint for want of food.

Then, in their desperation and anguish of suffering,
Isfendiyar and his warriors, with heads exposed, prostrated
themselves in solemn prayer unto the Almighty. And
verily Heaven was kind, for soon the snow and mighty
wind entirely ceased, enabling the heroes to leave the caves
of the mountain safe and unharmed. But when asked of
the final stage of the Heft-Khan, Karugsar said:

"Alas, O Valorous One! Forty farsangs yet lie between thee and the Brazen Fortress, and every inch of the
road is full of peril.

> "Along those plains of burning sand,
>   No bird can move, nor ant, nor fly;
> No water slakes the fiery land,
>   Intensely glows the flaming sky.
>
> No tiger fierce, nor lion ever
>   Could breathe that pestilential air;
> Even the unsparing vulture never
>   Ventures on blood-stained pinions there."

Now though the picture thus painted was dark, Isfendiyar determined to press forward. And lo! when they
were come unto the place said to be covered with burning
sand, they found the ground cool and pleasant unto their

feet, for the storm in its fury had lessened the burning heat, making the last stage of the Heft-Khan the easiest of all.

But though the Heft-Khan was now accomplished, there remained yet to be taken the Brazen Fortress. And as no accessible point of attack could be discovered, Isfendiyar quickly transformed his warlike cavalcade into a caravan of peaceful merchantmen, thus gaining admission into the fort. And being generous of heart, he arranged to give a great banquet unto Arjasp and the demon chiefs, feasting them right merrily. Then, when no man was master of his fate save Isfendiyar alone, suddenly the Persians fell upon the Deevs, completely annihilating them.

And now, this glorious victory achieved, Isfendiyar made haste to return unto Iran, taking with him his sisters and much treasure. And lo! the mouths of all men overflowed with praise for the brave young hero of the Heft-Khan who once more had saved Iran from her foes.

THE COMBAT OF ISFENDIYAR
AGAINST RUSTEM

BEHOLD! it is recorded that Gushtasp the Shah, after the return of his glorious son Isfendiyar from the triumphs of his great Heft-Khan, instead of resigning unto him the throne, as he had sworn to do, at once sent him forth upon a new adventure, which was nothing less than to slay, or bring unto him in chains, Rustem, the Champion of the World. For he said:

"Verily, in former days, this Mighty One was obedient unto the Shahs, but now doth he hold himself superior. For did he not decline to come unto my aid against Arjasp? Go, therefore, and conquer him, be it by strategem or by force, bringing him bound before me. Then shalt thou be Shah of Iran."

Now Isfendiyar was grieved when he heard these words of his father, and, unchaining the door of his lips, he hastened to remind his sire of all the hero's glorious deeds. And he said:

"O my father, I pray thee ask of me anything else than this—that I should make war against the King of China, or against any other ruler under the sun; but do not ask me to lay hands upon this grand old champion, who hath been the glory and the defence of Iran for hundreds of years. Sooner would I relinquish the glories of sovereignty forever."

But Gushtasp would not give ear unto the words of his son, saying angrily unto him:

"Verily, thou forgettest that a son oweth ever obedience, without question, unto his father! Go, therefore, and let me not behold thy face until thou presentest this Haughty One before me in chains, for I will that his pride be brought low, that he may recognize that still there is a Shah in Iran."

Then Isfendiyar, perceiving his father's intention, said unto him coldly:

"Alas, my father! now truly I perceive that thou sendest me forth in guile. For well thou knowest that no champion in all these long years hath ever been able to stand before the might of Rustem, and so thou thinkest thus to rid thyself of Isfendiyar, and the necessity of abandoning unto him the throne. I say unto thee, therefore, that Isfendiyar desireth it no longer. Nevertheless, since he is thy slave, he will go forth at thy bidding, and if peradventure he falleth, then truly wilt thou be the murderer of thy son, and his blood will be upon thy head."

So, though against the wishes of his mother, Isfendiyar placed himself at the head of a mighty host and set forth upon his disagreeable errand. But behold! when they had gone but a little way, the camel upon which the Hero was seated laid him down in the dust, refusing to rise from the ground, though the driver struck him many times. Now as this was regarded by all as an evil omen, lo! the head of the beast was cut off that the evil might fall upon it and not upon his rider. Nevertheless, Isfendiyar was troubled at this misfortune, pondering what the sign might mean.

Now when the cavalcade drew nigh unto Seistan, Isfendiyar called unto him Bahman, his son, giving unto him a message to carry unto Rustem. And behold, the message contained none but kind words, for Isfendiyar hoped that thus all might yet be well. So Bahman sped forth, but when he was come unto the courts of Rustem he found only Zal within, for the great Pehliva was absent with his followers upon a hunting trip. Now the aged Prince would have entertained the youth until his son's return, but Bahman declared the need of haste, so without tarrying he set forth for Rustem's camp.

And behold! after a long day's travel, the youth arrived at the halting-place of the hunters of Seistan. Now it was evening as he drew nigh, and at once he perceived about the blazing fire a man, like unto a mountain, roasting a wild ass for his supper. Yea, and about him were many brave heroes all gaily preparing their evening meal. But lo! as he gazed, what was Bahman's astonishment to behold that Rustem, of himself, devoured the whole of a wild ass for his meal; nor did this wondrous feat appear to be anything out of the ordinary.

Then was the youth filled with consternation, for he thought as he gazed upon Rustem, who seemed unto him as a huge mountain of might, that not even Isfendiyar, his gallant father, could stand before such an elephant of war. So, in his fear, Bahman hastily loosened a large rock from the mountain-side and sent it rolling unto the place where Rustem sat, hoping thus to save his father from harm.

But Rustem, when warned by his followers as to the speeding rock, smiled, and rising leisurely, with his foot he sent it spinning far out upon the plain. Then was Bahman still more amazed, and also affrighted, so that for

long he dared not come forth from his hiding-place. Yet
when his courage finally allowed him to present himself
before the Pehliva, Rustem welcomed him warmly. And
as he entertained his guest, behold, again he ate as though
his day's fast had but now been broken, and once more
Bahman marvelled at the might and majesty of the great
hero of Seistan. But, the meal being ended, the youth
delivered at once his father's message. Then was Rustem
filled with wrath and amazement, yet restrained he his
anger, replying courteously unto Bahman:

"O Noble Youth! I pray thee bear greeting unto Isfendiyar, thy gallant sire, whose glory hath added such lustre
unto the crown of Iran, and say unto him that Rustem rejoiceth that at last he is to behold his face. But as for his
demand, surely it is the device of the Evil One, and can in
nowise come to pass, for no man shall ever behold Rustem
in chains. Wherefore, say unto thy glorious sire that the
Pehliva of Seistan beg him to honor their house as his
guest, and when we shall have feasted together, then will
I go forth unto Gushtasp. And his anger, which is unjust,
will vanish like unto the morning mist, and all will again
be well.

So Bahman sped back unto his father, and Rustem fol-
lowed after to present, in person, his homage unto the
Prince. And behold! when he was come near unto the
royal camp, the Pehliva dismounted from Rakush, going
forward upon foot to pay his respects unto Isfendiyar.
For he wished to pay honor unto him, not only as his
Prince, but also as the brave hero of the Heft-Khan.
Now when the two had embraced, Rustem said:

"O Valorous Prince, whose wondrous deeds have filled
the world with glory, behold, I have a boon to ask at thy

hands, for I desire that thou enter into my house as my honored guest."

But Isfendiyar, whose eyes could not cease from gazing upon the mighty form of Rustem, nevertheless replied unto him:

"O Champion of the World! Unfortunately my errand forbiddeth me to eat of thy bread and salt, otherwise my soul would joy in thy hospitality. And alas! though it is grievous unto me, yet must I be faithful unto my mission."

Then Rustem replied unto Isfendiyar, speaking still more earnestly, and he said:

"Yet again, O brave Isfendiyar, do I entreat thee to enter into my house in friendship. Then will I do all that thou desirest, except only that I cannot submit unto the chains, for that would be neither fitting nor right—as thou well knowest."

Now unto this Isfendiyar replied:

"Alas! not only can I not feast with thee, O Mighty One, but, furthermore, if thou wilt not hearken unto my demands, then must I fall upon thee in enmity. But, as my soul goeth out to thee on account of thy deeds of valor, to-day let there be peace between us, and do thou feast with me in my tent."

So Rustem, hoping that thus unpleasantness might yet be avoided, replied:

"Gracious Prince, gladly will I come unto thee, but first must I change my robes, for, as thou seest, I am attired for the chase, and not as is fitting unto the guest of a Prince. When thy banquet is ready, therefore, send forth a messenger, and I will come unto thee with joy."

But behold! when Rustem was gone, Isfendiyar pondered over that which was come to pass, and his heart was full of care. So he said unto his brother:

"Verily, since the sword must decide our strife, not only have I no place in the house of Rustem, but neither is it fitting that he should enter into mine. Wherefore, I shall not send for him to come unto my feast!"

But Bashutan, shaking his head sadly, replied unto Isfendiyar:

"O my brother, truly it seemeth unto me a pity that heroes like unto Rustem and Isfendiyar should meet in enmity. I counsel thee, therefore, to disregard the unjust demands of our father, for much I fear that he seeketh but to ensnare thee."

Then Isfendiyar was thoughtful, but finally he said:

"Truly I am not deceived as to the desires of Gushtasp, but if I obey not my father it will be a reproach unto me in this world, and in the next I shall have to render account for it before God, my Maker—for so teacheth Zerdusht the Holy One."

So, though Isfendiyar prepared him a feast, when it was ready he sent not to summon his guest. And behold! when Rustem had waited long, he was angry because the messenger came not. Nevertheless, he tarried not at home, but hastened unto the tent of Isfendiyar to see what had befallen.

Now when the warriors of the Prince beheld Rustem draw near, lo, they gazed in open-eyed admiration, saying among themselves:

"Saw you ever such limbs, and such a chest on mortal man? Surely Gushtasp is bereft of reason, or never would he send Isfendiyar thus unto his death. But alas! the old Shah huggeth his throne and his treasure ever

closer as age creepeth on, caring naught for the welfare
of Iran."

But, all unconscious of the admiration and fear he was
exciting, Rustem, hot and angry, presented himself before
the Prince, saying:

"O Young Man, thou mayest be a hero, but certainly
thou seemest not to be acquainted with the laws of courtesy
due unto an invited guest, since thou deemest him not
worthy of a messenger. But perhaps thou knowest not
that it is Rustem whom thou treatest thus disdainfully?—
Rustem, whose glorious deeds have made the throne of
Iran to shine as a beacon light unto all the world!"

Now Isfendiyar, abashed at the anger of the Great Pehliva, excused himself for his breach of courtesy, saying:

"O Mighty One, verily I had thought to save thee the
long, hot journey hither; but since thou art come, pray
enter, and let us drink a cup of wine together."

Now, thus speaking, behold! Isfendiyar offered unto
Rustem a place at his left hand, smiling courteously:

But Rustem, advancing proudly, said quietly unto
Isfendiyar:

"Not at thy left, O Prince, for never yet hath Rustem
sat save at the right hand of the Shahs of Iran."

Thus spake Rustem, and behold! so majestic was the
mien of the old Hero, as he thus calmly asserted his rights,
that at once a chair of gold was brought and placed at
Isfendiyar's right hand. But, though outwardly calm, the
heart of Rustem burned at the dishonor done unto him,
and even the wine soothed not his ruffled spirit. Yea, and
the unfavorable impression made by the Prince was further increased by his words. For, after drinking for a
few minutes in silence, he said:

"So thou hast ever sat at the right hand of Kings, Old Warrior! Strange! for surely it hath been said unto me that Rustem is sprung of evil stock. Now, truly, is not Zal, thy father, of demon extraction? And was he not reared by a vile bird that gave unto him garbage for nourishment? So, at least, it hath been reported unto me."

Alas! this was an insult too biting for Rustem to bear with any degree of patience, so, frowning angrily, he said:

"Thou and I, O Prince, can boast of the same origin, as thou well knowest, since we are both descended from Husheng the Shah. Why, then, use such injurious language? Yea, and would it not, perhaps, be becoming for Isfendiyar to remember that but for the honor and fidelity of Rustem and his house unto the Shahs, Isfendiyar of the Heft-Khan would not be numbered among the heroes of Iran? But, after all, what hath he done? Why! he hath slain Arjasp, one puny King, while over against that is the long record of Rustem's glorious deeds, which need not to be recounted."

Now Rustem's vehemence and the disdainful tone of his voice made it hard for Isfendiyar to remember the courtesy due unto a guest, but, restraining his anger, he said softly unto him:

"O Modest One! Why dost thou raise thy voice so high and speak so loftily? For, after all, thou wert, and art still, but the slave of the Shah, dependent for thy very breath upon his clemency. And after all, what were thy seven boasted labors to my terrible Heft-Khan? And who, I ask you,—by the power of his sword—diffused the blessings of the faith of Zerdusht throughout the world? Verily, Rustem hath performed the duties of a warrior and a servant, but Isfendiyar the holy functions of a sovereign and a prophet. But now have we boasted enough, for behold, the day is almost ended and I am hungry. Let us eat and drink, therefore, for to-morrow will we meet in enmity upon the field of battle."

So a great banquet was spread, and the two heroes sat down to feast, Rustem astonishing Isfendiyar greatly, for never had the Prince dreamed that mortal man could eat and drink so much, and he wondered not now that Rustem's might was reckoned equal to that of a hundred strong men. When the time of departure was come, however, once more Rustem begged Isfendiyar to be his guest on the morrow, but again the Prince refused. Then the Hero knew that words were idle, and he was sorrowful in his soul, for within himself he said:

"Truly the Evil One is in this whole affair, and no good can come of it. Now if I suffer these chains, men will mock that Rustem permitted a boy to bind him, and the dishonor of it can never be wiped out. Yet if I slay this stripling on the morrow, the glory of a lifetime will be tarnished, for men will say that in his last days Rustem lifted up his hand against one of the royal house."

Nevertheless, concealing his sorrow and dismay, he replied gaily unto Isfendiyar, saying:

"So be it then, O Stubborn One! to-morrow will we meet in conflict, since naught else will content thee. And behold! when I shall have lifted thee lightly from off thy saddle, straight will I convey thee unto Silver-crowned Zal, who shall place thee upon the ivory throne, while upon thy head a crown of gold shall glitter. Yea, and when that we have feasted, right loyally our troops shall fight for thee as King, and we will serve thee faithfully as thy Pehliva forever and a day."

But Isfendiyar, thinking that Rustem mocked, said angrily:

"Old Man! Verily thou hadst best save thy breath for combat, since to-morrow, by the aid of Zerdusht, will I make the world dark unto thine eyes."

Then Rustem, laughing, said:

"O Foolish Youth, when Rustem wieldeth his mace, behold, the world trembleth, and the head of his enemy falls. Consider, therefore, thy course."

Now when he had thus spoken, Rustem rode forth from out the tents of Isfendiyar, and though his lips smiled, his heart was heavy with foreboding. Nevertheless, when he was come unto his palace, he commanded that his armor and implements of war be brought before him. Then, as he gazed upon them, sighing, he said:

"O my raiment of battle, verily thou hast rested long, yet once again must I don thee for combat. And alas! I greatly fear me that it is for my last fight."

But behold! when sunshine once more flooded the world, then the Pehliva threw off his sadness, for he resolved once more to speak persuasive words unto the Prince. So, having received his father's blessing, he armed himself for battle, and rode forth unto the tents of Isfendiyar, and lo! when he was come near, he shouted gaily:

"Ho, Brave Isfendiyar! Why sleepest thou when the hero with whom thou wouldst try thy strength hath come forth to meet thee?"

Now Isfendiyar, at this call, quickly issued from his tent, and, leaping upon his charger, rode like the wind unto his waiting antagonist. So the two met, the old warrior and the young, and truly they were a doughty pair. But

Rustem's efforts at persuasion were vain, for Isfendiyar
would hear of naught but battle.

So, after the useless controversy, behold, the Champions
began their combat. Now they began the fight with their
spears, but as the contest lasted for long hours, they tested
their strength and skill successively with their swords, clubs,
and lassos; but still the end came not. For, though they
fought until both they and their horses were worn out with
weariness, neither could prevail. So they stopped them
awhile to rest.

But behold! as they rested, Bahman, the son of Isfendiyar, rushed up to his father, informing him that Rustem's
lieutenants had provoked a battle between the two armies,
and that as a consequence two valiant youths, sons of
Isfendiyar, were slain, and the Shah's troops put to rout
with great slaughter. Then was Isfendiyar transported
with rage. Calling aloud unto Rustem, therefore, he said:

"Ho, Old Man! Dost thou hear this? Thy chiefs have
fallen upon my troops, killing my two brave sons. Verily,
I had thought such treachery beneath the Mighty Rustem."

Now when Rustem heard these words, behold, he
trembled like a leaf. But he said:

"O Isfendiyar, I swear unto thee by the head of the
King, by the sun, and by my conquering sword, that no
part have I had in this matter. Yea, and to prove it unto
thee, I swear that whoever hath been in fault, even though
it be my dearest, lo, he shall be bound hand and foot and
given over unto thee for vengeance."

But, unplacated, the Prince cried angrily unto Rustem:

"Verily, O Treacherous One, thy words have a pleasant sound, but I say unto thee, it is idle to kill the snake

that the peacock's death may be avenged. Thine own blood, therefore, shall pay for that of my sons, for verily my arrows shall make the world dark unto thine eyes."

Now thus saying, Isfendiyar seized his bow, and whiz! whiz! went a shower of arrows through the air, fastening themselves in the body of Rustem and Rakush, his steed. Yea, twice thirty arrows were there in all, and not one of them was there that did not wound the Hero or his horse, while Rustem's missiles fell harmless upon Isfendiyar, because that Zerdusht had charmed his body against all danger so that it was like unto brass.

Then Rustem, seeing that Rakush was like to perish of his wounds, and feeling also his own strength going from loss of blood, cried unto Isfendiyar:

"Behold, night is at hand, O Angry One, and since even heroes cannot combat in the darkness, go thy way, and we will meet again in the morning."

But Isfendiyar, seeing that Rustem staggered in his saddle, said:

"Old Man, think not to escape me thus, for yet there is light enough to finish our combat."

But Rustem replied unto the Eager One:

"Not so, O Isfendiyar! Farewell, therefore, until morning."

Now so saying, quickly Rustem turned him and swam across the stream. And behold! Isfendiyar was amazed, for he knew that both steed and rider were sore wounded. Then, standing upon the bank, with his lips he reviled the fleeing Hero, but lo! in his heart he was filled with admiration and wonder at his prowess.

And now, Rustem having escaped him, sorrowfully Isfendiyar returned unto his tent, where he mourned over

Isfendiyar seized his bow, and whiz! whiz! went a shower of arrows.

the bodies of his two sons. But when the night was far
spent, lo, he placed them on biers of ebony, in coffins of
gold, and sent them unto the Shah with this message:

"O King of Evil Devices! Behold, I am sending unto
thee the first fruits of thy seeds of guile. Isfendiyar is yet
alive, but Heaven alone knoweth what may befall to-
morrow."

Then the Prince said unto his brother:

"O Bashutan, my brother! Verily this Rustem is not
mortal. For neither with my sword nor javelin could I do
harm unto his body formed of rock and iron. But, thanks
unto Zerdusht, the charmed arrows have done their work,
and it will indeed be wonderful if the Mighty One liveth
throughout the night."

Meanwhile, when the wounded Hero, of whom Isfendiyar
spoke thus feelingly, was come into the presence of Zal and
Rudabeh, behold, they rent the air with their cries of woe;
for never yet had Rustem returned unto them vanquished;
neither had any man e'er done such harm unto his body.
Now they cried out sore in their distress, and Rustem, too,
lamented, for the pain of his wounds was great. Presently, however, seeing that the case of his son was indeed
serious, Zal bethought him of a remedy. So he said:

"O my glorious son, mourn not so bitterly, for yet
there is hope for thee, since in this, our extremity, once
more I shall call unto our aid the Wondrous Bird of God."

So at once Zal went forth unto a high mountain, taking
with him three golden censers filled with fire, and as many
mighty magicians, who caused the fires to glow brighter
and ever brighter. And lo! at the end of the first watch of
the night, Silver-crowned Zal dropped into the brightly
glowing fire the glorious golden feather of the Simurgh.

Then instantly a mighty stir of wings filled all the air, and the Wondrous Bird of God dropped down beside her child, listening sympathetically unto his plaint. And, the story being told, the Simurgh said:

"Let the Mighty Rustem and his glorious steed be brought unto me, for lo! there is healing in my wings."

So quickly the magicians hastened back unto the palace, and though Rustem and Rakush had scarcely strength to move, yet went they unto the mountain with all the speed they could, pausing not until they were come into the presence of the Bird of God.

And now the glorious Simurgh, swiftly passing her golden beak over the body of the wounded Hero, drew thence four wicked arrow-heads. Then caressing the wounds softly and lightly with her fluffy wings, lo, in a moment, Rustem felt all his strength return. Yea, and Rakush, too, rejoiced, neighing, and tossing his mighty head for gladness when that the six charmed arrow-heads troubled his peace no more; and then, the work of healing done, the Simurgh said unto Rustem:

"Alas, O Son of Zal! Wherefore hast thou entered upon combat with the son of the Shah, and the beloved of Zerdusht? For verily it can bring thee naught but woe; and there is little that even I can do to aid thee. For never hath there appeared in the world so brave and so perfect a hero as Isfendiyar. Yea, and the favor of Heaven is with him also, for in his great Heft-Khan, by some clever artifice, he succeeded in killing a Simurgh, and the farther thou art removed from his invincible arm, therefore, the greater will be thy safety. For alas! in the Book of Fate it is written that whosoever sheddeth the blood of Isfendiyar, he also shall perish miserably, never again knowing

joy in this life, and also suffering pangs in the life to come.
But if this fate dismay thee not, come forth with me, and
I will reveal unto thee a way to lay thine enemy low—if the
stars decree that his hour is come."

So, wishing not to face defeat, Rustem mounted into the
golden chariot of which he had heard so oft from his
father, and the Simurgh bare him far, far away, even unto
the shores of a mighty sea. Now there she put the Hero
down softly in a garden wherein grew a tamarisk-tree,
whose roots were in the ground, but whose branches
pierced unto heaven. Then the Simurgh said:

"O Glorious Son of Zal, I pray thee choose from this
tree the longest, straightest and finest branch that thou
canst find, for to this tamarisk bough is bound the fate of
Isfendiyar. Yea, and after thou hast secured it, make it
yet straighter before the fire, search out a well-tempered
arrow-head, feather it well, and if Isfendiyar's hour is
come, this is the weapon which, when directed unto his
forehead, will cause him to perish, for only through his eye
can this hero be wounded, since Zerdusht hath made the
rest of his body invulnerable. But yet once more I counsel
thee, bring this matter to a good end, for so shalt thou
escape much sorrow."

Now having thus spoken, behold, the Simurgh carried
Rustem safely back unto the palace of Zal, bidding him
be of good cheer. After her departure, however, the Hero
hastened to carry out her commands as to the fashioning
of the fateful arrow.

But behold! when morning was come, Rustem mounted
upon fiery Rakush, and rode serenely forth unto the camp
of Isfendiyar. And lo! his antagonist yet slumbered, for
he thought of a surety that Rustem must have perished

from his wounds during the night. So, beholding that Isfendiyar yet slept, Rustem, lifting up his voice of thunder, cried:

"Ho, Brave Crocodile of War! Is it a time to slumber when thou hast challenged a hero to combat? Get thee up, for verily Rustem is not accustomed thus to be kept waiting."

Now when Isfendiyar, thus awakened, beheld that it was really Rustem who awaited him without the tent, he was amazed. But quickly donning his armor, and mounting his horse, he soon appeared in the presence of Rustem, saying unto him:

"O Elephant-limbed Warrior! Yesterday thou wert wounded almost unto death by my arrows, and to-day there is no trace of them either upon thee or thy steed. Pray how is this?

> "But, then, thy father, Zal, is a sorcerer,
>   And he by charm and spell
> Hath cured all the wounds of the warrior,
>   And now he is safe and well.
> For the wounds I gave could never be
> Closed up except by sorcery.
> Yea, the wounds I gave thee in every part
> Could never be cured but by magic art."

Then Rustem, replying unto Isfendiyar, said:

"O Royal Archer! Know that if thou wert to shoot at me a thousand arrows, they would all drop harmless unto the ground. Therefore, let us be friends, and not only shalt thou be placed upon the throne, but all the treasure of the house of Zal shall be thine."

But Isfendiyar replied impatiently unto Rustem:

"Brave Prater! Wilt thou never cease from thy idle

talk? Now once for all I say unto thee that never will I forsake the paths of God by disobeying my father. Choose, therefore, between chains and battle."

Then Rustem, seeing that his submission was not accepted, though he had offered to sacrifice much, bent his bow, and laid the arrow of tamarisk in rest, and so held it while he prayed unto God. And lo! the Prince, noting that the Hero delayed, thought that he did so from fear, and he taunted him. Then Rustem, hesitating no longer, let his arrow fly toward his enemy, and behold! it sped straight unto its mark, piercing the eye of Isfendiyar, so that the bow dropped from his hand, and he clutched at his horse's mane. Yea,

> "And darkness overspread his sight,
> The world to him was hid in night;
> The bow dropped from his slackened hand,
> And down he sank upon the sand."

Now long Isfendiyar swooned, and his kinsmen and chiefs, beholding what had befallen, rent the air with their woe. But the Prince, when he revived, said unto them calmly:

"O Heroes of Iran, trouble not yourselves on account of my death, for it is not Rustem who hath slain me, nor the Simurgh, nor yet the magic arrow, but my father, who knowingly sent me forth unto my death, and verily the curse of the Great Prophet shall fall upon his head. As for thee, O Rustem, being but the instrument of fate, thou art guiltless in this matter, and that thou mayest know how I honor thee, I desire that thou take unto thee Bahman, my son, and rear him for Iran, even as thou didst noble Siawush, for lo! it hath been revealed unto me that

Bahman will sit upon the throne that hath been denied unto me."

Alas! having thus spoken, behold, Isfendiyar sighed, and the sun of his life was set, and great was the lamentation for the brave young hero lost unto Iran. As for Rustem, sorrowfully he made ready for Isfendiyar a coffin of gold, causing it to be lined with silken stuffs and perfumed with amber. Then he laid therein the valiant hero-prince of the Heft-Khan, and all beholding him wept with bitter sorrow. Tenderly then the coffin of gold was placed upon the back of a slow-moving dromedary, forty others following in its wake. And lo! there followed after them the brave army of the Prince, clad in robes of mourning, while Bashutan marched at the head of the sorrowful train, leading Isfendiyar's horse, whose saddle was reversed and whose mane and tail were shorn, while from its sides hung the armor of the vanquished one. Now thus it was that they brought brave Isfendiyar back unto the palace of his fathers, and behold! all the world mourned this great loss unto Iran.

But while Iran sorrowed for Isfendiyar, behold, Bahman grew up in the courts of Rustem, the Pehliva loving him as a son. For in his heart he grieved bitterly that by his hand brave Isfendiyar had fallen. Yea, and he gloried not in his last great fight, even though he knew that now his star would shine on undimmed unto the end, and that the children of Ormuzd would sing his praises through all the ages as the one great unconquered hero of the Persians.

THE DEATH OF RUSTEM

LO! it is chronicled by Firdusi, who, in his great epic
poem, hath made immortal the heroes and kings of
Persia, that Zal in his old age had born unto him
a son of remarkable beauty. But alas! when the astrologers
cast the horoscope of this beautiful babe, they read therein
that few and evil would be the days of Shughad; that he
would be the ruin of the house of his fathers, also bringing
destruction upon the land of Iran.

Now Zal was overwhelmed with dismay when this message of the stars was communicated unto him, and he
prayed continually unto Ormuzd that he would avert this
terrible fate from the head of his boy. Yea, and he reared
him carefully, sparing no pains to inculcate in the youth
the principles of truth, honor, loyalty unto his house and
unto the King.

Then, when Shughad was come unto man's estate, Zal
sent him unto the King of Kabul, who, when he saw that
he was tall and handsome, and fit in every way to sit upon
the throne, showed unto him great kindness, even giving
unto him his daughter in marriage, and providing for him
bountifully.

Now the King of Kabul paid tribute unto Rustem,
every year being required to send unto the Hero of Seistan
a bull's hide as a token of sovereignty. And alas! this was
a great grievance unto his soul, for he was proud in his
spirit and desired to be bondsman unto none. So it was

not alone kindness which prompted him to take Shughad unto him as his son, for in his heart he hoped thus to have the tribute remitted.

But behold! when the proper time came, Rustem sent his messenger as usual to demand the bull's hide, which made the King very angry. So, in his disappointment, he hesitated not to express his opinion of Rustem's conduct unto Shughad, stirring up his mind against his brother. Then Shughad, becoming angry and discontented also, said unto the King:

"Verily, since my elder brother hath behaved unto me thus unkindly, in my heart he shall be unto me no more than a stranger. Let us consider, therefore, how we may ensnare him."

So all night the King and Shughad talked and pondered how they might rid the world of Rustem, and at last they decided upon a scheme.

Consequently, it came to pass that presently the King of Kabul gave a great feast, and when all had become excited with wine, behold, Shughad, the son of Zal, began to boast of his lineage, saying:

"Verily, Shughad alone of all this great company should be toasted! Yea, and I except not even the King, our host! For is not the Mighty Rustem my brother? And do I not come from a long line of heroes, extending from Husheng the Shah even unto Zal of the white hair?"

Now hearing this, lo, the King sprang up in pretended wrath, saying:

"Upstart! Thinkest thou to lord it over me, the King of Kabul? Verily, nay! For thou art really no brother unto Rustem, since thy mother was but a slave in thy father's household. Therefore, boast not so loudly."

Then Shughad, feigning great anger, hastily left the banqueting-halls, threatening to call forth Rustem to avenge the insulting words of the King. So, with guile in his heart, the Prince rode forth unto the palace of his brother. And behold! after they had exchanged greetings, Rustem said:

"And how fares it with thee at Kabul, O my brother? Art thou still happy and contented in the King's palace?"

Then Shughad, rejoicing at the opening thus given him, said:

"I pray thee do not speak unto me of Kabul, for the word is hateful unto mine ears. For verily this night hath the King insulted me beyond bearing. Yea, and thee, too, and my father! So I came away in a rage, and never will I return until the vile words which he spake of my family are avenged."

Now when Rustem learned what had been spoken by the King of Kabul, he said unto Shughad:

"O my brother, trouble not thyself concerning this matter, for verily it shall bring thee naught but gain. Alas! ever hath the King of Kabul been vain and arrogant of spirit, but for this he shall be humbled unto the dust, for no longer shall he reign in Kabul, since his crown shall henceforth grace thine own fair brow."

So, at once Rustem set forth to avenge the wrongs of his brother, but lo! when they were yet far from Kabul, they were met by the King, who, bowing himself low in the dust, said unto Rustem:

"O Lord of the World! Thou beholdest before thee, with uncovered head and bare feet, the proud King of Kabul. Pardon, therefore—thou who art gracious as the River Nile—the foolish words of thy slave, spoken when

his head was troubled with wine. For lo! his mouth is
filled with dust and his soul with sorrow and repentance."

Now hearing these words of humility, Rustem's anger
was appeased. Granting unto the King forgiveness, therefore, he graciously consented to be his guest. So a great
banquet was made ready to celebrate the reconciliation,
and as they feasted the King lauded his wondrous hunting-
grounds, wherein the deer and the wild ass furnished such
excellent sport, and he invited Rustem to hunt therein for
a day before returning unto Seistan.

So Rustem, who loved the chase almost as well as the
field of battle, consented to remain the King's guest for
yet another day, for he suspected not that poison lurked in
the honey of the monarch's words. But alas! in a certain
part of these beautiful hunting-grounds, the schemers had
caused to be dug treacherous pits, lined thickly with
swords and lances and hunting-spears, yet no man would
have suspected their existence, so cleverly were they
covered over.

On the following day, therefore, the King directed the
hunt unto the place in the forest where the pits were hidden.
And behold! Shughad ran beside the horse of Rustem to
show unto him the path. But when they were come unto
the place of peril, Rakush, smelling the newly-turned
earth, reared high in the air, refusing to advance. Then
Rustem, thinking he was afraid, commanded him to go
forward; but Rakush, backing, refused to give ear unto
his master's voice. Now this made Rustem angry so that
lightly he struck him with his whip, though never before
in all their long wanderings together had he done so. Then,
alas! surprised and maddened by the stroke, Rakush sprang
forward, but only to fall into one of the treacherous pits.

Now sinking into the midst of this cruel bed of pointed weapons, many a ghastly stab and many a cut in limb and body received Rustem and his gallant steed. Yet from this awful grave, at one prodigious spring, Rakush escaped with his master still upon his back. But alas! what availed that mighty effort? For, down again into another pit, yet deeper, both fell together. And though again they rose, and yet again, it was only to be engulfed once more, and yet again. Yea, seven times down prostrate, seven times bruised and maimed, did Rakush struggle on, until mounting up the edge of the seventh pit, all covered with deep wounds, both horse and rider lay exhausted, Rustem swooning in his agony.

But when once more the mighty Hero opened his horror-stricken eyes upon the world, lo, he beheld Shughad his brother, smiling in triumph at his side. Then knew he unto whom he owed this infamous treachery, and he said:

"Thou Wicked One! Is it possible that thou, the son of Zal, hast contrived and wrought this evil deed against thy brother? Verily thy heart is as black as thy shadow, which shall not long darken the earth."

Then the treacherous Shughad, trying to justify his cruel deed, said sternly unto the dying Hero:

"Verily, God hath decreed this awful vengeance to recompense thee for all the blood that thou hast shed in thy long life as a warrior. Not I, but He, hath determined thy fate."

Now at this moment the King of Kabul drew near, feigning great anger and sorrow when he beheld the dying one. And he wailed:

"Alas the day! That the Mighty Rustem should perish so ignobly, and as my guest! Quick, bring the matchless balm for Rustem's cure, for the great Champion of Iran must not be allowed to die a death so wretched!"

But Rustem, smiling scornfully, said unto the treacherous King:

"O Man of Wile! Right well thou knowest that Death, that cometh unto all men in their turn, is the only physician that now can heal the great Rustem of his wounds. But why should the mighty son of Zal complain of Fate? For verily, many a mighty King hath died and left me still triumphant, still in power unconquerable. And behold! yet there liveth valiant Feramurz, who will be revenged upon thee for his father's death."

And now the Mighty Rustem sighed, saying unto Shughad in a weak and mournful voice:

"Verily, my spirit will soon be free! But alas! it grieveth me sore that my faithful body may this night be food unto the wolves and lions. String, therefore, my bow, and place it in my hands that I may appear unto the wild beasts that would devour me, even as a live warrior, ready to defend his life. For our father's sake, O Shughad, refuse not thy brother this last request."

So, suspecting naught, Shughad drew the great bow from its case, and placed it in Rustem's hands, smiling with satisfaction to think that his brother's end was so nigh. But verily he smiled not but a moment, for noting the strength with which Rustem gripped his bow, and the peculiar look of his eye, shuddering with terror, quickly Shughad dodged behind a plane-tree close at hand. But useless was the shelter, for though the dimness of death was come over the eyes of the Hero, he yet spied Shughad where he hid, and whiz! went an arrow, straight through the tree and the wicked Shughad, transfixing them together. And Rustem, when he saw the fate of his brother, was content, knowing that he could do no more harm unto his house.

But alas! of all that mighty hunting-party not a knightly follower escaped. For Zuara and all the others perished in the treacherous pits of the traitor King, save only one, who quickly fled with the dire news unto Seistan.

Then Zal, in agony, tore his white hair and rent his garments, lamenting bitterly for Rustem, crying again and again:

"Why was I not present, fighting at his side? Why could I not die for him? Wherefore, alas, am I left alone to mourn his memory?"

But behold! though bowed to the earth with grief, quickly the white-haired old warrior sent Feramurz forth with a great army to avenge the death of his father. And verily the work of the Hero was complete. For not only did he make of Kabul a desert, but he laid low the head of the treacherous King and all his race. Then the work of vengeance finished, lo, he sought out the body of Rustem, and of Rakush his gallant steed, and bare them back in sorrow unto Seistan, where they were placed in a noble tomb.

And alas! never was there such wailing in the land of Iran as for Rustem the Mighty. Nay, not even for the glorious Shahs of Old! And well might it be so, for never again did Persia rejoice in such an unbroken line of heroes, and never did she achieve such telling victories, for with Rustem her glory departed; yea, for many long years!